Praise for the Christmas novels of
#1 *New York Times* bestselling author Debbie Macomber

"[Macomber] displays her usual gift for tugging on the heartstrings. This...
should please fans of the series as well as new readers."
—*Publishers Weekly* on *Buffalo Valley*

"Macomber brings readers once again to this very special town and allows
us to catch up on the lives of characters who have quickly become like
family. This romance displays the warmth and depth that her readers
expect."
—*RT Book Reviews* on *Buffalo Valley*

"Sometimes the best things come in small packages. Such is the case here,
as Macomber returns readers to Promise, Texas, a small ranching town
filled with loving, friendly people and down-home Texas charm."
—*Publishers Weekly* on *Return to Promise*

"It's just not Christmas without a Debbie Macomber story."
—*Armchair Interviews*

"Macomber's latest charming contemporary Christmas romance is a
sweetly satisfying, gently humorous story that celebrates the joy and love of
the holiday season."
—*Booklist* on *Christmas Letters*

"A funny, touching tale...overflows with holiday warmth and puts a new
twist on the classic Christmas letter."
—*Library Journal* on *Christmas Letters*

"Macomber's take on *A Christmas Carol*...adds up to another tale of
romance in the lives of ordinary people, with a message that life is like a
fruitcake: full of unexpected delights."
—*Publishers Weekly* on *There's Something About Christmas*

"No one pens a Christmas story like Macomber—truly special and
guaranteed to warm even Scrooge's heart."
—*RT Book Reviews* on *There's Something About Christmas*

"A delightful seasonal story of friendship and love. Macomber is a master
storyteller.... A warm and loving novel that is destined to quickly become a
Christmas favorite."
—*Times Record News* on *The Christmas Basket*

X

DEBBIE MACOMBER

A Country Christmas

mira

mira

Recycling programs for this product may not exist in your area.

ISBN-13: 978-0-7783-6870-0

A Country Christmas

First published in 2014. This edition published in 2019.

Copyright © 2014 by Harlequin Books S.A.

Return to Promise
First published in 2000. This edition published in 2019.
Copyright © 2000 by Debbie Macomber

Buffalo Valley
First published in 2001. This edition published in 2019.
Copyright © 2001 by Debbie Macomber

For questions and comments about the quality of this book, please contact us at CustomerService@Harlequin.com.

BookClubbish.com

Printed in U.S.A.

**Also available from
Debbie Macomber and MIRA Books**

Blossom Street

The Shop on Blossom Street
A Good Yarn
Susannah's Garden
Back on Blossom Street
Twenty Wishes
Summer on Blossom Street
Hannah's List
"The Twenty-First Wish"
 (in *The Knitting Diaries*)
A Turn in the Road

Cedar Cove

16 Lighthouse Road
204 Rosewood Lane
311 Pelican Court
44 Cranberry Point
50 Harbor Street
6 Rainier Drive
74 Seaside Avenue
8 Sandpiper Way
92 Pacific Boulevard
1022 Evergreen Place
Christmas in Cedar Cove
 (*5-B Poppy Lane* and
 A Cedar Cove Christmas)
1105 Yakima Street
1225 Christmas Tree Lane

The Dakota Series

Dakota Born
Dakota Home
Always Dakota
Buffalo Valley

The Manning Family

The Manning Sisters
 (*The Cowboy's Lady* and
 The Sheriff Takes a Wife)
The Manning Brides
 (*Marriage of Inconvenience*
 and *Stand-In Wife*)

The Manning Grooms
 (*Bride on the Loose* and
 Same Time, Next Year)

Christmas Books

A Gift to Last
On a Snowy Night
Home for the Holidays
Glad Tidings
Christmas Wishes
Small Town Christmas
When Christmas Comes
 (now retitled *Trading
 Christmas*)
There's Something About Christmas
Christmas Letters
The Perfect Christmas
Choir of Angels
 (*Shirley, Goodness and Mercy,*
 Those Christmas Angels and
 Where Angels Go)
Call Me Mrs. Miracle

Heart of Texas

Texas Skies
 (*Lonesome Cowboy*
 and *Texas Two-Step*)
Texas Nights
 (*Caroline's Child* and *Dr. Texas*)
Texas Home
 (*Nell's Cowboy* and *Lone Star Baby*)
Promise, Texas
Return to Promise

Midnight Sons

Alaska Skies
 (*Brides for Brothers* and
 The Marriage Risk)
Alaska Nights
 (*Daddy's Little Helper* and
 Because of the Baby)
Alaska Home
 (*Falling for Him, Ending in
 Marriage* and *Midnight Sons
 and Daughters*)

CONTENTS

RETURN TO PROMISE

To Ruthanne Devlin
For blessing my life with your friendship
Happy Birthday!

One

Cal Patterson knew his wife would be furious. Competing in the annual Labor Day rodeo, however, was worth Jane's wrath—although little else was.

Bull riding had always enticed him, even more than bronc riding or roping or any of the other competitions. It was the thrill that got to him, the danger of riding a fifteen-hundred-pound bull, of staying on for eight seconds and sometimes longer. He craved the illusion that for those brief moments he was in control. Cal didn't do it for the trophy—if he was fortunate enough to take top prize—or to hear his name broadcast across the rodeo grounds. He was drawn by the challenge, pitting his will against the bull's savage strength, and yes, the risk. Jane would never understand that; she'd been raised a city girl and trained as a doctor, and she disapproved of what she called *unnecessary* risk. In her opinion, bull riding fell squarely into that category. He'd tried to explain his feelings about it, but clearly he'd failed. Jane still objected fervently whenever he mentioned his desire to enter rodeo competitions. Okay, okay, so he'd busted a rib a few years back and spent several pain-filled weeks recuperating. Jane had been angry with him then, too. She'd gotten over it, though, and she would again—but not without inducing a certain amount of guilt first.

He watched her out of the corner of his eye as she ushered their three-year-old son, Paul, into the bleachers. Cal dutifully followed behind, carrying eighteen-month-old Mary Ann, who was sound asleep in his arms. As soon as his family was settled, he'd be joining the other competitors near the arena. A few minutes later, Jane would open the program and see his name. Once she did, all hell would break loose. He sighed heavily. His brother and sister-in-law would be arriving shortly, and if he was lucky, that'd buy him a couple of minutes.

"Glen and Ellie are meeting us here, aren't they?" Jane asked, her voice lowered so as not to disturb the baby. His daughter rested her head of soft blond curls against his shoulder, thumb in her mouth. She looked peaceful, downright angelic—quite a contrast to her usual energetic behavior.

"They'll be here soon," Cal answered, handing Mary Ann to Jane.

With two children demanding her time and attention, plus the ranch house and everything else, Jane had cut back her hours at the medical clinic to one weekend a month. Cal knew she missed practicing medicine on a more frequent basis, but she never complained. He considered himself a lucky man to have married a woman so committed to family. When the kids were in school, she'd return to full-time practice, but for now, Paul and Mary Ann were the focus of her life.

Just then, Jane reached for the schedule of rodeo events and Cal tensed, anticipating her reaction.

"Cal Patterson, you *didn't!*" Her voice rose to something resembling a shriek as she turned and glared at him.

"Cal?" She waited, apparently hoping for an explanation.

However, he had nothing to say that he hadn't already said dozens of times. It wouldn't do any good to trot out his rationalizations yet again; one look told him she wouldn't be easily appeased. His only option was to throw himself on her good graces and pray she'd forgive him quickly.

"You signed up for the *bull ride?*"

"Honey, now listen—"

"Are you *crazy?* You got hurt before! What makes you think you won't get hurt this time, too?"

"If you'd give me a chance to—"

Jane stood, cradling Mary Ann against her. Paul stared up at his parents with a puzzled frown.

"Where are you going?" he asked, hoping he could mollify her without causing a scene.

"I refuse to watch."

"But, darling..."

She scowled at him. "Don't you darling me!"

Cal stood, too, and was given a reprieve when Glen and Ellie arrived, making their way down the long row of seats. His brother paused, glancing from one to the other, and seemed to realize what was happening. "I take it Jane found out?"

"You knew?" Jane asked coldly.

Ellie shook her head. "Not me! I just heard about it myself."

"Looks like Jane's leaving me," Cal joked, trying to inject some humor into the situation. His wife was overreacting. There wasn't a single reason she should walk out now, especially when she knew how excited their three-year-old son was about seeing his first rodeo.

"That's exactly what you deserve," she muttered, bending to pick up her purse and the diaper bag while holding Mary Ann tightly against her shoulder.

"Mommy?"

"Get your things," she told Paul. "We're going home."

Paul's lower lip started to quiver, and Cal could tell that his son was struggling not to cry. "I want to see the rodeo."

"Jane, let's talk about this," Cal murmured.

Paul looked expectantly from his father to his mother, and Jane hesitated.

"Honey, please," Cal said, hoping to talk her into forgiveness—or at least acceptance. True, he'd kept the fact that he'd signed up for bull riding a secret, but only because he'd been intent on delaying a fight. *This* fight.

"I don't want Paul to see you injured," she said.

"Have a little faith, would you?"

His wife frowned, her anger simmering.

"I rode bulls for years without a problem. Tell her, Glen," he said, nodding at his brother.

"Hey," Glen said, raising both hands in a gesture of surrender. "You're on your own with this one, big brother."

"I don't blame you for being mad," Ellie said, siding with Jane. "I'd be furious, too."

Women tended to stick together, but despite Ellie's support, Cal could see that Jane was weakening.

"Let Paul stay for the rodeo, okay?" he cajoled. "He's been looking forward to it all week. If you don't want him to see me compete, I understand. Just leave when the bull riding starts. I'll meet you at the chili cook-off when I'm done."

"Please, Mommy? I want to see the rodeo," Paul said again, eyes huge with longing. The boy pleaded his case far more eloquently than *he* could, and Cal wasn't fool enough to add anything more.

Jane nodded reluctantly, and with a scowl in his direction, she sat down. Cal vowed he'd make it up to her later.

"I'll be fine," he assured her, wanting Jane to know he loved and appreciated her. He slid his arm around her shoulders, hugging her close. But all the while, his heart thundered with excitement at the thought of getting on the back of that bull. He couldn't keep his gaze from wandering to the chute.

Jane might have been born and raised in the big city, but she was more than a little bit country now. Still, she'd probably never approve of certain rodeo events. Cal recognized her fears, and as a result, rarely competed anymore—hadn't in five years. But he expected Jane to recognize the impulses that drove him, too.

Compromise. Wasn't that what kept a marriage intact?

Jane had no intention of forgetting Cal's deceit, but now wasn't the time or place to have it out with her husband. He knew how she felt about his competing in the rodeo. She'd made her views completely clear, even before they were married.

Still, she'd acquiesced and held her tongue. She glanced at Cal's brother and sister-in-law and envied them. Their kids were with a baby-sitter, since they planned to attend the dance later that evening. Jane would've preferred to stay, too, but when she'd mentioned it to Cal, he'd balked. Dancing wasn't his favorite activity and he'd protested and complained until she dropped it.

Then he'd pulled *this* stunt. Men!

Partway through the rodeo, Paul fell asleep, leaning against her side. Cal had already left to wait down by the arena with the other amateur riders. As the time approached for him to compete, she considered leaving, but then decided to stay. Her stomach would be in knots whether she was there watching him or not. Out of sight wasn't going to put her risk-taking husband out of mind, and with Paul asleep, there was no reason to go now.

"Are you worried?" Ellie asked, casting her a sympathetic look.

She nodded. "Of course, I don't know what Cal was thinking."

"Who said he was thinking at all?" Ellie teased.

"Yeah—it's the testosterone," Jane muttered, wondering what her husband found so appealing about riding such dangerous beasts. Her nerves were shattered, and that wasn't going to change. Not until she knew he was safe.

"I was hoping you and Cal would come to the dance."

Ellie was obviously disappointed, but no more than Jane herself. She would've loved an evening out. Had she pressed the issue, Cal would eventually have given in, but it hadn't seemed worth the arguments and the guilt. Besides, getting a sitter would've been difficult, since nearly everyone in Promise attended the annual Labor Day rodeo—and Ellie had managed to snag the services of Emma Bishop, one of the few teenagers available for baby-sitting.

"Cal didn't want to leave the kids," she explained. There'd be other dances, other opportunities, Jane reassured herself.

"He's up next," Glen said.

"Go, Cal!" Ellie squealed. Despite her sister-in-law's effort to sound sympathetic, Jane could tell she was excited.

When Cal's name was announced, Jane didn't want to look but couldn't stop herself. Cal was inside the pen, sitting astride the bull, one end of a rope wrapped around the saddle horn and the other around his hand. She held her sleeping child more tightly and bit her lower lip hard enough to draw blood. Suddenly the gate flew open and fifteen hundred pounds of angry bull charged into the arena.

Almost immediately, Glen and Ellie were on their feet, shouting. Jane remained seated, her arms around her children. "What's happening?" she asked Ellie in a tight, urgent voice.

"Cal's doing great!" she exclaimed. Jane could barely hear her over the noise of the crowd. Ellie clapped wildly when the buzzer went. "He stayed on!" she crowed. "So far, he's ahead!"

Jane nodded. How he'd managed to last all those seconds, she had no idea.

"Whew. Glad that's over." Ellie sank down next to Jane.

"My brother's got a real flair for this," Glen said to no one in particular. "He could've gone on the circuit if..." He let the rest fade.

"If he wasn't married," Jane said, completing his thought. Actually Glen's assessment wasn't really accurate. Her husband was a long-established rancher before she'd come on the scene. He'd competed in rodeos since he was in his teens, but if he'd been interested in turning professional, he would have done so when he was much younger. She had nothing to do with that decision.

"Glen," Ellie said, squeezing her husband's arm, "who's that woman over there?" Ellie was staring at a brunette standing near the fence.

"What woman?" Glen asked.

"The one talking to Cal."

Jane glanced over, and even from this distance she could see that the other woman was lovely. Tall and slender, she looked like a model from the pages of a Western-wear catalog in her tight jeans, red cowboy boots and brightly checked shirt. It was more than just her appearance, though. Jane noticed the confidence with which she held herself, the flirtatious way she flipped back her long brown hair. This was a woman who knew she looked good—especially to men.

"She seems familiar," Ellie said, nudging Glen. "Don't you think?"

"She does," he agreed, "but I can't place her."

"Apparently she's got a lot to say to Cal," Ellie added, then glanced apologetically toward Jane as though she regretted mentioning it.

Jane couldn't help being curious. The woman wasn't anyone she recognized. She wasn't the jealous type, but she found herself wondering how this Rodeo Princess knew her husband. It was clear that the woman was speaking animatedly to Cal, gesturing freely; for his part, Cal seemed more interested in what was happening with the rodeo than in listening to her.

Jane supposed she should be pleased by his lack of interest in another woman, and indeed she was. Then, as if aware of her scrutiny, her husband turned toward the bleachers and surveyed the crowd. His face broke into a wide grin when he caught her eye, and he waved. Earlier she'd been annoyed with him—in fact, she still was—but she'd never been able to resist one of Cal's smiles. She waved in return and blew him a kiss.

An hour later, after Cal had been awarded the trophy for the amateur bull-riding competition, they decided to leave. With Mary Ann in the stroller and Paul walking between them, they made one last circuit of the grounds before heading toward the parking lot. They passed the chili cook-off tent, where the winner's name was posted; for the first time in recent memory, it wasn't Nell Grant. But then, Jane understood that Nell had declined to enter this year.

It was near dusk and lights from the carnival rides sparkled, delighting both Paul and Mary Ann. Cal's arm was around Jane's shoulder as they skirted the area set aside for the dance. The fiddle players were entertaining the audience while the rest of the musicians set up their equipment. People had gathered around, tapping their feet in anticipation.

The lively music had Jane swaying to the beat. "I wish we were staying," she murmured, swallowing her disappointment.

"We'd better get home," Cal said, swinging his trophy at his side. "I didn't want to say anything before, but I'm about as sore as a man can get."

"Your rib?" she asked.

He grimaced, obviously in pain. "Are you going to lecture me?"

"I should," she told him. "But I won't. You knew the risks."

He leaned forward and kissed her cheek. "You're right. I did."

What really bothered her was that he'd known—and participated, anyway. He was fully aware that he could've been badly injured, or worse. And for what? She simply didn't understand why a man would do anything so foolish when he had so much to lose.

"I'm ready to go home," he said. "How about you?"

Jane nodded, but glanced longingly over her shoulder at the dance floor. Maybe next year.

The phone rang, shattering the night silence. Cal bolted upright and looked at the glowing digital numbers of the clock radio, then snatched the receiver from its cradle without bothering to check call display. It went without saying that anyone phoning at 3:23 a.m. was calling with bad news.

"Pattersons'," he barked gruffly.

"Cal? It's Stephanie."

Jane's mother. Something was very wrong; he could hear it in her voice. "What's happened?"

"It's…it's Harry," she stammered.

Jane awoke and leaned across the bed to turn on the bedside lamp. "Who is it?" she asked.

He raised one hand to defer her question. "Where are you?"

"At the hospital," Stephanie said, and rattled off the name of a medical facility in Southern California. "Harry's fallen—he got up the way he sometimes does in the middle of the night and…and he slipped."

"Is he all right?"

"No," his mother-in-law answered, her voice trembling. She took a moment to compose herself. "That's why I'm calling. His hip's broken—and it's a very bad break. He's sedated and scheduled for surgery first thing in the morning, but… but the doctors told me it's going to be weeks before he's back on his feet."

"Cal?" Jane was watching him, frowning, her hair disheveled, her face marked by sleep.

"It's your mother," he said, placing his hand over the mouthpiece.

"Is this about my dad?"

Cal nodded.

"Let me talk to her," Jane demanded, instantly alert.

"Stephanie, you'd better talk to Jane yourself," he said, and handed his wife the phone.

Cal was pretty much able to follow the conversation from that point. With her medical background, Jane was the best person to talk to in circumstances like this. She asked a number of questions concerning medication and tests that had been done, explained the kind of orthopedic surgery her dad would undergo and reassured her mother. She spoke with such confidence that Cal felt his own sense of foreboding diminish. And then she hesitated.

"I'll need to talk to Cal about that," she told her mother, voice dropping as though he wasn't supposed to hear.

"Talk to me about what?" he asked after she'd replaced the receiver.

Jane paused for a moment, then took a deep breath.

"Mom wants me and the kids to fly home."

"For how long?" The question was purely selfish; still, he needed to know. Being separated would be a hardship on all of them. He understood the situation and was willing to do whatever he could, but he didn't like the thought of being apart for any length of time.

"I don't know. A couple of weeks, maybe longer."

"Two *weeks?*" He hated the telltale irritation in his voice, but it was too late to take back the words.

Jane said nothing. Then, as though struck by some brilliant idea, she scrambled onto her knees and a slow smile spread across her face.

"Come with us," she said.

"To California? Now?" That was out of the question, but he hated to refuse his wife—especially after what he'd done at the rodeo. "Honey, I can't. Glen and I are getting ready for the bull sale this week. I'm sorry, but this just isn't a good time for me to be away."

"Glen could handle the sale."

What she said was true, but the prospect of spending two weeks at his in-laws' held little appeal. Cal got along with Jane's mother and he liked her father well enough, but Harry had a few annoying mannerisms. Plus, the two of them tended to become embroiled in ridiculous arguments that served no real purpose and usually went nowhere. Cal suspected it was more a matter of competing for Jane's attention. Jane was Harry's only daughter and he doted on her. Cal figured he'd be doing Harry a favor by staying away. Besides, what would he do with himself in a place like Los Angeles?

"Don't be so quick to say no," she said. "We could make this a family vacation. We always talk about going somewhere and it never happens." She knew he found it hard to leave the ranch for longer than a few days, but still...

"A vacation? I don't think so, not with your father laid up and your mother as worried as she is. Besides, Stephanie doesn't want *me* there."

"That's not true."

"It's not me she needs, it's you. Having the kids around will boost your father's spirits, and your mother's too. I'd just be in the way."

Jane's disappointment was obvious. "You're sure?"

He nodded. "You go. A visit with you and the kids will be the best thing for your parents, and you'll have a chance to connect with your friends, too. It'll do everyone good."

Still Jane showed reluctance. "You're *sure* you don't mind me being gone that long?"

"I'll hate it," he admitted, and reached for the lamp to turn off the light. Then he drew his wife into his arms.

Jane released a deep sigh. "I'm going to hate it, too."

Cal closed his eyes, already experiencing a sense of loss, and Jane and the children hadn't even left yet.

The next morning was hectic. The minute she got up, Jane arranged the flight to California and threw clothes, toiletries, toys and baby supplies into several suitcases. No sooner had she finished than Cal piled them all into the car, and drove his family to San Antonio. Paul was excited about riding in an airplane, and even Mary Ann seemed to realize there was adventure ahead.

As always, San Antonio International Airport was bustling with activity. Cal quickly ushered Jane and the kids to the airline's check-in counter, where they received their boarding passes.

Kneeling down to meet his son at eye level, Cal put both hands on Paul's shoulders. "You be good for Mommy, understand?"

His three-year-old nodded solemnly, then threw his small arms around Cal's neck, hugging him fiercely.

"I'm counting on you to be as much help to your grandma and grandpa as you can," Cal added. He felt a wrenching in his stomach. This would be the first time he'd been apart from his children.

"I will," Paul promised.

Cal noted that his son's "blankey" was tucked inside his backpack, but said nothing. The blanket was badly worn. It'd been a gift from Jane's friend Annie Porter, and a point of contention between him and Jane. Cal didn't like the idea of the boy dragging it around, and Jane felt that Paul would give it up when he was ready.

Cal stood and scooped Mary Ann into his arms. His daughter squirmed, eager to break free and explore this wonderful new place.

"I'll phone often," Jane said when he'd kissed her.

"We'll talk every day."

Saying goodbye to his family was even more difficult than Cal had expected.

"I'm going to miss you," he murmured.

"Two weeks will go quickly."

"Right," Cal agreed, but at the moment those weeks loomed before him in all their emptiness.

Juggling two bags and clutching both children, Jane moved toward the security area. Cal left then, waving to the kids as he did. The feeling of emptiness stayed with him, and he knew he'd let his wife down. He should have gone with her; it was what she'd wanted, what she'd asked of him, but he'd refused. He shook his head miserably. This wasn't the first time he'd disappointed Jane.

As he made his way to the parking garage, Cal couldn't shake his reaction to seeing his wife leave. He didn't want to go to California, and yet he regretted not being on that plane with his family.

"You heard about Jane, didn't you?" Dovie Hennessey asked her husband. Frank had just come home from the golf course, where he'd played eighteen holes with Phil Patterson, Cal's father.

Frank, who'd retired three years earlier from his position as sheriff, nodded and walked straight to the refrigerator. "According to Phil, Cal drove Jane and the kids to the airport yesterday morning."

"I give him a week."

Frank turned around, a pitcher of iced tea in his hand. "A week before what?"

"Before Cal comes into town."

"Why?"

Exasperated, Dovie rolled her eyes. "Company. He's going to rattle around that house like a lost soul."

"Cal? No way!" Frank argued, pouring himself a glass of tea. "You seem to forget he was a confirmed bachelor before he met Jane. I was as surprised as anyone when he decided to marry her. Don't get me wrong. I think it was the smartest thing he ever did...."

"But?" Dovie said.

"Cal isn't any stranger to living alone," Frank continued, sitting down at the kitchen table with his tea and the newspaper. "He did it for years. Now, I know he loves Jane and the kids, but my guess is he's looking forward to two weeks of peace and quiet."

Dovie couldn't help herself. *Peace and quiet?* Frank made it sound as though Cal would welcome a vacation from his own family. Hands on her hips, she glared at her husband. "Frank Hennessey, what a rotten thing to say."

He glanced up from his paper, a puzzled expression on his face. "What was so terrible about that?"

"Jane and the children are *not* a nuisance in Cal's life," she said in a firm voice. "Don't you realize that?"

"Now, Dovie—"

"Furthermore, you seem to be implying that he's going to *enjoy* having them gone."

"I said no such thing," Frank insisted. "Cal's going to miss Jane—of course he is. The children, too. What I was *trying* to say is that spending a couple of weeks without his wife might not be all that bad." Flustered and avoiding her eyes, Frank rubbed his face. "That didn't come out right, either."

Dovie suppressed a smile. She knew what he meant, but she liked giving him a hard time once in a while—partly because he made it so easy. He'd remained a bachelor for the first sixty years of his life. Like Cal, he'd grown accustomed to his own company. He and Dovie had been involved for more than ten years, but Frank had resisted marriage until Pastor Wade McMillen had offered a solution. They became husband and wife but kept their own residences. In the beginning, that had worked beautifully, but as time passed, Frank ended up spending more and more nights with her, until it seemed wasteful to maintain two homes. Since he'd retired, Dovie, who owned an antique store, had reduced her hours. They were traveling frequently now, and with Frank taking a role in local politics and becoming active in the senior citizens' center, why, there just weren't enough hours in a day.

Patting her husband's arm as she passed, Dovie said, "I thought I'd make Cal one of my chicken pot pies and we could take it out to him later this week."

Frank nodded, apparently eager to leave the subject behind. "Good idea." Picking up his paper, he claimed the recliner and stretched out his legs. Almost immediately, Buttons, the black miniature poodle they'd recently acquired, leaped into Frank's lap and circled a couple of times before settling into a comfortable position.

"Nap time?" Dovie asked with a grin.

"Golf tires me out," Frank said.

Dovie laughed. "I meant the dog."

"I guess we're both tired...."

"You promised to drive me to the grocery store," she reminded him, although she was perfectly capable of making the trip on her own. It was the small things they did together that she enjoyed most. The ordinary domestic chores that were part of any marriage.

"In a while," Frank said sleepily, lowering the newspaper to the floor.

True to his word, an hour later Frank sought her out, obviously ready to tackle a trip to the supermarket. Once they got there, he found a convenient parking spot, accompanied her inside and grabbed a cart. Dovie marched toward the produce aisle, with Frank close behind.

"Do you have any idea what Cal would enjoy with his chicken pot pie?" she asked.

"I know what I'd enjoy," Frank teased and playfully swatted her backside.

"Frank Hennessey," Dovie protested, but not too loudly, since that would only encourage him. She didn't really mind, though. Frank was openly affectionate, unlike her first husband. Marvin had loved her, she'd never doubted that, but he'd displayed his feelings in less overt ways.

"Who's that?" Frank asked, his attention on a tall brunette who stood by the oranges, examining them closely.

It took Dovie a moment to remember. "Why, that's Nicole Nelson."

"Nicole Nelson," Frank repeated slowly, as though testing the name. "She's from Promise?"

"She lived here a few years back," Dovie said, taking a plastic bag and choosing the freshest-looking bunch of celery.

"She seems familiar. How do I know her?" Frank asked, speaking into her ear.

Which told Dovie that Nicole had never crossed the law. Frank had perfect recall of everyone he'd encountered in his work as sheriff.

"She was a teller at the bank."

"When?"

"Oh, my." Dovie had to think about that one. "Quite a few years ago now...nine, maybe ten. She and Jennifer Healy were roommates."

"Healy. Healy. Why do I know that name."

Dovie whirled around, sighing loudly. "Frank, don't tell me you've forgotten Jennifer Healy!"

He stared back at her, his expression blank.

"She's the one who dumped Cal two days before their wedding. It nearly destroyed the poor boy. I still remember how upset Mary was, having to call everyone and tell them the wedding had been canceled." She shook her head. "Nicole was supposed to be Jennifer's maid of honor."

Frank's gaze followed the other woman as she pushed her cart toward the vegetables. "When Jennifer left town, did Nicole go with her?"

Dovie didn't know, but it seemed to her the two girls had moved at about the same time.

"Cal was pretty broken up when Jennifer dumped him," Frank said. "Good thing she left Promise. Wonder why this one came back…"

"Mary was worried sick about Cal," Dovie murmured, missing her dearest friend more than ever. Cal's mother had died almost three years ago, and not a day passed that Dovie didn't think of her.

"I know it was painful when it happened, but Jennifer's leaving was probably a lucky break for Cal."

Dovie agreed with him. "I'm sure Jane thinks so, too."

Frank generally didn't pay much attention to other women—unless they were potential or probable felons. His noticing Nicole was unusual enough, but it was the intensity of his focus that perturbed her.

She studied Nicole. Dovie had to admit that the years had been kind to Jennifer's friend. Nicole had been lovely before, but immature. Time had seasoned her beauty and given her an air of casual sophistication. Even the way she dressed had changed. Her hair, too.

Dovie saw that her husband wasn't the only man with his eye on this woman; half the men in the store had noticed her—and Nicole was well aware of it.

"I'll admit she looks attractive," Dovie said with a certain reluctance.

When Frank turned back to her, he was frowning. "What is it?" she asked.

"What she looks like to me," he said, ushering her down the aisle, "is trouble."

Two

Cal had lived in this ranch house his entire life, and the place had never seemed as big or as empty as it did now. Jane hadn't been gone a week but he couldn't stand the silence, wandering aimlessly from room to room. Exhausted from a day that had started before dawn, he'd come home and once again experienced a sharp pang of loneliness.

Normally when Cal got back to the house, Paul rushed outside to greet him. The little boy always launched himself off the porch steps into his father's arms as if he'd waited for this moment all day. Later, after Cal had showered and Jane got dinner on the table, he spent time with his daughter. As young as Mary Ann was, she had a dynamic personality and persuasive powers to match. Cal knew she was going to be a beauty when she grew up—and he'd be warding off the boys. Mary Ann was like her mother in her loveliness, her energy... and her stubborn nature.

Cal's life had changed forever the day he married Jane. Marriage wasn't just the smartest move of his life, it was the most comfortable. Being temporarily on his own made him appreciate what he had. He'd gotten used to a great many things, most of which he hadn't stopped to consider for quite a while: shared passion, the companionship of the woman he loved, a family that gave him a sense of purpose and belonging. In addition, Jane ran their household with efficiency and competence, and he'd grown used to the work she did for her family—meals, laundry, cleaning. He sighed. To say he missed Jane and the kids was an understatement.

He showered, changed clothes and dragged himself into the kitchen. His lunch had been skimpy and his stomach felt hollow, but he wasn't in the mood to cook. Had there been time before she left, Jane would have filled the freezer with precooked dinners he could pop into the microwave. When they heard he was a temporary bachelor, Frank and Dovie had dropped off a meal, but that was long gone. The cupboards were full, the refrigerator, too, but nothing seemed simple or appealing. Because he didn't want to bother with anything more complicated, he reached for a bag of microwave popcorn. That would take the edge off his hunger, he decided. Maybe later he'd feel like putting together a proper meal.

The scent of popped corn enticed him, but just as he was about to start eating it, the phone rang. Cal grabbed the receiver, thinking it might be Jane.

"Pattersons'," he said eagerly.

"Cal, it's Annie."

Annie. Cal couldn't squelch the letdown feeling that came over him. Annie Porter was his wife's best friend and a woman he liked very much. She'd moved to Promise a few years back and had quickly become part of the community. The town had needed a bookstore and Annie had needed Promise. It wasn't long before she'd married the local vet. Cal suddenly remembered that Jane had asked him to phone Annie. He'd forgotten.

"I just heard about Jane's dad. What happened? Dovie was in and said Jane went to stay with her parents—she assumed I knew. I wish someone had told me."

"That's my fault," Cal said. "I'm sorry, Annie. On the way to the airport, Jane asked me to call...." He let his words drift off.

"What happened?" Annie asked again, clearly upset. Cal knew she was close to Jane's parents and considered them a second family.

Cal told her everything he could and apologized a second time for not contacting her earlier. He hoped Annie would see that the slight hadn't been intentional; the fact was, he hated making phone calls. Always had.

"I can't imagine why Jane hasn't called me herself," she said in a worried voice.

Cal had figured she would, too, which only went to show how hectic Jane's days must be with her parents and the children.

"Jane will be home in a week," Cal said, trying to sound hopeful and reassuring—although a week seemed like an eternity. He pushed the thought from his mind and forced himself to focus on their reunion. "Why don't you give her a call?" he suggested, knowing Annie was going to want more details. "I'm sure she'd love to hear from you."

"I'll do that."

"Great... Well, it's been good talking to you," he said, anxious to get off the phone.

"Before we hang up, I want to ask you about Nicole Nelson."

"Who?" Cal had no idea who she was talking about.

"You don't know Nicole? She came into the bookstore this afternoon and applied for a job. She put you and the bank down as references."

"Nicole Nelson." The name sounded vaguely familiar.

"I saw you talking to her at the rodeo," Annie said, obviously surprised that he didn't remember the other woman.

"Oh, yeah—her," he said, finally recalling the incident. Then he realized how he knew Nicole. She'd been a good friend of Jennifer's. In fact, they'd been roommates when he and Jennifer were engaged. "She put my name down as a job reference?" He found that hard to believe.

"She said she's known you for quite a while," Annie added.

"Really?" To be fair, Cal's problem hadn't been with Nicole but with Jennifer, who'd played him for a fool. He'd been too blinded by his first encounter with love to recognize the kind of woman she was.

"Nicole said if I had any questions I should ask you."

"It's been years since I saw her—other than at the rodeo last week." He did remember talking to her briefly. She'd said something about how good it was to be back in Promise, how nice to see him, that sort of thing. At the time Cal had been distracted. He'd been more interested in watching the rodeo and cheering on his friends than in having a conversation with a woman he'd had trouble recognizing. Besides, Jane was upset with him, and appeasing her had been paramount. He'd barely noticed Nicole.

"Did she list any other personal references?" he asked.

"No, I told her you and the bank were the only ones I needed," Annie said. "So can you vouch for her?"

"I guess so. It's just that I haven't seen her in a long time. We—"

"You went out with her?"

Leave it to Annie to ask a question like that. "No, with her best friend. We almost got married." No need to go into details. Jennifer had taught him one of the most valuable lessons of his life. The worth of that experience could be measured in the pain and embarrassment that resulted when she'd callously canceled the wedding. He could've lived with her breaking their engagement—but why did she have to wait until they were practically at the altar?

"I talked with Janice over at Promise First National about her job history," Annie said, interrupting his thoughts. "She doesn't have anything negative to say about Nicole, but if you're uncomfortable giving her a recommendation…"

"Oh, I'm sure Nicole will do a great job for you."

The length of Annie's hesitation told him he hadn't been very convincing.

"Nicole's fine, really," he said. He didn't actually remember that much about her. She always seemed to be there whenever he picked up Jennifer, but he couldn't say he *knew* her. Years ago she'd been a sweet kid, but that was the extent of his recollection. He certainly couldn't dredge up anything that would prevent her from selling books. He'd never heard that she was dishonest or rude to customers, and those were things that would definitely have stuck in his mind. It was difficult enough to attract good employees; Cal didn't want to be responsible for Annie's turning someone down simply because he had negative feelings about that person's friends.

"I was thinking of hiring her for the bookstore."

"Do it," Cal said.

"She seems friendly and helpful."

"Yeah, she is," Cal said, and glanced longingly at the popcorn.

"Thanks, Cal, I appreciate the input."

"No problem." He didn't know what it was about women and the telephone. Even Jane, who had a sensible approach to everything and hated wasting time, could spend hours chatting with her friends. He sighed. Thinking about his wife produced a powerful yearning. Nothing seemed right without her.

"I'll call Jane tomorrow," Annie was saying.

"Good plan." He checked his watch, wondering how much longer this would take.

"Thanks again."

"Give Nicole my best," he said, thinking this was how to signal that he was ready to get off the phone.

"I will," Annie promised. "Bye, now."

Ah, success. Cal replaced the receiver, then frowned as he attempted to picture Nicole Nelson. Brown hair—or blond? He hadn't paid much attention to her at the rodeo. And he couldn't imagine what would bring her back to Promise. Not that she needed to justify the move, at least to him. His one hope was that Annie wouldn't regret hiring her.

Mary Ann's squeal of delight woke Jane from a deep sleep. She rolled over and looked bleary-eyed at the clock radio and gasped. Ten o'clock. She hadn't slept this late since she was in high school. Tossing back the covers, she grabbed her robe and headed out of the bedroom, yawning as she went.

"Mom!" she called.

"In here, sweetheart," her mother said from the kitchen.

Jane found the children and her mother busily playing on the tile floor. Mary Ann toddled gleefully, chasing a beach ball, intent on getting to it before her brother. Because he loved his little sister, Paul was letting her reach it first, then clapping and encouraging her to throw it to him.

"You should've woken me up," Jane said.

"Why? The children are fine."

"But, Mom, I'm supposed to be here to help you," she protested. The last week had been difficult. Taking Paul and Mary Ann away from home and the comfort of their normal routines had made both children irritable. The first night, Mary Ann hadn't slept more than a few hours, then whined all the next day. Paul had grown quiet and refused to talk to either grandparent. The children had required several days to adjust to the time change, and with the stress of her father's condition, Jane was completely exhausted.

"You needed the sleep," her mother said.

Jane couldn't argue with that. "But I didn't come all this way to spend the whole morning in bed."

"Stop fussing. Paul, Mary Ann and I are having a wonderful visit. If you intend to spoil it, then I suggest you go back to bed."

"Mother!"

"I'm the only grandma they have. Now, why don't you let us play and get yourself some breakfast?"

"But—"

"You heard me." Stephanie crawled over to the lower cupboards, then held on to the counter, using that as leverage to get up off the floor. "I'm not as limber as I once was," she joked.

"Oh, Mom…" Watching her, Jane felt guilty. She gathered Mary Ann into her arms, although the child immediately wanted to get down. Paul frowned up at her, disgruntled by the interruption.

"I called your father, and he's resting comfortably," her mother informed her. "He wants us to take the day for ourselves."

"Dad said that?" He'd been demanding and impatient ever since Jane had arrived.

"He did indeed, and I intend to take him up on his offer. I promised the kids lunch at McDonald's."

"Dad *must* be feeling better."

"He is," her mother said. "By the way, Annie phoned earlier."

"Annie?" Jane echoed. "Is everything all right at home?"

"Everything's just fine. She wanted to know how your father's doing. Apparently no one told her—"

"I asked Cal to tell her. I meant to phone her myself, but... you know how crazy it's been this week."

"I explained it all, so don't you worry. She'd already talked to Cal, who apologized profusely for not phoning her. She sounds well and has some news herself."

Jane paused, waiting, although she had her suspicions.

"Annie's pregnant again. She says they're all thrilled— Annie, Lucas and the children. She's reducing her hours at work, hiring extra help. It was great to chat with her."

"A baby. That's wonderful." Annie was such a good mother, patient and intuitive. And such a good friend. Her move to Texas had been a real blessing to Jane.

Thinking about Promise made Jane's heart hunger for home. A smile came as she recalled how out of place she'd once felt in the small Texas town. She'd accepted a job in the medical clinic soon after she'd qualified. It wasn't where she'd wanted to settle, and she'd only taken the assignment so she could pay off a portion of her huge college loans. The first few months had been dreadful—until she'd become friends with Dovie, who'd introduced her to Ellie.

This was networking at its finest. Soon afterward, Ellie and Glen had arranged Jane's first date with Cal. What a disaster that had been! Cal wasn't the least bit interested in a blind date. Things had changed, however, when Cal and his brother and Ellie had started to teach her how to act like a real Texan. When she'd decided to take riding lessons, Cal had volunteered to be her teacher.

Jane had never meant to fall in love with him. But they were a good match, bringing out the best in each other, and they'd both realized that. Because of Cal, she was a better person, even a better physician, and he reminded her often how her love had enriched his life. They were married within a year of meeting.

After the children were born, Jane felt it necessary to make her career less of a priority, but she didn't begrudge a moment of this new experience. In fact, she enjoyed being a full-time wife and mother—for a while—and managed to keep up her medical skills with a few weekend shifts.

Annie, too, had found love and happiness in their small town. The news of her latest pregnancy pleased Jane.

"Have you connected with Julie and Megan yet?" her mother asked.

Along with Annie, Julie and Megan had been Jane's best friends all through high school. Julie was married and lived ten minutes away. Megan was a divorced single mother. Jane hadn't seen either woman in three years—make that four. How quickly time got away from her.

"Not yet," Jane told her.

"I want you to have lunch with your friends while you're home."

"Mom, that isn't necessary. I'm not here to be entertained."

"I don't want you to argue with me, either."

Jane grinned, tempted to follow her mother's suggestion.

Why not? She'd love to see her friends. "I'll try to set something up with Julie and Megan this week."

"Good." Her mother gently stroked Jane's cheek. "You're so pale and exhausted."

The comment brought tears to her eyes. *She* wasn't the one suffering pain and trauma, like her father, who'd broken his hip, or her mother who'd had to deal with the paramedics, the hospital, the surgeon and all the stress.

"I came here to help *you*," Jane reiterated.

"You have, don't you see?" Her mother hugged Paul. "It's time with my precious grandbabies that's helping me cope with all this. I don't see nearly enough of them. Having the grandkids with me is such a treat, and I fully intend to take advantage of it."

Jane went to take a shower, looking forward to visiting with her friends. She missed Cal and Promise, but it was good to be in California, too.

The metallic whine of the can opener made Cal grit his teeth. This was the third night in a row that he'd eaten soup and crackers for dinner. The one night he'd fried himself a steak, he'd overcooked it. A few years back he'd been a pretty decent cook, but his skills had gotten rusty since his marriage. He dumped the ready-to-heat soup into the pan and stared at it, finding it utterly unappetizing.

Naturally he could always invite himself to his brother's house for dinner. Glen and Ellie would gladly set an extra plate at their table. He'd do that when he got desperate, but he wasn't, at least not yet. For that matter, he could call his father. Phil would appreciate the company, but by the time Cal was finished with his chores on the ranch, dinner had already been served at the retirement home.

Come to think of it, he was in the mood for Mexican food, and no place was better than Promise's own Mexican Lindo. His mouth had begun to water at the mere thought of his favorite enchiladas, dripping with melted cheese. He could practically taste them. Needing no other incentive, he set the pan of soup inside the refrigerator and grabbed his hat.

If he hurried, he'd be back in time for Jane's phone call. Her spirits had seemed better these past few days. Her father was improving, and today she'd met a couple of high-school friends for lunch.

Soon Harry would be released from the rehab center, and once his father-in-law was home, Jane and the children would return to Texas. Cal sincerely wished Jane's father a speedy recovery—and his good wishes weren't entirely selfish, either. He liked Harry Dickinson, despite their long-winded arguments and despite his father-in-law's reservations about Jane's choice in a husband. He'd never actually said anything, but Cal knew. It was impossible not to. Still, Harry's attitude had gotten friendlier, especially after the children were born.

Promise was bustling when Cal drove up Main Street. All the activity surprised him, although it shouldn't have. It was a Thursday night, after all, and there'd been strong economic growth in the past few years. New businesses abounded, an area on the outskirts of town had been made into a golf course, and the city park had added a swimming pool and tennis courts. Ellie's feed store had been remodeled, but it remained the friendly place it'd always been. She'd kept the wooden rockers out front and his own father was among the retired men who met there to talk politics or play a game of chess. The tall white steeple of the church showed prominently in the distance. Cal reflected that it'd been a long time since he'd attended services. Life just seemed to get in the way. Too bad, because he genuinely enjoyed Wade McMillen's sermons.

The familiar tantalizing aroma of Texas barbecue from the Chili Pepper teased his nostrils, and for a moment Cal hesitated. He could go for a thick barbecue sandwich just as easily as his favorite enchiladas, but in the end he stuck with his original decision.

When he walked into the stucco-walled restaurant, he was immediately led to a booth. He'd barely had time to remove his hat before the waitress brought him a bowl of corn chips and a dish of extra-hot salsa. His mouth was full when Nicole Nelson stepped into the room, eyed him boldly and smiled. After only the slightest pause, she approached his table.

"Hello, Cal." Her voice was low and throaty.

Cal quickly swallowed the chip, almost choking as he did. The attractive woman standing there wasn't the kid he'd known all those years ago. Her jeans fit her like a second skin, and unless he missed his guess, her blouse was one of those designer numbers that cost more than he took to the bank in an average month. If her tastes ran to expensive clothes like that, Cal couldn't imagine how she was going to live on what Annie Porter could afford to pay her.

"Nicole," he managed. "Uh, hi. How're you doing?"

"Great, thanks." She peered over her shoulder as though expecting to meet someone. "Do you have a couple of minutes?"

"Uh...sure." He glanced around, grateful no one was watching.

Before he realized what she intended, Nicole slid into the booth opposite him. Her smile was bright enough to make him blink.

"I can't *tell* you how wonderful it is to see you again," she said.

"You, too," he muttered, although he wasn't sure he would've recognized her if he'd passed her in the street.

"I guess you're surprised I'm back in Promise."

"A little," he said. "What brings you to town?" He already knew she'd made the move without having a job lined up.

She reached for a chip, then shrugged. "A number of things. The year I lived in Promise was one of the best of my life. I really did grow to love this town. Jennifer and I got transferred here around the same time, but she never felt the way I did about it."

"Jennifer," he said aloud. "Are you still in touch with her?"

"Oh, sure. We've been friends for a lot of years."

"How is she?"

"Good," Nicole told him, offering no details.

"Did she ever marry?" He was a fool for asking, but he wanted to know.

Nicole dipped the chip in his salsa and laughed lightly. "She's been married—and divorced—twice."

"Twice?" Cal could believe it. "Someone told me she was living with a computer salesman in Houston." He'd heard that from Glen, who'd heard it from Ellie, who'd heard it from Janice at the bank.

"She married him first, but they've been divorced longer than they were ever married."

"I'm sorry to hear that." He wasn't really, but it seemed like something he should say.

"Then she met Mick. He was from Australia."

"Oh," he said. "Australia, huh?"

"Jennifer thought Mick was pretty hot," Nicole continued. "They had a whirlwind courtship, got married in Vegas and divorced a year later."

"I'll bet she was upset about that," Cal said, mainly because he didn't know how else to comment.

"With Jennifer it's hard to tell," Nicole said.

The waitress approached the table and Nicole declined a menu, but asked for a margarita. "Actually I'm meeting someone later, but I saw you and thought this was a good opportunity to catch up on old times."

"Great." Not that they'd *had* any "old times." Then, because he wasn't sure she knew he was married, he added, "I could use the company. My wife and kids are in California with her family for the next week or so."

"Oh..."

He might've been wrong, but Cal thought he detected a note of disappointment in her voice. Surely she'd known he was married; surely Annie had told her. But then again, maybe not.

"My boy's three and my daughter's eighteen months."

"Congratulations."

"Thanks," Cal said, feeling a bit self-conscious about dragging Jane and the kids into this conversation. But it was the right thing to do—and it wouldn't hurt his ego if the information got back to Jennifer, either.

Nicole helped herself to another chip. "The last time Jennifer and I spoke, she said something that might interest you." Nicole loaded the chip with salsa and took a discreet nibble. Looking up, she widened her eyes. "Jen said she's always wondered what would've happened if she'd stayed in Promise and you two *had* gotten married."

Cal laughed. He knew the answer, even if Nicole and Jennifer didn't. "I would've been husband number one. Eventually she would have moved on." In retrospect, it was easy to see Jennifer's faults and appreciate anew the fact that they weren't married.

"I don't agree," Nicole said, shaking her head. "I think it might've been a different story if she'd stayed with you."

The waitress brought her drink and Nicole smiled. She took a sip, sliding her tongue along the salty edge of the glass. "Jennifer's my best friend," she went on, "but when it comes to men she's not very smart. Take you, for example. I couldn't *believe* it when she told me she was calling off the wedding. Turns out I was right, too."

Cal enjoyed hearing it, but wanted to know her reasoning. "Why's that?"

"Well, it's obvious. You were the only man strong enough to deal with her personality. I think the world of Jennifer, don't get me wrong, but she likes things her own way and that includes relationships. She was an idiot to break it off with you."

"Actually it was fortunate for both of us that she did."

"Fortunate for you, you mean," Nicole said with a deep sigh. "Like I said, Jennifer was a fool." After another sip, she leaned toward him, her tone confiding. "I doubt she'd admit it, but ever since she left Promise, Jennifer's been looking for a man just like you."

"You think so?" Her remark was a boost to his ego and superficial though that was, Cal couldn't restrain a smile.

The waitress returned with his order, and Nicole drank more of her margarita, then said, "I'll leave now and let you have your dinner."

She started to slip out of the booth, but Cal stopped her. "There's no need to rush off." He wasn't in any hurry and the truth was, he liked hearing what she had to say about Jennifer. If he missed Jane's call, he could always phone her back.

Nicole smiled. "I wanted to thank you, too," she murmured.

"For what?" He cut into an enchilada with his fork and glanced up.

"For giving me a recommendation at Tumbleweed Books."

"Hey," he said, grinning at her. "No problem."

"Annie called me this morning and said I have the job."

"I'm glad it worked out."

"Me, too. I've always loved books and I look forward to working with Annie."

He should probably mention that the bookstore owner was Jane's best friend, and would have, but he was too busy chewing and swallowing—and after that, it was too late.

Nicole checked her watch. "I'd better be going. Like I said, I'm meeting a...friend. If you don't mind, I'd like to buy your dinner."

Her words took him by surprise. He wondered what had prompted the offer.

"As a thank-you for the job reference," she explained.

"It was nothing—I was happy to do it. I'll get my own meal. But let me pay for your drink."

She agreed, they chatted a few more minutes, and then Nicole left. She hadn't said whom she was meeting, and although he was mildly curious, Cal didn't ask.

He sauntered out of the restaurant not long after Nicole. He'd been dragging when he arrived, but with his belly full and his spirits high, he felt almost cheerful as he walked toward his truck. He supposed he was sorry about Jennifer's marital troubles—but not *very* sorry.

As it happened, Cal did miss Jane's phone call, but was quick to reach her once he got home. In her message she'd sounded disappointed, anxious, emotionally drained.

"Where were you?" she asked curtly when he returned her call.

Cal cleared his throat. "I drove into town for dinner. Is everything okay?"

"Mexican Lindo, right?" she asked, answering one question and avoiding the other.

"Right."

"Did you eat alone?"

"Of course." There was Nicole Nelson, but she hadn't eaten with him, not exactly. He'd bought her a drink, that was all. But he didn't want to go into a lengthy explanation that could only lead to misunderstandings. Perhaps it was wrong not to say something about her being there, but he didn't want to waste these precious minutes answering irrelevant questions. Jane might feel slighted or suspicious, although she had no reason. At any rate, Annie would probably mention that she'd hired Nicole on his recommendation, but he could deal with that later. Right now, he wanted to know why she was upset.

"Tell me what's wrong," Cal urged softly, dismissing the thought of Nicole as easily as if he'd never seen her. Their twenty minutes together had been trivial, essentially meaningless. Not a man-woman thing at all but a pandering to his ego. Jane was his wife, the person who mattered to him.

"Dad didn't have a good day," Jane said after a moment. "He's in a lot of pain and he's cranky with me and Mom. A few tests came back and, well, it's too early to say, but I didn't like what I saw."

"He'll be home soon?"

"I don't know—I'd thought, no, I'd hoped..." She let the rest fade.

"Don't worry about it, sweetheart. Take as long as you need. I'll manage." That offer wasn't easy to make, but Cal could see she needed his support. These weeks apart were as hard on her as they were on him. This was the only way he could help.

"You *want* me to stay longer?" Jane demanded.

"No," he returned emphatically. "I thought I was being noble and wonderful."

The tension eased with her laugh. "You seem to be getting along far too well without me."

"That isn't true! I miss you something fierce."

"I miss you, too," Jane said with a deep sigh.

"How did lunch with your friends go?" he asked, thinking it might be a good idea to change the subject.

"All right," she said with no real enthusiasm.

"You didn't enjoy yourself?"

Jane didn't answer immediately. "Not really. We used to be close, but that seems so long ago now. We've grown apart. Julie's into this beauty-pageant thing for her daughter, and it was all she talked about. Every weekend she travels from one state to another, following the pageants."

"Does her daughter like it?"

"I don't know. It's certainly not something I'd ever impose on *my* daughter." She sighed again. "I don't mean to sound judgmental, but we have so little in common anymore."

"What about Megan?"

"She came with her twelve-year-old daughter. She's terribly bitter about her divorce. She dragged her husband's name into the conversation at every opportunity, calling him 'that jerk I was married to.'"

"In front of her kid?" Cal was shocked that any mother could be so insensitive.

"Repeatedly," Jane murmured. "I have to admit I felt depressed after seeing them." She paused, then took a deep breath. "I wonder what they thought of me."

"That concerns you?" Cal asked, thinking she was being ridiculous if it did.

"Not at all," Jane told him. "Today was a vivid reminder that my home's not in California anymore. It's in Promise with you."

Three

"I hate to trouble you," Nicole said to Annie. She sat in front of the computer in the bookstore office, feeling flustered and annoyed with herself. "But I can't seem to find this title under the author's name."

"Here, let me show you how it works," Annie said, sitting down next to Nicole.

Nicole was grateful for Annie Porter's patience. Working in a bookstore was a whole new experience for her. She was tired of banking, tired of working in a field dominated by women but managed by men. Her last job had left her with a bitter taste—not least because she'd had an ill-advised affair with her boss—and she was eager to move on to something completely new. Thus far, she liked the bookstore and the challenge of learning new systems and skills.

Annie carefully reviewed the instructions again. It took Nicole a couple of tries to get it right. "This shouldn't be so difficult," she mumbled. "I mean, I've worked with lots of computer programs before."

"You're doing great," Annie said.

"I hope so."

"Hey, I can already see you're going to be an asset to the business," Annie said cheerfully, taking the packing slip out of a shipment of books. "Since you came on board, we've increased our business among young single men by two hundred percent."

Nicole laughed and wished that was true. She'd dated a handful of times since her return to Promise, but no one interested her as much as Cal Patterson. And he was married, she reminded herself. Married, married, married.

She should've known he wouldn't stay single long. She'd always found Cal attractive, even when he was engaged to Jennifer. However, the reason she'd given him for moving back to Promise was the truth. She had fallen in love with the town. She'd never found anywhere else that felt as comfortable. During her brief stint with the Promise bank, she'd made friends within the community. She loved the down-home feel of the feed store and the delights of Dovie's Antiques. The bowling alley had been a blast, with the midnight Rock-and-Bowl every Saturday night.

Jennifer Healy had never appreciated the town or the people. Her ex-roommate had once joked that Promise was like Mayberry RFD, the setting of that 60s TV show. Her comment had angered Nicole. These people were sincere, pleasant and kind. *She* preferred life in a town where people cared about each other, even if Jen didn't.

Only it wasn't just the town that had brought her back. She'd also returned because of Cal Patterson.

Almost ten years ago, she'd been infatuated with him, but since he was engaged to her best friend, she couldn't very well do anything about it. When Jennifer had dumped Cal, that would've been the perfect time to stick around and comfort him. Instead, she'd waited—and then she'd been transferred again, to a different branch in another town. Shortly after she'd left Promise, she'd had her first affair, and since then had drifted from one dead-end relationship to another. That was all about to change. This time she intended to claim the prize—Cal Patterson.

At the Mexican restaurant the other night, Nicole had told Cal that Jennifer compared every man she met to him, the one she'd deserted. Nicole hadn't a clue if that was the case or not. *She* was the one who'd done the comparing. In all these years she hadn't been able to get Cal Patterson out of her mind.

So he was married. She'd suspected as much when she made the decision to return to Promise, but dating a married man wasn't exactly unfamiliar to her. She would have preferred if he was single, although his being married wasn't a deterrent. It made things more…interesting. More of a challenge. Most of the time the married man ended up staying with his wife, and Nicole was the one who got hurt. This was something she knew far too well, but she'd also discovered that there were ways of undermining a marriage without having to do much of anything. And when a marriage was shaken, opportunities might present themselves….

"Nicole?"

Nicole realized Annie was staring at her. "Sorry, I got lost in my thoughts."

"It's time for a break." Annie led the way into the back room. Once inside, she reached for the coffeepot and gestured toward one of two overstuffed chairs. "Sit down and relax. If Louise needs any help, she can call us."

Nicole didn't have to be asked twice. She'd been waiting

for a chance to learn more about Cal, and she couldn't think of a better source than Annie Porter.

Annie handed her a coffee in a ceramic mug, and Nicole added a teaspoon of sugar, letting it slowly dissolve as she stirred. "How do you know Cal?" she asked, deciding this was the best place to start.

"His wife. You haven't met Jane, have you?"

Nicole shook her head. "Not yet," she said as though she was eager to make the other woman's acquaintance.

"We've been friends nearly our entire lives. Jane's the reason I moved to Promise."

Nicole took a cookie and nibbled daintily. "Cal said he has two children."

"Yes."

The perfect little family, a boy and a girl. Except that wifey seemed to be staying away far too long. If the marriage was as wonderful as everyone suggested, she would've expected Cal's wife to be home by now.

"This separation has been hard on them," Annie was saying.

"They're separated?" Nicole asked, trying to sound sympathetic.

She was forced to squelch a surge of hope when Annie explained, "Oh, no! Not that way. Just by distance. Jane's father has been ill."

"Yes, Cal mentioned that she was in California with her family." Nicole nodded earnestly. "She's a doctor, right?" She'd picked up that information without much difficulty at all. The people of Promise loved their Dr. Jane.

"A very capable one," Annie replied. "And the fact that she's with her parents seems to reassure them both."

"Oh, I'm sure she's a big help."

"I talked to her mom the other day, who's *so* glad she's

there. I talked to Jane, too—I wanted to tell her about the baby and find out about her dad. She's looking forward to getting home."

"I know I'd want to be with my husband," Nicole said, thinking if she was married to Cal, she wouldn't be foolish enough to leave him for a day, let alone weeks at a time.

"The problem is, her father's not doing well," Annie said, then sipped her coffee. She, too, reached for a cookie.

"That's too bad."

Annie sighed. "I'm not sure how soon Jane will be able to come home." She shook her head. "Cal seems at loose ends without his family."

"Poor guy probably doesn't know what to do with himself." Nicole would love to show him, but she'd wait for the right moment.

"Do you like children?" Annie asked her.

"Very much. I hope to have a family one day." Nicole knew her employer was pregnant, so she said what she figured Annie would want to hear. In reality, she herself didn't plan to have children. Nicole was well aware that, unlike Annie, she wouldn't make a good mother. If she was lucky enough to find a man who suited her, she'd make damn sure he didn't have any time on his hands to think about kids—or to be lured away by another woman.

"I understand you're seeing Brian Longstreet," Annie murmured.

"We had dinner the other night." The night she'd run into Cal. It was to Brian's disadvantage that she'd met him directly afterward, when Cal was all she could think about.

"Do you like him?"

Nicole shrugged. "Brian's okay."

"A little on the dull side?"

"A little." She'd already decided not to date the manager of the grocery store again. He was engaging enough and not unattractive, but he lacked the *presence* she was looking for. The strength of character. His biggest fault, Nicole readily admitted, was that he wasn't Cal Patterson.

"What about Lane Moser?"

Nicole had dated him the first week she'd returned. She'd known him from her days at the bank. "Too old," she muttered. She didn't mind a few years' difference, but Lane was eighteen years her senior and divorced. "I'm picky," she joked.

"You have a right to be."

"I never seem to fall for the guys who happen to be available. I don't know what my problem is," Nicole said, and even as she spoke she recognized this for a bald-faced lie. Her problem was easily defined. She fell for married men because of the challenge, the chase, the contest. Single guys stumbled all over themselves to make an impression, whereas with married men, *she* was the one who had to lure them, had to work to attract their attention.

Over the years she'd gotten smart, and this time it wouldn't be the wife who won. It would be her.

"Don't give up," Annie said, breaking into her thoughts.

"Give up?"

"On finding the right man. He's out there. I was divorced when I met Lucas and I had no intention of ever marrying again. It's too easy to let negative experiences sour your perspective. Don't let that happen to you."

"I won't," Nicole promised, and struggled to hide a smile. "I'm sure there's someone out there for me—only he doesn't know it yet." But Cal would find out soon enough.

"We'd better get back," Annie said, glancing at her watch.

Nicole set aside her mug and stood. Cal had been on his

own for nearly two weeks now, if her calculations were correct. A man could get lonely after that much time without a woman.

He hadn't let her pay for his meal at the Mexican restaurant. Maybe she could come up with another way to demonstrate just how grateful she was for the job reference he'd provided.

"How long's Jane going to be away?" Glen asked Cal as they drove along the fence line. The bed of the pickup was filled with posts and wire and tools; they'd been examining their fencing, and doing necessary repairs all afternoon.

Cal didn't want to think about his wife or about their strained telephone conversations of the last few nights. Yesterday he'd hung up depressed and anxious when Jane told him she wouldn't be home as soon as she'd hoped. Apparently Harry Dickinson's broken hip had triggered a number of other medical concerns. Just when it seemed his hip was healing nicely, the doctors had discovered a spot on his lung, and in the weeks since, the spot had grown. All at once, the big *C* loomed over Jane's father. *Cancer.*

"I don't know when she'll be back," Cal muttered, preferring not to discuss the subject with his brother. Cal blamed himself for their uncomfortable conversations. He'd tried to be helpful, reassuring, but hadn't been able to prevent his disappointment from surfacing. He'd expected her home any day, and now it seemed she was going to be delayed yet again.

"Are you thinking of flying to California yourself?" his brother asked.

"No." Cal's response was flat.

"Why not?"

"I don't see that it'd do any good." He believed that her parents had become emotionally dependent on her, as though it was within Jane's power to take their problems away. She loved her parents and he knew she felt torn between their needs and his. And here he was, putting more pressure on her....

He didn't mean to add to her troubles, but he had.

"Do you think I'm an irrational jerk?"

"Yes," Glen said bluntly, "so what's your point?"

That made Cal smile. Leave it to his younger brother to say what he needed to hear. "You'd be a lot more sympathetic if it was *your* wife."

"Probably," Glen agreed.

Normally Cal kept his affairs to himself, but he wasn't sure about the current situation. After Jane had hung up, he'd battled the urge to call her back, settle matters. They hadn't fought, not really, but they were dissatisfied with each other. Cal understood how Jane felt, understood her intense desire to support her parents, guide them through this difficult time. But she wasn't an only child—she had a brother living nearby—and even if she had been, her uncle was a doctor, too. The Dickinsons didn't need to rely so heavily on Jane, in Cal's opinion—and he'd made that opinion all too clear.

"What would you do?" he asked his brother.

Glen met his look and shrugged. "Getting tired of your own cooking, are you?"

"It's more than that." Cal had hoped Jane would force her brother to take on some of the responsibility.

She hadn't.

Cal and Glen reached the top of the ridge that overlooked the ranch house. "Whose car is that?" Glen asked.

"Where?"

"Parked by the barn."

Cal squinted and shook his head. "Don't have a clue."

"We'd better find out, don't you think?"

Cal steered the pickup toward the house. As they neared the property, Cal recognized Nicole Nelson lounging on his porch. Her *again?* He groaned inwardly. Their meeting at the Mexican Lindo had been innocent enough, but he didn't want her mentioning it to his brother. Glen was sure to say something to Ellie, and his sister-in-law would inevitably have a few questions and would probably discuss it with Dovie, and... God only knew where this would all end.

"It's Nicole Nelson," Cal said in a low voice.

"The girl from the rodeo?"

"You met her before," he told his brother.

"I did?" Glen sounded doubtful. "When? She doesn't look like someone I'd forget that easily."

"It was a few years ago," Cal said as they approached the house. "She was Jennifer Healy's roommate. She looked different then. Younger."

He parked the truck, then climbed out of the cab.

"Hi," Nicole called, stepping down off the porch. "I was afraid I'd missed you."

"Hi," Cal returned gruffly, wanting her to know he was uncomfortable with her showing up at the ranch like this. "You remember my brother, Glen, don't you?"

"Hello, Glen."

Nicole sparkled with flirtatious warmth and friendliness, and it was hard not to react.

"Nicole." Glen touched the rim of his hat. "Good to see you again."

"I brought you dinner," Nicole told Cal as she strolled casually back to her car. She seemed relaxed and nonchalant. The way she acted, anyone might assume she made a habit of stopping by unannounced.

Glen glanced at him and raised his eyebrows. He didn't need to say a word; Cal knew exactly what he was thinking.

"After everything you've done for me, it was the least I could do," Nicole said. "I really am grateful."

"For what?" Glen looked sharply at Cal, then Nicole.

Nicole opened the passenger door and straightened. "Cal was kind enough to give me a job recommendation for Tumbleweed Books."

"Annie phoned and asked if I knew her," Cal muttered under his breath, minimizing his role.

"I hope you like taco casserole," Nicole said, holding a glass dish with both hands. "I figured something Mexican would be a good bet, since you seem to enjoy it."

"How'd she know *that?*" Glen asked, glaring at his brother.

"We met at the Mexican Lindo a few nights ago," Cal supplied, figuring the news was better coming from him than Nicole.

"You did, did you?" Glen said, his eyes filled with meaning.

"I tried to buy his dinner," Nicole explained, "but Cal wouldn't let me."

Cal suspected his brother had misread the situation. "We didn't have dinner together if that's what you're thinking," he snapped. He was furious with Glen, as well as Nicole, for putting him in such an awkward position.

Holding the casserole, Nicole headed toward the house.

"I can take it from here," Cal said.

"Oh, it's no problem. I'll put it in the oven for you and get everything started so all you need to do is serve yourself."

She made it sound so reasonable. Unsure how to stop her, Cal stood in the doorway, arms loose at his sides. Dammit, he felt like a fool.

"There's plenty if Glen would like to stay for dinner," Nicole added, smiling at Cal's brother over her shoulder.

"No, thanks," Glen said pointedly, "I've got a wife and family to go home to."

"That's why I'm here," Nicole said, her expression sympathetic. "Cal's wife and children are away, so he has to fend for himself."

"I don't need anyone cooking meals for me," Cal said, wanting to set her straight. This hadn't been his idea. Bad enough that Nicole had brought him dinner; even worse that she'd arrived when his brother was there to witness it.

"Of course you don't," Nicole murmured. "This is just my way of thanking you for welcoming me home to Promise."

"Are you actually going to let her do this?" Glen asked, following him onto the porch.

Cal hung back. "Dovie brought me dinner recently," he said, defending himself. "Savannah, too."

"That's a little different, don't you think?"

"No!" he said. "Nicole's just doing something thoughtful, the same as Dovie and Savannah."

"Yeah, right."

"I'm not going to stand out here and argue with you," Cal muttered, especially since he agreed with his brother and this entire setup made him uncomfortable. If she'd asked his preference, Cal would have told Nicole to forget it. He was perfectly capable of preparing his own meals, even if he had little interest in doing so. He missed Jane's dinners—but it was more than the food.

Cal was lonely. He'd lived by himself for several years and now he'd learned, somewhat to his dismay, that he no longer liked it. At first it'd been the little things he'd missed most— conversation over dinner, saying good-night to his children, sitting quietly with Jane in the evenings. Lately, though, it was *everything*.

"I'll be leaving," Glen said coldly, letting Cal know once again that he didn't approve of Nicole's being there.

"I'll give you a call later," Cal shouted as Glen got into his truck.

"What for?"

His brother could be mighty dense at times. "Never mind," Cal said, and stepped into the house.

Nicole was in the kitchen, bustling about, making herself at home. He found he resented that. "I've got the oven preheating to 350 degrees," she said, facing him.

He stood stiffly in the doorway, anxious to send her on her way.

"As soon as the oven's ready, bake the casserole for thirty minutes."

"Great. Thanks."

"Oh, I nearly forgot."

She hurried toward him and it took Cal an instant to realize she wanted out the door. He moved aside, but not quickly enough to avoid having her brush against him. The scent of her perfume reminded him of something Jane might wear. Roses, he guessed. Cal experienced a pang of longing. Not for Nicole, but for his wife. It wasn't right that another woman should walk into their home like this. *Jane* should be here, not Nicole—or anyone else.

"I left the sour cream and salsa in the car," Nicole said breathlessly when she returned. She placed both containers on the table, checked the oven and set the glass dish inside. "Okay." She rubbed her palms together. "I think that's everything."

Cal remained standing by the door, wanting nothing so much as to see her go.

She pointed to the oven. "Thirty minutes. Do you need me to write that down?"

He shook his head and didn't offer her an excuse to linger.

"I'll stay if you like and put together a salad."

He shook his head. "I'll be fine."

She smiled sweetly. "In that case, enjoy."

This time when she left, Cal knew to stand several feet away to avoid any physical contact. He watched her walk back to her car, aware of an overwhelming sense of relief.

Life at the retirement residence suited Phil Patterson. He had his own small apartment and didn't need to worry about cooking, since the monthly fee included three meals a day. He could choose to eat alone in his room or sit in the dining room if he wanted company. Adjusting to life without Mary hadn't been easy—wasn't easy now—but he kept active and that helped. So did staying in touch with friends. Particularly Frank Hennessey. Gordon Pawling, too. The three men played golf every week.

Frank's wife, Dovie, and Mary had been close for many years, and in some ways Mary's death from Alzheimer's had been as hard on Dovie as it was on Phil. At the end, when Mary no longer recognized either of them, Phil had sat and wept with his wife's dear friend. He hadn't allowed himself to break down in front of his sons, but felt no such compunction when he was around Dovie. She'd cried with him, and their shared grief had meant more than any words she might have said.

Frank and Dovie had Phil to dinner at least once a month, usually on the first Monday. He found it a bit odd that Frank had issued an invitation that afternoon when they'd finished playing cards at the seniors' center.

"It's the middle of the month," Phil pointed out. "I was over at your place just two weeks ago."

"Do you want to come for dinner or not?" Frank said.

Only a fool would turn down one of Dovie's dinners. That woman could cook unlike anyone he knew. Even Mary, who was no slouch when it came to preparing a good meal, had envied Dovie's talent.

"I'll be there," Phil promised, and promptly at five-thirty, he arrived at Frank and Dovie's, a bouquet of autumn flowers in his hand.

"You didn't need to do that," Dovie said when she greeted him, lightly kissing his cheek.

As he entered the house, Phil caught a whiff of something delicious—a blend of delightful aromas. He smelled bread fresh from the oven and a cake of some sort, plus the spicy scent of one of her Cajun specialties.

Frank and Phil settled down in the living room and a few minutes later Dovie brought them an appetizer plate full of luscious little things. A man sure didn't eat this well at the retirement center, he thought. Good thing, too, or he'd be joining the women at their weekly weight-loss group.

Phil helped himself to a shrimp, dipping it in a spicy sauce. Frank opened a bottle of red wine and brought them each a glass.

They chatted amiably for a while, but Phil knew there was something on Dovie's mind. He had an inkling of what it was, too, and decided to break the ice and make it easier for his friends.

"It's times like this that I miss Mary the most," he murmured, choosing a brie-and-mushroom concoction next.

"You mean for social get-togethers and such?" Frank asked.

"Well, yes, those, too," Phil said. "The dinners with friends and all the things we'd planned to do…"

Dovie and Frank waited.

"I wish Mary was here to talk to Cal."

His friends exchanged a glance, and Phil realized he'd been right. They'd heard about Cal and Nicole Nelson.

"You know?" Frank asked.

Phil nodded. It wasn't as though he could *avoid* hearing. Promise, for all its prosperity and growth, remained a small town. The news that Nicole Nelson had delivered dinner to Cal had spread faster than last winter's flu bug. He didn't like it, but he wasn't about to discuss it with Cal, either. Mary could have had a gentle word with their son, and Cal wouldn't have taken offense. But Phil wasn't especially adroit at that kind of conversation. He knew Cal wouldn't appreciate the advice, nor did Phil think it was necessary. His son loved Jane, and that was all there was to it. Cal would never do anything to jeopardize his marriage.

"Apparently Nicole brought him dinner—supposedly to thank Cal for some help he recently gave her," Dovie said, her face pinched with disapproval.

"If you ask me, that young woman's trying to stir up trouble," Frank added.

"Maybe so," Phil agreed, but he knew his oldest son almost as well as he knew himself. Cal hadn't sought out this other woman; she was the one who'd come chasing after him. His son would handle the situation.

"No one's suggesting they're romantically involved," Frank said hastily.

"They aren't," Phil insisted, although he wished again that

Mary could speak to Cal, warn him about the perceptions of others. That sort of conversation had been her specialty.

"Do you see Nicole Nelson as a troublemaker?" Phil directed the question to Dovie.

"I don't know... I don't *think* she is, but I do wish she'd shown a bit more discretion. She's still young—it's understandable."

Phil heard the reluctance in her response and noticed the way she eyed Frank, as though she expected him to leap in and express his opinion.

"Annie seems to like her," Dovie went on, "but with this new pregnancy, she's spending less and less time at the bookstore. Really, I hate to say anything...."

"I tell you, the woman's a homewrecker," Frank announced stiffly.

"Now, Frank." Dovie placed her hand on her husband's knee and shook her head.

"Dovie, give me some credit. I was in law enforcement for over thirty years. I recognized that hungry look of hers the minute I saw her."

Phil frowned, now starting to feel worried. "You think Nicole Nelson has her sights set on Cal?"

"I do," Frank stated firmly.

"What an unkind thing to say." Still, he sensed that Dovie was beginning to doubt her own assessment of Nicole.

"The minute I saw her, I said to Dovie, 'That woman's trouble,'" Frank told him.

"He did," Dovie confirmed, sighing.

"Mark my words."

"Frank, please," she said. "You're talking as though Cal wasn't a happily married man. We both know he isn't the type to get involved with another woman. He's a good husband and father."

"Yes," Frank agreed.

"How did you hear about her bringing dinner out to Cal?" Phil asked. It worried him that this troublemaker was apparently dropping Cal's name into every conversation, stirring up speculation. Glen was the one who'd mentioned it to Phil—casually, but Phil wasn't fooled. This was his youngest son's way of letting him know he sensed trouble. Phil had weighed his options and decided his advice wasn't necessary. But it seemed that plenty of others had heard about Nicole's little trip to the ranch. Not from Glen and not from Ellie, which meant Nicole herself had been spreading the news. She had to be incredibly naive or just plain stupid or... Phil didn't want to think about what else would be going on in the woman's head. He didn't know her well enough to even guess. Whatever the reason for her actions, if Jane heard about this, there could be problems.

"Glen told Ellie," Dovie said, "and she was the one who told me. Not in any gossipy way, mind you, but because she's concerned. She asked what I knew about Nicole."

"Do you think anyone will tell Jane?"

Dovie immediately rejected that idea. "Not unless it's Nicole Nelson herself. To do so would be cruel and malicious. I can't think of a single person in Promise who'd purposely hurt Jane. This town loves Dr. Texas." Dr. Texas was what Jane had affectionately been called during her first few years at the clinic.

"The person in danger of getting hurt here is Cal," Frank said gruffly. "Man needs his head examined."

Phil had to grin at that. Frank could be right; perhaps it *was* time to step in, before things got out of hand. "Mary always was better at talking to the boys," he muttered. "But I suppose I could have a word with him...."

"You want me to do it?" Frank offered.

"Frank!" Dovie snapped.

"*Someone* has to warn him he's playing with fire," Frank blurted.

Phil shook his head. "Listen, if anyone says anything, it'll be me."

"You'll do it, won't you?" Frank pressed.

Reluctantly Phil nodded. He would, but he wasn't sure when. Sometimes a situation righted itself without anyone interfering. This might be one of those cases.

He sincerely hoped so.

Four

Jane stood at the foot of her father's hospital bed, reading his medical chart. Dr. Roth had allowed her to review his notes as a professional courtesy. She frowned as she studied them, then flipped through the test results, liking what they had to say even less.

"Janey? Is it that bad?" her father asked. She'd assumed he was asleep; his question took her by surprise.

Jane quickly set the chart aside. "Sorry if I woke you," she murmured.

He waved off her remark.

"It's bad news, isn't it?" he asked again. "You can tell me, Jane."

His persistence told her how worried he was. "Hmm. It says here you've been making a pest of yourself," she said, instead of answering his question.

He wore a sheepish grin. "How's a man supposed to get any rest around here with people constantly waking him up for one thing or another? If I'd known how much blood they were going to take or how often, I swear I'd make them pay me." He paused. "Do you have any idea what they charge for all this—all these X-rays and CAT scans and tests?"

"Don't worry about that, Dad. You have health insurance." However, she was well aware that his real concern wasn't the expense but the other problems that had been discovered as a result of his broken hip.

"I want to know what's going on," he said, growing agitated.

"Dad." Jane placed one hand on his shoulder.

He reached for her fingers and squeezed them hard. For a long moment he said nothing. "Cal wants you home, doesn't he?"

She hesitated, not knowing what to say. Cal had become restive and even a bit demanding; he hadn't hidden his disappointment when she'd told him she couldn't return to Promise yet. Their last few conversations had been tense and had left Jane feeling impatient with her husband—and guilty for reacting that way.

"Your mother and I have come to rely on you far too much," her father murmured.

"It's all right," Jane said, uncomfortably aware that Cal had said essentially the same thing. "I'm not just your daughter, I'm a physician. It's only natural that you'd want me here. What's far more important is for you and Mom not to worry."

Her father sighed and closed his eyes. "This isn't fair to you."

"Dad," she said again, more emphatically. "It's all right, really. Cal understands." He might not like it, but he did understand.

"How much time do I have?" he shocked her by asking

next. He was looking straight at her. "No one else will tell me the truth. You're the only one I can trust."

Her fingers curled around his and she met his look. "There are very effective treatments—"

"How much time?" he repeated, more loudly.

Jane shook her head.

"You won't tell me?" He sounded hurt, as if she'd somehow betrayed him.

"How do you expect me to answer a question like that?" she demanded. "Do I have a crystal ball or a direct line to God? For all we know, you could outlive me."

His smile was fleeting. "Okay, give me a ballpark figure."

Jane was uncomfortable doing even that. "Dad, you aren't listening to what I'm saying. You're only at the beginning stages of treatment."

"Apparently my heart isn't in great shape, either."

What he said was true, but the main concern right now was treating the cancer. He'd already had his first session of chemotherapy, and Jane hoped there'd be an immediate improvement. "Your heart is fine."

"Yeah, sure."

"Dad!"

He made an effort to smile. "It's a hard thing to face one's failing health—one's mortality."

When she nodded, he said quietly, "I worry about your mother without me."

Jane was worried about her mother, too, but she wasn't about to add to her father's burden. "Mom will do just fine."

Her father sighed and looked away. "You've made me very proud, Jane. I don't think I've ever told you that."

A lump formed in her throat and she couldn't speak.

"If anything happens to me, I want you to be there for your mother."

"Dad, please, of course I'll help Mom, but don't talk like that. Yes, you've got some medical problems, but they're all treatable. You trust me, don't you?"

He closed his eyes and nodded. "Love you, Janey."

"Love you, too, Dad." On impulse, she leaned forward and kissed his forehead.

"Tell your mother to take the kids to the beach again," he insisted. "Better yet, make that Disneyland."

"She wants to spend the time with you."

"Tell her not to visit me today. I need the rest." He opened his eyes and gave her an outrageous wink. "Now get out of here so I can sleep."

"Yes, Daddy," she said, reaching for her purse.

She might be a grown woman with children of her own, but the sick fragile man in that bed would always be the father she loved.

"Mommy, beach?" Paul asked as he walked into the kitchen a couple of mornings later, dragging his beloved blanket behind him. He automatically opened the cupboard door under the counter and checked out the selection of high-sugar breakfast cereals. Her mother had spoiled the children and it was going to take work to undo that once they got home.

Home. Jane felt so torn between her childhood home and her life in Promise, between her parents and her husband. She no longer belonged in California. Texas was in her blood now and she missed it—missed the ranch, her friends...and most of all, she missed Cal.

"Can we go to the beach?" Paul asked again, hugging the

box of sugar-frosted cereal to his chest as he carried it to the table.

"Ah…" Her father's doctor was running another set of tests that afternoon.

"Go ahead," her mother urged, entering the kitchen, already dressed for the day. "Nothing's going to happen at the hospital until later."

"But, Mom…" Jane's sole reason for being in California was to help her parents. If she was going to be here, she wanted to feel she was making some contribution to her father's recovery. Since their conversation two days ago, he'd tried to rely on her less, insisting she spend more time with her children. But the fewer demands her father made on her, the more her mother seemed to cling. Any talk of returning to Texas was met with immediate resistance.

"I'll stay with your dad this morning while you go to the beach," her mother said. "Then we can meet at the hospital, and I'll take the children home for their naps."

Jane agreed and Paul gave a shout of glee. Mary Ann, who was sitting in the high chair, clapped her hands, although she couldn't possibly have known what her brother was celebrating.

"Mom, once we get the test results, I really need to think about going home. I'm needed back in Promise."

Stephanie Dickinson's smile faded. "I know you are," she said with a sigh. "It's been so wonderful having you here…."

"Yes, but—"

"I can't tell you how much my grandkids have helped me cope."

"I'm sure that's true." Her mother made it difficult to press the issue. Whenever Jane brought up the subject of leaving, Stephanie found an even stronger reason for her to remain "a few extra days." Jane had already spent far more time away than she'd intended.

"We'll find out about Dad's test results this afternoon, and if things look okay, I'm booking a flight home."

Her mother lifted Mary Ann from the high chair and held her close. "Don't worry, honey," she said tearfully. "Your father and I will be fine."

"Mother. Are you trying to make me feel guilty?"

Stephanie blinked as if she'd never heard anything more preposterous. "Why would you have any reason to feel guilty?" she asked.

Why, indeed. "I miss my life in Texas, Mom—anyway, Derek's here," she said, mentioning her younger brother, who to this point had left everything in Jane's hands. Five years younger, Derek was involved in his own life. He worked in the movie industry as an assistant casting director and had a different girlfriend every time Jane saw him. Derek came for brief visits, but it was clear that the emotional aspects of dealing with their parents' situation were beyond him.

"Of course you need to get back," her mother stated calmly as she reached for a bowl and set it on the table for Paul, along with a carton of milk.

The child opened the cereal box and filled his bowl, smiling proudly at accomplishing this feat by himself. Afraid of what would happen if he attempted to pour his own milk, Jane did it for him.

"I want you to brush your teeth as soon as you're finished your breakfast," she told him. Taking Mary Ann with her, she left the kitchen to get ready for a morning at the beach.

Just as she'd hoped, the tests that afternoon showed some improvement. Jane was thrilled for more reasons than the obvious. Without discussing it, she called the airline and booked a flight home, then informed her parents as matter-of-factly as possible.

Stephanie Dickinson went out that evening for a meeting with her church women's group—the first social event she'd attended since Harry's accident. A good sign, in her daughter's opinion. Jane welcomed the opportunity to pack her bags and prepare for their return. Paul moped around the bedroom while she waited for a phone call from Cal. She'd promised her son he could speak to his father, but wondered if that had been wise. Paul was already tired and cranky, and since Cal was attending a Cattlemen's Association meeting, he wouldn't be back until late.

"I want to go to the beach again," he said, pouting.

"We will soon," Jane promised. "Aren't you excited about seeing Daddy?"

Paul's lower lip quivered as he nodded. "Can Daddy go to the beach with us?"

"He will one day."

That seemed to appease her son, and Jane got him settled with crayons and a Disney coloring book.

When the phone finally rang, she leaped for it, expecting to hear her husband's voice. Eager to hear it.

"Hello," she said. "Cal?"

"It's me." He sounded reserved, as if he wasn't sure what kind of reception he'd get.

"Hello, you," she said warmly.

"You're coming home?"

"Tomorrow."

"Oh, honey, you don't know what good news that is!"

"I do know. I'll give you the details in a minute. Talk to Paul first, would you?"

"Paul's still up? It's after nine, your time."

"It's been a long day. I took the kids to the beach this morning, and then this afternoon I was at the hospital with my dad when we got the test results." She took a deep breath. "Anyway, I'll explain later. Here's Paul."

She handed her son the receiver and stepped back while he chatted with his father. The boy described their hours at the beach, then gave her the receiver again. "Daddy says he wants to talk to you now."

"All right," she said. "Give me a kiss good-night and go to bed, okay? We have to get up early tomorrow."

Paul stood on tiptoe and she bent down to receive a loud kiss. Not arguing, the boy trotted down the hallway to the bedroom he shared with Mary Ann. Jane waited long enough to make sure he went in.

"I've got the flight information, if you're ready to write it down," she said.

"Yup—pen in hand," Cal told her happily. Hearing the elation in his voice was just the balm she needed.

She read off the flight number and time of arrival, then felt obliged to add, "I know things have been strained between us lately and—"

"I'm sorry, Jane," he said simply. "It's my fault."

"I was about to apologize to you," she said, loving him, anticipating their reunion.

"It's just that I miss you so much."

"I've missed you, too." Jane sighed and closed her eyes. They spoke on the phone nearly every night, but lately their conversations had been tainted by the frustration they both felt with their predicament. She'd wanted sympathy and understanding; he'd been looking for the same. They tended to keep their phone calls brief.

"I have a sneaking suspicion your mother's been spoiling the kids."

"She sees them so seldom..." Jane started to offer an excuse, then decided they could deal with the subject of their children's routines later.

"Your dad's tests—how were they?" Cal asked.

"Well, put it this way. His doctors are cautiously optimistic. So Dad's feeling a lot more positive."

"Your mother, too?"

"Yes." Despite Stephanie's emotional dependence on her, Jane admired the courage her mother had shown in the past few weeks. Seeing her husband in the hospital, learning that he'd been diagnosed with cancer, was a terrifying experience. At least, the situation seemed more hopeful now.

"I'll be at the airport waiting for you," Cal promised. "Oh, honey, I can't tell you how good it's going to be to have you back."

"I imagine you're starved for a home-cooked meal," Jane teased.

"It isn't your cooking I miss as much as just having my wife at home," Cal said.

"So you're eating well, are you?"

"I'm eating." From the evasive way he said it, she knew that most of his dinners consisted of something thrown quickly together.

"I'll see you tomorrow," Jane whispered. "At five o'clock."

"Tomorrow at five," Cal echoed, "and that's none too soon."

Jane couldn't agree more.

Cal was in a good mood. By noon, he'd called it quits for the day; ten minutes later he was in the shower. He shaved, slapped on the aftershave Jane liked and donned a crisp clean shirt. He was ready to leave for San Antonio to pick up his family. His steps lightened as he passed the bedroom, and he realized he'd be sharing the bed with his wife that very night. He hesitated at the sight of the disheveled and twisted sheets. Jane had some kind of obsession with changing the bed linens every week. She'd been away almost three weeks now and he hadn't made the bed even once. She'd probably appreciate clean sheets.

He stripped the bed and piled the dirty sheets on top of the washer. The laundry-room floor was littered with numerous pairs of mud-caked jeans and everything else he'd dirtied in the time she'd been away. No need to run a load, he figured; Jane liked things done her own way. He'd never known that a woman could be so particular about laundry.

The kitchen wasn't in terrific shape, either, and Cal regretted not using the dishwasher more often. Until that very moment, he hadn't given the matter of house-cleaning a second thought. He hurriedly straightened the kitchen and wiped the countertops. Housework had never been his forte, and Jane was a real stickler about order and cleanliness. When he'd lived with his brother, they'd divided the tasks; Cal did most of the cooking and Glen was in charge of the dishes. During the weeks his wife was away, Cal hadn't done much of either.

Still, he hadn't been totally remiss. He'd washed Savannah's and Dovie's dishes. Nicole Nelson's, too. He grabbed his good beige Stetson and started to leave yet again, but changed his mind.

He didn't have a thing to feel guilty about—but if Jane learned that Nicole had brought him a casserole, she'd be upset, particularly since he'd never mentioned it. That might look bad. He hadn't *meant* to keep it from her, but they'd been sidetracked by other concerns, and then they'd had their little spat. He'd decided just to let it go.

All Cal wanted was his wife and family home. That didn't strike him as unreasonable—especially when he heard about the way she seemed to be spending her days. How necessary was it to take the kids to Disneyland? Okay, once, maybe, but they'd gone three or four times. He'd lost count of their trips to the beach. This wasn't supposed to be a vacation. He immediately felt guilty about his lack of generosity. She'd had a lot of responsibility and he shouldn't begrudge her these excursions. Besides, she'd had to entertain the kids *somehow.*

Collecting the clean casserole dishes, Cal stuck them in the backseat of his car. He'd return them now, rather than risk having Jane find the dish that belonged to Nicole Nelson.

His first stop was at the home of Savannah and Laredo Smith. After a few minutes of searching, he found his neighbor in one of her rose gardens, winterizing the plants. They'd grown up next door to each other, and Savannah's brother, Grady Weston, had been Cal's closest friend his entire life.

Savannah, who'd been piling compost around the base of a rosebush, straightened when he pulled into the yard. She'd already started toward him by the time he climbed out of the car.

"Well, hello, Cal," she said, giving him a friendly hug.

"Thought I'd bring back your dish. I want you to know how much I appreciated the meal."

Savannah pressed her forearm against her moist brow. "I was glad to do it. I take it Jane'll be home soon?"

"This afternoon." He glanced at his watch and saw that he still had plenty of time.

"That's wonderful! How's her father doing?"

"Better," he said. He didn't want to go into all the complexities and details right now; he'd leave that for Jane.

"I should go," he told her. "I've got a couple of other stops to make before I head to the airport."

"Give Jane my best," Savannah said. "Ask her to call me when she's got a minute."

Cal nodded and set off again. His next stop was Dovie and Frank Hennessey's place. Besides a chicken pot pie, Dovie had baked him dessert—an apple pie. It was the best meal he'd eaten the whole time Jane was in California. Dovie had a special recipe she used for her crust that apparently included buttermilk. She'd passed it on to Jane, but despite several attempts, his wife's pie crust didn't compare with Dovie Hennessey's. But then, no one's did.

Frank answered the door and gave him a smile of welcome. "Hey, Cal! Good to see you." He held open the back door and Cal stepped inside.

"You, too, Frank." Cal passed him the ceramic pie plate and casserole dish. "I'm on my way to the airport to pick up Jane and the kids."

"So that's why you're wearing a grin as wide as the Rio Grande."

"Wider," Cal said. "Can't wait to have 'em back."

"Did Phil catch up with you?" Frank asked.

"Dad's looking for me?"

Frank nodded. "Last I heard."

"I guess I should find out what he wants," Cal said. He had enough time, since it was just after two and Jane's flight wasn't due until five. Even if it took him a couple of hours hours to drive to the airport, he calculated, he should get there before the plane landed. Still, he'd have to keep their visit brief.

Frank nodded again; he seemed about to say something else, then apparently changed his mind.

"What?" Cal asked, standing on the porch.

Frank shook his head. "Nothing. This is a matter for you and your dad."

Cal frowned. He had to admit he was curious. If his father had something to talk over with him, Cal wondered why he hadn't just phoned. From Frank and Dovie's house, Cal drove down Elm Street to the seniors' residence. He found his father involved in a quiet game of chess with Bob Miller, a retired newspaperman.

"Hello, Cal," Phil murmured, raising his eyes from the board.

"Frank Hennessey said you wanted to see me," Cal said abruptly. "Hi, Bob," he added. He hadn't intended any rudeness, but this was all making him a bit nervous.

Phil stared at him. "Frank said that, did he?"

"I brought back Dovie's dishes, and Frank answered the door. If you want to talk to me, Dad, all you need to do is call."

"I know, I know." Phil stood and smiled apologetically at Bob. "I'll be back in a few minutes."

Bob was studying the arrangement of chess pieces. "Take all the time you need," he said without looking up.

Phil surveyed the lounge, but there was no privacy to be had there. Cal checked his watch again, thinking he should preface their conversation with the news that he was on his way to the airport. Before he had a chance to explain why he was in town—and why he couldn't stay long—his father shocked him by saying, "I want to know what's going on between you and Nicole Nelson."

"Nicole Nelson?" Cal echoed.

Phil peered over his shoulder. "Perhaps the best place to have this discussion is my apartment."

"There's nothing to discuss," Cal said, his jaw tightening.

Phil ignored him and marched toward the elevator. "You take back her dinner dishes yet?" he pried. "Or have you advanced to sharing candlelit meals?"

Cal nearly swallowed his tongue. His father knew Nicole had brought him dinner. How? Glen wasn't one to waste time on idle gossip. Nor was Ellie. He didn't like to think it was common knowledge or that the town was feasting on this tasty tidbit.

His father's apartment consisted of a small living area with his own television and a few bookcases. His mother's old piano took up one corner. Double glass doors led to the bedroom and an adjoining bath. Although he didn't play the piano, Phil hadn't sold it when Cal's mother died. Instead, he used the old upright to display family photographs.

He walked over to a photo of Cal with Jane and the two children, taken shortly after Mary Ann's birth. "You have a good-looking family, son."

Cal knew his father was using this conversation to lead into whatever nonsense was on his mind. Hard as it was, he kept his mouth shut.

"It'd be a shame to risk your marriage over a woman like Nicole Nelson."

"Dad, I'm *not* risking my marriage! There's nothing to this rumor. The whole thing's been blown out of proportion. Who told you she'd been out to the ranch?"

"Does it matter?" Phil challenged.

"Is this something folks are talking about?" That was Cal's biggest fear. He didn't want Jane returning to Promise and being subjected to a torrent of malicious gossip.

"I heard the two of you were seen together at the Mexican Lindo, too."

"Dad!" Cal cried, yanking off his hat to ram his fingers

through his hair. "It wasn't *like* that. I was eating alone and Nicole happened to be there at the same time."

"She sat with you, didn't she?"

"For a while. She was meeting someone else."

Phil's frown darkened. "She didn't eat with you, but you bought her a drink, right?"

Reluctantly Cal nodded. He'd done nothing wrong; surely his father could see that.

"People saw you and Nicole in the Mexican Lindo. These things get around. Everyone in town knows she brought you a meal, but it wasn't Glen or Ellie who told them."

"Then who did?" Even as he asked the question, the answer dawned on Cal. He sank onto the sofa that had once stood in the library of his parents' bed-and-breakfast. "Nicole," he breathed, hardly able to believe she'd do something like that.

Phil nodded. "Must be. Frank thinks she's looking to make trouble." He paused, frowning slightly. "Dovie doesn't seem to agree. She thinks we're not being fair to Nicole."

"What do *you* think?" Cal asked his father. None of this made any sense to him.

Phil shrugged. "I don't know Nicole, but I don't like what I've heard. Be careful, son. You don't want to lose what's most important over nothing. Use your common sense."

"I didn't seek her out, if that's what you're thinking," Cal said angrily.

"Did I say you had?"

This entire situation was out of control. If he'd known that recommending Nicole for a job at the bookstore would lead to this, he wouldn't have said a word. It didn't help any that Jane's best friend, Annie Porter, owned Tumbleweed Books, although he assumed Annie would show some discretion. He could trust her to believe him—but even if she didn't, Annie would never say or do anything to hurt Jane.

"You plan on seeing Nicole again?"

"I didn't plan on seeing her the first time," Cal shot back. "I don't have any reason to see her."

"Good. Keep it that way."

Cal didn't need his father telling him something so obvious. Not until he reached the car did he remember the casserole dish. With his father's warning still ringing in his ears, he decided that returning it to Nicole could wait. When he had a chance, he'd tuck the dish in the cab of his pickup and drop it off at the bookstore. Besides, he no longer had the time. Because of this unexpected delay with his father, he'd have to hurry if he wanted to get to the airport before five.

Despite the likelihood that he'd now be facing rush-hour traffic, he had to smile.

His wife and family were coming home.

Exhausted, Jane stepped off the plane, balancing Mary Ann on her hip. The baby had fussed the entire flight, and Jane was pretty sure she had an ear infection. Her skin was flushed and she was running a fever and tugging persistently at her ear.

With Mary Ann crying during most of the flight, Paul hadn't taken his nap and whined for the last hour, wanting to know when he'd see his daddy again. Jane's own nerves were at the breaking point and she pitied her fellow passengers, although fortunately the plane had been half-empty.

"Where's Daddy?" Paul said as they exited the jetway.

"He'll be here," Jane assured her son. "He'll meet us at the entrance." The diaper bag slipped off her shoulder and tangled with her purse strap, weighing down her arm.

"I don't see Daddy," Paul cried, more loudly this time.

"Just wait, okay?"

"I don't want to wait," Paul complained. He crossed his arms defiantly. "I'm *tired* of waiting. I want my daddy."

"Paul, please, I need you to be my helper."

Mary Ann started to cry, tugging at her ear again. Jane did what she could to comfort her daughter, but it was clear the child was in pain. She had Children's Tylenol with her, but it was packed in the luggage. The checked luggage, of course.

She made her way to the baggage area; she'd get their suitcases, then she could at least take out the medication for Mary Ann.

With the help of a friendly porter, she collected the bags and brought them over to the terminal entrance, looking around for her husband. No Cal anywhere. She opened the smaller bag to get the Tylenol. She found it just as she heard her name announced over the broadcast system.

"That must be your father," she told Paul.

"I want my daddy!" the boy shrieked again.

Jane wanted Cal, too—and when she saw him she intended to let him know she was not pleased. She located a house phone, dragged over her bags and, kids in tow, breathlessly picked up the receiver.

She was put through to Cal.

"Where the hell are you?" he snapped.

"Where the hell are *you?*" She was tempted to remind him that she had two suitcases and two children to worry about, plus assorted other bags. The only items he had to carry were his wallet and car keys. She'd appreciate a little help!

"I'm waiting for you at the entrance," he told her a little more calmly.

"So am I," she said, her voice puzzled.

"You aren't at Terminal 1."

"No, I'm at 2! That's where I'm supposed to be." She tried to restrain her frustration. "How on earth could you get that wrong?"

"Stay right there and I'll meet you," Cal promised, sounding anxious.

Ten minutes later Paul gave a loud cry. "Daddy! Daddy!"

There he was. Cal strolled toward them, a wide grin on his face as Paul raced in his direction. He looked wonderful, Jane had to admit. Tanned and relaxed, tall and lean. At the moment all she felt was exhausted. He reached down and scooped Paul into his arms, lifting him high. The boy wrapped his arms around Cal's neck and hugged him fiercely.

"Welcome home," Cal said. Still holding Paul, he pulled her and the baby into his arms and embraced them.

"What happened?" Jane asked. "Where were you?"

"Kiss me first," he said, lowering his head to hers. The kiss was long and potent, and it told Jane in no uncertain terms how happy he was to have her back.

"I'm so glad to be home," she whispered.

"I'm glad you are, too." He put his son back on the floor and Paul gripped his hand tightly. "I'm sorry about the mixup." Cal shook his head. "I gave myself plenty of time, but I stopped off to see my dad and got a later start than I wanted. And then traffic was bad. And *then* I obviously wasn't thinking straight and I went to the wrong terminal."

Jane sighed. Knowing she was going to have her hands full, he might've been a bit more thoughtful.

The hour and a half ride into Promise didn't go smoothly, either. Keyed up and refusing to sleep, Paul was on his worst behavior. Mary Ann's medication took almost an hour to kick in, and until then, she cried and whimpered incessantly. Jane's nerves were stretched to the limit. Cal tried to distract both children with his own renditions of country classics, but he had little success.

When he pulled into the driveway, Jane gazed at the house with a sense of homecoming that nearly brought tears to her eyes. It'd been an emotional day from the first. Her mother had broken down when she dropped Jane and the kids off at LAX; seeing their grandmother weep, both children had begun to cry, too. Then the flight and Mary Ann's fever and her difficulties at the airport. Instead of the loving reunion she'd longed for with Cal, there'd been one more disappointment.

"You and the kids go inside, and I'll get the luggage," Cal told her.

"All right." Jane unfastened her now-sleeping daughter from the car seat and held her against one shoulder.

Paul followed. "How come Daddy's going to his truck?" he asked.

Jane glanced over her shoulder. "I don't know." He seemed to be carrying something, but she couldn't see what and, frankly, she didn't care.

What Jane expected when she walked into the house was the same sense of welcome and familiar comfort. Instead, she walked into the kitchen—and found chaos. Dishes were stacked in the sink and three weeks' worth of mail was piled on the kitchen table. The garbage can was overflowing. Jane groaned and headed down the hallway. Dirty clothes littered the floor in front of the washer and dryer.

Attempting to take a positive view of the situation, Jane guessed this proved how much Cal needed her, how much she'd been missed.

She managed to keep her cool until she reached their bedroom. The bed was torn apart, the bedspread and blankets scattered across the floor, and that was her undoing. She proceeded to their daughter's room and gently set Mary Ann in her crib; fortunately she didn't wake up. Jane returned to the kitchen and met Cal just as he was walking in the back door with the last of her bags.

Hands on her hips, she glared at him. "You couldn't make the bed?"

"Ah…" He looked a bit sheepish. "I thought you'd want clean sheets."

"I do, but after three hours on a plane dealing with the kids, I didn't want to have to change them myself."

"Mommy! I'm hungry."

Jane had completely forgotten about dinner.

"The house is, uh, kind of a mess, isn't it?" Cal said guiltily. "I'm sorry, honey, my standards aren't as high as yours."

Rather than get involved in an argument, Jane went to the linen closet for a clean set of sheets. "Could you fix Paul a sandwich?" she asked.

"Sure."

"I want tuna fish and pickles," Paul said.

"I suppose your mother let him eat anytime he wanted," Cal grumbled.

Stephanie had, but that was beside the point. "Let's not get into this now," she said.

"Fine."

By the time Jane finished unpacking, sorting through the mail and separating laundry, it was nearly midnight. Cal helped her make the bed. He glanced repeatedly in her direction, looking apologetic.

"I'm sorry, honey," he said again.

Jane didn't want to argue, but this homecoming had fallen far short of what she'd hoped. At least Mary Ann was sleeping soundly. But without a nap, Paul had been out of sorts. Cal had put him down and returned a few minutes later complaining that his son had turned into a spoiled brat.

Jane had had enough. "Don't even start," she warned him.

He raised both hands. "All right, all right."

They barely spoke afterward.

At last Cal undressed and slipped between the fresh sheets. "You ready for bed?"

Exhausted, Jane merely nodded; she didn't have the energy to speak.

He held out his arms, urging her to join him, and one look told her what he had in mind.

Jane hesitated. "I hope you're not thinking what I suspect you're thinking."

"Honey," he pleaded, "it's been nearly three weeks since we made love."

Jane sagged onto the side of the bed. "Not tonight."

Cal looked crestfallen. "Okay, I guess I asked for that. You're upset about the house being a mess, aren't you?"

"I'm not punishing you, if that's what you're saying." Couldn't he see she was nearly asleep on her feet?

"Sure, whatever," he muttered. Jerking the covers past his shoulder, he rolled over and presented her with a view of his back.

"Oh, Cal, stop it," she said, tempted to shake him. He was acting like a spoiled little boy—like their own son when he didn't get what he wanted. At this point, though, Jane didn't care. She undressed and turned off the light. Tired as she was, she assumed she'd be asleep the instant her head hit the pillow.

She wasn't.

Instead, she lay awake in the dark, wondering how their reunion could possibly have gone so wrong.

Five

To say that Jane's kitchen cupboards were bare would be an understatement. One of her first chores the next morning was to buy groceries. Cal kept Paul with him for the day, instead of taking him to preschool, and Jane buckled Mary Ann into her car seat and drove to town.

She was grateful to be home, grateful to wake up with her husband at her side and grateful that the unpleasantness of the night before seemed to be forgotten. With the washer and dryer humming and the children well rested, the day looked brighter all the way around. Even Mary Ann seemed to be feeling better, and a quick check of her ears revealed no infection.

Although she had a whole list of things to do, Jane took time to go and see Ellie. Later, when she'd finished with her errands, she planned to make a quick run over to Annie's.

"You look…" Ellie paused as she met Jane outside Frasier Feed.

"Exhausted," Jane filled in for her. "I'm telling you, Ellie, this time away was no vacation."

"I know," Ellie said, steering her toward the old-fashioned rockers positioned in front. "I remember what it was like. With my dad sick and my mother frantic, it was all I could do to keep myself sane."

Jane wished Cal understood how trying and difficult these weeks had been for her. He *should* know, seeing that his own mother had been so terribly ill, but then, Phil had protected his sons from the truth for far too long.

"I'm glad you're home." Ellie sank into one of the rockers.

"Me, too." Jane sat down beside her friend, balancing Mary Ann on her knee. She loved sitting right here with Ellie, looking out at the town park and at the street; she'd missed their chats. She could smell mesquite smoke from the Chili Pepper. California cuisine had nothing on good old Texas barbecue, she decided, her mouth watering at the thought of ribs dripping with tangy sauce. A bowl of Nell Grant's famous chili wouldn't go amiss, either.

"Everything will be better now," Ellie said.

Jane stared at her friend. "Better? How do you mean?"

Ellie's gaze instantly shot elsewhere. "Oh, nothing... I was thinking out loud. I'm just pleased you're back."

Jane was a little puzzled but let Ellie's odd remark slide. They talked about friends and family and planned a lunch date, then Jane left to get her groceries.

Buy-Right Foods had built a new supermarket on the outskirts of town, and it boasted one of the finest produce and seafood selections in the area. The day it opened, everyone in the county had shown up for the big event—not to mention the music, the clowns who painted kids' faces and, not least, the generous assortment of free samples. There hadn't been a parking space in the lot, which had occasioned plenty of complaints. People didn't understand that this kind of congestion

was a way of life in California. Jane had forgotten what it was
like to wait through two cycles at a traffic light just to make
a left-turn lane. A traffic jam in Promise usually meant two
cars at a stop sign.

Grabbing a cart at the Buy-Right, she fastened Mary Ann
into the seat and headed down the first aisle. Everyone who
saw Jane seemed to stop and chat, welcome her home. At this
rate, it'd take all day to get everything on her list. Actually she
didn't mind. If Cal had shown half the enthusiasm her friends
and neighbors did, the unpleasantness the night before might
have been averted.

"Jane Dickinson—I mean, Patterson! Aren't you a sight
for sore eyes."

Jane recognized the voice immediately. Tammy Lee Kollenborn. The woman was a known flirt and troublemaker.
Jane tended to avoid her, remembering the grief Tammy had
caused Dovie several years earlier. After a ten-year relationship,
Dovie had wanted to get married and Frank hadn't. Then,
for some ridiculous reason, Frank had asked Tammy Lee out.
The night had been a disaster, and shortly afterward Frank
had proposed to Dovie—although not before Tammy Lee
had managed to upset Dovie with her lies and insinuations.

"Hello, Tammy Lee."

The older woman's gold heels made flip-flop sounds as she
pushed her cart alongside Jane's. "My, your little one sure is a
cutie-pie." She peered at Mary Ann through her rhinestone-
rimmed glasses. "I swear I'd die for lashes that long," she said,
winking up at Jane.

Trying to guess Tammy Lee's age was a fruitless effort.
She dressed in a style Jane privately called "Texas trash" and
wore enough costume jewelry to qualify her for a weight-
lifting award.

"From what I hear, it's a good thing you got home when you did," Tammy Lee said.

Jane frowned. "Why?"

Tammy Lee lowered her voice. "You mean to say no one's mentioned what's been going on with Cal and that other woman while you were away?"

Jane pinched her lips. If she was smart, she'd make a convenient excuse and leave without giving Tammy the pleasure of spreading her lies. They *had* to be lies. After five years of marriage, Jane knew her husband, and Cal was not the type of man to cheat on his wife.

"Her name's Nicole Nelson. Pretty little thing. Younger than you by, oh, six or seven years." Tammy Lee studied her critically. "Having children ages a woman. My first husband wanted kids, but I knew the minute I got pregnant I'd eat my way through the whole pregnancy. So I refused."

"Yes, well…listen, Tammy Lee, I've got a lot to do."

"I saw Cal with her myself."

"I really do need to be going—"

"They were having dinner together at the Mexican Lindo."

"Cal and Nicole Nelson?" Jane refused to believe it.

"They were *whispering*. This is a small town, Jane, and people notice these things. Like I said, I'm surprised no one's mentioned it. I probably shouldn't, either, but my fourth husband cheated on me and I would've given anything for someone to tell me sooner. You've heard the saying? The wife is always the last to know."

"I'm sure there's a very logical reason Cal was with Nicole," Jane insisted, not allowing herself to feel jealous. Even if she was, she wouldn't have said anything in front of Tammy Lee.

"When my dear friend finally broke down and told me about Mark seeing another woman, I said the very same thing," Tammy Lee went on. "Wives are simply too trusting. We assume our husbands would never betray us like that."

"I really have a lot to do," Jane said again.

"Now, you listen to me, Jane. Later on, I want you to remember that I'm here for you. I know what you're feeling."

Jane was sure that couldn't be true.

"If you need someone to talk to, come to me. Like I said, I've been down this road myself. If you need a good attorney, I can recommend one in San Antonio. When she's finished with Cal Patterson, he won't have a dime."

"Tammy Lee, I don't have time for this," Jane said, and forcefully pushed her cart forward.

"Call me, you hear?" Tammy Lee gently patted Jane's shoulder. Jane found it a patronizing gesture and had to grit her teeth.

By the time she'd finished paying for her groceries, she was furious. No one needed to tell her who Nicole Nelson was; Jane had no trouble figuring it out. The other woman had approached Cal the afternoon of the rodeo. Jane had sat in the grandstand with her two children while that woman flirted outrageously with her husband.

For now, Jane was willing to give Cal the benefit of the doubt. But as she loaded the groceries into the car, she remembered Ellie's strange comment about everything being "better" now. So *that* was what her sister-in-law had meant.

The one person she trusted to talk this out with was Dovie. Jane hurried to her friend's antique store, although she couldn't stay long.

Dovie greeted her with a hug. The store looked wonderful, thanks to Dovie's gift for display. Her assortment of antiques, jewelry, dried flowers, silk scarves and more was presented in appealing and imaginative ways.

They chatted a few minutes while Dovie inquired about Jane's parents.

"I ran into Tammy Lee Kollenborn at the grocery store," Jane announced suddenly, watching for Dovie's reaction. It didn't take her long to see one. "So it's true?"

"Now, Jane—"

"Cal's been seeing Nicole Nelson?"

"I wouldn't say that."

"According to Tammy Lee, they were together at the Mexican Lindo. Is that right?"

Hands clenched in front of her, Dovie hesitated, then nodded.

Jane couldn't believe her ears. She felt as though her legs were about to collapse out from under her.

"I'm sure there's a perfectly logical reason," Dovie murmured, and Jane realized she'd said the very same words herself not ten minutes earlier.

"If that's the case, then why didn't Cal mention it?" she demanded, although she didn't expect an answer from Dovie.

The older woman shrugged uncomfortably. "You'll have to ask him."

"Oh, I intend to," Jane muttered as she headed out the door. She'd visit Annie another day. Right now, she was more interested in hearing what Cal had to say for himself.

When she pulled off the highway and hurtled down the long drive to the ranch house, the first thing she noticed was that the screen door was open. Cal and Paul walked out to the back porch to greet her. She saw that her husband's expression was slightly embarrassed, as if he knew he'd done something wrong.

"Don't be mad," he said when she stepped out of the car, "but Paul and I had a small accident."

"What kind of accident?" she asked.

"We decided to make lunch for you and...well, let me just say that I think we can save the pan." A smile started to quiver at the corners of his mouth. "Come on, honey, it's only a pan. I'm sure the smoke will wash off the walls."

"Tell me about Nicole Nelson," Jane said point-blank.

The amusement vanished from his eyes. He stiffened. "What's there to say?"

"Plenty, from what I hear."

"Come on, Jane! You know me better than that."

"Do I?" She glared at him.

"Jane, you're being ridiculous."

"Did you or did you not have dinner with Nicole Nelson?" Cal didn't answer.

"It's a simple question," she said, growing impatient.

"Yeah, but the answer's complicated."

"I'll bet it is!" Jane was angrier than she'd been in years. If they'd had a wonderful reunion, she might have found the whole matter forgettable. Instead, he hadn't even bothered to show up on time or at the right terminal. The house was a mess and all he could think about was getting her in the sack. She shifted Mary Ann on her hip, grabbed a bag full of groceries and stomped into the house.

"Jane!"

She stood in the doorway. "I have all the answers I need."

"Fine!" Cal shouted, angry now.

"Daddy, Daddy!" Paul cried, covering his ears. "Mommy's mad."

"Is this what you want our son to see?" Cal yelled after her.

"That's just perfect," Jane yelled back. "You're running around town with another woman, you don't offer a word of explanation and then you blame *me* because our son sees us fighting." Hurt, angry and outraged, she stormed into the bedroom.

* * *

It was obvious to Glen that things weren't going well between his brother and Jane. He saw evidence of the trouble in their marriage every morning when he drove to work at the Lonesome Coyote Ranch.

He and Cal were partners, had worked together for years, and if anyone knew that Cal could be unreasonable, it was Glen. More importantly, though, Glen was well aware that his older brother loved his wife and kids.

By late October the demands of raising cattle had peaked for the season, since the greater part of their herd had been sold off. Not that the hours Cal kept gave any indication of that. Most mornings when Glen arrived, Cal had already left the house.

"Are you going to talk about it?" Glen asked him one afternoon. Cal hadn't said more than two words to him all day. They sat side by side in the truck, driving back to the house.

"No," Cal barked.

"This has to do with Jane, right?" Glen asked.

Cal purposely hit a pothole, which made Glen bounce so high in his seat that his head hit the truck roof, squashing the crown of his Stetson.

"Dammit, Cal, there was no call for that," Glen complained, repairing his hat.

"Sorry," Cal returned, but his tone said he was anything but.

"If you can't talk to me, then who can you talk to?" Glen asked. It bothered him that his only brother refused to even acknowledge, let alone discuss, his problems. Over the years Glen had spilled his guts any number of times. More than once Cal had steered him away from trouble. Glen hoped to do him the same favor.

"If I *wanted* to talk, you mean," Cal said.

"In other words, you'd prefer to keep it all to yourself."

"Yup."

"Okay, then, if that's what you want."

They drove for several minutes in tense silence. Finally Glen couldn't stand it anymore. "This is your wife—your *family*. Doesn't that matter to you? What's going on?" He could feel his patience with Cal fading.

Cal grumbled something he couldn't hear. Then he said in a grudging voice, "Jane paid a visit to Tumbleweed Books the other day."

His brother didn't have to explain further. Nicole Nelson worked at the bookstore, and although Jane was a good friend of Annie Porter's, Glen suspected she hadn't casually dropped by to see her.

"She talk to Nicole?"

Cal spoke through clenched teeth. "I don't like my wife checking up on me."

Glen mulled this over and wondered if Cal had explained the situation. "Jane knows you didn't take Nicole to dinner, doesn't she?"

"Yes!" he shouted. "I *told* her what happened. The next thing I know, she's all bent out of shape, slamming pots and pans around the kitchen like I did something terrible."

"Make it up to her," Glen advised. If his brother hadn't learned that lesson by now, it was high time he did.

"I didn't do anything wrong," Cal snapped. "If she doesn't believe me, then…"

"Cal, get real! Do what you've got to do, man. You aren't the only one, you know. Ellie gets a bee in her bonnet every now and then. Darned if I know what I did, but after a while

I don't care. I want things settled. I want peace in the valley. Learn from me—apologize and be done with it."

Cal frowned, shaking his head. "I'm not you."

"Pride can make a man pretty miserable," Glen said. "It's... it's like sitting on a barbed-wire fence naked." He nodded, pleased with his analogy.

Cal shook his head again, and Glen doubted his brother had really heard him. Changing the subject, Glen tried another approach. "How's Jane's father?"

"All right, I guess. She talks to her mother nearly every day."

The ranch house came into view. Glen recalled a time not so long ago when they'd reached this same spot and had seen Nicole Nelson's vehicle parked down below. A thought occurred to him, a rather unpleasant one.

"Are you still in love with Jane?" Glen asked.

Cal hit the brakes with enough force to throw them both forward. If not for the restraint of the seat belts, they might have hit their heads on the windshield.

"What kind of question is that?" Cal roared.

"Do you still love Jane?" Glen yelled right back.

"Of course I do!"

Glen relaxed.

"What I want is a wife who trusts me," Cal said. "I haven't so much as looked at another woman since the day we met, and she damn well knows it."

"Maybe she doesn't."

"Well, she should" was his brother's response.

To Glen's way of thinking, there was plenty a wife should know and often didn't. He figured it was the man's job to set things straight and to make sure his wife had no doubt whatsoever about his feelings.

In the days that followed it was clear that the situation between Jane and Cal hadn't improved. Feeling helpless, Glen decided to seek his father's advice. He found Phil at the bowling alley Friday afternoon, when the senior league was just finishing up. It didn't take much to talk Phil into coffee and a piece of pie. The bowling alley café served the best breakfast in town and was a popular place to eat.

As they slid into the booth, the waitress automatically brought over the coffeepot.

"We'll each have a slice of pecan pie, Denise," Phil told her.

"Coming right up," she said, filling the thick white mugs with an expert hand. "How you doin', Phil? Glen?"

"Good," Glen answered for both of them.

No more than a minute later they were both served generous slices of pie. "Enjoy," she said cheerily.

Phil reached for his fork. "No problem there."

Glen wasn't as quick to grab his own fork. He had a lot on his mind.

"You want to talk to me about something?" Phil asked, busy doctoring his coffee.

Glen left his own coffee black and raised the mug, sipping carefully.

"I didn't think you were willing to buy me a slice of pecan pie for nothing."

Glen chuckled. Of the two sons, he shared his father's temperament. Their mother had been a take-charge kind of woman and Cal got that from her, but she'd never held her hurts close to the chest, the way Cal did.

"I take it you're worried about your brother." Phil picked up his fork again and cut into his pie.

"Yeah." Glen stared down at his favorite dessert and realized he didn't have much of an appetite. "What should I say to him?"

"Listen." Phil leaned forward to rest his elbows on the table. "When your mother was alive and we had the bed-and-breakfast, she was constantly trying new recipes."

Glen couldn't understand what his mother's cooking had to do with the current situation, but he knew better than to ask. Phil would get around to explaining sooner or later.

"No matter what time of day it was, she'd sit down and eat some of whatever new dish she'd just made. When I asked her why, she said it was important to try a little of it herself before she served it to anyone else."

"Okay," Glen said, still wondering about the connection between his mother's culinary experiments and Cal and Jane.

"Advice is like that. Take some yourself before you hand it to others."

"I haven't given Cal any advice." Not for lack of trying, however. Cal simply wasn't in the mood to listen.

"I realize that. The advice is going to come from me, and I'm giving it to you—free of charge."

Glen laughed, shaking his head.

"Let Cal and Jane settle this themselves."

"But, Dad…"

Phil waved his fork at him. "Every couple has problems at one time or another. You and Ellie will probably go through a difficult patch yourselves, and when you do, you won't appreciate other people sticking their noses in your business."

"Do you think Cal and Jane are going to be okay?"

"Of course they are. Cal loves Jane. He won't do anything to jeopardize his family. Now eat your pie, or I just might help myself to a second slice."

Glen picked up his fork. His father knew what he was talking about; Cal did love Jane, and whatever was wrong would eventually right itself.

★ ★ ★

Jane noticed a change in Cal the moment he came into the house. They'd been ignoring each other all week. The tension was taking its toll, not only on her but on the children.

Cal paused in the middle of the kitchen, where she was busy putting together Halloween costumes for the children. As usual the church was holding a combined harvest and Halloween party.

Jane didn't leave her place at the kitchen table, nor did she speak to Cal. Instead, she waited for him to make the first move, which he did. He walked over to the stove and poured himself a cup of coffee, then approached the table.

"What are you doing?" he asked in a friendly voice.

"Making Mary Ann a costume for the church party." She gestured at a piece of white fabric printed with spots. "She's going as a dalmatian," Jane said.

Cal grinned. "One of the hundred and one?" They'd recently watched the Disney animated feature on DVD.

Jane nodded and held up a black plastic dog nose, complete with elastic tie.

"What about Paul?"

"He's going as a pirate."

Cal cradled his mug in both hands. "Do you mind if I sit here?"

"Please."

He pulled out the chair and set his coffee on the table. For at least a minute, he didn't say another word. When he finally spoke, his voice was low, deliberate. "This whole thing about Nicole Nelson is totally out of control. If you need reassurances, then I'll give them to you. I swear to you not a thing happened."

Jane said nothing. It'd taken him nearly two weeks to tell

her what she already knew. His unwillingness to do so earlier had hurt her deeply. In her heart she knew she could trust her husband, but his pride and stubbornness had shut her out.

This situation with Nicole was regrettable. Not wanting to put Annie in the middle—it was awkward with Nicole working at Tumbleweed Books—Jane had asked general questions about the other woman. Annie had told her she liked Nicole. After their talk, Jane was convinced that the encounter between Nicole and Cal, whatever it was, had been completely innocent.

Because they lived in a small town, the story had spread quickly and the truth had gotten stretched out of all proportion; Jane understood that. What troubled her most was Cal's attitude. Instead of answering her questions or reiterating his love, he'd acted as if *she'd* somehow wronged him. Well, she hadn't been out there generating gossip! Still, Jane felt a sense of relief that their quarrel was ending.

She caught her husband staring at her intently.

"Can we put this behind us?" Cal asked.

Jane smiled. "I think it's time, don't you?"

Cal's shoulders relaxed, and he nodded. Seconds later, Jane was in her husband's arms and he was kissing her with familiar passion. "I'm crazy about you, Jane," he whispered, weaving his fingers into her thick hair.

"I don't like it when we fight," she confessed, clinging to him.

"You think I do?" he asked. "Especially over something as stupid as this."

"Oh, Cal," she breathed as he bent to kiss her again.

"Want to put the kids to bed early tonight?"

She nodded eagerly and brought her mouth to his. "Right after dinner."

Afterward, Jane felt worlds better about everything. They'd both been at fault and they both swore it wouldn't happen again.

For the next few days Cal was loving and attentive, and so was Jane, but it didn't take them long to slip back into the old patterns. The first time she became aware of it was the night of the church party.

Amy McMillen, the pastor's wife, had asked Jane to arrive early to assist her in setting up. She'd assumed Cal would be driving her into town. Instead, he announced that he intended to stay home and catch up on paperwork. Jane made sure Cal knew she wanted him to attend the function with her, that she needed his help. Supervising both children, plus assisting with the games, would be virtually impossible otherwise. But she decided not to complain; she'd done so much of that in the past couple of months.

When it came time for her to leave, Cal walked her and the children out to the car. Once she'd buckled the kids into their seats, she started the engine, but Cal stopped her.

"You've got a headlight out."

"I do? Oh, no…"

"I don't want you driving into town with only one head-light."

Jane glanced at her watch.

"Take the truck," he said. "I'll change the car seats."

"But—"

"Sweetheart, please, it'll just take a minute." Fortunately his truck had a large four-door cab with ample space for both seats.

"What's this?" Jane asked. In front, on the passenger side, was a cardboard box with a glass casserole dish.

Cal took one look at it and his eyes rushed to meet hers. "A dish," he muttered.

"Of course it's a dish. *Whose* dish?"

He shrugged as if it was no big deal. "I don't know if I mentioned it, but Dovie and Savannah brought me meals while
you were away," he said, wrapping the safety belt around Mary
Ann's car seat and snapping it in place.

"You mean to say half the town was feeding you and you
still managed to nearly destroy my kitchen?"

Cal chuckled.

"I meant to return the dish." He kissed Jane and closed
the passenger door. "I'll see to that headlight first thing tomorrow morning," he promised, and opened the door on the
driver's side.

Jane climbed in behind the wheel. Normally she didn't like
driving Cal's vehicle, which was high off the ground and had a
stick shift. She agreed, however, that in the interests of safety,
it was the better choice.

The church was aglow when Jane drove up. Pastor Wade
McMillen stood outside, welcoming early arrivals, and when
he saw Jane, he walked over and helped her extract Mary Ann
from her seat.

"Glad to have you back, Jane," he said. "I hope everything
went well with your father."

"He's doing fine," she said, although that wasn't entirely
true. She was in daily communication with her mother. It
seemed her father wasn't responding to the chemotherapy anymore and grew weaker with every treatment. Her mother was
at a loss. Several times she'd broken into tears and asked Jane
to talk Cal into letting her and the children come back for a
visit over Christmas. Knowing how Cal would feel, she hadn't
broached the subject yet.

"Would you like me to carry in that box for you?" Wade
asked.

"Please." Both Dovie and Savannah would be at the church party, and there was no reason to keep the casserole dish in the truck.

"I'll put it in the kitchen," Wade told her, leading the way.

Paul saw the display of pumpkins and dried cornstalks in the large meeting room and shouted with delight. Although it was early, the place was hopping with children running in every direction.

Jane followed the pastor into the kitchen, and sure enough, found Dovie there.

"I understand this is yours," Jane said when Wade set the box down on the counter.

Dovie shook her head.

"Didn't you send dinner out to Cal?"

"I did, but he already returned the dishes."

"It must belong to Savannah, then," she said absently.

Not until much later in the evening did Jane see Savannah and learn otherwise. "Well, for heaven's sake," she muttered to Ellie as they were busy with the cleanup. "I don't want to drag this dish back home. Do you know who it belongs to?"

Ellie went suspiciously quiet.

"Ellie?" Jane asked, not understanding at first.

"Ask Cal," her sister-in-law said.

"Cal?" Jane repeated and then it hit her. She knew *exactly* who owned that casserole dish. And asking Cal was what she intended to do. Clearly more had gone on while she was away than he'd admitted. How dared he do this to her!

Glen carried the box containing the dish back to the truck for her. Tired from the party, both Paul and Mary Ann fell asleep long before she turned off the highway onto the dirt road that led to the house.

No sooner had she parked the truck than the back door

opened and Cal stepped out. Although it was difficult to contain herself, she waited until the children were in bed before she brought up the subject of the unclaimed dish.

"I ran into Dovie and Savannah," she said casually as they walked into the living room, where the television was on. Apparently her husband didn't have as much paperwork as he'd suggested.

"Oh? How was the party?"

Jane ignored the question. "Neither one of them owns that casserole dish."

Jane watched as Cal's shoulders tensed.

"Tell me, Cal, who does own it?"

Not answering, Cal strode to the far side of the room.

"Don't tell me you've forgotten," Jane said.

He shook his head.

A sick feeling was beginning to build in the pit of her stomach. "Cal?"

"Sweetheart, listen—"

"All I want is a name," she interrupted, folding her arms and letting her actions tell him she was in no mood to be cajoled.

Cal started to say something, then stopped.

"You don't need to worry," Jane said without emotion. "I figured it out. That dish belongs to Nicole Nelson."

Six

Cal couldn't believe this was happening. Okay, so his wife had cause to be upset. He should've mentioned that Nicole Nelson had brought him a meal. The only reason he hadn't was that he'd been hoping to avoid yet another argument. He knew how much their disagreements distressed her, and she'd been through so much lately. He was just trying to protect her!

Without a word to him, Jane had gone to bed. Cal gave her a few minutes to cool down before he ventured into the bedroom. The lights were off, but he knew she wasn't asleep.

"Jane," he said, sitting on the edge of the bed. She had her back to him and was so far over on her side it was a wonder she hadn't tumbled out. "Can we talk about this?" he asked, willing to take his punishment and be done with it.

"No."

"You're right, I should've told you Nicole came to the ranch, but I swear she wasn't here more than ten minutes. If that. She brought over the casserole and that was it."

Jane flopped over onto her back. "Are you sure, or is there something *else* you're conveniently forgetting?"

Cal could live without the sarcasm, but let it drop. "I thought we'd decided to put this behind us." He could always hope tonight's installment of their ongoing argument would be quickly settled. The constant tension between them had worn his patience thin.

Jane suddenly bolted upright in bed. She reached for the lamp beside her bed and flipped the switch, casting a warm light about the room. "You have a very bad habit of keeping things from me."

That was unfair! Cal took a deep calming breath before responding. "It's true I didn't tell you Nicole fixed me dinner, but—"

"You didn't so much as mention her name!"

"Okay...but when was I supposed to do that? You were in California, remember?"

"We talked on the phone nearly every night," Jane said, crossing her arms. "Now that I think about it, you kept the conversations short and sweet, didn't you? Was there a reason for that?"

Again, Cal resented the implication, but again he swallowed his annoyance and said, "You know I'm not much of a conversationalist." Chatting on the phone had always felt awkward to him. That certainly wasn't news to Jane.

"What else haven't you told me about Nicole Nelson? How many other times have you two met without my knowing? When she brought you dinner, did she make a point of joining you? Did you *accidentally* bump into each other in town?"

"No," he answered from between gritted teeth.

"You're sure?"

"You make it sound like I'm having an affair with her! I've done nothing wrong, not a damn thing!"

"Tell me why I should believe you, seeing how you habitually conceal things from me."

"You think I purposely hid the truth?" Their marriage was in sad shape if she made such assumptions. Jane was his partner in life; he'd shared every aspect of his business, his home and his ranch with her, fathered two children with her. It came as a shock that she didn't trust him.

"What about the rodeo?" she asked. "You signed up for the bull-riding competition and you deliberately didn't tell me."

"I knew you didn't want me participating in the rodeo and—"

"What I don't know won't hurt me, right?"

She had a way of twisting his words into knots no cowhand could untangle, himself included. "Okay, fine, you win. I'm a rotten husband. That's what you want to hear, isn't it?"

Her eyes flared and she shook her head. "What I want to hear is the truth."

"I tell you the truth!" he shouted, losing his temper.

"But not until you're backed into a corner."

"I've been as honest with you as I know how." Cal tried again, but he'd reached his limit. Glen had advised him to say what he had to say, do what he had to do—whatever it took to make up with Jane. He'd attempted that once already, but it hadn't been enough. Not only wasn't she satisfied, now she was looking to collect a piece of his soul along with that pound of flesh.

"Why didn't you attend the church party with me and the kids?" she asked.

He frowned. Jane knew the answer to that as well as he did. "I told you. I had paperwork to do."

"How long did it take you?"

Cal ran a hand down his face. "Is there a reason you're asking?"

"A very good one," she informed him coolly. "I'm trying to find out if you slipped away to be with Nicole."

Cal couldn't have been more staggered if his wife had pulled out a gun and shot him. He jumped off the bed and stood there staring, dumbstruck that Jane would actually suggest such a thing.

"I noticed you had the television on," she continued. "So you finished with all that paperwork earlier than you expected. Did you stop to think about me coping with the children alone? Or did you just want an evening to yourself—while I managed the children, the party and everything else on my own."

"Would you listen to yourself?" he muttered.

"I *am* listening," she shouted. "You sent me off to California with the kids, then you're seen around town with another woman. If *that* isn't enough, you lie and mislead me into thinking I'm overreacting. All at once everything's beginning to add up, and frankly I don't like the total. You're interested in having an affair with her, aren't you, Cal? That's what I see."

Cal had no intention of commenting on anything so ludicrous.

"What's the matter? Am I too close to the truth?"

Shaking his head, Cal looked down at her, unable to hide his disgust. "Until this moment I've never regretted marrying you." He headed out the door, letting it slam behind him.

Almost immediately the bedroom door flew open again. "You think *I* don't have regrets about marrying *you?*" Jane railed. "You're not alone in that department, Cal Patterson."

Once again the door slammed with such force that he was sure he'd have to nail the molding back in place.

Not knowing where to go or what else to say, Cal stood in the middle of the darkened living room. In five years of marriage he and Jane had disagreed before, but never like this. He glanced toward their bedroom and knew there'd be hell to pay if he tried to sleep there.

Cal sat in his recliner, raised the footrest and covered himself with the afghan he'd grabbed from the back of the sofa.

Everything would be better in the morning, he told himself.

Cal had left the house by the time Jane got up. It was what she'd expected. What she *wanted,* she told herself. Luckily the children had been asleep and hadn't heard them fighting. She removed her robe from the back of the door and slipped it on. Sick at heart, she felt as though she hadn't slept all night.

The coffee was already made when she wandered into the kitchen. She was just pouring herself a cup when Paul appeared, dragging his favorite blanket.

"Where's Daddy?" he asked, rubbing his eyes.

"He's with Uncle Glen." Jane crouched down to give her son a hug.

Paul pulled away and met her look, his dark eyes sad. "Is Daddy mad at you?"

"No, darling, Daddy and Mommy love each other very much." She was certain Cal felt as sorry about the argument as she did. She reached for her son and hugged him again.

Their fight had solved nothing. They'd both said things that should never have been said. The sudden tears that rushed into Jane's eyes were unexpected, and she didn't immediately realize she was crying. The children *had* heard their argument. At least Paul must have, otherwise he wouldn't be asking these questions.

"Mommy?" Paul touched his fingers to her face, noticed her tears, then broke away and raced into the other room. He returned a moment later with a box of tissues, which made Jane weep all the more. How could her beautiful son be so thoughtful and sweet, and his father so insensitive, so unreasonable?

After making breakfast for Paul and Mary Ann and getting them dressed, Jane loaded the stroller and diaper bag into the car and prepared to drive her son to preschool. The truck was parked where she'd left it the night before. Apparently Cal had gone out on Fury, his favorite gelding. He often rode when he needed time to think.

Peering into the truck, Jane saw that the casserole dish was still there. She looked at it for a moment, then took it out and placed it in the car. While Paul was in his preschool class, she'd personally return it to Nicole Nelson. And when she did, Jane planned to let her know how happily married Cal Patterson was.

After dropping Paul off, Jane drove to Tumbleweed Books. Cal had indeed replaced her headlight, just as he'd promised, and for some reason that almost made her cry again.

"Hello," Nicole Nelson called out when Jane walked into the bookstore. Jane recognized her right away. The previous time she'd seen the other woman had been at the rodeo, and that was from a distance. On closer inspection, she had to admit that Nicole was beautiful. Jane, by contrast, felt dowdy and unkempt. She wished she'd made more of an effort with her hair and makeup, especially since she'd decided to meet Nicole face-to-face.

"Is there anything I can help you find?" Nicole asked, glancing at Mary Ann in her stroller.

"Is Annie available?" Jane asked, making a sudden decision that when she did confront Nicole, she'd do it looking her best.

"I'm sorry, Annie had a doctor's appointment this morning. I'd be delighted to assist you if I can."

So polite and helpful. So insincere. Jane didn't even know Nicole Nelson, and already she disliked her.

"That's all right. I'll come back another time." Feeling foolish, Jane was eager to leave.

"I don't think we've met," Nicole said. "I'm Annie's new sales assistant, Nicole Nelson."

Jane had no option but to introduce herself. She straightened and looked directly at Nicole. "I'm Jane Patterson."

"Cal's wife," Nicole said, not missing a beat. A knowing smile appeared on her face as she boldly met Jane's eye.

Standing no more than two feet apart, Jane and Nicole stared hard at each other. In that moment Jane knew the awful truth. Nicole Nelson wanted her husband. Wanted him enough to destroy Jane and ruin her marriage. Wanted him enough to deny his children their father. Cal was a challenge to her, a prize to be won, no matter what the cost.

"I believe I have something of yours," Jane said.

Nicole's smile became a bit cocky. "I believe you do."

"Luckily I brought the casserole dish with me," Jane returned just as pointedly. She bent down, retrieved it from the stroller and handed it to Nicole.

"Did Cal happen to mention if he liked my taco casserole?" Nicole asked, following Jane to the front of the bookstore.

"Oh," Jane murmured, ever so sweetly, "he said it was much too spicy for him."

"I don't think so," Nicole said, opening one of the doors. "I think Cal might just find he prefers a bit of spice compared to the bland taste he's used to."

Fuming, Jane pushed Mary Ann's stroller out the door and discovered, when she reached the car, that her hands were trembling. This was even worse than she'd thought it would be. Because now she had reason to wonder if her husband had fallen willingly into the other woman's schemes.

Jane had a knot in her stomach for the rest of the day. She was sliding a roast into the oven as Cal walked into the house at four-thirty—early for him. He paused when he saw her, then lowered his head and walked past, ignoring her.

"I...think we should talk," she said, closing the oven, then leaning weakly against it. She set the pot holders aside and forced herself to straighten.

"Now?" Cal asked, as though any discussion with her was an unpleasant prospect.

"Paul...heard us last night," she said. She glanced into the other room, where their son was watching a children's nature program. Mary Ann sat next to him, tugging at her shoes and socks.

"It's not surprising he heard us," Cal said evenly. "You nearly tore the door off the hinges when you slammed it."

Cal had slammed the door first, but now didn't seem to be the time to point that out. "He had his blankey this morning."

"I thought you threw that thing away," Cal said, making it sound like an accusation.

"He...found it. Obviously he felt he needed it."

Cal's eyes narrowed, and she knew he'd seen through her explanation.

"That isn't important. What *is* important, at least to me," she said, pressing her hand to her heart, "is that we not argue in front of the children."

"So you're saying we can go into the barn and shout at each other all we want? Should we arrange for a baby-sitter first?"

Jane reached behind her to grab hold of the oven door. The day had been bad enough, and she wanted only to repair the damage that had been done to their relationship. This ongoing dissatisfaction with each other seemed to be getting worse; Jane knew it had to stop.

"I don't think I slept five minutes last night," she whispered.

Cal said nothing.

"I...I don't know what's going on between you and Nicole Nelson, but—"

Cal started to walk away from her.

"Cal!" she cried, stopping him.

"Nothing, Jane. There's nothing going on between me and Nicole Nelson. I don't know how many times I have to say it, and frankly, I'm getting tired of it."

Jane swallowed hard but tried to remain outwardly calm. "She wants you."

Cal's response was a short disbelieving laugh. "That's crazy."

Jane shook her head. There'd been no mistaking what she'd read in the other woman's expression. Nicole had decided to pursue Cal and was determined to do whatever she could to get him. Jane had to give her credit. Nicole wasn't overtly trying to seduce him. That would have gotten her nowhere with Cal, and somehow she knew it. Instead, Nicole had attacked the foundation of their marriage. She must be pleased with her victory. At this point Jane and Cal were barely talking.

"Just a minute," Cal said, frowning darkly. "Did you purposely seek out Nicole?"

Jane's shoulders heaved as she expelled a deep sigh. "This is the first time I've met her."

"Where?"

"I went by the bookstore after I dropped Paul off at preschool."

"To see Annie?"

"No," she admitted reluctantly. "I thought since I was in town, I'd return the casserole dish."

Jane watched as Cal's gaze widened and his jaw went white with the effort to restrain his anger.

"That was wrong?" she blurted.

"Yes, dammit!"

"You wanted to bring it back yourself, is that it?"

He slapped the table so hard that the saltshaker toppled onto its side. "You went in search of Nicole Nelson. Did you ever stop to think that might embarrass me?"

Stunned, she felt her mouth open. "You're afraid I might have embarrassed *you?* That's rich." Despite herself, Jane's control began to slip. "How dare you say such a thing?" she cried. "What about everything you've done to embarrass *me?* I'm the one who's been humiliated here. While I'm away dealing with a family crisis, my husband's seen with another woman. And everyone's talking about it."

"I'd hoped you'd be above listening to malicious gossip."

"Oh, Cal, how can you say that? I was thrust right into the middle of it, and you know what? I didn't enjoy the experience."

He shook his head, still frowning. "You had no business confronting Nicole."

"No business?" she echoed, outraged. "How can you be so callous about my feelings? Don't you see what she's doing? Don't you understand? She wants you, Cal, and she didn't hide the fact, either. Are you going to let her destroy us? Are you?"

"This isn't about Nicole!" he shouted. "It's about trust and commitment."

"*Are* you committed to me?" she asked.

The look on his face was cold, uncompromising. "If you have to ask, that says everything."

"It does, doesn't it?" Jane felt shaky, almost light-headed. "I never thought it would come to this," she said, swallowing the pain. "Not with us..." She felt disillusioned and broken. Sinking into a chair, she buried her face in her hands.

"Jane." Cal stood on the other side of the table.

She glanced up.

"Neither of us got much sleep last night."

"I don't think—"

The phone rang, and Cal sighed irritably as he walked over and snatched up the receiver. His voice sharp, he said, "Hello," then he went still and his face instantly sobered. His gaze shot to her.

"She's here," he said. "Yes, yes, I understand."

Jane didn't know what to make of this. "Cal?" she said getting to her feet. The call seemed to be for her. As she approached, she heard her husband say he'd tell her. *Tell her what?*

Slowly Cal replaced the receiver. He put his hands on her shoulders and his eyes searched hers. "That was your uncle Ken," he said quietly.

"Uncle Ken? Why didn't he talk to me?" Jane demanded, and then intuition took over and she knew without asking. "What's wrong with my dad?"

Cal looked away for a moment. "Your father suffered a massive heart attack this afternoon."

A chill raced through her, a chill of foreboding and fear. The numbness she felt was replaced by a sense of purpose. She thought of the cardiac specialists she knew in Southern California, doctors her family should contact. Surely her uncle Ken had already reached someone. He was an experienced physician; he'd know what to do, who to call.

"What did he say?"

"Jane—"

"You should've let me talk to him."

"Jane." His hands gripped her shoulders as he tried to get her attention. "It's too late. Your father's gone."

She froze. Gone? Her father was dead? No! It couldn't be true. Not her father, not her daddy. Her knees buckled and she was immediately overwhelmed by deep heart-wrenching sobs.

"Honey, I'm so sorry." Cal pulled her into his arms and held her as she sobbed.

Jane had never experienced pain at this level. She could barely think, barely function. Cal helped her make the necessary arrangements. First they planned to leave the children with Glen and Ellie; later Jane decided she wanted them with her. While Cal booked the flights, she packed suitcases for him and the kids. Only when he started to carry the luggage out to the car did she realize she hadn't included anything for herself. The thought of having to choose a dress to wear at her own father's funeral nearly undid her. Unable to make a decision, she ended up stuffing every decent thing she owned into a suitcase.

"We can leave as soon as Glen and Ellie get here," Cal said, coming into the house for her bag.

"The roast," she said, remembering it was still in the oven.

"Don't worry about it. Glen and Ellie are on their way. They'll take care of everything—they'll look after the place until we're back."

"Paul and Mary Ann?" The deep pain refused to go away, and she was incapable of thinking or acting without being directed by someone else.

"They're fine, honey. I'll get them dressed and ready to go."

She looked at her husband, and to her surprise felt nothing.

Only a few minutes earlier she'd been convinced she was about to lose him to another woman. Right now, it didn't matter. Right now, she couldn't dredge up a single shred of feeling for Cal. Everything, even the love she felt for her husband, had been overshadowed by the grief she felt at her father's death.

Cal did whatever he could to help Jane, her younger brother and her mother with the funeral arrangements. Jane was in a stupor most of the first day. Her mother was in even worse shape. The day of the funeral Stephanie Dickinson had to be given a sedative.

Paul was too young to remember Cal's mother, and Cal doubted Mary Ann would recall much of Grandpa Dickinson, either. All the children knew was that something had happened that made their mother and grandmother cry. They didn't understand what Cal meant when he explained that their grandfather had died.

The funeral was well attended, as was the reception that followed. Cal was glad to see that there'd been flowers from quite a few people in Promise—including, of course, Annie. Harry Dickinson had been liked and respected. Cal admired the way Jane stepped in and handled the social formalities. Her mother just couldn't do it, and her brother, Derek, seemed trapped in his own private pain.

Later, after everyone had left, he found his wife sitting in the darkened kitchen. Cal sat at the table beside her, but when he reached for her, she stiffened. Not wanting to upset her, he removed his hand from her arm.

"You must be exhausted," he said. "When's the last time you ate?"

"I just buried my father, Cal. I don't feel like eating."

"Honey—"

"I need a few minutes alone, please."

Cal nodded, then stood up and walked out of the room. The house was dark, the children asleep, but the thought of going to bed held no appeal. Sedated, his mother-in-law was in her room and his wife sat in the shadows.

The day he'd buried his own mother had been the worst of his life. Jane had been by his side, his anchor. He didn't know how he could have survived without her. Yet now, with her father's death, she'd sent him away, asked for time alone. It felt like a rejection of him and his love, and that hurt.

Everyone handled grief differently, he reminded himself. People don't know how they'll react until it happens to them, he reasoned. Sitting on the edge of the bed, he mulled over the events of the past few days. They were a blur in his mind.

His arms ached to hold Jane. He loved his wife, loved his children. Their marriage had been going through a rough time, but everything would work out; he was sure of it. Cal waited for Jane to come to bed, and when she didn't, he must have fallen asleep. He awoke around two in the morning and discovered he was alone. Still in his clothes, he got up and went in search of his wife.

She was sitting where he'd left her. "Jane?" he whispered, not wanting to startle her.

"What time is it?" she asked.

"It's ten after two. Come to bed."

She responded with a shake of her head. "No. I can't."

"You've haven't slept in days."

"I know how long it's been," she snapped, showing the first bit of life since that phone call with the terrible news.

"Honey, please! This is crazy, sitting out here like this. You haven't changed your clothes. This has been a hard day for you...."

She looked away, and in the room's faint light, he saw tears glistening on her face.

"I want to help you," he said urgently.

"Do you, Cal? Do you really?"

Her question shocked him. "You're my wife! Of course I do."

She started to sob then, and Cal was actually glad to see it. She needed to acknowledge her grief, to somehow express it. Other than when she'd first received the news, Jane had remained dry-eyed and strong. Her mother and brother were emotional wrecks, and her uncle Ken had been badly shaken. It was Jane who'd held them all together, Jane who'd made the decisions and arrangements, Jane who'd seen to the guests and reassured family and friends. It was time for her to let go, time to grieve.

"Go ahead and cry, Jane. It'll do you good." He handed her a clean handkerchief.

She clutched it to her face and sobbed more loudly.

"May I hold you?"

"No. Just leave me alone."

Cal crouched in front of her. "I'm afraid I can't do that. I want to help you," he said again. "Let me do that, all right?"

She shook her head.

"At least come to bed," he pleaded. She didn't resist when he clasped her by the forearms and drew her to her feet. Her legs must have gone numb from sitting there so long because she leaned heavily against him as he led her into the bedroom.

While she undressed, Cal turned back the covers.

She seemed to have trouble unfastening the large buttons of her tailored jacket. Brushing her hands aside, Cal unbuttoned it and helped take it off. When she was naked, he pulled the nightgown over her head, then brought her arms through the sleeves. He lowered her onto the bed and covered her with the blankets.

She went to sleep immediately—or that was what he thought.

As soon as he climbed into bed himself and switched off the light, she spoke. "Cal, I'm not going back."

"Back? Where?"

"To Promise," she told him.

This made no sense. "Not going back to Promise?" he repeated.

"No."

"Why not?" he asked, his voice louder than he'd intended. He stretched out one arm to turn on the lamp again.

"I can't deal with all the stress in our marriage. Not after this."

"But, Jane, we'll settle everything...."

"She wants you."

At first he didn't understand that Jane was talking about Nicole Nelson. Even when he did, it took him a while to control the anger and frustration. "Are you saying she can have me?" he asked, figuring a light approach might work better.

"She's determined, you know—except you *don't* know. You don't believe me."

"Jane, please, think about what you're saying."

"I have thought about it. It's all I've thought about for days. You're more worried about me embarrassing you than what that woman's doing to us. I don't have the strength or the will to fight for you. Not after today."

Patience had never been his strong suit, but Cal knew he had to give her some time and distance, not force her to resume their normal life too quickly. "Let's talk about it later. Tomorrow morning."

"I won't feel any differently about this in the morning. I've already spoken to Uncle Ken."

For years her uncle had wanted Jane to join his medical practice and had been bitterly disappointed when she'd chosen to stay in Texas, instead. "You're going to work for your uncle?"

"Temporarily."

Jane had arranged all this behind his back? Unable to hide his anger now, Cal tossed aside the sheet and vaulted out of bed. "You might've said something to me first! What the hell were you thinking?"

"Thinking?" she repeated. "I'm thinking about a man who lied to me and misled me."

"I never lied to you," he declared. "Not once."

"It was a lie of omission. You thought that what I didn't know wouldn't hurt me, right? Well, guess what, Cal? It does hurt. I don't want to be in a marriage where my husband's more concerned about being embarrassed than he is about the gossip and ridicule he subjects me to."

He couldn't believe they were having this conversation. "You're not being logical."

"Oh, yes, I am."

Cal strode to one end of the bedroom and stood there, not knowing what to do.

"You'll notice that even now, even when you know how I feel, you haven't once asked me to reconsider. Not once have you said you love me."

"You haven't exactly been proclaiming your love for me, either."

His words appeared to hit their mark, and she grew noticeably paler.

"Do you want me to leave right now?" he asked.

"I...I..." She floundered.

"No need to put it off," he said, letting his anger talk for him.

"You're right."

Cal jerked his suitcase out of the closet and crammed into it whatever clothes he could find. That didn't take long, although he gave Jane ample opportunity to talk him out of leaving, to say she hadn't really meant it.

Apparently she did.

Cal went into the bedroom where the children slept and kissed his daughter's soft cheek. He rested his hand on his son's shoulder, then abruptly turned away. A heaviness settled over his heart, and before he could surrender to regret, he walked away.

Seven

"I know how hard this is on you," Jane's mother said. It was two weeks since the funeral. Two weeks since Jane had separated from her husband. Stephanie busied herself about the kitchen and avoided eye contact. "But, Jane, are you sure you did the right thing?" She pressed her lips together and concentrated on cleaning up the breakfast dishes. "Ken's delighted that you're going to work with him, and the children are adjusting well, but…"

"I'm getting my own apartment."

"I won't hear of it," her mother insisted. "If you're going through with this, I want you to stay here. I don't want you dealing with a move on top of everything else."

"Mother, it's very sweet of you, but you need your space, too."

"No…" Tears filled her eyes. "I don't want to live alone—I don't think I can. I never have, you know. Not in my entire life and…well, I realize I'm leaning on you, but I need you so desperately."

"Mother, I understand."

"It's not just that. I'm so worried about you and Cal."

"I know," Jane whispered. She tried not to think of him, or of the situation between them. There'd been no contact whatsoever. Cal had left in anger, and at the time she'd wanted him out of her life.

"Did you make an appointment with an attorney?" her mother asked.

Jane shook her head. It was just one more thing she'd de-layed doing. One more thing she couldn't make a decision about. Most days she could barely get out of bed and see to the needs of her children. Uncle Ken was eager to have her join his practice. He'd already discussed financial arrange-ments and suggested a date for her to start—the first Mon-day in the new year. Jane had listened carefully to his plans; however, she'd felt numb and disoriented. This wasn't what she wanted, but everything had been set in motion and she didn't know how to stop it. Yet she had to support herself and the children. So far she hadn't needed money, but she would soon. Cal would send support if she asked for it. She lacked the courage to call him, though. She hated the idea of their first conversation being about money.

"You haven't heard from Cal, have you?" Her mother broke into her thoughts.

"No." His silence wasn't something Jane could ignore. She'd envisioned her husband coming back for her, proclaiming his love and vowing never to allow any woman to stand be-tween him and his family. Ignoring Jane was bad enough, but the fact that he hadn't seen fit to contact the children made everything so much worse. It was as though he'd wiped his family from his mind.

Two months ago Jane assumed she had a near-perfect marriage. Now she was separated and living with her mother. Still, she believed that, if not for the death of her father, she'd be back in Texas right now. Eventually they would've worked out this discord; they would have rediscovered their love. Instead, in her pain and grief over the loss of her father, she'd sent Cal away.

She reminded herself that she hadn't needed to ask him twice. He'd been just as eager to escape.

Nicole Nelson had won.

At any other time in her life Jane would have fought for her husband, but now she had neither the strength nor the emotional energy to do so. From all appearances, Cal had made his choice—and it wasn't her or the children.

"We should talk about Thanksgiving," her mother said. "It's next week...."

"Thanksgiving?" Jane hadn't realized the holiday was so close.

"Ken and Jean asked us all to dinner. What do you think?"

Jane had noticed that her mother was having a hard time making decisions, too. "Sounds nice," she said, not wanting to plan that far ahead. Even a week was too much. She couldn't bear to think about the holidays, especially Christmas.

The doorbell chimed and Jane answered it, grateful for the interruption. Facing the future, making plans—it was just too difficult. A deliveryman stood with a box and a form for her to sign. Not until Jane closed the door did she see the label addressed to Paul in Cal's distinctive handwriting.

She carried the package into the bedroom, where her son sat doing a jigsaw puzzle. He glanced up when she entered the room.

"It's from Daddy," she said, setting the box on the carpet.

Paul tore into the package with gusto and let out a squeal

when he found his favorite blanket. He bunched it up and hugged it to his chest, grinning hugely. Jane looked inside the box and saw a short letter. She read it aloud.

Dear Paul,
I thought you might want to have your old friend with you. Give your little sister a hug from me.
   Love,
   Daddy

Jane swallowed around the lump in her throat. Cal's message in that letter was loud and clear. He'd asked Paul to hug Mary Ann, but not her.

Jane was on her own.

The post office fell silent when Cal stepped into the building. The Moorhouse sisters, Edwina and Lily, stood at the counter, visiting with Caroline Weston, who was the wife of his best friend, as well as the local postmistress. Caroline had taken a leave of absence from her duties for the past few years, but had recently returned to her position.

When the three women saw Cal, the two retired schoolteachers pinched their lips together and stiffly drew themselves up.

"Good day, ladies," Cal said, touching the brim of his hat.

"Cal Patterson," Edwina said briskly. "I only wish you were in the fifth grade again so I could box your ears."

"How're you doing, Cal?" Caroline asked in a friendlier tone.

He didn't answer because anyone looking at him ought to be able to tell. He was miserable and getting more so every day. By now he'd fully expected his wife to come to her senses and return home. He missed her and he missed his kids. He barely ate, hadn't slept an entire night since he got back and was in a foul mood most of the time.

Inserting the key in his postal box, he opened the small door. He was about to collect his mail when he heard Caroline's voice from the post-office side of the box. "Cal?"

He reached for the stack of envelopes and flyers, then peered through. Sure enough, Caroline was looking straight at him.

"I just wanted to tell you how sorry Grady and I are."

He nodded, rather than comment.

"Is there anything we can do?"

"Not a thing," he said curtly, wanting Caroline and everyone else, including the Moorhouse sisters, to know that his problems with Jane were his business...and hers. No one else's.

"Cal, listen—"

"I don't mean to be rude, but I'm in a hurry." Not waiting for her reply, Cal locked his postal box and left the building.

When he'd first returned from California, people had naturally assumed that Jane had stayed on with the children to help Mrs. Dickinson. Apparently news of the separation had leaked out after Annie called Jane at her mother's home. From that point on, word had spread faster than a flash flood. What began as simple fact became embellished with each retelling. Family and friends knew more about what was happening—or supposedly happening—in his life than he did, Cal thought sardonically.

Only yesterday Glen had asked him about the letter from Paul. Cal hadn't heard one word from his wife or children, but then he hadn't collected his mail, either. When Cal asked how Glen knew about this letter, his brother briskly informed him that he'd heard from Ellie. Apparently Ellie had heard it from Dovie, and Dovie just happened to be in the post office when Caroline was sorting mail. That was life in a small town.

As soon as he stepped out of the post office, Cal quickly shuffled through the envelopes and found the letter addressed to him in Jane's familiar writing. The return address showed Paul's name.

Cal tore into the envelope with an eagerness he couldn't hide.

Dear Daddy,
Thank you for my blankey. I sleep better with it. Mary Ann likes it, too, and I sometimes share with her. Grandma still misses Grandpa. We're spending Thanksgiving with Uncle Ken and Aunt Jean.
      Love,
      Paul

Cal read the letter a second time, certain he was missing something. Surely there was a hidden message there from Jane, a subtle hint to let him know what she was thinking. Perhaps the mention of Thanksgiving was her way of telling him that she was proceeding with her life as a single woman. Her way of informing him that she was managing perfectly well without a husband.

Thanksgiving? Cal had to stop and think about the date. It'd been nearly three weeks since he'd last talked to Jane. Three weeks since he'd hugged his children. Three weeks that he'd been walking around in a haze of wounded pride and frustrated anger.

Not wanting to linger in town, Cal returned to the ranch. He looked at the calendar and was stunned to see that he'd nearly missed the holiday. Not that eating a big turkey dinner would've made any difference to him. Without his wife and children, the day would be just like all the rest, empty and silent.

Thanksgiving Day Cal awoke with a sick feeling in the pit of his stomach. Glen had tried to talk him into joining his family. Ellie's mother and aunt were flying in from Chicago for the holiday weekend, he'd said, but Cal was more than welcome. Cal declined without regrets.

He thought he might avoid Thanksgiving activities altogether, but should have known better. Around noon his father arrived. As soon as he saw the truck heading toward the house, Cal stepped onto the back porch to wait for him.

"What are you doing here, Dad?" he demanded, making sure his father understood that he didn't appreciate the intrusion.

"It's Thanksgiving."

"I know what day it is," Cal snapped.

"I thought I'd let you buy me dinner," Phil said blithely.

"I thought they served a big fancy meal at the retirement residence."

"They do, but I'd rather eat with you."

Cal would never admit it, but despite his avowals, he wanted the company.

"Where am I taking you?" he asked, coming down the concrete steps to meet Phil.

"Brewster."

Cal tipped back his hat to get a better look at his father. "Why?"

"The Rocky Creek Inn," Phil said. "From what I hear, they cook a dinner fit to rival even Dovie's."

"It's one of the priciest restaurants in the area," Cal muttered, remembering how his father had announced Cal would be footing the bill.

Phil laughed. "Hey, I'm retired. I can't afford a place as nice as the Rocky Creek Inn. Besides, I have something to tell you."

"Tell me here," Cal said, wondering if his father had news about Jane and the children. If so, he wanted it right now.

Phil shook his head. "Later."

They decided to leave for Brewster after Cal changed clothes and shaved. His father made himself at home while he waited and Cal was grateful he didn't mention the condition of the house. When he returned wearing a clean, if wrinkled, shirt and brand-new Wranglers, Phil was reading Paul's letter, which lay on the kitchen table, along with three weeks' worth of unopened mail. He paused, expecting his father to lay into him about leaving his family behind in California, and was relieved when Phil didn't. No censure was necessary; Cal had called himself every kind of fool for what he'd done.

The drive into Brewster took almost two hours and was fairly relaxing. They discussed a range of topics, everything from politics to sports, but avoided anything to do with Jane and the kids. A couple of times Cal could have led naturally into the subject of his wife, but didn't. No need to ruin the day with a litany of his woes.

The Rocky Creek Inn had a reputation for excellent food and equally good service. They ended up waiting thirty minutes for a table, but considering it was a holiday and they had no reservation, they felt that wasn't bad.

Both men ordered the traditional Thanksgiving feast and a glass of wine. Cal waited until the waiter had poured his chardonnay before he spoke. "You had something you wanted to tell me?" He'd bet the ranch that whatever it was involved the situation with Jane. But he didn't mind. After three frustrating weeks, he hoped Phil had some news.

"Do you remember when I had my heart attack?"

Cal wasn't likely to forget. He'd nearly lost his father. "Of course."

"What you probably don't know is that your mother and I nearly split up afterward."

"You and Mom?" Cal couldn't hide his shock. As far as he knew, his parents' marriage had been rock-solid from the day of their wedding until they'd lowered his mother into the ground.

"I was still in the hospital recovering from the surgery and your mother, God bless her, waltzed into my room and casually said she'd put earnest money down on the old Howe place."

Cal reached for his wineglass in an effort to stifle a grin. He remembered the day vividly. The doctors had talked to the family following open-heart surgery and suggested Phil think about reducing his hours at the ranch. Shortly after that, his parents decided to open a bed-and-breakfast in town. It was then that Cal and his brother had taken over the operation of the Lonesome Coyote Ranch.

"Your mother didn't even *ask* me about buying that monstrosity," his father told him. "I was on my death bed—"

"You were in the hospital," Cal corrected.

"All right, all right, but you get the picture. Next thing I know, Mary comes in and tells me, *tells* me, mind you, that I've retired and the two of us are moving to town and starting a bed-and-breakfast."

Cal nearly burst out laughing, although he was well aware of what his mother had done and why. Getting Phil to cut back his hours would have been impossible, and Mary had realized that retirement would be a difficult adjustment for a man who'd worked cattle all his life. Phil wasn't capable of spending his days lazing around, so she'd taken matters into her own hands.

"I didn't appreciate what your mother did, manipulating me like that," Phil continued. "She knew I never would've agreed to live in town, and she went ahead and made the decision, anyway."

"But, Dad, it was a brilliant idea." The enterprise had been a money-maker from the first. The house was in decent condition, but had enough quirks to keep his father occupied with a variety of repair projects. The bed-and-breakfast employed the best of both his parents' skills. Phil was a natural organizer and his mother was personable and warm, good at making people feel welcome.

His father's eyes clouded. "It *was* brilliant, but at the time I didn't see it that way. I don't mind telling you I was mad enough to consider ending our marriage."

Cal frowned. "You didn't mean it, Dad."

"The hell I didn't. I would've done it, too, if I hadn't been tied down to that hospital bed. It gave me time to think about what I'd do without Mary in my life, and after a few days I decided to give your mother a second chance."

Cal laughed outright.

"You think I'm joking, but I was serious and your mother knew it. When she left the hospital, she asked me to have my attorney contact hers. The way I felt right then, I swear I was determined to do it, Cal. I figured there are some things a man won't let a woman interfere with in life, and as far as I was concerned at that moment, Mary had crossed the line."

Ah, so this was what Cal was meant to hear. In her lack of trust, Jane had crossed the line with him, too. Only, *he* hadn't been the one who'd chosen to break up the family. That decision had rested entirely with Jane.

"I notice you haven't pried into my situation yet," Cal murmured.

"No, I haven't," Phil said. "That's your business and Jane's. If you want out of the marriage, then that's up to you."

"Out of the marriage!" Cal shot back. "Jane's the one who wants out. She decided not to return to Promise. The day of her father's funeral, she told me she was staying with her mother...indefinitely."

"You agreed to this?"

"The hell I did!"

"But you left."

Cal had replayed that fateful night a hundred times, asking himself these same questions. Should he have stayed and talked it out with her? Should he have taken a stand and insisted she listen to reason? Three weeks later, he still didn't have the answer.

"Don't you think Jane might have been distraught over her father's death?" Phil wanted to know.

"Yeah." Cal nodded. "But it's been nearly a month and she hasn't had a change of heart yet."

"No, she hasn't," Phil said, and sighed. "It's a shame, too, a real shame."

"I love her, Dad." Cal was willing to admit it. "I miss her and the kids." He thought of the day he'd found Paul's blankey. After all the distress that stupid blanket had caused him, Cal was so glad to see it he'd brought it to his face, breathing in the familiar scent of his son. Afterward, the knot in his stomach was so tight he hadn't eaten for the rest of the day.

"I remember when Jennifer left you," Phil said, growing melancholy, "just a couple of days before the wedding. You looked like someone had stabbed a knife straight through your gut. I knew you loved her, but you didn't go after her."

"No way." Jennifer had made her decision.

"Pride wouldn't let you," Phil added. "In that case, I think it was probably for the best. I'm not convinced of it this time." His father shook his head. "I loved your mother, don't misunderstand me—it damn near killed me when she died—but as strong as my love for her was, we didn't have the perfect marriage. We argued, but we managed to work out our problems. I'm sure you'll resolve things with Jane, too."

Cal hoped that was true, but he wasn't nearly as confident as his father.

"The key is communication," Phil said.

Cal held his father's look. "That's a little difficult when Jane's holed up halfway across the country. Besides, as I understand it, communication is a two-way street. Jane has to be willing to talk to me and she isn't."

"Have you made an effort to get in touch with her?"

He shook his head.

"That's what I thought."

"Go ahead and say it," Cal muttered. "You think I should go after her."

"Are you asking my opinion?" Phil asked.

"No, but you're going to give it to me, anyway."

"If Jane was my wife," Phil said, his eyes intent on Cal, "I'd go back for her and settle this once and for all. I wouldn't return to Promise without her. Are you willing to do that, son?"

Cal needed to think about it, and about all the things that had been said. "I don't know," he answered, being as honest as he could. "I just don't know."

Nicole Nelson arrived for work at Tumbleweed Books bright and early on the Friday morning after Thanksgiving.

With the official start of the Christmas season upon them, the day was destined to be a busy one. She let herself in the back door, prepared to open the bookstore for Annie, who was leaving more and more of the responsibility to her, which proved—to Nicole's immense satisfaction—that Annie liked and trusted her.

Nicole had taken a calculated risk over Thanksgiving and lost. In the end she'd spent the holiday alone, even though she'd received two dinner invitations. Her plan had been to spend the day with Cal. She would've made sure he didn't feel threatened, would have couched her suggestion in compassionate terms—just two lonely people making it through the holiday. Unfortunately it hadn't turned out that way. She'd phoned the ranch house twice and there'd been no answer, which made her wonder where he'd gone and who he'd been with. Needless to say, she hadn't left a message.

At any rate, the wife was apparently out of the picture. That had been surprisingly easy. Jane Patterson didn't deserve her husband if she wasn't willing to fight for him. Most women did fight. Usually their attempts were just short of pathetic, but for reasons Nicole had yet to understand, men generally chose to stay with their wives.

Those who didn't…well, the truth was, Nicole quickly grew bored with them. It was different with Cal, had always been different. Never before had she shown her hand more blatantly than she had with Dr. Jane. Nicole felt almost sorry for her. Really, all she'd done was enlighten Jane about a few home truths. The woman didn't value what she had if she was willing to let Cal go with barely a protest.

The phone rang. It wasn't even nine, the store didn't officially open for another hour, and already they were receiving calls.

"Tumbleweed Books," Nicole answered.

"Annie Porter, please." The voice sounded vaguely familiar.

"I'm sorry, Annie won't be in until ten."

"But I just phoned the house and Lucas told me she was at work."

"Then she should be here any minute." Playing a hunch, Nicole asked, "Is this Jane Patterson?"

The hesitation at the other end confirmed her suspicion. "Is this Nicole Nelson?"

"It is," Nicole said, then added with a hint of regret, "I'm sorry to hear about you and Cal."

There was a soft disbelieving laugh. "I doubt that. I'd appreciate it if you'd tell Annie I phoned."

"Of course. I understand your father recently passed away. I am sorry, Jane."

Jane paused, but thanked her.

"Annie was really upset about it. She seems fond of your family."

Another pause. "Please have her call when it's convenient."

"I will." Nicole felt the need to keep Jane on the line. *Know your enemy,* she thought. "My friend Jennifer Healy was the one who broke off her engagement with Cal. Did you know that?"

The responding sigh told Nicole that Jane was growing impatient with her. "I remember hearing something along those lines."

"Cal didn't go after Jennifer, either."

"Either?" Jane repeated.

"Cal never said who wanted the separation—you or him. It's not something we talk about. But the fact that he hasn't sent for you says a great deal, don't you think?"

"What's happening between my husband and me is none of

your business. Goodbye, Nicole." Her words were followed
by a click and then a dial tone.

So Dr. Jane had hung up on her. That didn't come as a
shock. If anything, it stimulated Nicole. She'd moved to Promise, determined to have Cal Patterson. Through the years,
he'd never strayed far from her mind. She'd lost her fair share
of married men to their wives, but that wasn't going to happen *this* time.

So far she'd been smart, played her cards right, and her patience had been rewarded. In three weeks, she'd only contacted Cal once and that was about a book order. Shortly after
he'd returned from California alone, the town had been filled
with speculation. The news excited Nicole. She'd planted the
seeds, let gossip water Jane's doubts, trusting that time would
eventually bring her hopes to fruition. With Jane still in California, Nicole couldn't help being curious about the status of
the relationship, so she'd phoned to let him know the book
Jane had ordered was in. Only Jane hadn't ordered any book...

Playing dumb, Nicole had offered to drop it off at the ranch,
since she was headed in that direction anyway—or so she'd
claimed. Cal declined, then suggested Annie mail it to Jane at
her mother's address in California. Despite her efforts to keep
Cal talking, it hadn't worked. But he'd been in a hurry; he
must've had things to do. And he probably felt a bit depressed
about the deterioration of his marriage. After all, no man enjoyed failure. Well, she'd just have to comfort him, wouldn't
she? She sensed that her opportunity was coming soon.

It was always more difficult when there were children involved. In all honesty, Nicole didn't feel good about destroying a family. However, seeing how easy it'd been to break up
this marriage made her suspect that the relationship hadn't
been very secure in the first place.

She'd bide her time. It wouldn't be long before Cal needed someone to turn to. And Nicole had every intention of being that someone.

After speaking to that horrible woman, Jane felt wretched. Nicole had implied—no, more than implied—that she and Cal were continuing to see each other. Sick to her stomach, Jane hurried to her bedroom.

"Jane." Her mother stepped into the room. "Are you all right? Was that Cal on the phone? What happened? I saw you talking and all of a sudden the color drained from your face and you practically ran in here."

"I'm fine, Mom," Jane assured her. "No, it wasn't Cal. It wasn't anyone important."

"I finished writing all the thank-you notes and decided I need a break. How about if I take you and the children to lunch?"

The thought of food repelled her. "I don't feel up to going out, Mom. Sorry."

"You won't mind if I take the kids? Santa's arriving at the mall this afternoon and I know Paul and Mary Ann will be thrilled."

An afternoon alone sounded wonderful to Jane. "Are you sure it won't be too much for you?"

"Time with these little ones is *exactly* what I need."

"Is there anything you want me to do while you're out?" Jane asked, although she longed for nothing so much as a two-hour nap.

"As a matter of fact, there is," Stephanie said. "I want you to rest. You don't look well. You're tired and out of sorts."

That was putting it mildly. Jane felt devastated and full of despair, and given the chance, she'd delight in tearing Nicole

Nelson's hair out! What a lovely Christian thought, she chastised herself. For that matter, what a cliché.

"Mom." Paul stood in the doorway to her bedroom.

"Aren't you going with Grandma?" Jane asked.

Paul nodded, then came into the room and handed her his blankey. "This is for you." Jane smiled as he placed the tattered much-loved blanket on her bed.

"Thank you, sweetheart," she said and kissed his brow.

Jane heard the front door close as the children left with her mother. Taking them to a mall the day after Thanksgiving was the act of an insane woman, in Jane's opinion. She wouldn't be caught anywhere near crowds like that. As soon as the thought formed in her mind, Jane realized she hadn't always felt that way. A few years ago she'd been just as eager as all those other shoppers. Even in medical school she'd found time to hunt down the best buys. It'd been a competition with her friends; the cheaper an item, the greater the bragging rights.

Not so these days. None of that seemed important anymore. The closest mall was a hundred miles from the ranch, and almost everything she owned was bought in town, ordered through a catalog or purchased over the Internet. The life she lived now was based in small-town America. And she loved it.

She missed Promise. She missed her husband even more.

Her friends, too. Jane could hardly imagine what they must think. The only person she'd talked to after the funeral had been Annie, and then just briefly. When Annie had asked about Cal, Jane had refused to discuss him, other than to say they'd separated. It would do no good to talk about her situation with Annie, especially since Nicole worked for her now.

With her son's blanket wrapped around her shoulders, Jane did sleep for an hour. When she woke, she knew instantly who she needed to talk to—Dovie Hennessey.

The older woman had been her first friend in Promise, and Jane valued her opinion. Maybe Dovie could help her muddle her way through the events of the past few months. She was sorry she hadn't talked to her before. She supposed it was because her father's death had shaken her so badly; she'd found it too difficult to reach out. Dealing with the children depleted what energy she had. Anything beyond the most mundane everyday functions seemed beyond her. As a physician, Jane should have recognized the signs of depression earlier, but then, it was much harder to be objective about one's own situation.

To her disappointment Dovie didn't answer. She could have left a message but decided not to. She considered calling her husband, but she didn't have the courage yet. What would she say? What would *he* say? If Nicole answered, it would destroy her, and just now Jane felt too fragile to deal with such a profound betrayal.

Her mother was an excellent housekeeper, but Jane went around picking up toys and straightening magazines, anything to keep herself occupied. The mail was on the counter and Jane saw that it included a number of sympathy cards. She read each one, which renewed her overwhelming sense of loss and left her in tears.

Inside one of the sympathy cards was a letter addressed to her mother. Jane didn't read it, although when she returned it to the envelope, she saw the signature. Laurie Jo. Her mother's best friend from high school. Laurie Jo Spencer was the kind of friend to her mother that Annie had always been to Jane. Lately, though, Annie had been so busy dealing with the changes in her own life that they hadn't talked nearly as often as they used to.

Laurie Jo had added a postscript asking Stephanie to join

her in Mexico over the Christmas holidays. They were both recent widows, as well as old friends; they'd be perfect companions for each other.

Jane wondered if her mother would seriously consider the trip and hoped she would. It sounded ideal. Her father's health problems had started months ago, and he'd required constant attention and care. Stephanie was physically and emotionally worn out.

If her mother did take the trip, it'd be a good time for Jane to find her own apartment. That way, her moving out would cause less of a strain in their relationship. So far, Stephanie had insisted Jane stay with her.

In another four weeks it'd be Christmas. Jane would have to make some decisions before then. Painful decisions that would force her to confront realities she'd rather not face. This lack of energy and ambition, living one day to the next, was beginning to feel like the norm. Beginning to feel almost comfortable. But for her own sake and the sake of her children, it couldn't continue.

Jane glanced at the phone again. She dialed Dovie's number, but there was still no answer.

It occurred to her that Dovie's absence was really rather symbolic. There didn't seem to be anyone—or anything—left for her in Promise, Texas.

Eight

Cal had never been much of a drinking man. An occasional beer, wine with dinner, but he rarely broke into the hard stuff. Nor did he often drink alone. But after six weeks without his family, Cal was considering doing both. The walls felt like they were closing in on him. Needing to escape and not interested in company, Cal drove to town and headed straight for Billy D's, the local watering hole.

The Christmas lights were up, Cal noticed when he hit Main Street. Decorations were everywhere. Store windows featured Christmas displays, some of them quite elaborate. Huge red-and-white-striped candy canes and large wreaths dangled from each lamppost. Everything around town looked disgustingly cheerful, which only depressed him further. He'd never been all that fond of Christmas, but Jane was as bad as his mother. A year ago Jane had decided to make ornaments for everyone in the family. She'd spent hours pinning brightly colored beads to red satin balls, each design different, each ornament unique. Even Cal had to admit they were works of art.

His wife's talent had impressed him, but she'd shrugged off his praise, claiming it was something she'd always planned to do.

Last Christmas, Paul hadn't quite understood what Christmas was about, but he'd gotten into the spirit of it soon enough. Seeing the festivities through his son's eyes had made the holidays Cal's best ever. This year would be even better now that both children—the thought pulled him up short. Without Jane and his family, this Christmas was going to be the worst of his life.

Cal parked his truck outside the tavern and sat there for several minutes before venturing inside. The noise level momentarily lessened when he walked in as people noted his arrival, then quickly resumed. Wanting to be alone, Cal chose a table at the back of the room, and as soon as the waitress appeared, he ordered a beer. Then, after thirty minutes or so, he had another. Even this place was decorated for Christmas, he saw, with inflated Santas and reindeer scattered about.

He must have been there an hour, perhaps longer, when an attractive woman made her way toward him and stood, hands on her shapely hips, directly in front of his table.

"Hello, Cal."

It was Nicole Nelson. Cal stiffened with dread, since it was this very woman who'd been responsible for most of his problems.

"Aren't you going to say it's nice to see me?"

"No."

She wore skin-tight jeans, a cropped beaded top and a white Stetson. At another time he might have thought her attractive, but not in his present frame of mind.

"Mind if I join you?"

He was about to explain that he'd rather be alone, but apparently she didn't need an invitation to pull out a chair and sit down. He seemed to remember she'd done much the same thing the night she'd found him at the Mexican Lindo. The woman did what *she* wanted, regardless of other people's preferences and desires. He'd never liked that kind of behavior and didn't understand why he tolerated it now.

"I'm sorry to hear about you and Jane."

His marriage was the last subject he intended to discuss with Nicole. He didn't respond.

"You must be lonely," she went on.

He shrugged and reached for his beer, taking a healthy swallow.

"I think it's a good idea for you to get out, mingle with friends, let the world know you're your own man."

She wasn't making any sense. Cal figured she'd leave as soon as she realized he wasn't going to be manipulated into a conversation.

"The holidays are a terrible time to be alone," she said, leaning forward with her elbows on the table. She propped her chin in her hands. "It's hard. I know."

Cal took another swallow of beer. She'd get the message eventually. At least he hoped she would.

"I always thought you and I had a lot in common," she continued.

Unable to suppress his reaction, he arched his eyebrows. She leaped on that as if he'd talked nonstop for the past ten minutes.

"It's true, Cal. Look at us. We're both killing a Saturday night in a tavern because neither of us has anyplace better to go. We're struggling to hold in our troubles for fear anyone else will know the real us."

The woman was so full of malarkey it was all Cal could do not to laugh in her face.

"I can help you through this," she said earnestly.

"Help me?" He shouldn't have spoken, but he couldn't even guess what Nicole had to offer that could possibly interest him.

"I made a terrible mistake before, when Jennifer broke off the engagement. You needed me then, but I was too young to know that. I'm mature enough to have figured it out now."

"Really?" This entire conversation was laughable.

Her smile was coy. "You want me, Cal," she said boldly, her unwavering gaze holding him captive. "That's good, because I want you, too. I've always wanted you."

"I'm married, Nicole." That was a little matter she'd conveniently forgotten.

"Separated," she corrected.

This woman had played no small part in that separation, and Cal was seeing her with fresh eyes.

"I think you should leave," he said, not bothering to mince words. Until now, Cal had assumed Jane was being paranoid about Nicole Nelson. Yes, they'd bumped into each other at the Mexican Lindo. Yes, she'd baked him a casserole and delivered it to the house. Both occasions meant nothing to him. Until today, he'd believed that Jane had overreacted, that she'd been unreasonable. But at this moment, everything Jane had said added up in his mind.

"Leave?" She pouted prettily. "You don't mean that."

"Nicole, I'm married and I happen to love my wife and children very much. I'm not interested in an affair with you or anyone else."

"I...I hope you don't think that's what I was saying." She revealed the perfect amount of confusion.

"I know exactly what you were saying. What else is this 'I want you' business? You're right about one thing though—I know what I want and, frankly, it isn't you."

"Cal," she whispered, shaking her head. "I'm sure you misunderstood me."

He snickered softly.

"You're looking for company," she said, "otherwise you would've done your drinking at home. I understand that, because I know what it's like to be alone, to want to connect with someone. You want someone with a willing ear."

Cal had any number of family and friends with whom he could discuss his woes, and he doubted Nicole had any viable solutions to offer. He groaned. Sure as hell, Jane would get wind of this encounter and consider it grounds for divorce.

"All right," Nicole said, and pushed back her chair. "I know this is a difficult time. Separation's hard on a man, but when you want to talk about it, I'll be there for you, okay? Call me. I'll wait to hear from you."

As far as Cal was concerned, Nicole would have a very long wait. He paid his tab, and then, because he didn't want to drive, he walked over to the café in the bowling alley.

"You want some food to go with that coffee?" Denise asked pointedly.

"I guess," he muttered, realizing he hadn't eaten much of anything in days. "Bring me whatever you want. I don't care."

Ten minutes later she returned with a plate of corned-beef hash, three fried eggs, plus hash browns and a stack of sourdough toast. "That's breakfast," he said, looking down at the plate.

"I figured it was your first meal of the day. Your first decent one, anyhow."

"Well, yeah." It was.

Denise set the glass coffeepot on the table. "You okay?"

He nodded.

"You don't look it. You and I went all the way through

school together, Cal, and I feel I can be honest with you. But don't worry—I'm not going to give you advice."

"Good." He'd had a confrontation with his brother earlier in the day about his marriage. Then he'd heard from Nicole. Now Denise. Everyone seemed to want to tell him what to do.

"I happen to think the world of Dr. Jane. So work it out before I lose faith in you."

"Yes, Denise." He picked up his fork.

Cal was half finished his meal when Wade McMillen slipped into the booth across from him. "Hi, Cal. How're you doing?"

Cal scowled. This was the very reason he'd avoided coming into town until tonight. People naturally assumed he was looking for company, so they had no compunction about offering him that—and plenty of unsolicited advice.

"Heard from Jane lately?" Wade asked.

Talk about getting straight to the point.

"No." Cal glared at the man who was both pastor and friend. At times it was hard to see the boundary between the two roles. "I don't remember inviting you to join me," he muttered and reached for the ketchup, smearing a glob on the remains of his corned-beef hash.

"You didn't."

"What is it with people?" Cal snapped. "Can't they leave me the hell alone?"

Wade chuckled. "That was an interesting choice of words. Leave you *the hell alone*. I imagine that's what it must feel like for you about now. Like you're in hell and all alone."

"What gives you that impression?" Cal dunked a slice of toast into the egg yolk, doing his best to appear unaffected.

"Why else would you come into town? You're going stir-crazy on that ranch without Jane and the kids."

"Listen, Wade," Cal said forcefully, "I wasn't the one who

wanted a separation. Jane made that decision. I didn't want this or deserve it. In fact, I didn't do a damn thing."

His words were followed by silence. Then Wade said mildly, "I'm sure that's true. You didn't do a damn thing."

Cal met his gaze. "What do you mean by that?"

"That, my friend, is for you to figure out." Wade stood up and left the booth.

For the tenth time that day, Dovie Hennessey found herself staring at the phone, willing it to ring, willing Jane Patterson to call from California.

"You're going to do it, aren't you?" Frank said, his voice muted by the morning paper. "Never mind everything you said earlier—you're going to call Jane."

"I don't know what I'm going to do," Dovie murmured, although she could feel her resolve weakening more each day. When she learned that Cal and Jane had separated, Dovie's first impulse had been to call Jane. For weeks now, she'd resisted. After all, Jane was with her mother and certainly didn't need advice from Dovie. If and when she did, Jane would phone her.

Everything was complicated by Harry Dickinson's death. Jane was grieving, and Dovie didn't want to intrude on this private family time. First her father and then her marriage. Her friend was suffering, but she'd hoped that Jane would make the effort to get in touch with her. She hadn't, and Dovie was growing impatient.

Few people had seen Cal, and those who did claimed he walked around in a state of perpetual anger. That sounded exactly like Cal, who wouldn't take kindly to others involving themselves in his affairs.

Dovie remembered what he'd been like after his broken engagement. He'd hardly ever come into town, and when he did, he settled his business quickly and was gone. He'd been unsociable, unresponsive, impossible to talk to. Falling in love with Jane had changed him. Marrying Dr. Texas was the best thing that had ever happened to him, and Dovie recalled nostalgically how pleased Mary had been when her oldest son announced his engagement.

"Go ahead," Frank said after a moment. "Call her."

"Do you really think I should?" Even now Dovie was uncertain.

"We had two hang-ups recently. Those might've been from Jane."

"Frank, be reasonable," Dovie said, laughing lightly. "Not everyone likes leaving messages."

"You could always ask her," he said, giving Dovie a perfectly reasonable excuse to call.

"I could, couldn't I?" Then, needing no more incentive, she reached for the phone and the pad next to it and dialed the long-distance number Annie Porter had given her.

On the third ring Jane answered.

"Jane, it's Dovie—Dovie Hennessey," she added in case the dear girl was so distraught she'd forgotten her.

"Hello, Dovie," Jane said, sounding calm and confident.

"How are you?" Dovie cried, unnerved by the lack of emotion in her friend. "And the children?"

"We're all doing fine."

"Your mother?"

Jane sighed, showing the first sign of emotion. "She's adjusting, but it's difficult."

"I know, dear. I remember how excruciating everything was those first few months after Marvin died. Give your mother my best, won't you?"

"Of course." Jane hesitated, then asked, "How's everyone in Promise?"

Dovie smiled; it wasn't as hopeless as she'd feared. "By everyone, do you mean Cal?"

The hesitation was longer this time. "Yes, I suppose I do."

"Oh, Jane, he misses you so much. Every time I see that boy, it's all I can do not to hug him...."

"So he's been in town quite a bit recently." Jane's voice hardened ever so slightly. The implication was there without her having to say it.

"If that's your way of asking whether he's seeing Nicole Nelson, I can't really answer. However, my guess is he's not."

"You don't know that, though, do you? I...I spoke with Nicole myself and, according to her, they've been keeping each other company."

"Hogwash! What do you expect her to say? You and I both know she's after Cal."

"You think so, too?" Jane's voice was more emotional now.

"I didn't see it at first, but Frank did. He took one look at Nicole and said that woman was going to be trouble."

"Frank said that? Oh, Dovie, Cal thinks..." Jane inhaled a shaky breath. Then she went quiet again. "It doesn't matter anymore."

"What do you mean? Of course it matters!"

"I made an appointment with a divorce attorney this morning."

Stunned, Dovie gasped. "Oh, Jane, no!" This news was the last thing she'd wanted to hear.

"Cal made his choice."

"I don't believe that. You seem to be implying that he's chosen Nicole over you and the children, and Jane, that simply isn't so."

"Dovie—"

"You said Nicole claimed she was seeing Cal. Just how trustworthy do you think this woman is?"

"Annie trusts her."

"Oh, my dear, Annie hasn't got a clue what's happening. Do you seriously believe she'd stand by and let Nicole ruin your life if she knew what was going on? Right now all she's thinking about is this pregnancy and the changes it'll bring to *her* life. I love Annie, you know that. She's a darling girl, but she tends to see the best in everyone. Weren't you the one who told me about her first husband? You said everyone knew what kind of man he was—except Annie. She just couldn't see it."

"I…I haven't discussed this with her."

"I can understand why. That's probably a good idea, the situation being what it is," Dovie said. "Now, let's get back to this business about the lawyer. Making an appointment—was that something you really *wanted* to do?"

"Actually, my uncle Ken suggested I get some advice. He's right, you know. I should find out where I stand legally before I proceed."

"Proceed with what?"

"Getting my own apartment, joining my uncle's medical practice and…" She didn't complete the thought.

"Filing for divorce," Dovie concluded for her.

"Yes." Jane's voice was almost inaudible.

"Is a divorce what you want?"

"I don't know anymore, Dovie. I just don't know. Cal and I have had plenty of disagreements over the years, but nothing like this."

"All marriages have ups and downs."

"I've been gone nearly six weeks and I haven't even heard from Cal. It's almost as…as if he's blotted me out of his life."

Dovie suspected that was precisely what he'd been try-ing to do, but all the evidence suggested he hadn't been very successful. "What about you?" she asked. "Have you tried to reach him?"

Jane didn't want to answer; Dovie could tell from the length of time it took her to speak. "No."

"I see." Indeed she did. Two stubborn, hurting people, both intent on proving how strong and independent they were. "What about the children? Do they miss their father?"

"Paul does the most. He asks about Cal nearly every day. He...he's taken to sucking his thumb again."

"And Mary Ann?"

"She's doing well. I don't think she realizes her father's out of the picture."

"You don't seriously believe that, do you?"

Jane breathed in deeply and Dovie could tell she was hold-ing back tears. "I'm not sure anymore, Dovie." There was a pause. "She's growing like a weed, and she looks so much like Cal."

"She deserves to know her father."

"And I deserve a husband."

"Exactly," Dovie said emphatically. "Then what are you doing seeing an attorney?"

"Cal will never do it. He'll be content to leave things as they are. He seems to think if he ignores me long enough, I'll come to my senses, as he puts it, and return home. But if I did that, I'm afraid everything would go back the way it was before. My feelings wouldn't matter. He'd see himself as the long-suffering husband and me as a jealous shrew. No, Dovie, I'm not going to be the one to give in. Not this time."

"So this is a battle of wills?"

"It's much more than that."

Dovie heard the tears in her voice, and her heart ached for Jane, Cal and those precious children. "This is all because of Nicole Nelson," she said.

"Partially. But there's more."

"There's always more," Dovie agreed.

"I guess Nicole crystallized certain...problems or made them evident, anyway." Jane paused. "She as good as told me she wants him."

That Dovie could believe. "So, being the nice accommodating woman you are, you're just stepping aside and opening the door for her?"

This, too, seemed to unsettle Jane. After taking a moment to consider her answer, she said, "Yes, I guess I am. You and everyone else seem to think I should fight for Cal, that I have too much grit to simply step aside. At one time I did, but just now...I don't. If she wants him and he wants her, then far be it from me to stand between them."

"Oh, Jane, you don't mean that!"

"I do. I swear to you, Dovie, I mean every word." She stopped and Dovie heard her blowing her nose then, a murmured "I'm fine, sweetheart, go watch Mary Ann for me, all right?"

"That was Paul?" Dovie asked. The thought of this little boy, separated from his father for reasons he didn't understand, brought tears to her eyes.

"Yes. He gave me a tissue." She took a deep breath. "Dovie, I have to go now."

"Sounds like you've made up your mind. You're keeping that appointment with the divorce attorney, then?"

"Yes. I'll be getting an apartment right after Christmas, and I'll move in the first of the year."

"You aren't willing to fight for Cal," she said flatly.

"We've been over this, Dovie. No, as far as I'm concerned, he's free to have Nicole if he wants, because he's made it quite plain he isn't interested in me."

"Now, you listen, Jane Patterson. You're in too much pain to deal with this right now. You've just lost your father. That's trauma enough without making a decision about your marriage. And isn't it time you thought about your children?"

"My children?"

"Ask yourself if they need their father and if he needs them. You won't have to dig very deep to know the answers to those questions. Let them be your guide."

To Dovie's surprise, Jane started to laugh. Not the bright humorous laughter she remembered but the soft knowing laughter of a woman who's conceding a point. "You always could do that to me, Dovie."

"Do what?"

Jane sniffled. "Make me cry until I laugh!"

Cal knew something was wrong the minute Grady Weston pulled into the yard. The two men had been neighbors and best friends their whole lives. As kids, they'd discovered a ghost town called Bitter End, which had since become a major focus for the community. Along with Nell Bishop and the man she'd married, writer Travis Grant, they'd uncovered the secrets of the long-forgotten town. It was the original settlement—founded by Pattersons and Westons, among others— and later re-established as Promise.

Grady jumped out of his pickup, and Cal saw that he had a bottle of whiskey in his hand.

"What's that for?" Cal asked, pointing at the bottle.

"I figured you were going to need it," Grady said. "Remember when I was thirteen and I broke my arm?"

Cal nodded. They'd been out horseback riding, and Grady had taken a bad fall. Both boys had realized the bone was broken. Not knowing what to do and fearful of what would happen if he left his friend, Cal had ridden like a madman to get help.

"When you brought my dad back with you, he had a bottle of whiskey. Remember?"

Cal nodded again. Grady's dad had given him a couple of slugs to numb the pain. It was at this point that Cal made the connection. "You've got something to tell me I'm not going to want to hear."

Grady moved onto the porch, and although it was chilly and the wind was up, the two of them sat there.

"I'm not getting involved in this business between you and Jane," Grady began. "That's your affair. I have my own opinion, we all do, but what happens between the two of you... well, you know what I mean."

"Yeah."

"Savannah was in town the other day and she ran into Dovie."

Cal was well aware that Dovie and Jane were good friends, had been for years. "Jane's talked to Dovie?"

"Apparently so."

"And whatever Jane told Dovie, she told Savannah and Savannah told Caroline and Caroline told you. So, what is it?"

Grady hesitated, as though he'd give anything not to be the one telling him this. "Jane's filing for divorce."

"The hell she is." Cal bolted upright, straight off the wicker chair. "That does it." He removed his hat and slapped it against his thigh. "Enough is enough. I've tried to be patient, wait this out, but I'm finished with that."

"Finished?"

"We start getting lawyers involved, and we'll end up hating each other, sure as anything."

Grady chuckled. "What are you going to do?"

"What else can I do? I'm going after her." He barreled into the house, ready to pack his bags.

"You're bringing her home?" his friend asked, following him inside. The screen door slammed shut behind Grady.

"You bet I'm bringing her home. Divorce? That's just crazy!" So far, Cal had played it cool, let Jane have the distance she seemed to need. Obviously that wasn't working. He hadn't thought out his response to the situation, had merely reacted on an emotional level. In the beginning he was too angry to think clearly; then his anger had turned to bitterness, but that hadn't lasted long. Lately, all he'd been was miserable, and he'd had about as much misery as a man could take.

Grady gave him a grin and a thumbs-up. "Good. I wasn't keen on handing over my best bottle of bourbon, so if you have no objection, I'll take this back with me."

"You do that," Cal said.

"Actually this is perfect."

"How do you mean?"

Grady laughed. "A Christmas reunion. Just the kind of thing that makes people feel all warm and fuzzy." The laughter died as Grady looked around the kitchen.

"What?" Cal asked, his mood greatly improved now that he'd made his decision. He loved his wife, loved his children, and nothing was going to keep them apart any longer.

"Well…" Grady scratched his head. "You've got a bit of a mess here."

Cal saw the place with fresh eyes and realized he'd become careless again with Jane away. Their previous reunion had been tainted by a messy house. "I'd better do some cleaning before she gets home. She was none too happy about it the last time."

"You're on your own with this," Grady said. He headed out the door, taking his whiskey with him.

"Grady," Cal said, following him outside. His friend turned around. Cal was unsure how to say this other than straight out. "Thank you."

Grady nodded, touched the brim of his hat and climbed into his truck.

Almost light-headed with relief, Cal went back to the kitchen and tackled the cleaning with enthusiasm. He started a load of dishes, put away leftover food, took out the garbage, mopped the floor. He was scrubbing away at the counter when it occurred to him that after three weeks of caring for her parents, Jane must have been completely worn out. Upon her return to Promise, she'd faced a gigantic mess. *His* mess.

Cal hadn't understood why she'd been so upset over a few dishes and some dirty laundry. He recalled the comments she'd made and finally grasped what she'd really been saying. She'd wanted to be welcomed home for herself and not what she could do to make his life more comfortable. He'd left her with the wrong impression, hadn't communicated his love and respect.

He had to do more than just straighten up the place, Cal decided now. Glancing around, he could see plenty of areas that needed attention. Then it hit him—what Grady had said about a Christmas reunion. God willing, his family would be with him for the holidays, and when Jane and the children walked in that door, he wanted them to know they'd been in his thoughts every minute of every day.

Christmas. Jane was crazy about Christmas. She spent weeks

decorating the house, and while he didn't have time for that, he could put up the tree. Jane and the kids would love that.

Hauling the necessary boxes down from the attic was no small task. He assembled the tree and set it in the very spot Jane had the year before. The lights were his least-favorite task, but he kept thinking of Jane as he wove the strands of tiny colored bulbs through the bright green limbs.

Several shoe boxes were carefully packed with the special beaded ornaments she'd made. He recalled the time and effort she'd put into each one and marveled anew at her skill and the caring they expressed. In that moment, his love for her nearly overwhelmed him.

When he'd finished with the tree, he hung a wreath on the front door. All this activity had made him hungry, so he threw together a ham sandwich and ate it quickly. As he was putting everything back in the fridge—no point in undoing the work of the past few hours—he remembered his conversation with Wade McMillen a week earlier. Cal had stated vehemently that he hadn't "done a damn thing," and Wade had said that was the problem. How right his friend had been.

This separation was of his own making. All his wife had needed was the reassurance of his love and his commitment to her and their marriage. Until now, he'd been quick to blame Jane—and of course the manipulative Nicole—but he'd played an unsavory role in this farce, too.

Because of the holidays, he had to pay an exorbitant price for a plane ticket to California the next day, December twenty-second. The only seat available was in business class; and considering that he was plunking down as much for this trip as he would for a decent horse, he deserved to sit up front.

The next phone call wasn't as easy to make. He dialed his

mother-in-law's number and waited through four interminable rings.

Voice mail came on. He listened to the message, taken aback when Harry Dickinson's voice greeted him. Poor Harry. Poor Stephanie.

He took a deep breath. "Jane, it's Cal. I love you and I love my children. I don't want to lose you. I'll be there tomorrow. I just bought a ticket and when I arrive, we can talk this out. I'm willing to do whatever it takes to save our marriage and I mean that, Jane, with all my heart."

Nine

"Dovie! Have you heard anything?" Ellie asked, making her way along the crowded street to get closer to Dovie and Frank Hennessey. She had Johnny by the hand and Robin in her stroller. Both children were bundled up to ward off the December cold.

The carolers stood on the opposite corner. Glen was with the tenors, and Amy McMillen, the pastor's wife, served as choral director. Carol-singing on the Saturday night before Christmas had become a tradition for Promise Christian Church since the year Wade married Amy. The event was free of charge, but several large cardboard boxes were positioned in front of the choir to collect food and other donations for charity.

"I did talk to Jane," Dovie murmured for Ellie's ears only.

"Again?" Ellie asked, unable to hide her excitement.

Dovie nodded. "She's feeling very torn. I gather her mother's relying on her emotionally."

"But..."

"Don't worry, Ellie," Dovie whispered. "She's halfway home already. I can just feel it!"

"How do you mean?" Ellie was anxious to learn what she could. This episode between Cal and Jane had taken a toll on her own marriage. Glen was upset, so was she, and they'd recently had a heated argument over it, each of them taking sides.

It'd all started when Ellie and Glen decorated their Christmas tree, and Ellie had found the beautiful beaded ornament Jane had made for her the previous year. She'd felt a rush of deep sadness and regret and had said something critical of Cal. Glen had instantly defended his brother.

She was baffled by how quickly their argument had escalated. Within minutes, what had begun as a mere difference of opinion had become a shouting match. Not until later did Ellie realize that this was because they were so emotionally connected to Cal and Jane. She wasn't sure she could ever put that special ornament on the tree again and not feel a sense of loss, especially if the situation continued as it was.

"Did she keep the appointment with the attorney?" Ellie asked. The fact that Cal and Jane had allowed their disagreement to escalate this far horrified her; at the same time it frightened her. Ellie had always viewed Cal and Jane's marriage as stable—like her own. If two people who loved each other could reach this tragic point so quickly, she had to wonder if the same sad future was in store for her and Glen.

The intensity of their own quarrel had shocked her, and only after their tempers had cooled were Ellie and Glen able to talk sensibly. Her husband insisted they had nothing to worry about, but Ellie still wondered.

Dovie shrugged. "I don't know what happened with the attorney. Doesn't Cal discuss these things with Glen?"

Ellie shook her head. "Cal won't, and every time Glen brings up the subject, they argue. When I told Glen about Jane seeing an attorney, he was furious."

"With Jane?"

"No, with Cal, but if Glen said anything to him, he didn't tell me."

"Oh, dear." Dovie wrapped her scarf around her neck.

The singing began and Ellie lifted Robin out of the stroller and held her up so the child could see her father. Johnny clapped with delight at the lively rendition of "Hark Go the Bells," and Robin imitated her brother.

Ellie's eyes met her husband's. Even though he stood across the street, she could feel his love and it warmed her. This ordeal of Cal's had been difficult for him. They both felt terrible about it. She wished now that she'd done something earlier, *said* something.

A warning about Nicole Nelson, maybe. A reassurance that this problem would pass. Anything.

"I have a good feeling," Dovie said, squeezing Ellie's arm. "In my heart of hearts, I don't think Cal or Jane will ever let this reach the divorce courts."

"I hope you're right," Ellie murmured and shifted Robin from one side to the other.

The Christmas carols continued, joyful and festive, accompanied by a small group of musicians. The donation boxes were already filled to overflowing.

"You're bringing the children over for cookies and hot chocolate, aren't you?" Dovie asked.

Ellie sent her a look that suggested she wouldn't dream of missing it. So many babies had been born in Promise recently, and several years ago, Dovie and Frank started holding their own Christmas party for all their friends' children.

Dovie wore a Mrs. Claus outfit and Frank Hennessey made an appearance as Santa. Even Buttons, their poodle, got into the act, sporting a pair of stuffed reindeer antlers. For a couple who'd never had children of their own, Dovie and Frank did a marvelous job of entertaining the little ones.

"Johnny and Robin wouldn't miss it for the world," Ellie assured her. "I wish…"

Ellie didn't need to finish that thought; Dovie knew what she was thinking. It was a shame that Paul and Mary Ann wouldn't be in Promise for the Hennesseys' get-together.

"I'm just as hopeful as you are that this will be resolved soon," Ellie said, forcing optimism in her words. She wanted so badly to believe it.

"Me, too," Nell Grant said, standing on the other side of Dovie. "The entire community is pulling for them." She blushed. "I hope you don't mind me jumping into the middle of your conversation."

"Everyone's hoping for the best," Dovie said with finality. Then, looking over at the small band of musicians, she turned back to Nell. "Don't tell me that's Jeremy playing the trumpet? It can't be!"

Nell nodded proudly. "He's quite talented, isn't he?"

"Yes, and my goodness, he's so tall."

"Emma, too," Nell said, pointing at the flute player.

"That's Emma?" Ellie asked, unable to hide her shock. Heavens, it hadn't been more than a couple of months since she'd seen Nell's oldest daughter, and the girl looked as though she'd grown several inches.

With this realization came another. It'd been nearly six weeks since Cal had seen his children. At their ages, both were growing rapidly, changing all the time. She could only guess how much he'd missed—and felt sad that he'd let it happen.

Despite her disagreement with Glen, Ellie still blamed Cal. Eventually he'd come to his senses. She hoped that when he did, it wouldn't be too late.

Her mother's mournful expression tugged at Jane's heart as she finished packing her suitcase.

"You're sure this is what you want?" Stephanie Dickinson asked. Tears glistening in her eyes, she stood in the doorway of Jane's old bedroom.

"Yes, Mom. I love my husband. Things would never have gone this far if—"

"It's my fault, isn't it, honey?"

"Oh, Mom, don't even think that." Jane moved away from the bed, where the suitcases lay open, and hugged her mother. "No one's to blame. Or if anyone is, I guess I am. I let everything get out of control. I should've fought for my husband from the first. Cal was angry that I doubted him."

"But he—" Her mother stopped abruptly and bit her lip.

"You heard his message. He loves me and the children, and Mom...until just a little while ago I didn't realize how *much* I love him. It's taken all this time for us both to see what we were doing. I love you and Derek and Uncle Ken, but Los Angeles isn't my home anymore. I love Promise. My friends are there, my home and my husband."

Jane could tell that it was difficult for her mother to accept her decision. Stephanie gnawed on her lower lip and made an obvious effort not to weep.

"You talked to Cal? He knows you're coming?"

"I left him a message."

"But he hasn't returned your call?"

"No." There was such wonderful irony in the situation. Her mother had taken the children on an outing while Jane was scheduled to meet with the attorney. But as she'd sat in the waiting room, she'd tried to picture her life without Cal, without her family and friends in Promise, and the picture was bleak. She could barely keep from dissolving in tears right then and there.

Everything Dovie had said came back to her, and she'd known beyond a doubt that seeing this attorney was wrong. Paul and Mary Ann needed their father, and she needed her husband. For the first time since her father's illness, Jane had felt a surge of hope, the desire to win back her husband. If Nicole thought Jane would simply walk away, she was wrong. At that moment, she'd resolved to fight for her marriage.

Without a word of explanation, Jane left the attorney's office and rushed home. The message light alerted her to a call, and when she listened to it, Cal's deep voice greeted her. His beautiful loving voice, telling her the very things she'd longed to hear.

In her eagerness to return his call, her hand had shaken as she punched out the number. To her consternation she'd had to leave a message. She'd tried his cell phone, too, but Cal was notorious for never remembering to turn it on. Later phone calls went unanswered, as well. Her biggest fear was that he'd already boarded a plane, but she still hoped to stop him, and fly home with the children and meet him in San Antonio. With that in mind, she'd booked her flight.

"I'll try to call him again."

"You could all spend Christmas here," her mother suggested hopefully.

"Mom, you're going with Laurie Jo to Mexico and that's the end of it."

"Yes, I know, but—"

"No buts, you're going. It's exactly what you need."

"But your father hasn't even been gone two months."

Jane shook her head sternly. "Staying here moping is the last thing Dad would want you to do."

Her mother nodded. "You're right...but I'm worried about you and the children."

"Mom, you don't have to be. We'll be fine."

"But you can't go flying off without knowing if Cal will be at the airport when you arrive!"

"I'll give Glen and Ellie a call. They'll see he gets the message. And if they can't reach him, don't worry—*someone* will be at the airport to pick us up." Jane sincerely hoped it would be Cal. And this time she'd make sure their reunion was everything the previous one wasn't.

Her mother frowned and glanced at her watch. "You don't have much time. I really wish you weren't in such a rush."

"Mother, I've been here nearly two months. Anyone would think you'd be glad to get rid of me." This wasn't the most sensitive of comments, Jane realized when her mother's eyes filled with tears and she turned away, not wanting Jane to see.

"I shouldn't have depended on you and the children so much," Stephanie confessed. "I'm sorry, Jane."

"Mom, we've already been through this." She closed the largest of the suitcases, then hugged her mother again. "I'll call Ellie right now and that should settle everything. She'll let Cal know which flight I'm on, or die trying."

She wished her husband would phone. Jane desperately wanted to speak to him, and every effort in the past three hours had met with failure. Funny, after all these weeks of no communication, she couldn't wait to speak with him.

"Mommy, Mommy!" Paul dashed into the bedroom and stuffed his blankey in the open suitcase. Then, looking very proud of himself, he smiled up at his mother. "We going home?"

"Home," she echoed and knelt to hug her son. She felt such joyful anticipation, it was all she could do to hold it inside.

Luckily, reaching Ellie wasn't difficult. Her sister-in-law was at the feed store and picked up on the second ring. "Frasier Feed," Ellie said in her no-nonsense businesswoman's tone of voice.

"Ellie, it's Jane."

"Jane!" Her sister-in-law nearly exploded with excitement.

"I'm coming home."

"It's about time!"

"Listen," Jane said, "I haven't been able to get hold of Cal. He left a message that he's flying to California, but he didn't say when. Just that he's coming today."

"Cal phoned you?"

"I wasn't here. This is so crazy and wonderful. Ellie, I was sitting in the attorney's office and all of a sudden I knew I could't go through with it. I belong with Cal in Promise."

"Whatever you need, I'll find a way to do it," Ellie said. "You have no idea how much we've all missed you. None of us had any idea what to think when we didn't hear from you."

"I know. I'm so sorry. It's just that…" Jane wasn't sure how to explain why she hadn't called anyone in Promise for all those weeks. Well, she'd tried to reach Dovie, but—

"Don't apologize. I remember what it was like after my father died. One night I sat and watched some old westerns he used to love and I just cried and cried. Even now I can't watch a John Wayne movie and not think of my dad."

"You'll make sure Cal doesn't leave Promise?" That was Jane's biggest concern. She hated the thought of getting home and learning he was on his way to California. If that did hap-

pen, he'd find an empty house, because her mother would
be in Mexico.

"You can count on it."

"And here, write down my flight information and give it
to Cal—if you catch him in time."

"I'll find him for you, don't you worry."

Jane knew her sister-in-law would come through.

Cal spent the morning completing what chores he could,
getting ready to leave. Glen was attending a cattlemen's con-
ference in Dallas and would be home that evening, but by
then Cal would be gone.

Now that his decision was made, he wondered what had
taken him so long to own up to the truth. His love for Jane
and their children mattered more than anything—more than
pride and more than righteousness. His friends and family had
tried to show him that, but Cal hadn't truly grasped it until
he learned how close he was to losing everything that gave
his life meaning.

His father had urged him to listen to reason with that conversation during Thanksgiving dinner, and Phil's advice hadn't
come cheap. Not when Cal was paying the bill at the Rocky
Creek Inn.

Glen had put in his two cents' worth, and his comments
had created a strain in their relationship. Cal hadn't been able
to listen to his younger brother, couldn't accept his judgment
or advice—although he wished he was more like Glen, easy-
going and quick to forgive.

Even Wade McMillen had felt obliged to confront Cal.
Every single thing his friends and family said had eventually
hit home, but the full impact hadn't been made until the night
Cal had gone to Billy D's.

Only when Nicole Nelson had approached his table had he seen the situation clearly. He'd been such a fool, and he'd nearly fallen in with her schemes. His wife was right: Nicole *did* want him. Damned if he knew why. It still bothered Cal that Jane hadn't trusted him. He hadn't even been tempted by Nicole, he could say that in all honesty, but he'd allowed her to flatter him.

Cal had made his share of mistakes and was more than willing to admit it. He regretted the things he'd said and done at a time when Jane had been weakest and most vulnerable. Thinking over the past few months, Cal viewed them as wasted. He wanted to kick himself for waiting so long to go after his family.

As he headed toward the house, he saw Grady's truck come barreling down the driveway. His neighbor eased to a stop near Cal, rolled down his window and shouted, "Call Ellie!"

"Ellie? What about?"

"No idea. Caroline called from town with the message."

"All right," he said, hurrying into the house.

Grady left, shouting "Merry Christmas" as his truck rumbled back down the drive.

When Cal reached his front door, he saw a large piece of paper taped there. "CALL ELLIE IMMEDIATELY," it read. "Good Luck, Nell and Travis."

What the hell? Cal walked into his house and grabbed the phone. He noticed the blinking message light, but not wanting to be distracted, he ignored it.

"Is that you, Cal?" Ellie asked, answering the phone herself.

"Who else were you expecting?"

"No one."

She sounded mighty cheerful.

"You doing anything just now?" his sister-in-law asked.

"Yeah, as a matter of act, I am. I've got a plane to catch. It seems I have some unfinished business in California."

He'd thought Ellie would shriek with delight or otherwise convey her approval, since she'd made her opinion of his actions quite clear.

But all she said was "You're going after Jane?"

He'd be on the road this very minute if he wasn't being detained. He said as much, although he tried to be polite about it. "What's with the urgency? Why is it so important that I call you?"

"Don't go!"

"What?" For a moment Cal was sure he'd misunderstood.

"You heard me. Don't go," Ellie repeated, "because Jane and the kids are on their way home."

"If this is a joke, Ellie, I swear to you—"

She laughed and didn't let him finish. "When was the last time you listened to your messages?"

The flashing light condemned him for a fool. He should have realized Jane would try to reach him. In his eagerness he'd overlooked the obvious.

"What flight? When does she land?" He'd be there to meet her and the children with flowers and chocolates and whatever else Dovie could recommend. Ah, yes, Dovie. Someone else who'd been on his case. He smiled, remembering her less-than-subtle approach.

Ellie rattled off the flight number and the approximate time Jane and the children would land, and Cal scribbled down the information. "How did she manage to get a flight so quickly?" With holiday travel, most flights were booked solid.

"I don't know. You'll need to ask Jane."

Cal didn't care what she'd had to pay; he wanted her home.

And now that the time was so close, he could barely contain himself.

As soon as he finished his conversation with Ellie, Cal listened to his messages. When he heard Jane's voice, his heart swelled with love. He could hear her relief, her joy and her love—the same emotions he was experiencing.

With his steps ten times lighter than they'd been a mere twenty-four hours ago, Cal jumped into the car and drove to town. Before he left, though, he carefully surveyed the house, making sure everything was perfect for Jane and the children. The Christmas tree looked lovely, and he'd even bought and wrapped a few gifts to put underneath. Not a single dirty dish could be seen. The laundry was done, and the sheets on the bed were fresh. This was about as good as it got.

Cal dropped in at Dovie's, and then—because he couldn't resist—he walked over to Tumbleweed Books. Sure enough, Nicole was behind the counter. Her face brightened when he entered the store.

"Cal, hello," she said with an eagerness she didn't bother to disguise.

"Merry Christmas."

"You, too." People were busy wandering the aisles, but Nicole headed directly toward him. "It's wonderful to see you."

He forced a smile. "About our conversation the other night…"

Nicole placed her hand on his arm. "I was more blunt than I intended, but that's only because I know what it's like to be lonely, especially at Christmastime."

"I'm here to thank you," Cal said, enjoying this.

Nicole flashed her baby blues at him with such adoration it was hard to maintain a straight face.

"You're right, I have been terribly lonely."

"Not anymore, Cal, I'm here for you."

"Actually," he said, removing her fingers from his forearm, "it was after our conversation that I realized how much I miss my wife."

"Your...wife?" Nicole's face fell.

"I phoned her and we've reconciled. You helped open my eyes to what's important."

Nicole's mouth sagged. "I...I wish you and Jane the very best," she said, obviously struggling to hide her disappointment. "So you decided to go back to her." She shrugged. "Too bad. It could have been great with us, Cal."

Her audacity came as a shock. She'd actually believed he'd give up his wife and family for her. If he hadn't already figured out exactly the kind of woman she was and what she'd set out to do, he would have known in that instant. He should have listened to Jane—and just about everyone else.

"Stay out of my life, Nicole. Don't *just happen* to run into me again. Don't seek me out. Ever."

"I'm sorry you feel this way," she mumbled, not meeting his eyes.

During the course of his life, Cal had taken a lot of flack for being too direct and confrontational. Today he felt downright pleased at having imparted a few unadorned facts to a woman who badly needed to hear them. He walked out of the bookstore, and with a determination that couldn't be shaken, marched toward his parked car. He was going to collect his wife and children.

Jane's flight landed in San Antonio after midnight. Both children were asleep, and she didn't know if anyone would be at the airport to meet her. During the long hours on the plane, she'd fantasized about the reunion with her husband, but she'd begun to feel afraid that she'd been too optimistic.

All the passengers had disembarked by the time she gathered everything from the overhead bins and awakened Paul. The three-year-old rubbed his eyes, and Jane suspected he was still too dazed to understand that they were nearly home. Dragging his small backpack behind him, he started down the aisle. Mary Ann was asleep against her shoulder.

Their baggage was already on the carousel, and with a porter's assistance, she got it all piled on a cart. Then she moved slowly into the main area of the airport. Her fear—that Cal might not be there—was realized when she didn't see him anywhere. Her disappointment was so intense she stopped, clutching her son's hand as she tried to figure out what to do next.

"Jane...Jane!" Cal's voice caught her and she whirled around.

He stood at the information counter, wearing the biggest smile she'd ever seen. "I didn't know what to think when you weren't here. I thought you—"

"This is your family?" the woman at the counter interrupted.

"Yes," he said happily.

Paul seemed to come fully awake then and let out a yell. Dropping his backpack, the boy hurled himself into Cal's waiting arms.

Cal wrapped his son in his embrace. Jane watched as his eyes drifted shut and he savored this hug. Then Paul began to chatter until his words became indistinguishable.

"Just a minute, Paul," Cal said as he walked toward Jane.

With their children between them—Paul on his hip, Mary Ann asleep on her shoulder—Cal threw one arm around Jane and kissed her. It was the kind of deep open kiss the movies would once have banned. A kiss that illustrated everything his phone message had already explained. A real kiss, intense and passionate and knee-shaking.

The tears, which had been so near the surface moments earlier, began to flow down her cheeks. But they were no longer tears of disappointment; they were tears of joy. She found she wasn't the least bit troubled about such an emotional display in the middle of a busy airport with strangers looking on.

"It's all right, honey," Cal whispered. He kissed her again, and she thought she saw tears in his eyes, too.

"I love you so much," she wept.

"Oh, honey, I love you, too. I'm sorry."

"Me, too— I made so many mistakes."

"I've learned my lesson," he said solemnly.

"So have I. You're my home, where I live and breathe. Nothing's right without you."

"Oh, Jane," he whispered and leaned his forehead against hers. "Let's go home."

They talked well into the night, almost nonstop, discussing one subject after another. Cal held her and begged her forgiveness while she sobbed in his arms. They talked about their mistakes and what they'd learned, and vowed never again to allow anyone—man, woman, child or beast—to come between them.

Afterward, exhausted though she was from the flight and the strain of the past months, Jane was too keyed up to sleep. Too happy and excited. Even after they'd answered all the questions, resolved their doubts and their differences, Jane had something else on her mind. When her husband reached for her, she went into his arms eagerly. Their kisses grew urgent, their need for each other explosive.

"Cal, Cal," she whispered, reluctantly breaking off the kiss.

"Yes?" He kissed her shoulder and her ear.

"I think you should know I stopped taking my birth control pills."

Cal froze. "You what?"

She sighed and added, "I really couldn't see the point."

It was then that her husband chuckled. "In other words, there's a chance I might get you pregnant again?"

She kissed his stubborn wonderful jaw. "There's always a chance."

"How would you feel about a third child?"

"I think three's a good number, don't you?"

"Oh, yes—and if it's a boy we'll name him after your father."

"Harry Patterson?" she asked, already picturing a little boy so like his father and older brother. "Dad would be pleased."

Two nights later Cal, Jane and the children drove into town to attend Christmas Eve services. Their appearance generated considerable interest from the community, Jane noted. Every head seemed to turn when they strolled into the church, and plenty of smiles were sent in their direction. People slipped out of their seats to hug Jane and slap Cal on the back or shake his hand.

When Wade stepped up to the pulpit, he glanced straight at Cal, grinned knowingly and acknowledged him with a brief nod. Jane saw Cal return the gesture and nearly laughed out loud when Wade gave Cal a discreet thumbs-up.

"You talked to Wade?" she asked, whispering in his ear.

Her husband squeezed her hand and nodded.

"What did he say?"

"I'll tell you later."

"Tell me now," Jane insisted.

Cal sighed. "Let's just say the good pastor's words hit their mark."

"Oh?" She raised her eyebrows and couldn't keep from smiling. Being here with her husband on Christmas Eve, sharing the music, the joy, love and celebration with her community, nearly overwhelmed her.

Not long after Jane and Cal had settled into the pew, Glen, Ellie and their two youngsters arrived, followed by her father-in-law. Phil's eyes met Jane's and he winked. Jane pressed her head to her husband's shoulder.

Cal slid his arm around her and reached for a hymnal, and they each held one side of the book. Organ music swirled around them, and together they raised their voices in song. "O, Come All Ye Faithful." "Silent Night." "Angels We Have Heard on High." Songs celebrating a birth more than two thousand years ago. Songs celebrating a rebirth, a reunion, a renewal of their own love.

The service ended with a blast of exultation from the trumpet players, and finally the "Hallelujah" chorus from the choir. More than once, Jane felt Cal's gaze on her. She smiled up at him, and as they gathered their children and started out of the church, she was sure she could feel her father's presence, as well.

Phil was waiting for them outside. Paul ran to his grandfather and Phil lifted the boy in his arms, hugging him.

"We have a lot to celebrate," he said quietly.

"Yes, Dad, we do," Cal agreed. He placed one arm around his father and the other around Jane, and they all headed for home.

★ ★ ★ ★ ★

BUFFALO VALLEY

In memory of my mom and dad, Ted and Connie Adler.
Boy, did I get lucky to have you for my parents!
I will always love you both.

One

So this was North Dakota. Gazing steadily ahead, Vaughn Kyle barreled down the freeway just outside Grand Forks. Within a few miles, the four lanes had narrowed to two. Dreary, dirt-smudged snow lay piled up along both sides of the highway. Fresh snow had begun to fall, pristine and bright, glinting in the late-afternoon sun.

His parents had retired earlier in the year, leaving Denver, where Vaughn had been born and raised, and returning to the state they'd left long ago. They'd moved north, away from the majestic peaks of the Rocky Mountains to the endlessly boring landscape of the Dakotas. *This* was supposed to be beautiful? Maybe in summer, he mused, when the fields of grain rippled with the wind, acre after acre. Now, though, in December, in the dead of winter, the beauty of this place escaped him. All that was visible was a winding stretch of black asphalt cutting through flat, monotonous terrain that stretched for miles in every direction.

After seven years as an Airborne Ranger in the U.S. Army's

Second Battalion based in Fort Lewis, Washington, Vaughn was poised to begin the second stage of his working life. He had his discharge papers and he'd recently been hired by Value-X, a mega-retailer with headquarters in Seattle. Value-X was one of America's most notable success stories. New stores were opening every day all across the United States and Canada.

His course was set for the future, thanks largely to Natalie Nichols. They'd met two years earlier through mutual friends. Natalie was smart, savvy and ambitious; Value-X had recognized her skills and she'd advanced quickly, being promoted to a vice presidency before the age of thirty.

Vaughn had been attracted by her dedication and purpose, and he'd admired her ambition. His own work ethic was strong; as he'd come to realize, that was increasingly rare in this age of quick fixes and no-fault living. Natalie was the one who'd convinced him to leave the army. He was ready. When he'd enlisted after finishing college, he'd done so intending to make the military his career. In the seven years since, he'd learned the advantages and drawbacks of soldiering.

He didn't mind the regimented life, but the career possibilities weren't all he'd hoped they would be. What he lacked, as Natalie had pointed out, was opportunity. He was limited in how far he could rise through the ranks or how quickly, while the private sector was wide-open and looking for promising employees like him. He'd been interviewed by three head-hunters who recruited candidates for a variety of corporations and in just a few weeks had six job offers.

At first he'd felt there might be a conflict of interest, taking a position with the same company as Natalie. However, she didn't view it that way; they would be a team, she'd told Vaughn, and with that remarkable persuasive skill of hers had convinced him to come on board. He wouldn't officially start until after the first of the year, but he was already on assignment.

Value-X was buying property in Buffalo Valley, North Dakota. Since Vaughn was going to be in the vicinity, visiting his parents in nearby Grand Forks, Natalie had asked him to pay the town a visit. It wasn't uncommon for a community to put up token resistance to the company's arrival. In most cases, any negative publicity was successfully handled, using a proven strategy that included barraging the local media with stories showing the company's "human face." After a recent public-relations disaster in Montana, Natalie was eager to avoid a repeat. She'd asked Vaughn to do a "climate check" in Buffalo Valley, but it was important, she insisted, that he not let anyone know he was now a Value-X employee, not even his parents. Vaughn had reluctantly agreed.

He'd done this because he trusted Natalie's judgment. And because he was in love with her. They'd talked about marriage, although she seemed hesitant. Her reasons for postponing it were logical, presented in her usual no-nonsense manner. She refused to be "subservient to emotion," as she called it, and Vaughn was impressed by her clear-cut vision of what she wanted and how to achieve it. They'd get married when the time was right for both of them.

He was eager to have her meet his family. Natalie would be joining him on December twenty-seventh, but he wished she could've rearranged her schedule to travel with him.

On this cold Friday afternoon two weeks before Christmas, Vaughn had decided to drive into Buffalo Valley. Because of Hassie Knight, he didn't need to invent an excuse for his parents. Hassie was the mother of his namesake. She'd lost her only son—his parents' closest friend—in Vietnam three years before Vaughn was born. Every birthday, until he'd reached the age of twenty-one, Hassie had mailed him a letter with a twenty-five-dollar U.S. Savings Bond.

In all that time, he'd never met her. From first grade on, he'd dutifully sent her a thank-you note for every gift. That was the extent of their contact, but he still felt a genuine fondness for her—and gratitude. Hassie had been the one to start him on a savings program. As a young adult Vaughn had cashed in those savings bonds and begun acquiring a portfolio of stocks that over the years had become a hefty nest egg.

An hour after he left Grand Forks, Vaughn slowed his speed, certain that if he blinked he might miss Buffalo Valley entirely. Value-X could put this place on the map. That was one benefit the company offered small towns. He wasn't sure what kind of business community existed in Buffalo Valley. He knew about Knight's Pharmacy of course, because Hassie owned that. Apparently the town was large enough to have its own cemetery, too; Hassie had mailed him a picture of her son's gravesite years earlier.

Buffalo Valley was directly off the road. You didn't take an exit the way you would in most places. You just drove off the highway. He slowed, made a right turn where the road sign indicated. The car pitched as it left the pavement and hit ruts in the frozen dirt road. He'd gone at least a hundred feet before the paved road resumed.

He passed a few scattered houses, and as he turned the corner, he discovered, somewhat to his surprise, a main street with businesses lining both sides. There was even a hotel of sorts, called Buffalo Bob's 3 of a Kind. The bank building, a sprawling brick structure, seemed new and quite extensive. This was amazing. He wasn't sure what he'd expected, but nothing like this. Buffalo Valley was a real town, not a cluster of run-down houses and boarded-up stores, like some of the prairie towns his parents had told him about.

Hassie's store caught his attention next. It was a quaint, old-fashioned pharmacy, with big picture windows and large white lettering. Christmas lights framed the window, flashing alternately red and green. In smaller letters below KNIGHT'S PHARMACY, a soda fountain was advertised. Vaughn hadn't tasted a real soda made with hand-scooped ice cream and flavored syrup since his childhood.

He parked, climbed out of his rental car and stood on the sidewalk, glancing around. This was a decent-size town, decorated for the holidays with festive displays in nearly every window. A city park could be seen in the distance, and the Buffalo Valley Quilting Company appeared to take up a large portion of the block across the street. He remembered an article about it in the file Natalie had given him.

The cold stung his face and snow swirled around him. Rather than stand there risking frostbite, Vaughn walked into the pharmacy. The bell above the door jingled and he was instantly greeted by a blast of heat that chased the chill from his bones.

"Can I help you?" He couldn't see who spoke, but the voice sounded young, so he assumed it wasn't Hassie. The woman or girl, whoever she was, stood behind the raised counter at the back of the store.

"I'm looking for Hassie Knight," Vaughn called, edging his way down the narrow aisle. This pharmacy apparently carried everything: cosmetics, greeting cards, over-the-counter medicine, gourmet chocolate, toothpaste and tissues—just about anything you might require.

"I'm sorry, Hassie's out for the day. Can I be of help?"

He supposed he didn't need to see Hassie, although it would have been nice.

"I'm Carrie Hendrickson." A petite blonde in a white jacket materialized before him, hand extended. "I'm an intern working with Hassie."

"Vaughn Kyle," he said, stretching out his own hand. He liked the way her eyes squarely met his. Her expression held a hint of suspicion, but Vaughn was prepared for that. Natalie had mentioned the North Dakota attitude toward strangers—a wariness that ranged from mild doubt to outright hostility. It was one reason she worried about this proposed building site.

"Hassie and I have never officially met, but she does know me," he added reassuringly. "I was named after her son."

"You're *the* Vaughn Kyle?" she asked, her voice revealing excitement now. "Did Hassie know you were coming and completely forget? I can't imagine her doing that."

"No, no, it was nothing like that. I just happened to be in the area and thought I'd stop by and introduce myself."

Her suspicion evaporated and was replaced with a wide, welcoming smile. "I'm so pleased to meet you. Hassie will be thrilled." She gestured to the counter. "Can I get you anything? Coffee? A soft drink?"

"Actually, I wouldn't mind an old-fashioned soda."

"They're Hassie's specialty, but I'll do my best."

"Don't worry about it." On second thought, he decided something warm might be preferable. "I'll have a coffee."

She led him to the soda fountain and Vaughn sat on a padded stool while Carrie ducked beneath the counter and reappeared on the other side.

"Do you know when Hassie's due back?" he asked.

"Around six," Carrie told him, lifting the glass pot and filling his cup. "You need space for cream?" she asked.

He answered with a quick shake of his head. She didn't cut off the steady stream of weak coffee until it'd reached the very brim of his cup.

The door opened, bells jingling, and a woman dressed in a black leather jacket walked into the store. She had three scarves wrapped around her neck, nearly obscuring her face.

"Hi, Merrily," Carrie called, then scrambled under the fountain barrier. "I'll have Bobby's prescription ready in just a moment." She hurried to the back of the store. "While you're waiting, introduce yourself to Vaughn Kyle."

Merrily glanced toward the counter and waved, and Vaughn raised his mug to her.

"That's *Hassie's* Vaughn Kyle," Carrie said emphatically. "Vaughn was named after her son," she added.

"Well, why didn't you say so?" Merrily walked over to shake his hand. "What are you doing here?" she asked, unwinding the woolen scarves.

Now, that was an interesting question, Vaughn thought. He certainly hadn't anticipated anyone knowing about him.

"He came to meet Hassie," Carrie said as she returned with the prescription. She handed Merrily a small white sack. "How's Bobby feeling?"

"Better, I think. Poor little guy seems prone to ear infections." She turned to Vaughn with a smile. "Nice meeting you," she said. She wrapped the mufflers around her face again before she headed out the door.

"You, too," Vaughn murmered.

Carrie reached across the counter and grabbed a second mug for herself. "Hassie told you about the War Memorial, didn't she? We're all proud of that." Not waiting for a response, she continued, "The town built the Memorial three years ago, and it honors everyone from Buffalo Valley who died in war.

The only one most of us actually remember is Hassie's son. But there were others. We lost Harvey Schmidt in the Korean War and five men in World War II, but none of their families live in the area anymore."

"You knew Vaughn Knight?" The blonde seemed far too young to have known Hassie's son.

"Not personally. But from the time I was small, Hassie told my brothers and me about Vaughn. It's been her mission to make sure he isn't forgotten."

Vaughn had heard about Vaughn Knight from his own parents of course, since they'd both been close to Hassie's son.

Carrie sipped her coffee. "Hassie told me it was one of the greatest honors of her life that your parents chose to remember her son through you."

Vaughn nodded, disappointed that he'd missed meeting the older woman. "What time did you say Hassie would be back?"

"Around six, I guess."

Vaughn checked his watch. He didn't intend to make an entire day of this.

"If Hassie had known you were coming, I don't think *anything* could've kept her away."

"I should have phoned beforehand," he muttered. "But..."

"I hope you'll wait."

Vaughn glanced at his watch again. Three hours was far longer than he wanted to stick around. "Tell her I'll come by some other time."

"*Please* stay. Hassie would feel terrible if she learned you'd left without meeting her." She hesitated, obviously thinking. "Listen," she said, "I'll phone Leta Betts and ask if she can fill in for me for a couple of hours."

Vaughn reconsidered. He might get all the information he needed from Carrie; then he could meet Hassie on strictly social terms. He'd been vaguely uncomfortable about questioning Hassie, anyway.

"Please," she said, "it would mean the world to Hassie, and I'd be delighted to give you a tour of town."

Perfect. He'd learn everything Natalie wanted to know and more. "That's a generous offer. Are you sure you don't mind?"

"I'd consider it a pleasure," she said, and smiled.

With her looking up at him that way , smiling and appreciative, Vaughn couldn't help noticing that Carrie Hendrickson was a very attractive woman. Not that Natalie had anything to worry about, he told himself staunchly.

Working closely with Hassie as an intern pharmacist, Carrie Hendrickson was keenly aware of how eager the older woman was to meet her son's namesake. A few months ago, Hassie had heard that the Kyles had retired in Grand Forks and she'd mailed off a note, inviting them to visit Buffalo Valley. Apparently they planned to do that sometime in the new year. Hassie would be ecstatic about finally meeting their son.

Carrie loved Hassie Knight, who was her mentor and her friend. Following Carrie's divorce, Hassie had given her sympathy—and good, brisk, commonsense advice. She'd guided her through the fog of her pain and encouraged her to look toward the future. Many an afternoon they'd spent talking, reminiscing, sitting quietly together. Hassie had shared the grief of her own losses and helped Carrie deal with Alec's betrayal in ways her own mother never could. Hassie was the person who'd suggested she return to college. Carrie had taken her advice; nearly six years ago she'd enrolled at the University of North Dakota in Grand Forks. Now she was about to finish her internship with Knight's Pharmacy and achieve her Pharm.D and become a Doctor of Pharmacy. The last few years had been bleak financially, but the reward would be worth all the sacrifices.

After her divorce, she'd moved back in with her parents. She felt deeply grateful for their generosity but she *was* twenty-seven years old and longed for more independence and a home of her own. Well, it would happen eventually; she'd just have to wait.

Meanwhile, working side by side with Hassie, Carrie had learned a great deal. When it came time for the older woman to retire, Carrie would be willing and able to assume her role in the pharmacy and in the town. People knew and trusted her. Already they approached her with their troubles and concerns as naturally as they did Hassie. Alec's infidelity had reinforced the importance of trust and honor for Carrie. Those were precepts she lived by. The people of Buffalo Valley knew she would keep their problems to herself.

The town was a success story in an area where there'd been few. The Hendrickson farm, like many others, had fallen victim to low crop prices. Unable to make a living farming the land that had supported them for three generations, her father had leased the acreage to his older sons and moved into town. Together with Carrie's two younger brothers, he'd opened a hardware store.

For as long as she could remember, Knight's Pharmacy had been the very heart of this town. Hassie was getting on in years and probably should've retired long ago. She wouldn't, though, not while the community still needed her, not only to dispense prescriptions and basic medical advice but also to be their counselor and confidante.

Carrie knew she could never replace Hassie, because that would be impossible. But she'd always been good at chemistry and math, and had done well at her pharmaceutical studies. She also cared about the town and had an intense interest in people. Hassie had often told her she was naturally intuitive and sensitive toward others; Carrie was pleased by that, although her intuition had been notably absent during her exhusband's affair. Hassie said she was exactly the pharmacist Buffalo Valley needed and had given her the faith in herself to believe she could complete the six years of schooling required to obtain her license.

"I'll get my coat and hat and be right back," she told Vaughn after calling Leta. Hassie's friend worked at the pharmacy part-time and was as eager as Carrie to make sure that Hassie met Vaughn.

"You're certain this isn't an imposition?"

"Absolutely certain," she told him.

Leta arrived promptly and after making swift introductions, Carrie removed the white pharmacist's jacket and put on her long wool coat.

"What would you like to see first?" she asked when she rejoined him.

"Whatever you'd like to show me."

"Then let's go to the City Park." Although there were a number of places she wanted to take him, the park seemed the best place to start. As they left the pharmacy, Carrie noticed it had stopped snowing, but she suspected the temperature had dropped several degrees. She led him across the street and then down a block, past the quilt store and several others.

"I know Hassie would want you to see the War Memorial," she said, glancing up at Vaughn. Now that she stood beside him, she was surprised to see how tall he was—possibly six-two. All four of her brothers were six feet, but Carrie took after her mother's side of the family and was small-boned and petite. His dark good looks didn't escape her notice, either.

"First came the park," she explained, walking briskly to ward off the cold. Carrie loved the City Park and everything it said about their community. The people of Buffalo Valley had worked together to make this barren plot of land a place of which to be proud. "The land itself was a gift from Lily Quantrill," she said. "Heath Quantrill, her grandson, is the president of Buffalo Valley Bank." She pointed toward the brick structure at the far end of Main Street.

"Isn't there a branch in Grand Forks?"

"There are branches all across the state," Carrie told him.

"The headquarters is here?"

She nodded. "Heath moved everything to Buffalo Valley two years ago. I know it was a hard decision, but this is his home now, and he was tired of commuting to Grand Forks three days a week."

"It's an impressive building."

"Heath's an impressive bank president. I hope you get the chance to meet him and his wife, Rachel."

"I do, too," Vaughn said.

"Heath donated the lumber for the children's play equipment," she said as they entered the park and strolled past the jungle gym, slides and swings. "But Brandon Wyatt, along with Jeb McKenna and Gage Sinclair, actually built all these things." She realized the names didn't mean anything to Vaughn, but she wanted him to get a sense of what the park stood for in this community. Each family had contributed something, from planting the grass to laying the concrete walkway.

"It looks well used."

An outsider like Vaughn couldn't possibly understand how much the children of Buffalo Valley cherished the park. "My family owns the hardware," she continued, pointing to the opposite side of the park toward the store. "We donated the wood for the picnic tables."

"I notice they aren't secured with chains," Vaughn said.

"We don't have much crime in Buffalo Valley." It distressed her to visit public areas where everything, including picnic tables and garbage cans, was tied down by chains to prevent theft. But no one had ever stolen from the park or any other public place in Buffalo Valley. There'd never been any real vandalism, either.

"No crime?" He sounded as though he didn't believe her.

"Well, some, but it's mostly petty stuff. A few windows soaped at Halloween, that kind of thing. The occasional fight or display of drunkenness. We did have a murder once, about eighty years ago. According to the stories, it was a crime of passion." Quickly changing the subject, she said, "The War Memorial was designed by Kevin Betts. I don't know if you've heard of him, but he was born and raised right here."

"Sorry, I haven't," Vaughn said with a shrug.

"He's Leta's son, and he's an artist who's making a name for himself." Everyone in town was proud of Kevin. "This sculpture—" she gestured as they neared it "—was one of his very first." She watched Vaughn's expression when he saw it and was stirred by the immediate appreciation that showed in his eyes.

Kevin was a gifted artist, not only because he was technically skilled but because his work evoked emotion in people. The bronze sculpture was simple and yet profound. Half-a-dozen rifles were stacked together, upright and leaning against one another, with a helmet balanced on top. Beside the guns a young soldier knelt, his shoulders bowed in grief. No one seeing the piece could fail to be moved, to respond with sorrow and a bittersweet pain.

Vaughn stood before the memorial and didn't say anything right away. Then he squatted down and ran his finger over the name of Vaughn Knight. "My parents still talk about him. He was the one who brought them together," Vaughn said, and slowly straightened. "I'm glad he won't be forgotten."

"He won't be," Carrie assured him. "With this memorial, his name will always be here to remind everyone."

Vaughn thrust his gloved hands into his coat pockets.

"Cold?" Carrie asked.

He shook his head. "I know about the pharmacy and you've mentioned the hardware store. Tell me about the other businesses in town."

They walked toward Main Street and Carrie told him about each one in turn, starting with Joanie Wyatt's video-rental and craft store and ending with her parents' place.

"It was a leap of faith for you to move into town, wasn't it?" Vaughn said.

Carrie nodded pensively. "Yeah, but it's paid off. My two oldest brothers are still farming and the two younger ones work exclusively with Mom and Dad. It's a good arrangement all around."

"Are you hungry?" Vaughn asked unexpectedly.

She laughed. "You offering to feed me?" It was a bit early, but dinner would pass the time until Hassie returned.

"Unless there's a reason for you to hurry home."

"No reason. I'm divorced." Even now, six years later, the words left a bitter taste on her tongue. She focused her gaze directly in front of her.

"I'm sorry," he said.

"I am, too." She forced a cheerful note into her voice, as if to say she was over it.

"I thought I'd suggest Buffalo Bob's 3 of a Kind. I was intrigued by what you told me about him."

"He's certainly a character," she agreed. "But before we go there, I'd like to show you Maddy's Grocery." Carrie loved the wonderful and witty Christmas display Maddy put up every year. Eight reindeer were suspended from the ceiling, with the front half of Santa's sleigh coming out of the wall.

Vaughn laughed when he saw it. His reaction was one of genuine enjoyment and not the short derisive laugh of someone mocking Maddy's efforts. On their way to 3 of a Kind, they strolled past the Buffalo Valley Quilting Company.

"This is the success story of the decade," Carrie boasted as she motioned to the holiday quilt displayed in the first set of windows. "Sarah Urlacher started the business in her father's house, dyeing the muslin herself from all-natural products. The designs are her own, too."

Vaughn stopped to look at the quilt in the window.

"It all began when Lindsay Sinclair introduced Sarah's quilts to her uncle. He owns an upscale furniture store in Atlanta, and before she knew it, Sarah had trouble keeping up with the demand. Now people all over the country buy her quilts."

"That's great."

"Sarah's business has boosted the economy of Buffalo Valley to the point that we can now afford things that are commonplace in other towns."

"Such as?"

"The sidewalks got refurbished last summer, and the town could never have paid for that without the tax revenue Sarah's business brings in." Carrie didn't mention the new community well and several other improvements that had taken place over the past few years.

"I'll let Leta know where we are so she can tell Hassie,"

Carrie said, and made a quick stop at the pharmacy. She was back within moments. Vaughn waited for her outside.

There was no one at the restaurant or in the bar when they arrived. Studying Buffalo Bob with fresh eyes, Carrie could only guess what Vaughn must think. The ex-biker was a burly man. He was an oddity here in a town where most men came off the farm. With his thinning hair drawn back into a ponytail and his muscular arms covered in tattoos, he looked as though he'd be more comfortable with a biker gang than waiting tables.

"How ya doin', Carrie?" he greeted her when she took a seat across the table from Vaughn.

"Good, Bob. Come meet Vaughn Kyle."

"Welcome to Buffalo Valley," Bob said, extending his hand for a hearty shake. "Merrily told me you'd dropped by." Bob gave them each a menu. "Take a look, but the special tonight is Salisbury steak. I don't mind telling you it's excellent." He grinned. "And who would know better than me?"

"I'm convinced," Vaughn told him with an answering smile. "I'll have the special."

"Me, too," Carrie said, returning the menu.

Bob left them, and Carrie tried to relax but found it difficult. She hadn't been alone with a man, other than her brothers, in a very long time. Following her divorce, she'd only dated twice, and both occasions had been awkward. Her schooling, plus her internship, didn't leave much room for a social life, anyway.

Vaughn sat back in his chair. "Tell me about Hassie," he suggested easily.

Carrie felt the tightness leave her shoulders. On the subject of Hassie, she could talk his ear off. "What would you like to know first?"

"Whatever you feel is important."

"She's been my hero for as long as I can remember. I don't know what would've happened to this town without her." Carrie wanted him to realize how deeply Hassie was loved by everyone in Buffalo Valley. "She's older now, and she's slowing down some." Carrie had seen the evidence of that in the months since she'd come to work as an intern. She almost suspected that Hassie had been holding on until she got there.

Vaughn glanced at Buffalo Bob as he brought their salads and nodded his thanks. "Every year, along with my birthday card and a U.S. Savings Bond, she wrote me a short message." His mouth lifted in a half smile. "She called it *words to live by*."

"Give me an example," Carrie said, curious.

"I don't remember them all, but...okay, she told me about the importance of being on time. Only, she did it by making up this little poem...." He hesitated and a slow grin crossed his face. "She once wrote that if at first I don't succeed, it just means I'm normal."

"That sounds like Hassie."

"She has a wonderful way of putting things." He paused, a reflective look on his face. "When I was sixteen, she told me the grass isn't greener on the other side of the fence, it's greener where it's watered."

"I think it's wonderful that you remembered them."

"How could I not, when she made them so much fun? She was like an extra grandmother."

Hearing that warmed Carrie's heart, because she knew Hassie felt toward him the way she would a grandson.

They were silent as they ate their salads. Buffalo Bob had made even a plain lettuce, cucumber and tomato salad taste delicious with the addition of a tart-sweet cranberry dressing. They were just finishing when Bob reappeared, carrying two plates heaped with food. He placed them in front of Vaughn and Carrie, then stepped back, and said, "Enjoy."

Vaughn stared after him as he returned to the kitchen. "He's not the typical sort of person you find in a place like this, is he?"

"Bob's a sweetheart," she said defensively. "He's hardworking and well-liked and a wonderful father and—"

"Tell me how he happened to land in Buffalo Valley," Vaughn broke in. He reached for his fork, tasting the fluffy mashed potatoes and tender gravy-covered steak.

"He came here when the town was at its lowest point. My uncle Earl owned this hotel and he'd been trying to sell it for years. Seeing that there weren't any buyers and he was losing money every month, my uncle devised an unusual poker game. It cost a thousand dollars to play, but the winner walked away with the hotel, restaurant and bar. Lock, stock and barrel."

Vaughn's brows arched. "And Bob won it with three of a kind."

"Exactly."

Vaughn shook his head. "More power to him."

"A lot has changed since then, all of it for the better. Bob married Merrily, and two and a half years ago, they had little Bobby."

"The one who's prone to ear infections?"

She nodded. "You've never seen better parents. Those two dote on that little boy something fierce. In fact, Bob and Merrily are terrific with all the kids in town." Carrie paused long enough to sample her dinner. "Hey, this is terrific."

Vaughn agreed with her. "In addition to his other talents, Buffalo Bob's a good cook. He wasn't kidding about that."

"I don't know what his life was like before he came to Buffalo Valley, but he's one of us now."

Vaughn was about to ask a question when the door opened and Hassie hurried inside.

Carrie was instantly on her feet. One look told her Hassie was exhausted. Her shoulders were slumped and she seemed close to collapse.

"Hassie," Carrie said, wrapping her arm protectively around the older woman's waist. "This is Vaughn Kyle."

It was almost as if Hassie didn't hear her at first. "Vaughn," she repeated, and then her face brightened visibly. "My goodness, did you let me know you were coming and it slipped my mind?"

Vaughn pulled out a chair for her to sit down. "No, I very rudely showed up without an invitation."

"I wish I'd known."

"It's no problem. Carrie was kind enough to spend the afternoon with me."

"Let me take a good look at you," Hassie said. She cupped his face with both hands and a smile emerged. "You're so handsome," she whispered. "You have such kind eyes."

If her praise embarrassed or flustered him, Vaughn didn't reveal it.

"How long can you stay?" she asked.

"Actually, I should probably think about heading back to Grand Forks soon."

"No," Hassie protested. "That's hardly enough time for me to show you everything."

"Carrie already gave me a tour of town."

"That's good, but I have a number of things I've saved that I'd like you to have—things that were my son's."

Her disappointment was unmistakeable, and Carrie glanced at Vaughn, trying to signal him, hoping he'd change his mind.

"I want to see them."

Carrie could have hugged him right then and there.

"But," he added, "you've had a long, tiring day. Perhaps it would be better if I came back later."

Hassie didn't bother to deny what was obvious. "Would it be too much to ask you to come here on Sunday?" Both her hands gripped his, as if she was afraid to let him go.

Carrie found herself just as eager to hear his response.

"I'll meet you at the store shortly after noon," he said. "I'll look forward to seeing you then."

Carrie felt a surge of relief—and anticipation. She couldn't help smiling, first at Hassie, then at Vaughn.

Happiness shimmered in the old woman's eyes as she placed one hand on Carrie's shoulder and leaned heavily against her.

"That would be perfect," she said quietly. "Thank you, Vaughn."

Two

Hassie felt old and weary, especially after a day like this. But God had rewarded her patience by sending Vaughn Kyle to Buffalo Valley. Seeing him, however briefly, had lifted her spirits. Best of all was his promise to return on Sunday afternoon.

Tired though she was, Hassie brewed herself a cup of tea and sat at her kitchen table, mulling over the events of the day. Ambrose Kohn had been a thorn in her side for many years. His family had lived and worked in town for generations, but with impeccable timing, the Kohns had moved to Devils Lake just before the economy in Buffalo Valley collapsed.

Ambrose owned several pieces of property here and a building or two. The theater belonged to him, and he'd been quick enough to close it down, despite the town council's efforts to convince him otherwise. The old building still had plenty of life in it, but it'd sat abandoned and neglected until the first year Lindsay Snyder came to Buffalo Valley as the high-school teacher. She'd wanted to use it for a Christmas play. If Hassie remembered correctly, Ambrose had demanded she go out with him first before he gave permission. That annoyed Hassie even now, several years later.

Lindsay had attended some social function with Ambrose, and it had nearly ruined her relationship with Gage Sinclair. But she and Gage had resolved their differences.They'd been married for more than five years now and were parents of two beautiful daughters.

Ambrose, despite his underhanded methods, had walked away a winner, as well. After the community had cleaned up that old theater and put on the high-school Christmas program, he'd reopened the movie house and it'd been in operation ever since.

Unfortunately Ambrose hadn't learned anything from that experience. He hadn't learned that people in Buffalo Valley loved their town and that they supported one another. He hadn't figured out that for them, Buffalo Valley was *home,* not just a place to live. Now the middle-aged bachelor held the fate of the community in his hands. Value-X, a huge retailer, wanted to move into town and they wanted to set up shop on land owned by Ambrose. The company had a reputation for sweeping into small towns and then systematically destroying independent and family-owned businesses. Six months earlier, Hassie had watched a television report on the effect the mega-retailer had on communities. At the time she'd never dreamed Buffalo Valley might be targeted. Naturally the company insisted this was progress and a boon to the town's economy. There were already articles in some of the regional papers, touting the company's supposedly civic-minded attitudes. Profit-minded was more like it.

No one needed to tell Hassie what would happen to Buffalo Valley if Value-X decided to follow through with its plans. All the small businesses that had recently started would die a fast and painful death. Her own pharmacy wouldn't be immune.

Ambrose owned twenty acres just outside of town; this was the property Value-X was interested in acquiring, and he wasn't opposed to selling it—no matter how badly it damaged the community.

Nothing Hassie said had the least bit of impact on him. Buffalo Bob, as president of the town council, had tried to reason with him, too, again without success. Heath Quantrill had thrown up his hands in frustration at the man's stubborn refusal to listen.

While Ambrose didn't live in Buffalo Valley, he did have a powerful influence on its future. For that reason alone, he should think carefully about his decision to sell that parcel of land. Progress or not, it wasn't the kind of future she or anyone here saw for Buffalo Valley. Jerry, her husband, might have been able to talk sense into Ambrose, but Jerry had died the year after Vaughn. She'd lost them both so close together.

The TV report on Value-X had made a strong impression on Hassie. What had stayed in her mind most clearly were the interviews with business owners, some with three- and four-generation histories. They'd been forced to close down, unable to compete. Local traditions had been lost, pride broken. Men and women wept openly, in despair and hopelessness. Downtown areas died out.

Hassie couldn't bear to think what would happen to Buffalo Valley if Ambrose sold that land to those outsiders. Why, it would undo all the work the town council had done over the past six years. The outcome was too dismal to consider.

Joanie Wyatt's video-rental and craft store would probably be one of the first to fold. And the Hend-ricksons—they'd sunk everything they had in this world and more into Ace-

Man Hardware. Value-X would undercut the lowest prices they could charge and ring the store's death knell for sure.

Dennis Urlacher supplied car parts to the community at his filling station. Although that was only a small portion of his business, Dennis had once mentioned that his largest profit margin came from the auto parts and not the fuel. It wouldn't be long before his business was affected, too. Even Rachel Quan-trill's new hamburger stand would lose customers. Maddy's Grocery would suffer, too; how long she'd be able to hold on depended on Value-X's plans. It was said that many of the newer stores included groceries.

None of that concerned Ambrose. All he knew was that he'd been offered a fair price for a piece of land that had sat vacant for years. He'd let it be known that he fully intended to sell those acres. If anyone else was interested, he'd entertain other offers. Ambrose had made one thing perfectly clear: the offer had to be substantially higher than the deal Value-X had proposed. No one in town, not even Heath Quantrill, had a thick-enough bankroll to get into a bidding war with the huge retailer.

Hassie sipped her tea and purposely turned her thoughts in a more pleasant direction. What a fine-looking young man Vaughn Kyle was. After all these years, she was grateful to finally meet him. His letters had meant so much to her, and she'd saved each thank-you note from the time he was six years old.

For a short while after her son was buried, Hassie and Barbara, the boy's mother, had been close. They'd stayed in touch, but then a year later the wedding announcement arrived. Barbara, the beautiful young woman her son had loved, was marrying Rick Kyle, who'd been one of Vaughn's best friends.

Hassie didn't begrudge the couple happiness, but she hadn't

attended the wedding. Their marriage was a painful reminder that life continues. If circumstances had been different, this might have been her own son's wedding.

Two years later, Rick and Barbara had mailed her the birth announcement. They'd named their first child after Hassie's son. Two years later came another birth announcement, this time for a girl they named Gloria. Sight unseen, Hassie had loved that boy and thought of him as the grandson Vaughn could never give her. Her own daughter, Valerie, had two girls and Hassie adored them, but since Val and her family lived in Hawaii, there was little opportunity to see them. Vaughn Kyle had assumed a special significance for her. Neither his parents nor anyone else knew how deep her feelings ran. With a determined effort, she'd remained on the sidelines of his life, writing occasional letters and sending gifts at the appropriate times.

Now she would have the opportunity to give Vaughn the things she'd set aside for him so many years ago. It'd been her prayer that they meet before she died.

She had to stop herself from being greedy. She would gladly accept whatever time Vaughn Kyle was willing to grant her.

Carrie found herself smiling as she walked into the family home shortly after six. She paused in the entryway to remove the handknit scarf from around her neck and shrug out of her coat. Softly humming a Christmas tune, she savored the warm feelings left by her visit with Vaughn. She'd enjoyed getting to know him. Even though it'd been years since she'd spent this much time in a man's company, the initial awkwardness between them had dissipated quickly.

Vaughn seemed genuinely interested in learning what he could about Hassie and Buffalo Valley. What she appreciated most was that he hadn't asked any prying questions about her divorce. A lot of people assumed she wanted to tell her side of it, but Carrie found no joy in reliving the most painful, humiliating experience of her life.

Their dinner conversation had flowed smoothly. He was easy to talk to, and Carrie loved telling him about Buffalo Valley. She was proud to recount its history, especially the developments of the past five years. The improvements could be attributed to several factors, but almost all of them went right back to Hassie Knight and her determination and optimism. Hassie refused to let the town fade into nothingness, refused to let it die like countless other communities throughout the Dakotas.

When Carrie walked into the living room, her mother glanced up from her needlework and her two younger brothers hurried in from the kitchen. All three fixed their eyes on her. Everyone seemed to be waiting for her to speak.

"What?" Carrie demanded.

"We're curious about your dinner date," her mother said mildly.

Carrie should've realized her family would hear she'd gone out with Vaughn. *How* they knew she could only speculate, but in a small town word traveled even faster than it did on the Internet.

"How'd it go?" Ken asked, looking as though he'd welcome the opportunity to defend her honor should the occasion arise.

Part of the pain of her divorce came from knowing that she was the first in their family's history to whom it had happened. Long-standing marriages were a tradition she would gladly have continued. But she couldn't stay married to a man who didn't honor his vows, a man whose unfaithfulness undermined her self-respect, as well as their marriage. Her four brothers had hinted that things with Alec would have worked out differently if they'd been around to see to it. Needless to say, the last thing she wanted was her brothers, much as she loved them, playing the role of enforcers.

"He's very nice," she said, carefully weighing her words. She didn't want to give the impression that there was more to their meeting than a simple, friendly dinner.

"He didn't try anything, did he?" Chuck asked.

Carrie nearly laughed out loud. "Of course he didn't. Where's Dad?" she asked, wondering why her father hadn't leaped into the conversation.

Before anyone could respond, her father shuffled into the room, wearing his old slippers, a newspaper tucked under his arm and his reading glasses perched on the end of his nose. He stopped abruptly when he saw her.

"So how was your hot date?" he asked. He stood in front of his easy chair and waited for her to answer.

"It was just dinner," she protested. "The only reason he asked me out was to kill time while he waited for Hassie." It was unlikely they'd be doing this again, which she supposed was just as well. She had to admit she *wanted* to, but from what he'd said, he was only in the area for the Christmas holidays and then he was going home to Seattle. There was no point in starting something you couldn't finish, she thought. Not that she knew if he was even interested in her...or available.

"Will you be seeing him again?" her mother asked, but Carrie wasn't fooled by her nonchalant tone.

"He's coming back Sunday afternoon to—"

"That's great." Her mother smiled, clearly pleased.

"He isn't returning to see *me*." It was important her family understand that she had nothing to do with his decision. The sole reason for his visit was to spend time with Hassie.

"That's a shame." Her father claimed his chair, turning automatically to the sports page.

"Did you invite him to the tree-lighting ceremony?" Ken asked.

Her father lowered the newspaper and her mother paused in the middle of a stitch to await her response.

"No," Carrie admitted reluctantly. She'd thought of mentioning it, but couldn't see the purpose. She glanced around the room, looking at each hopeful face.

What she didn't say was that she would've welcomed the opportunity to know Vaughn Kyle better. The few hours she'd spent with him had helped her realize that her heart was still capable of response, that it hadn't shriveled up inside her like an orange left too long in the fruit bowl.

For that she was grateful.

As Vaughn pulled the rental car into the long driveway that led to his parents' home, he saw that his mother had turned on the back porch light. It wasn't really necessary, since the outside of the entire house was decorated with Christmas lights.

He knew his mother had made tentative plans for a dinner with friends on Sunday afternoon and might not be pleased by his absence. However, Vaughn didn't mind returning to Buffalo Valley. He'd enjoyed meeting Carrie and learning some of the town's recent history. He'd report this information to Natalie; she might find it useful. Carrie Hendrickson was an interesting contrast to the women he'd met and dated in Seattle during the past few years—including Natalie, his sort-of fiancée. Carrie had shied away from talking about herself, which was a refreshing change from what he'd grown accustomed to hearing. A recent dinner date with Natalie had been spent discussing every aspect of her career and the Value-X corporation—as if their work was all they had to talk about. He'd come away with a letdown feeling, feeling, somehow, that he'd missed out on something important...only he didn't know quite what. After all, he *admired* Natalie's drive and ambition and her unemotional approach to life.

His mother was finishing the dinner dishes when he entered the kitchen. "How was your visit?" she asked, rinsing a pan before setting it on the drainboard.

"Wonderful."

"How's Hassie?" she asked, looking expectantly at him as she reached for the towel to dry her hands. "You did give her my love, didn't you?"

"She was exhausted." He explained that the pharmacist had been at a meeting when he arrived and that her assistant had convinced him to wait until she got back. Neither she nor Carrie had mentioned the reason for the meeting, but whatever it was had drained her, emotionally and physically.

His mother's brow furrowed with concern. "She's not ill, is she?"

"I don't think so, but I didn't want to tire her out any more than she already was, so I told her I'd be back on Sunday."

His mother's face clouded and he knew what was coming. The subject of Vaughn Knight always distressed her. Every time his name was brought up, she grew quiet. He suspected she'd postponed a promised visit to Hassie because, for whatever reason, she found it hard to talk about Vaughn. More than once he'd seen tears fill her eyes. His mother wasn't the only one; his father also tended to avoid conversations about Hassie's son. All Vaughn knew was that both his parents thought a great deal of the friend who'd lost his life in a rice paddy thirty-three years earlier. So much that it still caused them pain.

"I'm glad you're doing this," she said. "Over the years I've wanted to talk about Vaughn, but I get choked up whenever time I try."

She grabbed a bottle of hand lotion and occupied herself with that for a few moments, but Vaughn wasn't fooled. She didn't want him to see that her eyes were brimming with tears.

"Hassie will do a far better job of telling you about Vaughn than your father or I could."

Impulsively Vaughn hugged his mother, then joined his father, who was watching television in the living room.

On Sunday the drive into Buffalo Valley seemed to go faster than it had on Friday. He knew exactly where he needed to go, and the very landscape he'd found monotonous two days earlier now seemed familiar, even welcoming.

When he pulled into town, Buffalo Bob was spreading salt on the sidewalk in front of his own place and the businesses on either side. He waved, and Vaughn returned the gesture, then eased into a parking spot near the pharmacy. Once again he was struck by what an appealing town Buffalo Valley was. It felt as though he'd stepped back in time, to an era when family and a sense of community were priorities, when neighbor helped neighbor and people felt responsible for one another.

A sign on the door stated that the drugstore was open from noon until five on Sundays during December. When he walked inside, Vaughn found Hassie behind the counter. He automatically looked for Carrie and wasn't disappointed when he saw her over by the cash register, checking receipts. She paused in her task as soon as she saw him.

To his surprise, his mind had drifted toward her a number of times since Friday. He was attracted by her charm, which was real and uncontrived. She was genuine and warm, and he liked the pride in her eyes when she talked about her town.

She froze, as if she, too, had been thinking of him. That was a pleasant thought and one that sent a shiver of guilt through him. He was as good as engaged to Natalie, and the last thing he should be doing was flirting with another woman.

"Right on time," Hassie said, sounding much livelier this afternoon than she had two days earlier.

"I'm rarely tardy when I have a date with a beautiful woman," he teased, and watched both Hassie and Carrie smile. He generally didn't have much use for flattery, but occasionally it served a purpose. In this case, his rather silly statement had given everyone, including him, a moment of pleasure.

"You going to be all right here by yourself?" She turned to Carrie.

"Of course. You two go and visit, and don't you worry about a thing."

"I'll just get my coat," Hassie said, and disappeared to retrieve it. While she was gone, he had a few minutes with Carrie.

"I'm glad you're doing this for Hassie," she said. "It means so much to her to be sharing her son's life with you."

"I'm not doing it out of any sense of charity." Vaughn was truly interested in learning what he could about his namesake.

Hassie returned, wearing a long, dark coat, and they walked over to her house, which was one street off Main. Vaughn slowed his gait to match hers, tucking her arm in the crook of his elbow. Together they strolled leisurely down the newly shoveled sidewalk.

The house resembled something out of a 1950s movie. The furniture was large and bulky, covered in thick navy-blue fabric. Doilies decorated the back of the chair, and three were strategically placed across the back of the matching sofa. Even the television set was an old-fashioned floor model.

"It'll only take me a minute to make tea," Hassie announced heading toward the kitchen. He was given instructions to sit down and to look through the photo albums she'd already laid out.

Vaughn opened the biggest album. The first photograph he saw was a black-and-white version of a much younger Hassie standing with a baby cradled in her arms. A tall, handsome man stood awkwardly beside her, grinning self-consciously. His hand was on the shoulder of a little girl about four or five who stood in front of them, her dark brown hair in long braids.

Thereafter, photograph after photograph documented the life of Vaughn Knight. He was in Boy Scouts and active in his church. His school pictures showed increasing growth and maturity. When he reached high school, Vaughn had grown tall and athletic; a series of newspaper articles detailed his success on the basketball court and the football field. The year he was a senior, Buffalo Valley High School won the state football championship, with Vaughn Knight as the star quarterback. Another article named him Most Valuable Player.

His high-school graduation picture revealed the face of a young man eager to explore the world.

Hassie rejoined him, carrying a tray with a ceramic pot and two matching cups, as well as a plate of small cookies.

Vaughn stood and took the tray from her, placing it on the coffee table, and waited while she poured. He noticed that her hands were unsteady, but he didn't interrupt or try to assist her.

When she'd finished, she picked up a round, plain hatbox and removed the lid. "The top letter is the first one that mentions your mother."

Vaughn reached for the envelope.

September 30, 1966

Dear Mom and Dad,

I'm in love. Don't laugh when you read this. Rick and I
went to a hootenanny last night and there was this terrific girl there. Her name's Barbara Lowell, and guess
what? She's from Grand Forks. She's got long blond hair
and the most incredible smile you've ever seen. After
the hootenanny we drank coffee and talked for hours.
I've never felt like this about any other girl. She's smart
and funny and so beautiful I had a hard time not staring at her. Even after I left her, I was so wrapped up in
meeting her I couldn't sleep. First thing this morning,
I called her and we talked for two hours. Rick is thor-
oughly disgusted with me and I don't blame him, but
I've never been in love before.

  As soon as I can, I want to bring her home for you to
meet. You'll understand why I feel the way I do once
you see her for yourselves.
Love,
Vaughn

"The Rick he's writing about is my dad?" Vaughn asked.
  Hassie nodded. "Here's another one you might find interesting." She lifted a batch of letters from the box. It was apparent from the way she sorted through the dates that she'd
reread each letter countless times.

July 16, 1967

Dear Mom and Dad,
I've made my decision, but I have to tell you it was prob-

ably the most difficult I've ever had to make. I love Barb, and both of us want to get married right away. If I were thinking just of me, that's exactly what we'd do before I ship out. But I'm following your example, Dad. You and Mom waited until after the war to marry, and you came back safe and whole. I will, too.

Barb cried when I told her I felt it was best to delay the wedding until after my tour. Although you never advised me one way or the other, I had the feeling you thought it was better this way.

Vaughn stopped reading. "Did you want him to wait before marrying my mother?"

Hassie closed her eyes. "His father and I thought they were both too young. In the years that followed, I lived to regret that. Perhaps if Vaughn had married your mother, there might have been a grandchild. I realize that's terribly selfish, and I hope you'll forgive me."

"There's nothing to forgive."

"I always wondered if Jerry would've lived longer if we'd had grandchildren. Valerie was still in college at the time and wasn't married yet. A few years after that, she moved to Hawaii to take a job and met her husband there, but by then it was too late for Jerry."

"So your husband took the news of Vaughn's death very hard?"

"Once we received word about Vaughn, my husband was never the same. He was close to both children, but the shock of Vaughn's death somehow made him lose his emotional balance. Much as he loved Valerie and me, he couldn't get over the loss of his son. He went into a deep depression and started having heart problems. A year later, he died, too."

"Heart attack?"

"Technically, yes, but Vaughn's death is what really killed him, despite what that death certificate said. He simply gave up caring about anything. I wish…" Her voice trailed off.

"I'm sorry," Vaughn said, and meant it.

"Don't be." She patted his hand. "God knew better. Had your mother and my son married, you would never have been born."

It must have hit her hard that her son's fiancée and closest friend married each other within a year of his death. "Were you upset when my parents got married?" he asked.

"A little in the beginning, but then I realized that was exactly what Vaughn would have wanted. He did love her, and I know in my heart of hearts that she loved him, too."

"She did." Vaughn could say that without hesitation.

Hassie plucked a tissue from the nearby box and dabbed at her eyes. "I'd like you to have this." She reached for a second box and withdrew a heavy felt crest displaying the letters BVHS. It took Vaughn a moment to recognize that it was from a letterman's jacket.

"Vaughn was very proud of this. He earned it in wrestling. He was a natural at most sports. Basketball and football were barely a challenge, but that wasn't the case with wrestling. Many an afternoon he'd walk into the pharmacy and announce to his father and me that he was quitting. By dinnertime he'd change his mind and then he'd go back the next day." She paused, dabbing at her eyes again. "Our children were the very best of Jerry and me. Vaughn was a good son, and losing him changed all of us forever."

"I'd be honored to have this letter," Vaughn said.

"Thank you," Hassie whispered. She smiled faintly through her tears. "You must think me an old fool."

"No," he was quick to tell her. "I'm very glad you showed me all this." For the first time Vaughn Knight was more than a name, someone remembered who'd been lost in a war fought half a world away. He was alive in the words of his letters, in the photographs and in the heart of his mother.

"His letters from Vietnam are in this box," Hassie said. "They'll give you a feel for what it was like. If you're interested…"

Having served in the military, Vaughn was, of course, interested. He sat back and read the first letter. When he'd finally finished them all, it'd grown dark and Hassie was busy in the kitchen.

"What time is it?" he asked.

"It's after six."

"No." He found that hard to believe. "I had no idea I'd kept you this long. I apologize, Hassie. You should have stopped me."

She shook her head. "I couldn't. Your interest was a pleasure to me. Everything was fine with the store—Carrie's fully capable of handling anything that might come up. Besides, we're closed now."

"He could've been a writer, your son," Vaughn said, setting aside the last letter. For a few hours he'd been completely drawn into Vaughn Knight's descriptions of people and landscapes and events. Although the details were lightly sketched, a vivid picture of the young soldier's life had revealed itself through his words.

"I often thought that myself," Hassie agreed. After a brief silence she said, "I didn't want to interrupt you to ask about dinner. I hope it wasn't overly presumptuous to assume you'd join me."

"I'd like that very much."

Hassie nodded once, slowly, as if she considered his company of great worth.

While she put the finishing touches on the meal, Vaughn phoned his parents to tell them he'd be later than anticipated. "Be sure and give Hassie my love," his mother instructed. "Tell her your father and I plan to visit her soon."

"I will," he promised.

When he ended the phone conversation, he found Hassie setting the table. He insisted on taking over, eager to contribute something to their dinner. His admiration and love for the older woman had grown this afternoon in ways he hadn't thought possible on such short acquaintance. She'd opened his eyes to a couple of important things. First and foremost, he'd learned about the man he'd been named after and discovered he had quite a lot to live up to. Second, he'd come to see his parents in a new light. He understood how their fallen friend had shaped their lives and their marriage. It was no wonder they didn't often speak of Vaughn Knight. The years might have dulled the pain, but the sense of loss was as strong in them as it was in Hassie.

They chatted over dinner, and his mood lightened. Hassie was wise and considerate; she seemed to understand how serious his thoughts had become.

"The community is lighting the Christmas tree this evening," she said casually as Vaughn carried their dishes to the sink.

"Are you going?" he asked.

"I wouldn't miss it for the world," Hassie informed him. "The Christmas tree is set up beside the War Memorial. Nearly everyone in town will be there—" she paused and looked at him "—including Carrie."

"Are you playing matchmaker with me, Hassie Knight?"

he asked. He had a feeling she didn't miss much—and that she'd seen the way his gaze had been drawn to Carrie when he'd entered the pharmacy.

Hassie chuckled. "She's smitten, you know."

Smitten. What a wonderful old-fashioned word, Vaughn mused. It would take a better man than him not to feel flattered.

"You could do worse."

"And how do you know I don't already have a girlfriend waiting for me in Seattle?" he asked, and wondered what Hassie would think of Natalie. For some reason he had the impression she wouldn't think much of her sharp-edged sophistication. It'd taken him a while to see past Natalie's polished exterior; once he had, he'd realized she was just like everyone else, trying to be noticed and to make a name for herself.

"You don't," Hassie returned confidently.

He was about to tell her about Natalie, when Hassie said, "Come with me. Come and watch the community tree being lit. There's no better way to learn about Buffalo Valley."

Vaughn's purpose, other than meeting Hassie, was to do exactly that. Still, seeing Carrie again appealed to him, too—more than it should.

"That's just what I need to put me in the Christmas spirit," Vaughn said. "I'd consider it an honor to accompany you."

"Wonderful." Hassie clasped her hands together as though to keep herself from clapping with delight. "I can't tell you how happy this makes me."

He helped her on with her coat, then grabbed his own. Taking her arm again, Vaughn guided her out the door and down the front steps. By the time they rounded the corner to Main Street and the City Park, the town was coming to life. There were groups of people converging on the park and cars stopping here and there. The air was filled with festivity—carols played over a loudspeaker, kids shrieking excit-edly, shouts of welcome…and laughter everywhere. Vaughn could practically *feel* the happiness all around him.

"This is about as close as it gets to a traffic jam in Buffalo Valley," Hassie told him.

As soon as they appeared, it seemed everyone in town called a greeting to Hassie. Vaughn had never seen anything to compare with the reverence and love people obviously felt for her.

"You've been holding out on me, Hassie Knight," an older man teased as he approached. "I didn't realize I had competition."

"Cut it out, Joshua McKenna." Hassie grinned. "Meet Vaughn Kyle."

"Mighty pleased to meet you." The man thrust out his hand for Vaughn to shake.

"Nearly everyone in a fifty-mile radius is coming," Joshua said, glancing around him. More and more cars arrived, and the park was actually getting crowded.

"I don't see Calla. She's not going to make it home this year?"

"And miss spoiling her baby brother?" Joshua returned. "You're joking, right?"

Hassie laughed delightedly. "I should have known better."

"Jeb, Maddy and the kids are already here."

The names flew over Vaughn's head, but it was apparent that Hassie loved each family.

"Maddy owns the grocery," Joshua explained as they strolled across the street and entered the park. "She's married to my son. Best thing that ever happened to him."

"Oh, yes—I saw the grocery," Vaughn said. "Maddy. I remember. The fantastic reindeer."

Joshua grinned widely. "Yup, that's our Maddy. Loves any excuse to decorate—and does a great job."

"They have two of the most precious children you'll ever want to see," Hassie added, "with another on the way."

"The first pregnancy and this latest one were real surprises."

"I'll bet Jeb's developed a liking for blizzards," Hassie murmured, and the two older folks burst into laughter.

"You'd have to know the history of that family to understand what's so amusing," Carrie said, joining them.

"Hello again," Vaughn murmured.

"Hi."

Vaughn had trouble looking away.

"How about you and Carrie getting me some hot chocolate?" the older woman asked.

"Bring some for me, too, while you're at it," Joshua said.

"I think we just got our marching orders," Carrie told him, her eyes smiling. "Is that okay?"

"I don't mind if you don't," Vaughn replied.

The cold had brought color to her cheeks, and her long blond hair straggled out from under her wool hat. "It's fine with me. Buffalo Bob and Merrily are serving cocoa and cookies over there," she said a little breathlessly.

"I'll be right back," Vaughn said over his shoulder as he followed Carrie.

"Don't rush," Hassie called after him…and then he thought he saw her wink at him.

Three

The Christmas lights strung around the outside of the old house welcomed Vaughn back to his parents' home. His mother had been born and raised in Grand Forks, but his grandparents had moved to Arizona when he was six. Vaughn had no recollection of visiting the Dakotas, although he was certain they had. His memories centered on the Denver area and his father's family. Not until Rick was accepted for early retirement did they decide to return to the home that had been in the Lowell family for more than a hundred years.

The television blared from the living room as Vaughn let himself into the house, entering through the door off the kitchen after stomping the snow from his shoes on the back porch. He unzipped his jacket and hung it on a peg, along with his muffler.

"Is that you, Vaughn?" his mother called.

"No, it's Santa," he joked.

He watched as his mother, still holding her needlepoint, hurried into the kitchen. "You're not hungry, are you?"

"I filled up on cookies and hot chocolate."

His mother studied him as if to gauge how the meeting with Hassie had gone—the *real* question she wanted to ask, he suspected. "Did you have a...good visit?"

"Yes." He nodded reassuringly. "We talked before dinner, but afterward there was a tree-lighting ceremony in the park."

"You attended that?" His mother sounded pleased.

"Sure, why not?" His response was flippant, as though this was the very thing he'd normally do. In truth, though, Vaughn couldn't recall attending anything like it since he was in grade school. The evening had been quite an experience. The whole town had come alive with music and laughter and people enjoying one another's company. Christmas had never been a big deal to Vaughn—but he'd never seen an entire community join together like this, either. He knew it had made a lasting impression on him, that it left him longing for the same kind of warmth. For a true spirit of celebration, far removed from sophisticated parties and decorator-trimmed trees.

"How is Hassie?" his mother asked.

Vaughn wasn't sure what to say. Hassie was without a doubt one of the most dynamic women he'd ever met. She possessed character and depth and a heart that poured out love for her family and her community. He'd immediately seen how deeply she was loved and respected. After these hours in her company, Vaughn had understood why. "She's an extraordinary woman."

"I know." His mother's voice was soft, a little tentative. Before Vaughn could say more, she'd retreated into the living room.

Vaughn followed and his father muted the television, obviously waiting for him to enlighten them about his visit.

"Hassie let me read the letters her son wrote from Vietnam."

His mother resumed her needlepoint and lowered her head, as though the stitches demanded her full attention.

"They were riveting. I learned about the war itself, things I could never have learned from a book, and about the man who wrote them." At the time, Hassie's son had been younger than Vaughn was now. In his letters, Vaughn had recognized the other man's sense of humanity, his hatred of war and his desire to make a difference, to share in a struggle for freedom.

"We met at the University of Michigan during our freshman year of college," his father said, and his eyes went blank. He seemed to be back in a different place, a different time. Vaughn knew he hadn't been accepted into the service himself because of poor eyesight. "He was my roommate. Both of us were away from home for the first time and in an environment completely foreign and unfamiliar. I suppose it's only natural that we became close."

His mother added in a low voice, "He was the most generous person I've ever known."

"He got a part-time job tutoring a youngster who had leukemia," his father continued, his gaze focused on the television screen. "He was hired for three hours a week, but Vaughn spent much more time with him than that. He played games with Joey, talked to him, cheered him up, and when Joey died at thirteen, the boy's mother said Vaughn had been his best friend."

"That's the kind of person he was," his mother said.

"Hassie gave me the school letter he earned in wrestling. And then, after I walked her back home, she said there was something else she wanted me to have." His parents looked up when he paused. Even now, Vaughn could hardly believe Hassie would give him such a gift.

"What, son?"

"Her husband's gold pocket watch. It would've been Vaughn's had he lived." Hassie had placed it in his hands with tears filming her eyes, then closed his fingers around it.

"Treasure it, Vaughn," his mother whispered.

"I do." Vaughn's first reaction had been to refuse something that was clearly a valuable family heirloom, something that meant a great deal to the old woman. He'd felt the significance of her gift and was moved by the solemnity of her words and gestures when she'd presented it to him.

He would always keep it safe. And he would pass it down to his oldest son or daughter.

"What else did Hassie tell you?" his father asked.

"She...said how much Vaughn had loved Mom."

"He did."

Vaughn studied his father, looking for any sign of jealousy. If he'd been in his father's shoes—well, he wasn't entirely sure *how* he'd feel.

"We planned to marry," his mother said, "but Hassie probably told you that."

He nodded. "She showed me the letter in which Vaughn explains why it would be best to wait until he returned from Vietnam."

"Only, he didn't return. And everything worked out in a completely different way." His mother took his father's hand and held it and they gazed at each other for a moment. "But a good way," she said quietly.

"I often wondered what Hassie really thought about the two of us getting married," his father said. He stared at Vaughn as if, after meeting Hassie, he could supply the answer.

Indeed, Vaughn had seen the look that came over her face when she mentioned his parents' marriage. "At first I think she took it hard." This didn't appear to surprise either of his parents.

"Our marriage was a reminder that Vaughn was never coming home," his mother said, "and that no matter how much pain the world brings us, life continues."

"She said as much herself."

"I think...she was disappointed in us both."

"Perhaps in the beginning," Vaughn agreed, "but she changed her mind later. She told me she felt that her son approved."

"I'm sure he did," his mother whispered.

His father reached abruptly for the remote, indicating that the conversation was over. Sound flared back, and Vaughn got up and went to the kitchen to pour himself a cup of coffee before rejoining his parents.

"Oh, dear, I almost forgot to tell you," his mother said. "Natalie phoned."

Vaughn's first reaction was that he didn't want to talk to her. Not tonight. Not after such an emotionally overwhelming day. Knowing Natalie, she'd want to discuss business, and that was the last thing on his mind. He needed to think before he returned the call, needed to absorb what he'd learned first—about the town, about Hassie...about himself.

"It isn't too late to call her back," his mother said. "With the time difference, it's barely eight on the West Coast."

"I know," he said absently, his thoughts now on Carrie Hendrickson. Much of the evening had been spent with her. After they'd brought hot chocolate to Hassie and Joshua McKenna, she'd introduced him to her family.

Vaughn had seen the wary look in her brothers' eyes and realized how protective they were of her. He wished he'd had more of a chance to talk to Carrie, but they were constantly interrupted. She was a favorite with her nieces and nephews, who were forever running up to her, involving her in their games and their squabbles. She was a natural peacemaker, he observed, one of those people whose very presence brought out the best impulses in others. Like Hassie. And the people in town valued Carrie in much the same way; that was easy to tell. They came to her for advice and comfort. They were drawn to her just as he was.

"Your father and I are looking forward to meeting Natalie," his mother said, breaking into his musings.

Vaughn started guiltily. He was as good as engaged—although, he supposed, all they'd really done was discuss the possibility of marriage. He hadn't divulged his plans to either of his parents. At Natalie's request, he hadn't even told them about his job. "She's anxious to meet you, too," he said, but without a lot of enthusiasm. The contrast between Natalie and Carrie flashed like a neon sign in his brain. One was warm and personable and focused on the needs of her community, the other sharp, savvy and ambitious. When he'd arrived in North Dakota, he thought he knew what he wanted; all at once, he wasn't sure.

"You've been seeing her for two years now," his mother went on, watching him.

"Barbara, the boy doesn't need you to tell him that."

Vaughn sipped his coffee. This was one conversation he had no wish to continue. "Carrie and I are going Christmas shopping tomorrow," he said, instead.

His mother lowered the needlepoint to her lap and stared at him. "Carrie? Who's Carrie?"

Vaughn didn't realize his mistake until it was too late. "A friend."

His mother raised her eyebrows as if his answer didn't please her. "When did you have time to make friends?"

"She works with Hassie at the pharmacy."

"I see." It appeared his mother did see, because she said nothing more.

Vaughn wished he understood his own feelings. A week ago he would have rushed to return Natalie's call. He wasn't avoiding *her,* he decided, but the subject of Value-X and Buffalo Valley. In a matter of days—one day, really—he'd become oddly protective of the town...and its people. Hassie, of course, but Carrie, too. Natalie was bound to ask him questions he no longer wanted to answer.

One thing was clear; he needed to think the situation through very carefully.

Craving solitude, Vaughn swallowed the last of his coffee, then announced he was heading for bed.

His mother glanced up at the wall clock. "Aren't you calling Natalie?"

He frowned. "Later. Don't worry about it, Mom."

"Vaughn has to rest up for shopping," his father teased.

"Ah, yes, the great shopping expedition. Where will it be, by the way?"

"The mall here in town."

"You're actually going to a mall at this time of year?" His father looked at him as though he'd lost his sanity.

Vaughn gave a nonchalant shrug. He didn't know what had possessed him to suggest he and Carrie meet at Columbia Mall. His excuse had been that Carrie was a wonderful source of information about the town. He'd never had the opportunity to bring up the subject of Value-X, and wanted to get her reactions to it. Or so he told himself.

The truth was, he wanted to know her better.

★ ★ ★

Hassie sat up in bed, her eyes on the photograph of her son on the bedroom wall. She looked at Jerry's picture next and Valerie's, then turned back to Vaughn's. It was only natural that she'd be thinking about her son tonight.

Time passed with such inexorable swiftness, she reflected. She had startlingly clear memories of Vaughn as a toddler, stumbling toward her, arms outstretched. If she closed her eyes, she could almost hear his laughter. She'd loved to scoop him into her arms and hug him close until he squirmed, wanting to run and play with his older sister. As they grew older, Valerie had listened to his confidences and offered a big sister's sage advice.

How carefree life had been for her and Jerry in the early 1950s. Simple pleasures had meant a great deal back then. She could think of no greater comfort than sitting with her husband after a day at the pharmacy, a day they'd spent working together. Jerry would slip his arm around her shoulder and she'd press her head against his. He'd loved to whisper the sweetest words in her ear, and oh, she'd enjoyed being in his arms. In those days, it seemed the sun would never stop shining and the world would always be filled with happiness.

Turning out the light, Hassie nestled under the covers and let her memories take her back. Valerie and Vaughn used to come to the pharmacy every afternoon after school. To this day she could still picture the two of them sitting at the soda fountain, waiting to be served an after-school snack. They were a normal sister and brother, constantly bickering. Valerie always teased Vaughn, and when she did, he'd tug her pigtails hard enough to bring tears to her eyes. Then it would be up to Hassie to chastise them both. Softhearted Jerry had left the discipline to her. Hassie hated it, but knew her children needed to understand that their actions had consequences.

The years flew by so fast! Looking back, Hassie wished she'd appreciated each day a little more, treasured each moment with her children while they were young. Before she could account for all the years that had passed, it was 1960, and Vaughn was in high school.

Jerry was especially proud of Vaughn's athletic talent. He, too, had been a sports star in his youth. Vaughn had played team sports throughout his four years in high school, and they'd never missed a game. One or the other, and often both of them, were at his games, even if it meant closing the pharmacy, although they didn't do that often. They always sat in the same section of the stands so Vaughn would know where to find them. When his team came onto the field, it wasn't unusual for him to turn toward the bleachers and survey the crowd until he located his parents. Then he'd smile and briefly raise one hand.

Without even trying, Hassie could hear the crowds and recall the cheerleaders' triumphant leaps, while the school band played in the background.

Watching Vaughn play ball had been hard on Hassie's nerves. Twice that she could remember, her son had been injured. Both times Jerry had to stop her from running onto the field. She stood with the other concerned parents, her hands over her mouth, as the coaches assessed his injuries. On both occasions Vaughn had walked off the playing field unaided, but it'd been pride that had carried him. The first time his arm had been broken, and the second, his nose.

His high-school years had been wonderful. The girls always had eyes for Vaughn. Not only was he a star athlete and academically accomplished, he was tall and good-looking. The phone nearly rang off the hook during his junior and senior years. There'd never been anyone special, though, until he met Barbara Lowell in college. She'd been his first love and his last.

Hassie recalled how handsome he'd looked in his brand-new suit for the junior-senior prom, although he'd been uncomfortable in the starched white dress shirt. The photo from the dance revealed how ill at ease he'd been. His expression, Jerry had said, was that of someone who expected to be hit by a water balloon.

Hassie had suggested he ask Theresa Burkhart to the biggest dance of the year. He'd done so, but he'd never asked her out for a second date. When Hassie asked him why, Vaughn shrugged and had nothing more to say. Every afternoon for a week after the prom, Theresa had stopped at the soda fountain, obviuosly hoping to run into Vaughn. Each afternoon she left, looking disappointed.

Packing Vaughn's suitcase the day before he went off to the University of Michigan was another fond memory. She'd lovingly placed his new clothes in the suitcase that would accompany him on this first trip away from home. Although saddened by his departure, she took comfort in knowing he'd only be gone for a few years. This wasn't a new experience, since Valerie had left four years earlier and was attending Oregon State. She was working part-time and seemed in no particular hurry to finish her education. Jerry and Hassie had been reassured by Vaughn's promise to return as a pharmacist himself. He shared their commitment to community and their belief in tradition.

Soon the kitchen table was littered with his letters home. The letter in which he first mentioned meeting Barbara had brought back memories of Hassie's own—like meeting Jerry at college just before the war. The day that letter arrived, she'd sat at the kitchen table with her husband and they'd held hands and reminisced about the early days of their own romance.

Then the unthinkable happened. News of a war in a country she'd barely heard of escalated daily. The papers, television and radio were filled with reports, despite President Johnson's promises to limit the United States' involvement. Then the day came when Vaughn phoned home and announced, like so many young men his age, that he'd been drafted. A numbness had spread from Hassie's hand and traveled up her arm. It didn't stop until it had reached her heart. Vaughn was going to war. Like his father before him, he would carry a rifle and see death.

This wasn't supposed to happen. For a while, men in college were exempt, but with the war's escalation, they were now included. Vaughn took the news well, but not Hassie. He had to do his part, he told her. It was too easy to pass the burden onto someone else. Citizenship came with a price tag.

Suddenly bombs were exploding all around her. Terrified, Hassie hid her head in her hands, certain she was about to die. Bullets whizzed past her and she gasped, her heart cramping with a terrible fear. All at once she was cold, colder than she could ever remember being, and then she was flat on her back with the sure knowledge that she'd been hit. The sky was an intense shade of blue, and she was simultaneously lying there and hovering far above. But when she looked down, it wasn't her face she saw. It was the face of her dying son. His blood drained out of him with unstoppable speed as the frantic medic worked over him.

Her son, the child of her heart, was dying. He saw her and tried to smile, to tell her it was all right, but his eyes closed and he was gone. Her baby was forever gone.

A crushing load of grief weighed on Hassie's heart. She cried out and, groaning, sat upright.

It was then she realized she'd fallen asleep. This had all been a dream. Awash with memories, she'd drifted into a dream so real she could hear the fading echoes of exploding ammunition as she dragged herself out of a past world and back to reality.

As her eyes adjusted to the dark, her gaze darted from one familiar object to another. From the bedroom door where her housecoat hung on a hook to the dresser top with the silver mirror and brush set Jerry had given her on their tenth anniversary.

"Vaughn." His name was a broken whisper, and she realized that she couldn't remember what he looked like. His face, so well loved, refused to come. Strain as she might, she couldn't see him. Panic descended, and she tossed aside the blankets and slid out of bed. It wasn't her son's image that filled her mind, but the face of another young man. Another Vaughn.

Vaughn Kyle.

"Of course," she whispered, clutching the bedpost. Leaning against it, she heaved a deep, quivering sigh and climbed back into bed.

Wrapping the quilt around her, she tucked her arm beneath her pillow and closed her eyes. Yes, it made sense that she'd dream of Vaughn that night. Her Vaughn. It also made sense that it was Vaughn Kyle's face she now saw. After all, she'd spent much of the day with him.

Barbara and Rick had done a good job raising him. Vaughn was a fine man, honest and genuine, sensitive yet forthright. She was grateful she'd had the opportunity to meet him before she died.

Giving him the gold watch had been a spur-of-the-moment decision. It was the one possession of Jerry's she'd held back from Valerie and her two granddaughters. Valerie lived in Hawaii and although they were close, they rarely visited each other. Hassie had flown to the island once, but all those tourists and hordes of people had made her nervous. Not only that, she wasn't comfortable in planes, and the long flight made her nervous. A few years back, after a scare with Hassie's heart, Valerie had flown out to spend time with her, but had soon grown bored and restless.

Hassie didn't think Val's daughters, Alison and Charlotte, would have much interest in their grandfather's watch. But it was precious to her, so she'd kept it.

She knew when she pressed the watch into Vaughn's palm that this was the right thing to do. He looked as if he was about to argue with her, but he didn't and she was glad. Still, his hesitation told her more clearly than any words that he understood the significance of her gift.

Warm once more, Hassie stretched out her legs, enjoying the feel of the sheets against her bare skin. She smiled, remembering the exchange she'd witnessed between Carrie and Vaughn Kyle last night. She hoped something came of it. After her divorce Carrie was understandably wary about relationships, but Hassie felt confident that Vaughn would never intentionally do anything to hurt her.

"Can't something be done?" Carrie asked, pacing in front of Heath Quantrill's polished wood desk. As the president of Buffalo Valley Bank, he just might know of some way to stop Value-X from moving into town. In the past day or so, news of the retailer's plans had spread through town faster than an August brushfire. Carrie had first heard of it that morning. She suspected Hassie knew and had been protecting her; she also suspected there'd been rumors last night, but she'd been too involved with Vaughn to notice.

Heath's frown darkened. It went without saying that he wasn't any happier about this than she was. "I'm sorry, Carrie, but Ambrose Kohn is a difficult man to deal with. The town council has spoken to him several times. Hassie tried and I did, too, but he isn't willing to listen."

"You knew before this morning?" she fired back. "Hassie, too?" That was what she thought—and it explained a great deal. Hassie just hadn't been herself lately, but every inquiry was met with denial.

Heath nodded.

"Doesn't Mr. Kohn realize what he's doing?" Carrie found it hard to believe he could be so callous toward the town.

"He knows all too well."

"People have a right to know that the entire future of our town is at risk." She could only imagine what would happen to her father's store if Value-X set up shop.

Heath obviously agreed with her. "Hassie suggested we keep this under wraps until after Christmas, and the rest of the council decided to go along with her. I don't know how the news leaked." He scowled and rolled his gold pen between flat palms.

Delaying the bad news changed nothing. This morning at breakfast her father had announced what he'd learned. He was already alternating between depression and panic. He'd heard it from Joanie Wyatt at the treelighting ceremony. The Wyatts had sent away for stock information, and Joanie had read over a prospectus; she'd seen that Buffalo Valley was listed as a possible expansion site. She'd immediately phoned Buffalo Bob, who'd reluctantly confirmed it.

"Nothing's been signed yet," Heath said, as though that should make her feel better. It didn't.

She glanced at her watch, wishing she had more time to get all this straight in her mind. Although she was eager to meet Vaughn at the Columbia Mall as promised, she wasn't in the mood for Christmas activities. Not with this Value-X problem hanging over all their heads.

"Have you talked to anyone at the corporate office?" she asked.

Heath nodded.

"They weren't interested in listening, were they?" Heath's disheartened look was answer enough. "It's *progress,* right?"

"Right," Heath muttered. "Listen, I've got a meeting in ten minutes. I'm sorry, Carrie. I know what this will mean for your father's business and Knight's Pharmacy, too. I'm doing the best I can."

"Can't you buy the property yourself?"

"I approached Kohn about that, but..."

"He won't sell it to you?" Carrie asked in an outraged voice.

"Let's say he'd love a bidding war—one I'd be sure to lose." Heath stood and retrieved his overcoat from a closet.

Her gaze pleaded with his. "You've *got* to find a way to keep Value-X out of Buffalo Valley."

"Kohn hasn't heard the last of this," Heath promised as he escorted her out of the bank.

Carrie accompanied him to his four-wheel-drive vehicle.

"Is there anything *I* can do?" she asked, feeling the need to act.

Heath shook his head as he opened his car door. "Don't worry, Carrie, this isn't over yet. Not by a long shot."

All Carrie could do was trust that, somehow or other, he'd convince Ambrose Kohn to be reasonable.

The drive into Grand Forks passed in a fog. Burdened by the news, Carrie was surprised when the two lanes widened to four as she reached the outskirts of the big city.

Vaughn was waiting for her inside the mall at a coffee shop they'd designated as their meeting place. He stood as she approached. She was struck again by what an attractive man he was. Her ex-husband had been attractive, too, but Alec's good looks had belied his selfish, arrogant nature. She'd learned, the hard way, that a handsome face proved nothing about the inner man. No, handsome is as handsome does, her grandma always said. Which made Vaughn Kyle very handsome, indeed.

He'd been so gentle and caring with Hassie. He'd spent time with her, listened to her talk about her son. Carrie marveled at his patience and his good humor and the respect he seemed to genuinely feel for Hassie and for the town. When he'd asked her to meet him in Grand Forks to help him finish his shopping, she'd agreed. It'd been a long, long time since a man had impressed her as much as Vaughn Kyle.

"Thanks for coming," he said now.

Although it was relatively early, the mall was already frantic. With exactly a week left before Christmas, the entire population of Grand Forks had apparently decided to cram itself inside.

"The only person I still need to buy for is my mother," he told her, looking around as though he already regretted this.

"What about perfume?" Carrie wasn't feeling too inspired, either.

"She's allergic to a lot of those scents."

"Okay, how about…" Carrie proceeded to rattle off several other suggestions, all of which he categorically dismissed for one reason or another.

"Do you have any more ideas?" he asked, looking desperate.

"Not yet, but we might stumble across something while we're here."

Vaughn sighed. "That doesn't sound promising." He glanced around. "How about if we find a quiet restaurant and discuss it over lunch?"

He didn't need to ask twice. She was as anxious to get away from the crowds as he was. They found an Italian place Joanie and Brandon Wyatt had once recommended and were seated almost immediately. Sitting at their table with its red-and-white-checkered tablecloth, Carrie could see why her friends liked it here. The casual atmosphere was perfect. If the food was half as good as the smells wafting from the kitchen, she was in for a treat.

Carrie quickly made her decision and closed the menu. Lowering her gaze, she pushed thoughts of Value-X from her mind for the umpteenth time. Her worries kept intruding on the pleasant day she was hoping to have.

"You'd better tell me," Vaughn said. His hand reached for hers and he gently squeezed it. "Something's wrong."

Apparently she hadn't done a very good job of hiding her concerns. Rather than blurt everything out, she stared down at the tablecloth for a long moment.

"We learned this morning that Value-X is considering Buffalo Valley as a possible site," she finally said. "Apparently they've already negotiated for a piece of land. I don't need to tell you what that'll do to our community."

"It might be a good thing," he said slowly. "Try to think positive."

"If this is progress, we don't want anything to do with it," she muttered. Vaughn couldn't *possibly* understand. She was sorry she'd brought up the subject. "We happen to like our town just the way it is."

"It isn't that—"

"We're going to fight it," she said confidently.

"How?" Vaughn asked. "Isn't that a little like David fighting Goliath?"

"Perhaps, but like David, you can bet we aren't going to idly sit by and do nothing." Already plans had started to form in her mind. "Other communities have succeeded. We can, too."

"You're serious about this?"

"Damn straight I am."

"Don't you think you're overlooking the positive aspects of a company like Value-X opening a store in Buffalo Valley? They have a lot to offer."

Carrie glared at him. "You don't get it, do you?"

"I guess not. Help me understand." Vaughn leaned back in his chair, his expression serious.

"Value-X will ruin *everything*. We don't want it, we don't need it." Carrie struggled to keep her voice even.

Vaughn studied her. "I imagine you're a formidable opponent when you put your mind to something."

"It isn't only me," she told him. "The entire town is up in arms. We haven't come this far to let some heartless enterprise wipe out all our efforts."

Vaughn frowned. "Value-X will mean the end of Knight's Pharmacy, won't it?"

That was only the beginning as far as Carrie could tell. "And AceMan Hardware." She ran one finger across the tines of the fork. "The only business I can't see it affecting is the Buffalo Valley Quilting Company." Carrie shot him a look and wondered why she hadn't thought of this earlier. "That's it!"

"What is?"

"A quilt. It's the perfect Christmas gift for your mother."

Vaughn didn't appear convinced. "A quilt?"

"They're special. Hand-sewn, and you could go traditional or innovative."

"How much are they?"

"I don't know the full range of prices," she said, "but if the quilt is more than you want to spend, there're table runners and place mats and lap robes."

"Hmm." The idea seemed to take hold. "That does sound like a gift she'd enjoy."

"I'm sure she would," Carrie said. "I can't believe I didn't think of it earlier."

"So how do I go about this?"

"If you don't want to drive back to Buffalo Valley so soon, I could choose one for you," she offered.

"Perhaps Mom should pick it out herself."

"Great idea—and I know Hassie would love to see her."

"I think it would do my mother a world of good to renew her friendship with Hassie."

The waitress arrived and took their orders. Seafood linguine for her, lasagna for him. And a glass of red wine for each. "Hey, it's Christmas," Vaughn said with a grin.

He took his cell phone from his jacket and flipped it open. Within seconds, he had his mother on the line.

"What about tomorrow?" he asked, looking at Carrie.

"I'm sure that'll be fine."

"Hassie will be there, won't she?"

Carrie nodded. "She's scheduled to work in the morning, but she has the afternoon free. I'll cover for her, if need be."

He relayed the information to his mother, then ended the conversation and slid the phone back inside his jacket. Smiling at her, he said, "Thanks, Carrie."

A warm feeling came over her, and once again she lowered her gaze. Vaughn Kyle—kind to old women and a thoughtful son. He was exciting and he was interesting and he made her heart beat furiously. She could only regret that he was heading back to Seattle so soon after Christmas.

Four

"I suppose you heard," Hassie said when Leta Betts came bustling into the pharmacy late in the afternoon. The word about Value-X had filtered through Buffalo Valley, and the town was rife with speculation. Nearly everyone she knew had stopped by to talk it over with her, as though she had a solution to this perplexing problem.

"I don't like it," Leta muttered, walking behind the counter of the soda fountain and pulling out a well-used teapot. "Want me to make you a cup?"

"Please." Hassie had filled prescriptions all afternoon, between interruptions, and she was ready for a break. She'd known that Leta would come by at some point; fortunately, there was a lull just now, which made it a good time to talk to her dearest friend.

"Where's Carrie?" Leta found two mugs and set them on the counter.

"It's her day off."

"I heard she went to see Heath."

Hassie had heard about that, as well. Carrie had a good heart and cared about this community with the same intensity as Hassie did. Once Carrie received her Pharm.D., Hassie had planned to turn the business over to her. That was before the threat of Value-X, however. If that threat became a reality, Hassie couldn't sell the pharmacy, not in good conscience. In all likelihood the place would be out of business within a year after the big retailer moved in.

"It's a shame, you know," Leta murmured. She dragged a chair closer to the counter and perched on the seat. Leaning forward, she braced her elbows on the edge, sighing deeply. "Who'd have thought something like this would ever happen?"

Hassie shook her head helplessly. She'd worked so hard to save this town. And now, even if oblivion wasn't to be its fate, a corporation like Value-X could make Buffalo Valley unrecognizable, could turn it into something that bore no resemblance to the place it had been. The place it *should* be.

"What are we going to do?" Leta asked.

Hassie sat next to her and assumed the same slouched pose. Leta was her friend and employee, and there wasn't anything Hassie couldn't tell her. But this situation with the conglomerate had her poleaxed. She was at her wit's end. "I don't know," she admitted.

"We'll think of something," Leta insisted, and poured tea into the mugs. She set one in front of Hassie and then added a teaspoon of sugar to her own.

"Not this time," Hassie said as she reached for the mug, letting it warm her hands. She was too old and too tired. A few years back she'd fought for her town with determination and ingenuity, but this new war would have to be waged by someone else. She'd done her part.

"This was how we both felt when we learned Lindsay had decided to return to Atlanta, remember?" Leta prodded.

As though Hassie would ever forget. At the last minute Leta's son, Gage, had realized he'd be making the worst mistake of his life if he let Lindsay leave without telling her how much he loved her. As a result, Lindsay had not only stayed on as a high-school teacher, she'd married Gage. Leta was a grandmother twice over, thanks to the young couple.

"Value-X is too powerful for me." A bit of research had revealed that the retailer was accustomed to exactly this kind of local resistance. They had their battle plans worked out to the smallest detail. Hassie remembered from the television exposé that the company had a legal team, as well as public-relations people, all of them experts at squelching opposition. Hassie knew the town council couldn't afford any high-priced attorneys to plead their case. Even if they banded together, they were no match for the company's corporate attorneys. They were cutthroat, they'd seen it all, done it all. According to the documentary, they'd won in the majority of their cases. Like it or not, Value-X simply overran a community.

"We can't give up," Leta insisted. She glared at Hassie, as though waiting for some of the old fight to surface.

It wouldn't, though. Not anymore. Slowly Hassie lowered her gaze, refusing to meet her friend's eyes. "It's a lost cause," she murmured.

"This doesn't sound like you, Hassie."

"No," she agreed, glancing at her tired reflection in the mirror above the soda fountain, "but it won't matter that much if I lose the pharmacy."

Leta's jaw sagged open. "Wh-what—"

"I should've retired years ago. The only reason I held on as long as I did is the community needs a pharmacy and—"

"What about Carrie?"

Hassie had been so pleased and grateful when Carrie had come to work as an intern. This was what she'd always wanted for the pharmacy. Years ago she'd expected her son to take over, but Vietnam had robbed her of that dream. The hopelessness of the situation settled squarely over her heart.

"I'm sure Value-X will require a pharmacist. Carrie can apply there."

Silent, Leta stared into the distance.

"I'm tired," Hassie said. "Valerie's been after me to retire, move to Hawaii.... Maybe I should."

"You in Hawaii? Never!" Leta shook her head fiercely. "I've always followed your lead—we all have. I don't know what would've become of us if not for you."

"Fiddlesticks." Hassie forced a laugh. "Value-X is coming to town, and that's all there is to it. We might as well accept the inevitable. Not long from now, both of us will be shopping there and wondering how we ever lived without such a store in town."

"You're probably right," Leta returned, but her words rang false.

"Let's just enjoy Christmas," Hassie suggested, gesturing at the garlands strung from the old-fashioned ceiling lights. "What are your plans?"

"Kevin won't be home, but he'll call from Paris on Christmas Eve. Gage and Lindsay invited me to spend Christmas Day with them." Hassie knew that Leta would take delight in spoiling four-year-old Joy and two-year-old Madeline.

"Bob and Merrily invited me over in the morning to open gifts with them and Bobby," Hassie told her friend. They thought of her as Bobby's unofficial grandmother. Early in their marriage, Bob and Merrily had lost a son—although not to death. They'd fostered a child from an abusive environment and had wanted to adopt him, but in the end, the California authorities had seen fit to place the boy with another family. It'd been a difficult time for the couple. Having lost a son herself, Hassie had understood their grief as only someone who'd walked that path could understand it. She'd tried to bring them comfort and the example of her endurance. Bob and Merrily never forgot her kindness, little as it was. Over the past few years, they'd become as close to her as family.

"You finally met Vaughn Kyle," Leta said. "That's definitely a highlight of this Christmas season."

"Yes," Hassie agreed, somewhat cheered. It'd been an unanticipated pleasure, one she'd always remember. In the hours they'd spent with each other, she'd forged a bond with the young man. Meeting Vaughn had left Hassie feeling closer to her own son, although he'd been dead for thirty-three years. Hard to believe so much time had passed since his death....

"That was him with Carrie at the tree-lighting ceremony, wasn't it?"

Hassie felt a small, sudden joy, sending a ray of light into the gloom she'd experienced earlier. "She's spending the afternoon with him in Grand Forks."

"It's time she put the divorce behind her."

Hassie felt the same way but didn't comment.

"Do you think something might come of it?" Leta asked, her voice slightly raised.

Hassie couldn't answer. Her hours with Vaughn had been taken up with the past, and she hadn't discovered much at all about his future plans. She knew he'd been honorably discharged from the military and had accepted a position with a Seattle-based company, although he'd never said which one. Probably a big software firm, she decided. From what she understood, he'd be starting work after the first of the year. She felt it was a good sign that he'd come to spend two weeks with his parents.

"He's been to town twice already," Leta offered. "That's encouraging, don't you think?"

"I suppose."

A small smile quivered at the edges of Leta's mouth. "I remember when Gage first got interested in Lindsay. That boy drummed up a hundred excuses to drive into town."

"Remember Jeb and Maddy?" Hassie murmured, her eyes flashing with the memory. These were the thoughts she preferred to cling to. Stories with happy resolutions. Good things happening to good people.

Leta's responding grin brightened her face. "I'm not likely to forget. We hadn't seen hide nor hair of him in months."

"Years," Hassie corrected. Following the farming accident that cost Jeb McKenna his leg, the farmer-turned-buffalo-rancher became a recluse. Hassie recalled the days Joshua had to practically drag his son into town for Christmas dinner. Then Maddy Washburn bought the grocery and started her delivery service. After those two were trapped together in a blizzard, why, there was no counting the number of times Jeb showed up in Buffalo Valley.

"Do you remember the day Margaret Eilers stormed into town and yanked Matt out of Buffalo Bob's?" Leta asked, laughing outright.

"Sure do. She nearly beat him to a pulp." Tears of laughter filled Hassie's eyes. "Can't say I blame her. Those two certainly had their troubles."

Margaret had set her sights on Matt Eilers and wanted him in the worst way, faults and all. That was what she got, too. Not three months after they were married, Margaret found out that Matt had gotten a cocktail waitress pregnant. Granted, it had happened *before* the marriage, but Margaret had still felt angry and betrayed.

"Look at them now," Leta said, sobering. "I don't know any couple more in love." She drank a sip of her tea. "If Margaret and Matt can overcome their problems, why can't Buffalo Valley sort out this thing with Value-X?"

For the first time all week, Hassie felt hopeful. "Maybe you're right, Leta. Maybe you're right."

Carrie sat down at the kitchen table and reached for the cream, adding it to her coffee. Even though she was twenty-seven years old, she found it comforting to watch her mother stir up a batch of gingerbread cookies. The house was redolent with the scent of cinnamon and other spices.

Her morning had been busy. After a lengthy conversation with Lindsay Sinclair, who'd been in contact with the Value-X corporate offices, Carrie had spent an hour on the Internet learning what she could about the big retailer.

"Did you have a good time yesterday afternoon?" Diane Hendrickson asked. She set the mixing bowl in the refrigerator, then joined Carrie at the table.

"I had a *wonderful* time." She was surprised to realize how much she meant that. Lowering her eyes momentarily, she looked back up. "I told Vaughn about Alec."

Her mother held her gaze. Carrie didn't often speak of her failed marriage, especially not to new acquaintances.

"It came up naturally, and for the first time I didn't feel that terrible sense of…of defeat. I don't think I'll ever be the same person again, but after talking to Vaughn, I knew I don't want to be."

Her mother smiled softly. "There was nothing wrong with you, Carrie."

"That's true, Mom, but I was at fault, too. I suspected Alec was involved with someone else. I simply preferred not to *face* it. The evidence was right in front of my eyes months before he told me. I don't ever again want to be the kind of woman who ignores the truth."

"You've never—"

"Oh, Mom," she said, loving her mother all the more for her unwavering loyalty. "It's time to move forward."

"With Vaughn Kyle?"

Carrie had thought of little else in the past three days. "Too soon to tell."

"But you like him?" her mother pressed.

She nodded. "I do." It felt good to admit it. Good to think that her life wouldn't be forever weighed down by a mistake she'd made when she was too young to understand that her marriage was doomed. Her husband's betrayal had blindsided her. Outwardly she'd picked up the pieces of her shattered pride and continued her life, but in her heart, Carrie had never completely recovered. Alec had shattered her self-esteem. Somehow she'd convinced herself that there must've been something lacking in *her;* it'd taken her a long time to realize the lack had been his.

Carrie drank the rest of her coffee and placed the cup in the sink. "We spoke about Value-X, too, Vaughn and I. At first he didn't seem to see how a company like that would hurt Buffalo Valley. In fact, he felt it might even have a positive effect. If so, I don't see one. But he let me vent my frustrations and helped me clarify my thinking."

"Will you be seeing him again?" her mother asked innocently enough.

"Most likely. He's bringing his mother into town this morning. He's buying her one of Sarah's quilts for Christmas and thought she'd like to choose it herself."

"What a thoughtful gift."

Carrie didn't mention that she'd been the one to suggest it. "They're meeting Hassie later." They hadn't made any definite plans, but Carrie hoped to meet Vaughn's mother. She was almost sure he'd stop by, either here or at the store; in fact, she was counting on it.

The doorbell chimed right then, and fingers crossed, Carrie decided it had to be Vaughn. Her mother went to answer the door.

"Carrie," she called from the living room, "you have a visitor."

"I hope you don't mind me dropping by unexpectedly," he was saying to her mother when Carrie walked in. Vaughn stood awkwardly near the door. He removed his gloves and stuffed them in his pockets.

"Hello, Vaughn." Carrie didn't bother to disguise her pleasure at seeing him again.

"Hi." He looked directly into her eyes. "Would you be free to meet my mother? I left her a few moments ago, drooling over Sarah's quilts."

"I'd like that." Carrie reached into the hall closet for her coat and scarf. "What did you think of the quilts?" she asked, buttoning her coat. She wanted him to appreciate Sarah's talent.

"They're incredible. You're right, it's the perfect gift for Mom."

Carrie supposed she had no business feeling proud; the quilt shop wasn't hers and she had nothing to do with it. But everyone in Buffalo Valley took pride in Sarah's accomplishments.

It was more than the fact that Sarah had started the company in her father's living room. People viewed her success as a reflection of what had happened to the town itself—the gradual change from obscurity and scant survival to prosperity and acclaim. Her struggles were their own, and by the same token, her successes were a reason to celebrate.

"I wanted you to know how much I enjoyed our time together yesterday," Vaughn said, matching his steps to hers as they took a shortcut through the park. "I appreciate the suggestion about the quilt. And I learned a lot about you—and Buffalo Valley. You helped me see the town in an entirely different way."

"I was grateful you let me talk out my feelings about Value-X...and everything else."

Vaughn's arm came around her and he briefly squeezed her shoulder. There was no need to refer to the divorce. He understood what she meant.

"I talked to Lindsay Sinclair earlier," Carrie said, changing the subject. "She phoned the corporate office and asked if the rumors are true."

"I thought you said they were negotiating for property."

"That's what I told Lindsay, but she doesn't trust Ambrose Kohn. She said she wouldn't put it past him to let people *think* Value-X was interested in the property so Heath or someone else would leap forward and offer to buy it. He's not exactly the kind of person to generate a lot of trust."

"What did your friend find out when she talked to the corporate people?"

"First they said they didn't want to comment on their plans, but when Lindsay pressed the spokeswoman, she admitted that Buffalo Valley's definitely under consideration." Carrie's shoulders tensed. "Lindsay took the opportunity to let her know they aren't welcome in Buffalo Valley." When she'd heard about that part of the conversation, Carrie had cheered.

"What did the company spokeswoman say then?"

Carrie laughed. "Apparently Value-X's official response is that according to their studies, a growing community such as Buffalo Valley doesn't have enough retail choices."

Vaughn snorted.

"That's what I thought. They're sending a representative after Christmas. This person is supposed to win us over and show us everything Value-X can do for Buffalo Valley." She couldn't keep the sarcasm out of her voice.

"It wouldn't hurt to listen," he said mildly.

Carrie whirled on him. "We'll listen, but having a huge chain store in town is *not* what we want. Joanie Wyatt's already started a petition, so when the company representative arrives, he or she will be met with the signature of every single person in town."

Vaughn said nothing.

"What Value-X doesn't understand is that Buffalo Valley is a small town with small-town values and that's exactly the way we want to keep it. If they move in, they'll ruin everything that makes us who we are."

Vaughn stopped in front of a picnic bench, cleared away the snow with his arm and sat down. "What about jobs? Value-X will offer a lot of opportunity to young people. I've heard repeatedly that farming communities are seeing their young adults move away because of the lack of financial security."

"That's not necessarily true, the part about Value-X bringing jobs. After I talked to Lindsay, I got on the Internet and did some research myself. I learned that most of the positions Value-X brings into a town are part-time and low-paying.

They offer few benefits to their employees. The worst aspect is that they destroy more jobs than they create."

Vaughn's frown deepened.

"I apologize," she said. "I didn't mean to get carried away about our problems with Value-X."

Standing, Vaughn still seemed deep in thought. "No, I want to hear this. It bothers me that the company isn't listening to your concerns."

"They don't *want* to listen."

"But you said they're sending a representative."

"Right," she said with a snicker. "To talk to us, not to listen. They're under the mistaken impression that we'll be swayed by a few promises and slick words. They've decided we need to think bigger and bolder and stop acting like a small town."

"But Buffalo Valley *is* a small town."

Carrie gave a sharp nod. "Exactly."

As they approached the Buffalo Valley Quilting Compay, Carrie noticed the middle-aged woman standing inside by the window, looking out into the street. When Vaughn and Carrie appeared, she smiled and waved, then pointed to the quilt on display.

Carrie waved back, silently applauding his mother's choice.

Mrs. Kyle smiled. Her eyes moved to her son and then to Carrie; her expression grew quizzical. Carrie didn't have time to guess what that meant before Mrs. Kyle opened the glass door, stepped out and introduced herself.

Barbara Kyle knew that when she agreed to accompany Vaughn into Buffalo Valley, she'd be seeing Hassie Knight. A meeting was inevitable. They hadn't been together since the day they'd stood in the pouring rain as a military casket was lowered into the ground.

Following the funeral, she'd kept in touch with Vaughn's mother. They'd called each other frequently. But despite the war, despite her grief, Barbara's college courses had continued, and she'd had to immerse herself in a very different kind of reality.

Rick had lost his best friend, and they began to seek solace from each other. Falling in love with him was a surprise. Barbara hadn't expected that, hadn't thought it was possible to love again after losing Vaughn. Rick wasn't a replacement. No one could ever replace the man she'd loved. He understood, because in his own way he'd loved Vaughn, too.

When they announced their engagement, Hassie had pulled away from Barbara. Neither spoke of it, but they both knew that their relationship had fundamentally changed and that their former closeness could no longer exist. Vaughn's parents didn't attend the wedding, although they'd mailed a card and sent a generous check.

Barbara thought now that naming their son after Vaughn Knight had as much to do with Hassie as it did with their feelings for Vaughn. Perhaps she'd hoped to bridge the distance between them....

Until he was twenty-one, Hassie had remembered Vaughn Kyle every year on his birthday, but that was the only time Barbara and Rick heard from her. When Rick accepted early retirement and they'd decided to move back to North Dakota, Barbara recognized that, sooner or later, she'd see Hassie again. A month or so after they'd moved, Hassie had welcomed them with a brief note. It seemed fitting that Barbara's son had been the one to arrange this meeting, to bring them together again.

"Hassie wanted me to bring you to the house, instead of the pharmacy," Vaughn said as they left the quilting store.

"You're coming with us, aren't you?" Barbara asked Carrie. She'd quickly grasped that Vaughn was attracted to this woman, and she could understand why. However, she didn't pretend to know what was happening. Natalie had phoned several times, wanting to speak to Vaughn; she wasn't amused that he'd apparently turned off his cell phone. Barbara didn't feel it was her place to inform the other woman that Vaughn was out with someone else. The situation concerned her, but she couldn't interfere and had to trust that he was treating both women with honesty and fairness.

"I'd love to come to Hassie's with you," Carrie told them, "but I said I'd fill in at the store for her. You two go and have a good visit, and I'll see you later."

As they crossed the street, Carrie headed toward the pharmacy, and Barbara and Vaughn went in the opposite direction.

"Does the pharmacy still have the soda fountain?" Barbara asked her son.

"Sure does. In fact, I thought I'd leave you and Hassie to visit, and I'd steal away to Knight's to let Carrie fix me a soda."

"You're spending a lot of time with her, aren't you?" Barbara couldn't resist asking.

"Am I?"

Barbara didn't answer him. There was probably some perfect maternal response, but darned if she knew what it was.

Hassie's house came into view, and Barbara automatically slowed her pace. It'd been thirty-three years since she'd walked up these steps. Thirty-three years since she'd attended the wake, sat in a corner of the living room with Vaughn's older sister and wept bitter tears. At the end of a day that had been too long for all of them, Vaughn's mother had hugged her close and then instructed a family friend to make sure Barbara got safely home to Grand Forks.

"Mom?" Vaughn studied her and seemed to sense that something was wrong.

"It's all right," she said. Funny how quickly those old emotions resurfaced. Her stomach churned as if it'd been only a few months since she'd last walked this path. But thirty-three years, a lifetime, had passed.

Hassie opened the door before Barbara could ring the bell. They stood there for a moment, gazing into each other's eyes.

Hassie smiled then, a welcoming smile that seemed to reach deep inside her with its warmth and generosity. "Barbara," the older woman said, flinging open the screen door.

When she'd entered the house, Hassie hugged her for long minutes, and Barbara felt the tears gather in her eyes.

"I'm so glad you came." Hassie finally released her and embraced Vaughn, who stood quietly behind his mother. "I assume Vaughn told you about our visit?"

"Yes, he did. I can't tell you how honored we all are that you'd give him Mr. Knight's gold watch."

"It seemed right that he have it." She took Barbara's coat and hung it in the hall closet. "I won't take yours," she said to Vaughn, her back to them both. "You're probably planning to sneak over to the shop for a soda."

"How'd you guess?"

"I was young once myself," Hassie said, and shooed him out the door.

"Carrie's a wonderful young woman," Hassie told her as soon as Vaughn had left.

"They certainly seem to have taken a liking to one another," Barbara said noncommittally. She liked what she'd seen of Carrie—but what about Natalie? Well, that was Vaughn's business, she reminded herself again.

Hassie led her into the living room. "I hope you don't mind, but I've already poured the tea."

"Not at all."

The silver service was set up on the coffee table and two delicate china cups were neatly positioned, steam rising from the recently poured tea. A plate of cookies had been placed nearby.

"I don't often get an excuse to use my good tea service and china these days," Hassie murmured.

The two women sat side by side on the dark-blue sofa and sipped their tea. Neither really knew where to start, Barbara reflected. She took a deep breath.

"I've thought of you often," she said. "Especially since you were so generous with our son."

"He must have thought me a silly old woman, writing him little tidbits of advice."

"Hassie," Barbara said, and touched Hassie's forearm. "*No one* could think that." She shook her head. "He saved every birthday card you ever sent him. And he remembered what you wrote. He grew up honorable and generous, and I can't help thinking you played a part in that."

Hassie smiled her appreciation. "Nonsense, but it's very kind of you to say so."

Barbara glanced around the room. "Being here brings back so many memories," she said. The house, this room, was exactly as she remembered. She suspected that even after all these years, Vaughn's bedroom was virtually untouched. She remembered the high-school banner he had pinned to the wall and the bedroom set, old-fashioned even then. Valerie's old room was probably the same as it had been, as well, just like the rest of this house.

Hassie didn't comment, and Barbara sensed that the older woman had hung on to the past as much as she could and found comfort in what was familiar. Hassie's strength was considerable, but her loss had been too great. *Losses,* Barbara recalled. Jerry had died not long afterward, and Valerie had moved to Hawaii.

"Do you like living in Grand Forks?" Hassie asked, turning away from reminders of grief.

"Very much. My parents leased out the house when they moved to Arizona. Rick and I always intended to move here one day, and I'm really happy we did. This will be our first Christmas in North Dakota since Vaughn was five or six."

"With family again."

"Actually, there'll only be Rick, Vaughn and me. All my family has moved away, and Gloria, our daughter, lives in Dallas."

"Have Christmas here with me," Hassie urged, and then as if she regretted the impulse, she shook her head. "No, please forget I asked. I'm sorry to impose. It's just the rambling of an old woman."

"Hassie, if you're serious, we'd love nothing better than to spend the day with you."

Hassie's eyes shone. "You mean you'd actually consider coming?"

"We'd be honored. I know Rick would love to see you again. He wanted to join me today, but he was already committed to something else—some volunteer work he's doing."

"You're sure about Christmas?"

"Very sure," Barbara insisted. "But I can't allow you to do all the cooking."

"Oh," Hassie said, "it's no problem. I'd enjoy preparing my favorite recipes."

"We'll share the meal preparation, then," Barbara compromised, and Hassie aggreed.

"We'll be having Christmas dinner," Barbara murmured, "with a dear, dear friend."

"I can't think of anything I'd enjoy more."

Barbara couldn't, either.

Five

Carrie found Leta tending Knight's Pharmacy when she arrived after saying goodbye to Vaughn and his mother.

"Thanks for filling in for me," she said, hurrying to the back of the store. She stored her coat and purse and pulled on her white jacket.

"I don't mind staying," Leta told her. "In fact, Hassie asked me if I would. She thought you and Vaughn might like a few hours together." Leta wiped down the counter, and Carrie noticed how the other woman's eyes managed to evade hers.

"Aren't you two being just a little obvious?" she teased.

"Perhaps," Leta said, "but we both think it's high time you got into circulation again."

"Like a library book?" Carrie said with a grin. "I've been on the shelf too long?"

"Laugh if you want, but it's true. You've been avoiding a social life. That's not good for a woman of your age."

Carrie was about to explain that, while she appreciated their efforts, she'd already spent time with Vaughn. Before she could, though, the bell above the door chimed, and Lindsay Sinclair and her two daughters stepped into the warmth of the pharmacy.

"Grandma." Four-year-old Joy ran toward Leta, who scooped the girl up in her arms for an enthusiastic hug.

"I've had the most incredible morning," Lindsay announced.

"Value-X?" Carrie asked.

Lindsay nodded. "The spokeswoman actually phoned me back."

"She called you?" Leta asked, voice incredulous, as she set Joy back on the floor.

"Yes, and for some reason, she seemed to view me as a contact who represented the community. That's fine, since everyone in town shares my opinion." Lindsay removed her hat and shook out her hair. "She wanted me to understand that Value-X intends to be a good neighbor, quote, unquote."

"Yeah, right!" Carrie muttered sarcastically.

"I'll just bet," Leta added. "They assume we're nothing but a bunch of dumb hicks."

"To be fair," Lindsay said, glancing between the other two women, "we don't know *what* they think of us—not that we have any interest in their opinion. But we are fully capable of mounting a campaign to keep them out."

"I was thinking the same thing," Carrie said.

"Organization is the key," Leta put in.

"You'll be at the Cookie Exchange tonight, won't you?" Lindsay asked Carrie. "I know Leta will." She smiled at her mother-in-law. "I thought that would be the best time to get all the women together. We can talk then."

"Good idea. Mom and I will be there for sure." The women's group at the church held the cookie exchange every Christmas. Joyce Dawson, the pastor's wife, had been instrumental in organizing the event, and every woman in town and the surrounding community could be counted on to attend.

"Value-X won't know what hit them," Leta said happily.

The bell chimed a second time, and Vaughn entered the store. For a moment, he seemed startled to see the three women, but then his gaze sought out Carrie's. "Should I come back later?"

"Not at all," Leta said. "There's no need for Carrie to work today. I've got everything covered."

Carrie was grateful for what her friends were trying to do, but she did have responsibilities. Leta seemed to read her thoughts. "If any prescriptions get phoned in, I'll find you," she promised. "I'll leave a message with your mom."

"Ever hear the expression about not looking a gift horse in the mouth?" Lindsay whispered.

"Well, it appears I'm not wanted or needed around here," Carrie said before Leta and Hassie's intentions became any plainer than they already were. She walked past Lindsay, who winked at her. After collecting her coat and purse, Carrie left with Vaughn.

"Where would you like to go?" he asked as soon as they were outside.

She hadn't had lunch yet and suspected Vaughn hadn't, either. "I know we had Italian yesterday, but I love pizza."

"Me, too."

"Buffalo Valley has some of the best homemade pizza you'll ever eat."

He lifted his eyebrows. "Sounds good to me."

They started down the street, their pace relaxed. Snow had just begun to fall, drifting earthward in large, soft flakes. Christmas-card snow, Carrie thought. As they walked, she told him the story about Rachel's pizza, and how it had led to her restaurant and subsequent success.

"You mean she makes the sauce herself?"

Carrie nodded. "I worked for Rachel one summer and I watched her make a batch. She starts with fresh tomatoes straight from her garden. It's amazingly good. I think she could sell her recipe, but of course, she doesn't want to."

A pickup approached and slowed as it came alongside Vaughn and Carrie. Glancing over her shoulder, Carrie saw her two older brothers, Tom and Pete. She tried to ignore them, but that was impossible.

"Hey, Carrie," Tom called, leaning his elbow out the open passenger window.

She acknowledged his greeting with a short wave, hoping he'd simply move on. Not that this was likely. Apparently Chuck and Ken had mentioned Vaughn, and now they, too, were looking for an introduction.

"Don't you want us to meet your friend?"

"Not right now," she called back, and sent Vaughn an apologetic glance. Because she was the only girl, all four of her brothers were protective of her, even more so after her divorce.

"You ashamed of your family?" This came from Pete, who was driving.

Carrie sighed, praying that her brothers wouldn't say or do anything to further embarrass her. Pete parked the truck and both men climbed out, slamming their doors extra hard. Both wore thick winter coats and wool caps with the earflaps dangling. They were large men and did their best to appear intimidating.

She made the introductions, gesturing weakly toward her brothers. Vaughn stepped forward and shook hands with both of them.

"Nice to finally meet you," Tom said, resting his foot on the truck's bumper. "Now I'd like to know what your intentions are toward my sister."

"Tom!" Furious, Carrie clenched her fists. "This is *none* of your business."

"The day you stop being my sister is the day I stop caring who you date."

"Well..." Vaughn clearly had no idea what to say.

Her brothers putting him on the spot like this was outrageous. Picking up a handful of snow, Carrie immediately formed a ball and threw it at her oldest brother, hitting him square in the chest. Not waiting for his reaction, Carrie grabbed Vaughn's arm and shouted, "Run!"

"You asked for this, Carrie Ann," Tom shouted as Carrie and Vaughn raced across the street. They had just entered the park when Carrie felt her backside pelted by two snowballs.

"This is war," Vaughn yelled when he saw that she'd been hit. He leaned down and packed his own snow, then hurled two balls in quick succession, hitting both Pete and Tom. Her brothers reacted with stunned surprise.

Laughing and dodging around the play equipment with her brothers in hot pursuit, Carrie had trouble keeping pace with Vaughn. He yelled instructions and pointed toward the back of Hamburger Heaven. The stand was closed for the winter and offered ample protection, but a few moments later, her brothers found them and began to bombard them with a flurry of snowballs. Although most of them hit the side of the building, it was obvious that Vaughn and Carrie couldn't stay there long.

"You ready to surrender yet?" Pete demanded.

"Never," Vaughn answered for them.

"This way," Carrie told him. With the community Christmas tree blocking their movements, she led him across the street. Hidden by a loaded hay truck that passed behind them, Carrie steered him toward her parents' store.

"This is what I'd consider enemy territory," Vaughn whispered as they slipped behind the building and out of view.

"But it's the last place they'll look," she assured him.

"Smart thinking." Vaughn beamed her a delighted smile.

She smiled back—and realized she hadn't felt this kind of pure, uninhibited pleasure in…years. Since childhood, probably. When she didn't break eye contact and started to laugh, he said, "What?"

She shook her head, not wanting to put into words the joy she felt.

A sound startled them both, and they froze. Carrie was certain her brothers had found them again, but if it *was* Pete and Tom, they left without searching farther.

Relieved, Carrie sighed and slumped against the wall. "I believe we're safe for the moment. Are you still interested in that pizza?"

Vaughn nodded, but she saw a strange expression in his eyes as he continued to gaze down at her. Carrie tried to look away and couldn't. She knew he intended to kiss her, and she shut her eyes as he moved closer. She'd been waiting for this moment, anticipating it. Wrapping her arms around his neck, she leaned into him. He drew off his gloves and then her wool hat and dropped them. Weaving his hands into her hair, he kissed her…and deepened the kiss until they were both breathless. Carrie trembled and buried her face in his shoulder. Neither spoke. As he held her tight, it seemed for those few moments that their hearts beat in unison.

He kissed her again, his mouth both firm and soft. When he eased away, Carried noticed that his brow had furrowed, and she thought she read doubt in his eyes. Uncertainty. She touched his face, wondering at the confusion she saw in him. "Is anything wrong?" she asked.

He answered with a quick shake of his head. "Everything is right."

And yet he sounded reluctant. She wanted to ask him more, but he moved away from her and peeked around the back wall. "Do you think it's safe now?" he asked.

"It should be. Pete and Tom were just having fun with us."

"Protective older brothers."

"Exactly."

"I watched over Gloria, too," he said. "She's two years younger than me."

"Just imagine that four times over."

"I don't need to," Vaughn said, ostentatiously brushing evidence of the snow battle from his sleeves.

They didn't see Pete or Tom on their way over, so Carrie assumed they'd gone about their business. As she'd told Vaughn, it'd been all in fun and at least her brothers knew when to admit defeat.

Predictably enough, Vaughn raved about the pizza. In fact, he bought a second one to take home and reheat. When they'd eaten, they returned to Hassie's, where his mother had just finished her visit. All four of them walked to where Vaughn had parked the car outside Sarah's quilt store. When they reached it, Hassie and Barbara Kyle hugged for a long moment.

"Thank you for coming," Hassie said, dabbing at her eyes.

Carrie knew it had been an emotional visit for both women.

"No—thank *you* for...for being Hassie," Barbara said, and they hugged again. "I'll be in touch about Christmas."

Vaughn opened the car door for his mother and helped her

inside, an old-fashioned courtesy that reminded Carrie of her father and uncles.

Carrie stood on the sidewalk next to Hassie as Vaughn placed his pizza carefully on the backseat.

"They're coming to spend Christmas with me," Hassie said. "I haven't looked forward to anything so much in years. It'll be like when the children were still home."

Carrie knew Hassie intended to spend Christmas morning with Bob and Merrily and little Bobby, but she'd turned down invitations from almost everyone in town for dinner. Carrie was relieved that Hassie wouldn't spend the afternoon alone—and she envied her Vaughn's company.

He climbed into the car beside his mother and started the engine. Before he backed out of the parking space, his eyes met Carrie's. She raised her hand and he returned the gesture. She felt as if her heart was reaching out to him…and his to her.

Six

Hassie had been looking forward to this night. The Dawsons had moved to Buffalo Valley four years earlier; at that time the only church in town had been Catholic and was closed after Father McGrath's retirement. Then Reverend John Dawson and his wife had arrived.

What a blessing the couple had turned out to be! Joyce knew instinctively what to say to make people feel welcome. John's sermons were inspiring, and his advice was both sensitive and practical.

Her first Christmas in Buffalo Valley, Joyce had organized the Cookie Exchange, which had become a yearly event.

Hassie had baked oatmeal-cranberry cookies early that morning and set out a plate for her visit with Barbara. Both had gotten so involved in their conversation that they hadn't tasted a single one. Hassie shook her head, smiling. It was as though all those years of not seeing each other had simply vanished after their initial awkwardness had passed. The visit had gone by far too quickly; Barbara had to leave long before

Hassie was ready. What amazed Hassie was that she'd found herself saying things she hadn't even realized she felt.

Her daughter's decision to live in Hawaii was one example. She'd never understood what had prompted Valerie's choice. Yes, there'd been a job offer, but Valerie had *pursued* that job. The fact was, she'd wanted to get as far away from North Dakota as she possibly could. Hassie understood this for the very first time.

When Barbara had inquired about Valerie, Hassie explained that her daughter had chosen to remove herself from the pain of losing her only brother and then her father. Never before had Hassie consciously acknowledged that. Yet the moment she said the words, she knew they were true.

Later that evening when Hassie got to the church for the Cookie Exchange, the place was blazing with light. Although she was twenty minutes early, the parking lot was already half-full. The first person she saw once she'd set her platter of cookies on the table was Calla Stern. Sarah's once-rebellious daughter had become a lovely young woman. She was in her junior year of college now, if Hassie recalled correctly, and there was talk of her applying for admission to law school. She attended the University of Chicago and shared an apartment nearby, but at heart Calla remained a small-town girl.

As soon as Calla saw Hassie, she broke off her conversation and hurried across the room, arms outstretched.

"When did you get home?" Hassie asked, hugging her close.

"This afternoon. Oh, Hassie, I just heard about Value-X. What are we going to do?"

"I don't know, Calla, and this might shock you all, but I've decided I'm too old to fight them."

Calla frowned.

"That's what Leta told us."

"We can't stand in the way of progress." *If progress it is.* Change, anyway. Perhaps if Hassie repeated that often enough, she might come to accept it. This wasn't what she wanted, but as she'd learned long ago, the world didn't revolve around what she assumed was best.

"Let's enjoy this evening," Hassie urged, "and put these worries behind us until the new year."

"I'll try," the girl promised.

"Good." Hassie slid her arm through Calla's. "Now tell me, are you still seeing Kevin?" Calla had been dating Leta's boy off and on since her last year of high school.

"Occasionally. He's so busy, and I'm in school most of the time. Anyway, with him in Paris for six months…"

"Calla would make a wonderful daughter-in-law," Leta said, joining them.

"Oh, you!" Calla hugged her tightly, laughing as Hassie seconded Leta's remark.

"Stop it, you two," the girl chided. "I'm dating someone else at the moment and so is Kevin. We're good friends, but that's all. For now, anyway."

"Damn," Leta muttered.

"Give them time," Hassie told her.

"Exactly," Calla said with a soft smile, and after kissing them both, added, "Now excuse me while I go mingle."

Hassie watched her leave. She thought Calla and Kevin would eventually get married, but probably not for some years. Not until educations were completed and careers launched. Still, they understood each other and shared the experience of having grown up in Buffalo Valley.

No sooner had Calla wandered off than Maddy appeared with four-year-old Julianne. She was heavily pregnant with her third child, but she'd lost none of her composure or contentment.

"Maddy," Hassie said, pleased to see her. "Here, let me help you with all that." Maddy was juggling her coat and purse, plus a huge box of homemade cookies.

"Mommy, can I play with Joy?" Julianne asked, tugging at Maddy's sleeve.

"Yes, sweetheart, and tell Lindsay I'll be right there."

"Where's little Caleb?" Hassie asked.

"With his daddy. After all, this is a *girls'* night out," Maddy said. Hassie knew this third pregnancy was as unexpected as their first. With three babies in five years, Jeb and Maddy were sure to have their hands full for quite a while.

Jeb's mother must be looking down from heaven, mighty pleased with her son, Hassie mused. Thanks to Maddy, he'd gone from curmudgeonly recluse to good husband and proud father.

Hassie and Leta busied themselves arranging platters of cookies on the long tables. Joyce made several trips to the business office to run recipes off on the copier so they'd be available for whoever wanted them.

Margaret Eilers and her daughter, Hailey, were among the last to arrive. Hailey, at three, bore a strong resemblance to her father and to her brother, David. Looking at Margaret and the child, no one would guess she wasn't the girl's birth mother. Hassie had nothing but praise for the way Matt and Margaret had worked out the awkward situation involving their children.

In the beginning Hassie hadn't been keen on Matt Eilers. No one in town held a high opinion of the rancher. But Margaret had fallen hard for Matt; she wanted to marry him and nothing would change her mind. After Bernard died and left her the ranch, Matt started seeing more and more of her.

A few months later, there was a wedding. Then, lo and behold, Margaret turned up pregnant—at the same time as that woman in Devils Lake.

The babies were born within a few weeks of each other, Hailey first and then little David. Hailey had been living with the couple for most of her three years. She was a darling little girl, which Hassie attributed primarily to the love and attention Margaret lavished on her.

The room rang with laughter and cheer, and Hassie basked in the sounds that ebbed and flowed around her. Her day had started early and been an emotional one. When she noticed chairs arranged along the wall, she slipped quietly off and sat down. A few minutes later Leta came to sit beside her.

"Just listen," Hassie said, closing her eyes.

"What am I supposed to be listening to?" Leta asked.

"The joy," Hassie told her. "The friendship. These women are the very breath of this community." Hassie was grateful she'd lived long enough to witness the town's reversal of fortunes. It was because of women like Lindsay and Rachel and Maddy and Sarah and Joanie Wyatt.... And maybe she herself had played a small part.

"What I can't get over is all the babies," Leta said. "Future generations for Buffalo Valley."

"Rachel Quantrill is pregnant again," Hassie said, nodding at the young woman on the other side of the room talking with Sarah. Hassie was particularly fond of Rachel. She'd watched the young widow struggle to get by after the death of her first husband. She'd driven a school bus and worked as a part-time bookkeeper for Hassie. Later she'd opened the pizza-delivery service. That was how she'd met Heath. New to the banking business, Heath had rejected her loan application. His grandmother, who'd started the bank, had been furious with him, Hassie recalled. But things had a way of working out for the best. Lily Quantrill had lived to see her grandson and Rachel marry. Rachel had brought a son into the marriage, and later she and Heath had a daughter they'd named after Lily. A third child was expected in early summer.

"I'll have to remember that," Hassie murmured absently.

Leta gave her a puzzled look. "What?"

Hassie wasn't aware she'd spoken aloud. "About things working out for the best." Despite her efforts, her thoughts had returned to Value-X and the potential for disaster. All her hopes for this town and the people she loved so dearly were at stake.

"You feeling all right?" Leta asked in a concerned tone.

"I'm fine," Hassie assured her. "Just tired. It's been a busy day."

Joyce Dawson sat down at the piano, and soon the room was filled with sweetly raised voices. The women and children gathered around, breaking naturally into two-part harmony. To Hassie it sounded as though the very angels from heaven were singing.

"Hassie—" Carrie Hendrickson crouched by her chair "— are you ill?"

Leta answered for her. "She's just tired."

"No wonder," Carrie murmured. "She was up before dawn baking cookies and then there was the visit from Barbara Kyle, plus a big order came in for the pharmacy."

Hassie grinned, amused that they spoke as if she wasn't even there.

"Let me walk you home," Carrie suggested, taking her hand.

"Fiddlesticks. I'm perfectly capable of walking back on my own. No need for you to leave the party."

"I insist," Carrie said. "It'll only take a few minutes and no one will miss me."

Hassie was weary, wearier than she cared to admit, so she agreed. Carrie retrieved their coats and led the way outside, sliding her arm through Hassie's to lend her support. They walked slowly, in companionable silence. The night sky was bright and clear, the stars scattered against it like diamonds. Most of the snow had been swept aside and the sidewalks salted.

As they crossed the street, a truck pulled up to the curb and rolled down the window. "You two need a ride?" Chuck Hendrickson asked.

"We're fine, thanks, anyway," Carrie told her brother.

"Say, that fellow you had dinner with phoned a few minutes ago."

"Must be Vaughn," Hassie said. It did seem that Carrie and Vaughn were seeing a lot of each other, and that pleased her. From now on, Hassie resolved to look only at the positive side of things. She refused to let herself fret over situations she couldn't control.

"I'll call him back once I'm finished over at the church," Carrie told her brother, who drove off.

"You could do worse, Carrie," Hassie said. "He's a fine man."

"I think so, too."

"Not every man is another Alec."

"I know," she said.

Hassie patted Carrie's hand. She would go home and think good thoughts for the young woman and for Buffalo Valley. Happy, positive thoughts.

"It's about time you called," Natalie snapped. There'd been no word of greeting.

Vaughn sat on the bed in his parents' guest room and pressed his cell phone to his ear. He felt guilty about not returning Natalie's repeated calls. He'd delayed it, needing to put his thoughts in order first. He felt guilty about other things, too, but he didn't want to think about Carrie, not when he had to deal with Natalie.

No one in Buffalo Valley knew he'd taken a job with Value-X. Not his parents. Not Hassie. And certainly not Carrie. His visit to North Dakota at a time when the company was considering an outlet in this area had seemed a fortuitous coincidence. Now it felt like the very opposite. He'd agreed to check out the town, but that had been a mistake he regretted heartily. And Natalie was hounding him for information.

"You're right, I should've phoned sooner," he admitted.

"Yes, you should have." Her voice softened. "I've missed hearing from you."

He didn't have an excuse to offer her, and the truth was... well, difficult to explain. Not only did he have serious doubts about working for this company, he'd met Carrie, and the attraction between them was undeniable.

Just a few days ago his future had seemed assured, but now, after meeting Hassie and Carrie, his entire sense of what was right had been challenged. And his assumptions about love and marriage, about Natalie—they'd changed, too.

Natalie's voice was hard when she spoke again. "I was beginning to wonder if I made a mistake recommending you for this position. I put my reputation on the line."

"I assumed I'd been hired on my own merits."

"You were but..." She sighed heavily. "Let's forget all that, shall we? I didn't know what to think when you didn't phone." She gave a stilted laugh. "I realize you're not officially on the payroll until January, but it's so advantageous for you to be near this little town."

"The town has a name."

"I know that," she said, and some of the stiffness returned to her voice. "I'm sorry, Vaughn, but I've had a trying day. Apparently Buffalo Valley is mounting opposition against Value-X."

"I know."

"You do?" She slowly released her breath. "You can't imagine how hectic everything is here, with the holidays and everything else. Now *this*. I spoke with a woman in town. I can't remember her name exactly. Lesley, Lindy..."

"Lindsay Sinclair."

"You know her?"

"I've met her."

"She made the town's position very clear," Natalie continued. "It seems we've got some public-relations work ahead of us. Okay, we can deal with that—we've done it before. We know how to present our case in a positive light. It won't take much to change their attitude, and really, at this point, they really don't have much choice."

Vaughn was sorry to hear that. So it was too late; Value-X had obviously succeeded in buying the property. This was what he'd feared. "Lindsay told me Value-X is sending someone out after Christmas."

"I volunteered for the job myself," she said, excited now. "It was providential, don't you think? I can meet your parents and settle this unfortunate matter with Buffalo Valley at the same time. Combine business with pleasure, in other words." She sounded pleased with herself for having so neatly arranged this trip. "I've got everything in motion for a Value-X campaign."

"I hope you'll be willing to listen to the town's concerns."

"Well, yes, of course I'll listen, but I'm hoping to present our case, too. In fact, I've already authorized a letter to be delivered to every family in Buffalo Valley. It's scheduled to arrive just after the first of the year."

"A letter?"

"Everyone thinks it's a great idea." Her satisfaction was un-mistakable. "I wrote it myself for a personal touch. I want the town to understand that they've unfairly prejudged Value-X. I told them not to look at any negatives they might've heard about the company, but at the positives—everything we can do for their community. We plan to be a good neighbor."

Vaughn knew that Natalie's letter would most likely anger the people of Buffalo Valley, not reassure them. "I didn't real-ize you'd signed the deal on the land," he muttered. Without being completely aware of it, Vaughn had held out hope that the controversy would die a natural death if the land deal fell through. His heart sank. It looked as if he'd have no choice now but to get involved. The question was: on which side would he stand? If he followed his heart, he'd join Hassie and Carrie in their fight, but if he did that, he'd compromise his future with Value-X and Natalie...

Natalie hesitated before she answered. "There've been a few snags with the property deal. Mr. Kohn isn't an easy man to work with."

Vaughn's relief was swift. So there *was* hope. "That's what I hear about Ambrose Kohn."

"Have you met him?"

"No, he lives in Devils Lake. Listen, Natalie, I have to tell you I'm not convinced Buffalo Valley is a good site."

She laughed, but he could tell she wasn't amused. "You haven't even started work yet and you're already telling me my job?"

"*You* chose Buffalo Valley as a development site?"

"I sure did," she said smugly. "We did a study on small

towns that have shown substantial growth over the last five years. Buffalo Valley is a perfect target area for retail expansion."

Vaughn's hand tightened around the telephone receiver. "They don't have enough retail choices," he muttered.

"Exactly." Apparently she hadn't noticed the sarcasm in his voice.

Vaughn felt tension creeping across his shoulders. He probably couldn't influence her to change her letter or withdraw it; he was in no position to tell Natalie news she didn't want to hear.

She returned to the subject of Ambrose Kohn. "I'm interested in what you know about him," she said.

"I don't know him, but I have heard about him." Vaughn didn't feel comfortable saying anything more than he already had. As it was, he felt traitor enough.

"He *will* sign, and soon." Natalie's confidence sounded unshakable. "The transaction is as good as done."

Vaughn rotated his neck in order to ease the tension.

"I know what's happened," she said, catching him by surprise. "You've seen this little town and now you have doubts that Value-X is doing the right thing."

It was as though she'd read his mind. He found himself nodding.

"You're confused," Natalie continued. "It happens to a lot of us when we first hire on with the company. Don't worry, it's something we all work through. Trust me, Vaughn, Value-X knows what it's doing."

"Buffalo Valley is afraid of losing its character."

"Every town is in the beginning. They get over it. Sooner or later, each town comes to realize that we know what's best for them. Buffalo Valley will, too."

This was worse than he'd thought. Vaughn rubbed his hand down his face. Still sitting on the edge of his bed, he tilted his head back to stare up at the ceiling. This was *really* bad.

Value-X had no intention of listening to the concerns of Buffalo Valley's citizens. In its arrogance, the retailer had decided on a course of action, one that reflected solely its own interests.

"I'm looking forward to seeing you," Natalie told him, lowering her voice seductively.

It was almost more than Vaughn could do to echo the sentiment.

When he finished the conversation, he returned to the kitchen to find his mother dishing up ice cream.

"You interested?" she asked, holding up the scoop.

"Sure, why not?" he muttered. He took a third bowl from the cupboard and handed it to his mother, who pried open the carton lid.

"Tell me more about Natalie," she said.

Vaughn didn't know what to say. "You'll meet her soon enough."

"She's joining us after Christmas, right?" She studied him hard, and Vaughn knew what she was thinking. He'd spent almost every day of the past week with Carrie. He was with one woman and had another waiting in the wings—that was how it looked. His mother's eyes filled with questions.

"Natalie is coming, then?" she repeated when he didn't answer.

"So it seems." He sighed. She'd show up even if he asked her to stay home. Value-X was paying for the trip.

"You don't sound too happy about it," his mother murmured, her eyes narrowed. "What about Carrie?"

"Mom…"

"I know, I know, but I can't help wondering if you're really sure of what you want. I saw the look Carrie gave you as we left Buffalo Valley earlier today."

Vaughn frowned.

"She deserves your honesty."

He was in full agreement; he owed Carrie the truth, and not only about his relationship with Natalie. He had to tell her about Value-X.

As soon as his mother left the kitchen, Vaughn reached for the phone. Unfortunately Carrie wasn't home. He recalled now that she'd mentioned something about meeting with the church women's group, but that'd slipped his mind. He left a message with one of her brothers.

After that, he joined his parents in the living room. He settled on the sofa next to his mother and focused his attention on a television show about Christmas traditions around the world.

An hour later the phone pealed and his mother automatically rose to answer it. She returned almost immediately. "It's Carrie for you."

Vaughn went into the kitchen.

"Hi," she said excitedly when he picked up the receiver. "I just got back from the Cookie Exchange and got your message."

"How was it?"

"Great, as usual. There was a lot of talk about this Value-X problem. We're going to take active measures to keep the company out of town."

She'd given him the perfect lead. This was his chance to explain the whole confused mess. But Vaughn didn't. He couldn't, not over the phone. It was something that needed to be said face-to-face, he decided. Okay, so he was a coward.

Carrie seemed to be waiting for a response, so to keep the conversation going, he asked, "What can be done?"

"According to Hassie, nothing. She's afraid we can't win, especially after everything she's heard and read. According to all the news stories, the company practically always comes out on top. Still, there are a few towns that didn't give in, including one in Montana, I think." She paused. "Hassie's real problem is that she's just tired out. But I'm not, and neither are the rest of us."

Vaughn could hear the fighting spirit in her voice.

"I suggest you start with Ambrose Kohn." That was probably more than he should've said, but the words escaped before he could judge their wisdom.

"We're having an organizational meeting as soon as it can be arranged, and I'll recommend that."

"Great," he mumbled, wishing he could tell her he didn't want to hear any of this. It put him in a terrible position. He'd be a traitor to Value-X and Natalie if he withheld these facts, and a traitor to Carrie if he relayed them.

"...tomorrow night."

"I'm sorry," Vaughn said, trapped in his own dilemma. "What did you say?"

"Can you come? It's the high-school play. I know it doesn't sound like much, but we're all proud of it. The play's about the history of Buffalo Valley and the families that settled here. It'll give you a feel for the town."

Vaughn's own great-grandparents on his mother's side had settled in the Dakotas in the late 1800s. He pondered Carrie's words. Knowing more about the town's past might help him decide what to do about his relationship with Value-X—and Natalie. It was a faint hope—and maybe just another delaying tactic—but he had nothing else to cling to.

"Will you come as my guest?" she asked.

"I'll look forward to it."

She gave him the details and Vaughn hung up the phone feeling as vulnerable and unsure as ever.

"How'd it go?" his mother asked when he returned to the living room.

"Fine," he muttered. "Just fine."

Seven

The theater was filled to capacity. People crowded the aisle, chatting and visiting with one another. Carrie had been fortunate to get good seats for herself and Vaughn, thanks to Lindsay Sinclair.

"I didn't know there were this many people in Buffalo Valley," Vaughn said, twisting around to glance over his shoulder.

"There aren't. Folks come from all over. The Cowans drove down from Canada. Her great-grandmother is one of the main characters in the play."

Vaughn looked at his program. "So, Lindsay Sinclair is the producer and director of Dakota Christmas."

Carrie nodded. "Lindsay's the person responsible for all this," she said, gesturing toward her friend. "None of it would've happened without her."

Carrie went on to explain how the play had been created and described everything Lindsay had done to make sure it got performed. At the end of the story she told him that the theater belonged to Ambrose Kohn.

"*The* Ambrose Kohn?" Vaughn's brows arched.

"When Lindsay first arrived, the theater was nothing but cobwebs and dirt. She was a first-year teacher and one of the stipulations when she accepted the job was that the community would pitch in and help."

"In what way?"

"In whatever way she required. She asked the town's older people to talk to the kids. It started with Joshua McKenna. At the time he was president of the town council, plus he knows quite a bit of local history. After that, Lindsay lined up community representatives to come to the school on Friday afternoons. Joshua was the one who gave her the idea of having the kids write the play."

"The high-schoolers wrote the play?"

"The original script was created by the kids Lindsay taught six years ago. Each new group of students refines it a little bit."

"This is the sixth year?" He glanced around with what appeared to be renewed appreciation. "Pretty impressive audience."

"It's a fabulous play. Why else would so many people return year after year?"

"What's your favorite part?"

"I love all of it. There's a scene early on when a tornado hits the town and everything's destroyed. The people lose heart. Entire crops are wiped out and families are left homeless. You can just *feel* their agony." She didn't mean to get carried away, but no matter how often she'd seen it, the scene brought tears to Carrie's eyes.

"What happens then?" Vaughn asked.

"Everyone pulls together. The people whose fields were spared share their crops with the ones who lost everything.

With everyone working together, they rebuild the farms destroyed in the tornado and save the town."

Vaughn nodded slowly. "Teamwork," he murmured.

"That was a message that really hit home for all of us. So many of the farmers continue to struggle financially. The play helped remind us that we need to work together. Then and now."

"Are you talking about Value-X?"

Carrie shook her head. "Not only Value-X. We have more problems than just that. As you probably know, farm prices are low and have been for years. Most folks around here feel that no one appreciates the contribution of the small farmer anymore. A lot of people were demoralized by what was happening."

"Is it better now?"

"Yes, but only because farmers in the area have banded together. They still aren't getting decent prices for their crops, but they've found ways around that."

Carrie looked away; she had to swallow the lump in her throat. Her own family had been forced off the farm. The land had produced record yields, and it still wasn't enough to make ends meet. After several years of dismal wheat prices, the family had realized the farm could no longer support them all. That was when her parents and younger brothers had moved into town.

This had happened shortly after she'd filed for divorce. At first it had seemed inevitable that they'd have to sell the land, but then her two older brothers had decided to lease it. Pete and Tom were married by this time, and along with their wives, they'd made the decision to stay.

Buffalo Valley had started to show signs of new life—with the reopening of the hotel and bar, as well as Rachel's pizza restaurant. And Lindsay, of course, had brought fresh hope to the community in so many ways....

Carrie's mother had come into a small inheritance, and her parents chose to invest it in a business. Buffalo Valley was badly in need of an all-purpose hardware store. Carrie's father felt confident that if people could shop locally, they would, so the family had risked everything with this venture. To date, it had been a wise choice, but now with the mega-chain threatening to swallow up smaller businesses, the Hendricksons were in grave danger of losing it all.

"The American farmer refuses to be discounted," Carrie said, clearing her throat. "When was the last time you purchased pasta?"

"Pasta? As in noodles?" Vaughn asked in a puzzled voice. "Not recently. What makes you ask?"

"Ever hear of Velma brand?"

"Can't say I have."

Carrie tucked her arm through his. "It's made with wheat grown right here in Buffalo Valley. Brandon Wyatt and Gage Sinclair are part of the program. A year ago they joined several other local farmers, including my brothers, and some not so local, and cut out the middleman."

"You mean a group of farmers decided to start their own pasta company?"

"That's exactly what I mean."

"Ingenious," Vaughn said. "Incredible. So that's what you were talking about when you said they'd found ways around the poor prices."

"Yeah. There's often a solution—but sometimes you have to find it yourself."

"Carrie."

Carrie looked up to see Lindsay and Gage Sinclair standing in the aisle near them.

Carrie started to make the introductions, then remembered that Vaughn had met Lindsay in the pharmacy two days before.

"Vaughn, this is my husband, Gage," Lindsay said.

Vaughn stood and held out his hand to Gage. He and Carrie made their way into the aisle.

"I understand you're an Airborne Ranger," Gage said.

"Was," Vaughn corrected.

The two men began a conversation about military life, and Lindsay stepped closer to Carrie.

"Thanks for getting us such great seats," Carrie said. Lindsay was a substitute teacher now but still worked on the play every year.

"No problem." Lindsay glanced pointedly at Vaughn. "How's it going?"

Carrie didn't know how to answer. Her divorce had devastated her, and since then she'd thrown herself into her studies, forging ahead, insulating her heart. She'd been protecting herself from any risk of pain, but at the same time she'd eliminated any hope of finding love. Then Vaughn entered her life. His patience with Hassie had touched her. His willingness to hear her concerns about the changes that seemed to be coming to Buffalo Valley inspired her to fight for what she knew was right.

Carrie looked at Vaughn and sighed. "He gives me hope," she whispered.

"I remember the first time I saw Gage," Lindsay whispered back. "He looked at me and… I know it's a cliché, but it was as if someone had zapped me with an electrical jolt. I didn't even know this man's name and it was as though I'd *connected* with him."

The music started and Gage reached for Lindsay's hand. "We'd better find our seats."

Gage and Lindsay left, and Carrie and Vaughn returned to their own seats. No sooner had they settled in than the curtain went up.

Several times during the evening, Carrie caught Vaughn studying her. She felt his eyes on her, and when she turned to meet his gaze, he took her hand and entwined his fingers with hers. Carrie had the sensation that something was troubling him, but now wasn't the time to ask.

"Kids in high school actually wrote the play themselves?" Vaughn asked Carrie for the second time. He found it difficult to believe that a group of teenagers could have created and put on such a high-quality production. The acting was a bit amateurish, true, but the emotion and heart that went into each scene stirred him more than he would've thought possible.

After seeing the play, Vaughn realized he could no longer evade a decision regarding Value-X. Not after these vivid depictions of the struggles Buffalo Valley had faced. Through the years, bad weather and bouts of pestilence had plagued the land. The tales of the "dust bowl" years had given him a small taste of the hopelessness the farmers endured. The play ended with a farm family standing in the middle of a wheat field, their heads held high, their arms linked. Just thinking about that scene raised goose bumps onhis arms.

"High-school kids," he repeated before Carrie could respond.

"It was as good as I said it was, don't you agree?"

Words fell short of describing the powerful sensation he'd experienced throughout the play.

"Would you like to come over to Buffalo Bob's for hot

cider? A lot of folks do," Carrie said. "But I should warn you, Pete and Tom will be there."

Vaughn would enjoy going another round with Carrie's brothers, but unfortunately he had a long drive back to Grand Forks. "Another time," he told her. He wasn't in the mood to socialize.

As they stepped from the warmth of the theater into the cold night air, his breath became visible in foggy wisps. The cold seemed to press against him with an intensity he hadn't expected.

"Let me get you home," Vaughn said, placing his arm around her. He wasn't accustomed to cold so severe it made his lungs ache just to draw a breath.

Carrie wrapped her scarf more securely about her neck and pulled on her wool hat. Normally they would have walked the short distance, but not when the cold was so bitter, the wind so vicious.

Vaughn helped her into his rental car, then hurried around the front and climbed into the driver's seat.

Neither spoke as he drove the few short blocks to her family's home. Vaughn wondered if Carrie had realized no one would be there. The house was dark. Had he asked, she would've invited him inside, but he preferred talking to her there, in the dark.

"Carrie, listen, there's something I have to tell you." He stared straight ahead, unable to look at her.

"I know what you're going to say."

He jerked his gaze to hers. Her blue eyes were barely visible in the moonlight, but he saw enough to be aware that she only *thought* she knew.

"We've known each other a very short time," she said. "You'll be leaving soon."

"It doesn't have anything to do with you and me."

"Oh." He could hear her surprise and embarrassment. "I'm sorry. I didn't mean to speak out of turn."

"At the same time, it has *everything* to do with us," he said, and slid his arm around her neck and drew her to him. He breathed in her scent—clean and light and floral; he felt her body against him, softly yielding. After a moment of debating the wisdom of what he was about to do, he exhaled harshly.

"Vaughn, what is it?"

He didn't know where he'd find the courage to tell her. She raised her head to look at him, her eyes full of warmth and concern. Kissing her was wrong; he knew it even as he lowered his mouth to hers. He didn't care, he *had* to kiss her one last time before he was forced to watch the transformation that would come over her when she learned the truth. In a few seconds he was going to hurt and disillusion her.

His mouth was on hers with excitement, with need. The kiss was intense. Real. It seemed to him that the woman in his arms had flung open her life for him, and that thought left his senses reeling.

The guilt he felt was nearly overwhelming.

Her hat had fallen off, and Vaughn slipped his fingers into her hair. He held her close, refusing to release her. From the way she clung to him, she didn't want him to let her go.

"Tell me?" she pleaded.

"Carrie…" He shut his eyes and held his breath for a moment. "I came to Buffalo Valley for more reasons than you know."

"Hassie?"

"For Hassie, yes, but…I'd also been asked to check on something for a friend."

"Check on what?"

"The only way to say this is straight out. I work for Value-X."

Carrie froze. *"What?"* she asked, her voice confused. Uncomprehending.

"Value-X's corporate headquarters are in Seattle."

"I thought you were just discharged from the army."

"I was."

She pulled away from him and scraped the hair back from her face as though to see him more clearly. "I don't understand."

"I don't expect you to. I took a job with Value-X after my discharge."

"They sent you here?" Her back was stiff now, and she leaned away from him. A moment earlier she couldn't get close enough, and now she was as far from him as the confines of the vehicle would allow. "Are your parents involved in this?"

"No! They don't even know."

She shook her head over and over, raising both hands to her face. "I need to think," she said.

"I don't officially start with the company until January."

"You're a *spy?*"

"No. The vice president of new development asked me to check out the town. I was going to be in the area, anyway. It made perfect sense, and..."

"And so you did."

He couldn't very well deny it. "You have every right to be furious."

"You're damn straight I do," she said, grabbing the door handle.

Vaughn stopped her by reaching for her hand. "I can't do it."

She glared at him. "Can't do what?"

"Work for Value-X. I'm faxing in my resignation first thing

tomorrow morning." No one would be in the office to read it until after Christmas, but that couldn't be helped.

Carrie still appeared stunned. "I don't know what to say," she muttered. "I need time to think."

"All right. I know this is a shock. I won't blame you if you decide you want nothing more to do with me. That decision is yours." He sincerely hoped his honesty would prove his sincerity.

She climbed out of the car and without another word, ran toward the house. Vaughn waited at the curb until she was safely inside and then, with a heavy heart, he drove back to Grand Forks.

His parents were still up, playing a game of Scrabble at the kitchen table, when he walked in.

His mother looked up and smiled. "How was the play?"

"Excellent," he answered.

His father picked up four new alphabet squares. "I heard it was put on by a bunch of kids."

"That's true, but they did an incredible job." Vaughn turned a chair around and straddled it.

"How's Carrie?" his mother asked innocently enough.

Vaughn's response was so long in coming that Barbara frowned. She seemed about to repeat her question when he spoke, intending to forestall her.

"If no one minds," he said quickly, "I think I'll go to bed."

"Sure," his father said, concentrating on the game.

"You don't want a cup of tea first?" his mother asked, still frowning.

"I'm sure," he said.

Inside the guest room, Vaughn threw himself on the bed. The guilt and remorse that had haunted him on the sixty-minute drive from Buffalo Valley hadn't dissipated.

He folded his hands beneath his head and gazed up at the ceiling, his thoughts twisting and turning as he attempted to reason everything out. Now that Carrie knew the truth, he should feel better, but he didn't.

Resigning from Value-X was only a small part of what he had to do. He wouldn't be this attracted to Carrie if he truly loved Natalie. He closed his eyes and could only imagine what Natalie would say once she discovered what he'd done. Avoiding a confrontation with her would be impossible. She was coming to Buffalo Valley, and what was that old adage? *Hell hath no fury like a woman scorned.* He could feel the flames licking at his feet even now. Oh, yes, this was only the beginning.

He trusted that Carrie would eventually forgive him for his deception concerning Value-X and his role with the company. He'd been as candid with her as he could.

Unfortunately Value-X wasn't the only issue. He didn't have the courage to tell Carrie about Natalie. Not yet. He didn't want to force her to accept more than one disappointment at a time. Once she'd dealt with the fact that he was connected with Value-X, he'd explain his relationship to Natalie. By then, that relationship would be over.

Sitting up, Vaughn swung his legs over the side of the bed and sat there for several minutes. His mind wasn't going to let him sleep, so it was a waste of time to even try.

The kitchen light was off when he stepped into the hallway. He assumed his parents had finished their game and retired for the night. Perhaps if he had something to eat, it might help him relax. To his surprise, he found his father sitting in the darkened living room, watching the late-night news. The Christmas tree in the corner twinkled with festive lights that illuminated the gifts piled beneath.

"I thought you'd gone to bed," his father said.

"I thought I had, too," Vaughn answered, joining him. They both stared at the screen, although there was nothing on except a too-familiar commercial. Yet anyone might have thought they were viewing it for the first time.

His father suddenly roused himself and turned off the TV. "Something on your mind?" he asked after an uncomfortable moment of silence.

Vaughn hesitated, wondering if he should share his burden.

His father yawned loudly. "You'd better start talking soon if you're inclined to do so, because I'm about to hit the sack."

Vaughn laughed despite himself. "Go to bed. This is something I've got to settle myself."

"All right," Rick Kyle told him. "If you're sure…"

"'Night, Dad," Vaughn said, grateful for having been raised by two loving parents.

"You coming to bed or not?" Gage Sinclair called to his wife. Lindsay had been fussing ever since they'd driven back to the farm. After they'd put the girls down for the night, she'd decided to sort laundry. Then it was something in the kitchen. He had no idea what she was up to now.

"Lindsay," he shouted a second time, already in bed himself.

"I'll be there in a minute." Her voice came from the living room.

"That's what you said fifteen minutes ago."

Tossing aside the comforter, he got out of bed and reached for his robe before walking into the other room. Sure enough, he found her sitting on the sofa, knitting. This particular project looked like it was going to be a sweater for Joy. "Tell me what's bothering you," he said, sinking down in his recliner.

"Things," she returned a moment later.

"You're not upset with me, are you?"

She lowered her knitting and stared at him. "Has there *ever* been a time I was afraid to tell you exactly what I thought, Gage Sinclair?"

Gage didn't have to consider that for very long. "No," he said decisively.

"Exactly."

"Then what is it?" he pressed. All at once he knew. The answer should have been obvious. "Value-X?"

His wife nodded. "My mind's been buzzing ever since I talked to the company. That woman was so arrogant. I don't doubt for a moment that Value-X will be as ruthless as they need to be."

"Sweetheart, there isn't anything we can do about it now."

"I know, but I can't stop thinking. We've got to get organized."

"I agree."

"It's just that with Christmas only a few days away, everyone's so busy we can't find even a couple of hours."

"That's what happens this time of year."

"But the future of the entire *town* is at risk."

"Don't you think other towns have tried to keep them out?" He didn't mean to be a pessimist, but truth was truth. No matter what kind of slant they put on it, nothing was going to change.

"What worries me most is Hassie's attitude," Lindsay admitted. "I've never known her to give up without one hell of a fight."

"Sweetheart, she's single-handedly slayed dragons for this town. It's someone else's turn."

"I know." This was said with a sadness that tugged at his heart. Gage knew his wife had a special relationship with Hassie. He also knew that without Hassie Knight, he might never have married Lindsay. Now it was impossible to imagine his life without her and their daughters. It wasn't anything he even wanted to contemplate.

"I saw you talking to Maddy," Gage said. The two women had been friends nearly all their lives, and they still relied on each other when either had a problem. This problem, though, was shared by the whole town. Predictably, Lindsay had taken on Buffalo Valley's latest dilemma—taken on Hassie's role, too, he thought.

That was what he loved about her, and at the same time dreaded. His wife didn't know the meaning of the word *no*. She simply refused to give up. When she'd first moved to Buffalo Valley, they'd been constantly at odds; he was crazy about her, yet couldn't say a word to her without an argument erupting.

They'd met one hot summer afternoon at Hassie's. Lindsay had left town but she'd stayed in his mind. For weeks afterward she filled his thoughts, and if that wasn't bad enough, she invaded his dreams. When he learned she'd accepted the teaching position at the high school, he managed to convince himself that this Southern belle wouldn't last longer than the first snowflake. His behavior toward her had been scornful, even combative—an attempt to keep from making a fool of himself. It hadn't worked, since he'd done a mighty fine job of looking like a dolt.

Then there was the matter of finding their aunt, the illegitimate child of her grandmother and his grandfather. Gage had wanted no part of that. He'd violently disagreed with her decision to intrude on this unknown woman's life.

He'd been wrong about that, and during the past few years, Angela Kirkpatrick had become an important figure in their lives.

It didn't stop there. Lindsay had known what was best for Kevin, too. His much younger brother was never meant to be a farmer. Kevin hated what Gage loved most. But Kevin's talent meant that he would one day be named among the country's major artists. Lindsay had recognized his brother's gift when Gage had turned a blind eye to it.

Having seen the error of his ways—repeatedly—Gage had come to trust his wife's judgment and intuition. "What do you suggest we do?" he asked, getting up and sitting next to her on the sofa.

"I just don't know, and neither does Maddy," Lindsay told him, shrugging helplessly. She put aside her knitting, muttering that she couldn't concentrate anymore. Not *his* fault, she assured him. It was just this Value-X thing.

He clasped her hand and she gripped his hard. She scrambled into his lap, pressing her head against his shoulder. Gathering her close, Gage savored the feel of his wife in his arms.

"I tried to talk to Hassie about it, but she said I should turn my thinking around and try to look at the positive side of the situation."

"Have you?" Gage asked, dropping a kiss on her forehead.

"No. I can't get past what'll happen to Buffalo Valley once Value-X arrives."

The prospects for the future weren't bright in view of what had become of other communities the retailer had entered.

Neither spoke for several moments, then Gage changed the subject. "I enjoyed meeting Vaughn Kyle."

"You two certainly seemed to hit it off."

"We got to talking about army life."

"Wouldn't it be wonderful if he moved to Buffalo Valley and he and Carrie got married?" his wife said. Sometimes he forgot what a romantic she could be. And yet…time and again, her instincts about people proved to be correct. She was the one who'd claimed Maddy and Jeb were falling in love, although Gage would've sworn on a stack of Bibles that it wasn't happening.

"Carrie and Vaughn?" he repeated.

"Mark my words, Gage."

Lindsay wasn't going to get an argument out of him. "You ready for bed now?"

"Ready," she told him, kissing his jaw and sending shivers down his back.

"Me, too," he whispered.

Eight

"I've got a meeting in town this morning," Margaret Eilers announced at the breakfast table Saturday morning, three days before Christmas.

This came as news to Matt. His wife hadn't mentioned anything about going into Buffalo Valley. Something was in the air, though. The phone had been ringing off the hook for the better part of a week. He knew the women around here were up in arms about the Value-X problem, although Matt didn't see what could be done. Neither did any of the other men in town.

"Can you watch the kids for me, Sadie?" His wife smiled at the housekeeper, who'd been with the family since Margaret's childhood.

Sadie brought a stack of pancakes to the table and wiped her hands on her apron. "Not this morning," she said in that brusque way of hers.

Anyone who didn't know Sadie might assume she was put out by the request. She wasn't. This was simply her manner, and they were all used to it. Matt had learned more than one lesson from the highly capable housekeeper. She'd become an ally and friend shortly after he married Margaret, and he was forever grateful for all she'd done to see him through his troubles.

"I'm leaving at noon, remember?" Sadie reminded them.

"That's right," Margaret muttered, glancing at Matt.

"What's going on in town?" he asked. Margaret wasn't one to make unnecessary trips, nor was she the type of woman to find an excuse to shop.

"I'm meeting with the other women. We're going to discuss ideas on how to deal with the threat from Value-X," she told him.

"Sweetheart, that's already been discussed to death. The town council has tried, Hassie's—"

"Everyone's been talking to Ambrose Kohn individually. We've got to mount a defense as a community."

"And do what? Sign petitions?" He didn't mean to sound negative, but he sincerely doubted that Value-X cared what the community thought. They'd already set the wheels in motion. Matt suspected many a town such as theirs had tried to mount a defense, but it had been hopeless from the start. Value-X knew how to win.

"We can't sit by and do nothing," Margaret insisted.

"But it's almost Christmas."

"Exactly, and Value-X is counting on the community to delay a response until after the holidays. By then it could be too late. That's what the meeting's about. I'm willing to fight now, and so are the other women in town."

"What about the men?"

"You're welcome to join us, but..."

"But the women are spearheading this."

"That's because none of you men believe it can be done." Her smile belied the sharpness of her words. "You can still come if you want."

"No, thanks," Matt said, waving a hand in dismissal. "I've got the kids to look after."

Margaret smiled and reached over to spear a hotcake with her fork. They'd been married three years, and Matt fell more in love with her every day. Times had been hard in the beginning, but it seemed that once they'd survived that rough period, they'd grown closer than ever. Of one thing Matt was certain—his wife brought out the very best in him. He loved her with an intensity that gave him strength.

"So I can leave Hailey and David with you?"

"I did have plans this morning, but they can wait." He'd hoped to finish the gift he was working on for Margaret. The antique rocker had belonged to her father. Matt had stumbled upon it in the loft up in the barn, and Sadie had told him its history. Joshua McKenna had repaired it earlier, and Matt had sanded and varnished the wood. Sadie had sewed new cushions for the seat and back. Matt had hoped to add a final coat of varnish that morning so it would be ready for Margaret on Christmas morning. Well...he'd have to find time tonight.

"I don't know what you women think you're going to accomplish," he said, "but if you sincerely believe it'll make a difference, then I'll do my part—and I'll wish you well."

Margaret thanked him with a brilliant smile, rose from the table and kissed him. The kiss was deep and full of promise. She was letting him know he'd be rewarded a hundred times over at a more appropriate hour.

Soon afterward Margaret headed into town. Once the kids were up, dressed and fed, Matt decided he wanted to know exactly what the women intended. Reaching for the phone, he called Jeb McKenna, his closest neighbor.

"Is Maddy gone, too?" he asked. Matt heard children crying in the background.

"I've got my hands full."

"Me, too," Matt confessed.

"Do you know what they're planning?" Jeb asked.

"I don't have a clue, but I'm sorry now that I didn't go with her. They have great intentions, but what can they do that hasn't already been tried?"

"You signed the petition?"

"Along with everyone else in town," Matt told him.

"Buffalo Bob contacted the governor and asked for help."

"Did he hear back?" Now, that was promising.

"Not yet."

Matt sighed impatiently. "I feel like we should be there."

"I do, too."

"Daddy." Hailey tugged at his jeans. "Can we go to town and have a soda?"

Matt grinned at his daughter. "Just a minute, honey." What an inspiration. "I'll meet you at the soda fountain," Matt suggested. "That way we can keep the kids occupied and we can talk ourselves."

"Good idea," Jeb said.

Matt pushed a tape into the truck's console and sang Christmas songs with his children as he drove into town. When he parked outside Hassie's, he noticed several other vehicles there, too. The two youngsters followed him excitedly into the drugstore.

The soda fountain appeared to be the most popular place in town; Gage Sinclair was there with his two daughters, and Jeb McKenna had arrived ahead of him. So had Brandon Wyatt and six-year-old Jason. Every stool at the fountain was occupied.

Matt acknowledged his friends with a quick nod.

"Hey, Matt," Jeb said in a jocular tone, "seeing that you called us together, I'm hoping you've come up with a few ideas to share."

"Me?" Matt glanced at Jeb, who shifted his weight. "I called a couple of the other guys, too. I think we made a mistake by taking such a negative attitude. Now the women are stuck trying to cope with the problem all by themselves."

The door opened and Dennis Urlacher walked in with his three-year-old son. Little Josh might be named after Sarah's father, but he was the spitting image of his own.

"I'm not late, am I?" Dennis asked, taken aback by the sight of all the children.

Leta was doing her best to keep up with orders, but she was obviously overwhelmed. As soon as she delivered one soda, she got an order for two more. Apparently Hassie was at the meeting over at Sarah's shop, as well. The men stood in a small circle while the children sat at the counter. Their joyous laughter made all the fathers smile, none more than Matt.

"So, does anyone have any ideas?" Dennis asked.

"Did you get anywhere with the governor's office?" Jeb asked Bob.

Bob shook his head. "I got the runaround. Reading between the lines, I could tell the politicians don't want to get involved in this fight. Buffalo Valley is on its own."

"Okay," Matt said, "maybe the politicians don't want to take sides in this issue, but there are plenty of other influential people who aren't afraid of challenging Value-X."

"Who?"

A flurry of names followed—writers and filmmakers and

media personalities—along with a volunteer to contact each one immediately after the holidays. This was exactly the kind of pressure necessary to get the company's attention.

Soon the men were talking excitedly, their voices blending with those of their children. Various ideas were considered, discarded, put aside for research or further thought. The women were right—they had to become a united front.

"Do you seriously believe anyone at the corporate level will listen?" Gage asked. "They've dealt with organized opposition before."

Matt shrugged, although he suspected that if Margaret was the one doing the talking, those muck-a-mucks would soon learn she refused to be ignored. A smile formed on his face as he imagined Margaret standing before the conglomerate's board of directors. They'd listen, all right.

"What's so funny?" Brandon Wyatt asked.

"Nothing." Matt shook his head, dispelling the image.

"Joanie's been real upset about all this."

"Maddy, too," Jeb said. "I don't think the grocery will be too badly affected, but that's not the point. She's worried about how everyone else will fare."

"Value-X would ruin Joanie's and my business," Brandon said. "But I don't think a bunch of suits in some fancy office in Seattle really care what'll happen to a small video store in Buffalo Valley."

The other men agreed.

"We could hold a rally," Gage suggested.

"The women have already thought of that," Leta inserted, speaking from behind the counter. "They figured it wouldn't have enough impact unless we got major media coverage."

Several of the men nodded; others seemed prepared to argue.

"Hassie's probably got a few ideas," Gage said next. "When she comes back from the meeting, we'll—"

Leta broke in. "Hassie's not with the others," she informed them as she set a chocolate soda on the polished mahogany counter.

"She's not?" The question came from two or three men simultaneously, including Matt.

"Nope. She's at home this morning."

This was news to them all.

"Hassie's not with the other women?" Dennis repeated, frowning. "But..."

"How many of them are over at Sarah's, anyway?" Matt wanted to know.

"They're not at Sarah's," Dennis told them.

"Then where are they?" Matt had assumed that was where the women had met. Sarah had the most space for such a gathering.

"I think they're over at the church with Joyce Dawson," Brandon Wyatt said. "I'm not sure, but something Joanie said..."

Matt figured it wasn't all that important where the women had congregated. The community was coming together, bringing forth ideas. Value-X might be a powerful corporation, but the men and women of Buffalo Valley weren't going to submit humbly to this invasion.

Sleep had eluded Vaughn Kyle all night. The message of the Christmas play had stayed with him. A community standing together, enduring through hard times, its unique character created by that history of struggle and victory. Not *a* community, *this* community. Buffalo Valley.

His confession to Carrie after the performance had played

no small part in his inability to sleep. Unfortunately Carrie wasn't the only woman he needed to talk to, and the conversation with Natalie would probably be even harder.

He waited until eight, Seattle time, before calling her. His decision to resign and the reasons for it would infuriate her. And his plan to end their relationship—he didn't even want to think about her reaction to that. He wasn't convinced that she truly loved him, but the humiliation of being rejected would be difficult for her to accept. He sighed; he'd betrayed Carrie twice over and now he was doing the same to Natalie.

The house was still quiet when Vaughn brought the portable phone into his room. Sitting on the bed, he dialed Natalie's home number and waited four long rings before she picked up.

"Hello." Her voice was groggy with sleep. Normally she'd be awake by now. He'd already started off on the wrong foot, and he had yet to say a word.

"I got you up, didn't I," he said.

"Vaughn," she said sleepily, then yawned. "Hello, darling."

Vaughn tried to ignore the guilt that rushed forward. Mere hours ago, he'd been holding and kissing Carrie.

"This is a surprise," Natalie cooed. "You must really be missing me."

"I need to talk to you about Value-X," Vaughn said, getting directly to the point. There was no easy way to do this.

"Now?" she protested. "You're always telling me all I think about is work. I didn't get home until after eleven last night, and work is the last thing I want to think about now. You know we're under a lot of pressure just before the holidays. There's so much I have to get done, especially since I'll be leaving on this trip."

"I do know, and I apologize." He honestly felt bad about this. "I'll be sending in a fax this morning."

She sighed as if to say she was already bored. "Why?"

He hesitated, bracing himself for her angry outburst. "I've resigned."

"*What?*" Her shriek was loud enough to actually startle him. "If this is a joke, Vaughn, I am *not* amused."

In some ways he wished it was. He doubted this was one of those situations he'd look back on years from now and find amusing. "You asked me to check out Buffalo Valley."

"So?" she asked. "You mentioned an aunt or someone you knew who lived there. What's the big deal?"

"The big deal is that the town isn't interested in Value-X setting up shop."

Natalie didn't so much as pause. "Honey, listen, we've already been through this. Few communities fully appreciate everything we can do for them. Invariably there's a handful of discontented, ill-informed people who take it upon themselves to make a fuss. For the most part it's a token protest. Rarely is it ever a threat."

"If that's the case, why did you ask me to report back to you on Buffalo Valley?" She'd been worried, Vaughn knew; otherwise she'd never have suggested he check the place out.

"After the bad publicity in that Montana town, I overreacted. That was a mistake," she said quickly. "I see that now. A big mistake! I can't allow you to throw away the opportunity of a lifetime because I sent you into battle unprepared."

"Battle?"

"You know what I mean," she said irritably. "I wasn't thinking clearly. You were going to be in the area and it seemed like such a little thing. I should've known…"

"I'm grateful you asked me to do this," Vaughn countered. "I've learned a whole lot."

"No! No...this is all wrong." Natalie sounded desperate now.

"Buffalo Valley is a nice town. The people here are worried about what'll happen if Value-X moves in."

"But they don't understand that we—"

"They want someone to listen, and it's clear the company isn't going to do that." The purpose of Natalie's visit was to convince the people of Buffalo Valley that they needed Value-X.

"Of course the town wants us to listen, they all do, but what would happen to our jobs if we actually did?"

Natalie made her point without contradiction by Vaughn, although he doubted she recognized the real import of her words.

"Don't do anything stupid," Natalie pleaded. "At least wait until I get there and we can talk this out."

Her arrival was an entirely separate issue. "That brings up another...problem."

"Now what?" she snapped. "I suppose you're going to tell me you've met someone else and you want to dump me."

Vaughn rubbed his hand along his thigh and said nothing.

"This has *got* to be a joke." She gave a short, humorless laugh. "Talk about the Grinch stealing Christmas!"

"I realize my timing is bad—"

"Bad! You don't know the half of it."

"Natalie, listen, I'm genuinely sorry."

"You asked me to be your wife."

Technically, that wasn't true. They'd talked about marriage, but Natalie had shown no great enthusiasm. Now, however, didn't seem to be the time to argue the point. "If you'll recall, you were pretty lukewarm about the idea. That has to tell you something about your feelings for me."

"I was playing it cool," she insisted, sounding close to tears.

Vaughn had never known Natalie to cry, and he experienced deep pangs of regret. "I didn't mean to hurt you, but I had to say something before you showed up here." He hoped she'd cancel the trip, although he figured that was unlikely.

"I wanted you to be thrilled when I finally agreed to marry you. Now you're saying you don't love me."

"Not exactly…" He did hold tender feelings for her, but he knew with certainty that they were never meant to be together.

"You love me—but you love someone else more?"

Vaughn wasn't sure how to respond. He hadn't declared his feelings for Carrie, but the promise he felt with her outweighed his feelings for Natalie.

"I suppose she's one of the crusaders against Value-X. That would make sense, now that I think about it."

Vaughn didn't answer.

"I'm not giving up on us," Natalie insisted, "not until we've had a chance to speak face-to-face."

He'd already guessed she wouldn't make this easy. "I'd rather you just accepted my decision."

A painful pause followed. "Just what do you plan to do with your life if you resign from Value-X?" she demanded.

"I don't know." His future was as much a mystery to him as it was to her. All Vaughn could say was that he had no intention of remaining with the company.

"You're not thinking clearly," Natalie said.

"Actually, I'm thinking about settling here." He wasn't sure where the words had come from, but until he said them aloud the possibility hadn't even occurred to him.

"In North Dakota," she blurted out, as though he was suffering from temporary insanity. "Now I *know* this is all a bad joke. Who in their right mind would live there? You know the demographics as well as I do. *No one* lives in a place like that on purpose."

"I would."

"This is ridiculous! I wouldn't believe it if I wasn't hearing it with my own ears. You can't be serious."

Although he knew it was probably a waste of breath, Vaughn felt obliged to tell her about Buffalo Valley. He wanted her to know the people he'd met. She couldn't begin to grasp what he felt unless she understood who and what they were.

"This farming community is small-town America at its best," he said, and wondered if she was even listening. "They have a history of banding together in hard times—and there've been plenty of hard times." He wanted to make her understand the depth of his respect for them, so he relayed to her the plot of the Christmas play.

"That's all very interesting," Natalie told him, her tone bored, "but that was then and this is now. Value-X will come into Buffalo Valley with or without you. With or without me. It doesn't matter how many times you sit and watch a group of teenagers act out the town's history, nothing is going to change."

"It will," Vaughn said.

"I'm not letting you quit. One day you'll thank me."

"Natalie, what are you doing?"

"First I'm going into corporate headquarters to make sure no one reads your resignation letter. Then I'm flying out on the twenty-seventh, just the way I planned, so we can talk this out."

"I wish you wouldn't. Let it go, Natalie."

Her returning laugh sounded like a threat. "I don't think so.

You didn't really believe I'd allow you to cut me loose with a simple phone call, did you?"

He didn't bother to respond. What was the point?

"You see yourself as this hero, this knight in shining armor, and while that's fine and good, it isn't going to work."

Vaughn could see the storm clouds gathering on the horizon.

Sunday morning while his parents attended church, Vaughn drove into Buffalo Valley. He'd made the trek so often in the past week that it seemed almost second nature to head in that direction.

Everything about the town appealed to him. It'd started when he'd first met Hassie and accepted the gold watch that had belonged to her husband. With the watch came an implied trust. He refused to be part of anything that would betray their relationship.

He hadn't heard from Carrie, but he would once she was ready. He didn't think it would take her long to come to terms with his confession. Because of her ex-husband's betrayal, it was vital that he be as open and honest with her as possible. However…he still hadn't explained Natalie's role in his life. Poor Carrie was about to be hit with a second shock, but there wasn't a damn thing he could do to prevent it.

He parked just outside town, at the twenty-acre site for the proposed Value-X. With the wind howling, he climbed out of the car and walked onto the property. Either he was becoming accustomed to the bone-chilling weather or it'd warmed up in the past twenty-four hours. He discovered he could breathe now without feeling as though he was inhaling ice particles.

He'd been there for several minutes when he saw a truck pull up and park next to his vehicle. Two men climbed out and started toward him. He instantly recognized them as Carrie's younger brothers.

"Chuck and Ken, right?" he said as they approached.

Chuck, the older of the two, touched his hat. "Vaughn Kyle?"

Vaughn nodded.

"Did you have a falling-out with Carrie after the play?" Chuck asked. The man was nothing if not direct. His brow had furrowed and the teasing friendliness was gone. "You hurt her and you have me to answer to."

"I have no intention of hurting her."

"Good." He nodded once as if to suggest the subject was closed.

"What are you doing out here?" Ken muttered.

Vaughn wasn't sure what to tell him. He hadn't asked Carrie to keep the fact that he was employed by Value-X a secret, but it was apparent that she had. If either Chuck or Ken knew the truth, they'd have him tarred and feathered and run out of town.

"Just looking," Vaughn told him.

"Looking at what? Empty land?"

"If you had this twenty acres or any portion of it, how would you develop it?" Vaughn asked the pair.

"That's easy," Ken said. "This town needs a feed store—been needing one for years. Most everyone has to drive to Devils Lake for their feed."

A feed store. Now that was interesting. "Why don't you do it?" he suggested.

"No time. The hardware store keeps us busy. Dad needs us there, but if someone were to come along with enough investment capital and a head for business, they'd be guaranteed success."

"Dad carries some of the more common feed, but he doesn't have room for much."

"We got to talking about a feed store just the other day," Ken said, glancing at his brother. "Wondering who might be able to open one."

This morning, Vaughn had casually told Natalie that he might settle in Buffalo Valley. A few days earlier his future was set, and now all at once he was cast adrift. His carefully ordered life was in shambles, and Vaughn didn't like the uncomfortable feeling that gave him.

"It'd take someone with ready cash," Ken told him, his expression pensive, "and that's in short supply around here." He kicked at the snow with the toe of his boot. "People in these parts invest everything in their land."

"You interested?" Chuck asked him bluntly.

Vaughn looked in the direction of town, suddenly aware that this venture piqued his interest. He wanted to be part of Buffalo Valley, part of its future. It'd be a risk, but he'd never backed down from a challenge before and he wasn't planning to start now.

"I don't know a damn thing about running a feed store," he said, meeting the other men's eyes.

Chuck and Ken studied him for a long moment.

"You serious about this?" Chuck finally asked.

Vaughn nodded.

"Between Dad, me and my brothers, we could show you everything you need to know."

"You'd do that?" Vaughn found it hard to believe that these men, who were little more than strangers, would willingly offer him their expertise.

"I saw a light in my sister's eyes that hasn't been there since her divorce," Ken told him. "That made me decide you might be worth taking a chance on." He stared down at the ground, then raised his head. "Now, I realize you moving into town and opening a feed store might have absolutely nothing to do with Carrie. Personally, I hope it does, but I want you to know that whatever happens between you and my sister is your business."

"That's the way it would have to be."

Her two brothers shared a glance and seemed to reach the same conclusion. "You're right about that." Chuck spoke for the pair. "This has nothing to do with Carrie."

"There are a lot of *ifs* in all this," Vaughn reminded them. He could see that they were getting excited, but then so was he. Naturally, all of this depended on a dozen different factors. Right now it was little more than the glimmer of an idea. Little more than a possibility. But it gave him a glimpse of what he might do....

"At the moment the future doesn't look all that promising for Buffalo Valley," Ken said, surveying the bare land around them. It went without saying that if Value-X came to town, that would be the end of any talk about a feed store.

On the verge of leaving, Vaughn returned to the subject of their sister. "Have either of you seen Carrie?"

"She's gone for the day," Ken told him.

"All day?"

Chuck shrugged. "She's over with our brother Tom and his family. Did you two have plans?"

"No." How could he expect her to be at his beck and call? "I'll talk to her later," he said with reluctance. Their conversation had to take place soon. He'd rather this business with Natalie was over, but it now seemed that would require a protracted...discussion, for lack of a better word.

"She was upset when you dropped her off at the house after

the play." Ken frowned at him in an accusatory way, suggesting Vaughn had some explaining to do. "What happened? What did you do?"

"That's Carrie's and my business. Remember?"

Chuck agreed. "She'd have our heads if she knew we were talking to you about her. We'll stay out of it, but like I said, you hurt her and you'll have me to answer to."

Vaughn nodded and resisted the urge to laugh. Melodramatic though they sounded, her brothers were serious.

"I heard you and your parents are spending Christmas Day with Hassie," Ken said.

News sure traveled fast in a small town. "We're coming for dinner."

"Then I think we might be able to arrange something." The two brothers exchanged another look.

"Arrange what?" Vaughn asked.

"Nothing much, just an opportunity for you to have some time alone with our sister." Chuck and Ken left then, both of them grinning broadly.

Nine

Hassie spent Christmas morning with Buffalo Bob, Merrily and little Bobby, upstairs at the 3 of a Kind. Sitting around the Christmas tree with the family reminded her of what it'd been like years ago, when Valerie and Vaughn were young. The good feelings started right then, and she suspected this would be her best Christmas in a very long while.

Bobby's eyes got round as quarters when his father rolled out a shiny new miniature bicycle with training wheels. It amazed her that a three-year-old could actually ride a bicycle. In another three or four months, the park would be crowded with kids on bikes, enjoying the Dakota sunshine. When Hassie closed her eyes, she could almost hear the sound of their laughter. That would happen, she comforted herself, with or without Value-X.

She exchanged gifts with the family—magazine subscriptions for Bob and Merrily, a book of nursery rhymes for Bobby. Their gift to her was a new pair of lined leather gloves. After coffee and croissants—and hugs and kisses—she left.

Home again, Hassie set the dining-room table with her finest china. Not much reason to use it these days. Yet twice this week she'd had cause to bring it out of the old mahogany cabinet. The first time was her visit with Barbara and now Christmas dinner.

Already the kitchen counter was crowded with a variety of food. Carrie and her mother had thoughtfully dropped off a platter of decorated sugar cookies. Those cookies, plus the ones she'd collected the night of the exchange, added up to enough for the entire town.

Sarah Urlacher and Calla had given her a plate of home-made fudge. Maddy, Lindsay and several of the other women had stopped by with offerings, too—preserves and homemade bread and mincemeat tarts. It was far more than Hassie could eat in two or three Christmases.

Then word had leaked out about Vaughn Kyle and his parents coming for dinner. Before Hassie could stop them, her friends and neighbors had dropped off a plethora of side dishes. Joanie Wyatt sent over baked yams. Rachel Quant-rill delivered a green-bean-and-cauliflower casserole. Soon all that was required of Hassie was the bird and dressing. The tantalizing aroma of baking turkey, sage and onions drifted through the house.

Living alone, Hassie didn't bother much with meals. At night, after she closed the pharmacy, her dinner consisted of whatever was quick and easy. When Jerry had been alive and the children still lived at home, she'd been an accomplished cook. Now she considered cooking for one a nuisance. Many a night she dined on soup or a microwave entrée.

The doorbell chimed at exactly one o'clock, and Hassie, who'd been occupying herself with last-minute touches, was ready to receive her company.

"Merry Christmas," Barbara Kyle sang out, hugging Hassie as soon as she opened the front door.

"Merry Christmas. Merry Christmas." Hassie hugged them all.

For the next few minutes the men made trips back and forth between the car and the house. They hauled in festively wrapped presents, plus various contributions to the meal, including three beautiful pies.

"How in heaven's name are the four of us going to eat all these pies?" Hassie asked, giggling like a schoolgirl over such an embarrassment of riches. Pies, cookies, candies. Oh, my, she'd be on a diet till next June if she tasted everything in her kitchen.

"Pecan pie is Rick's favorite," Barbara explained.

"Pumpkin is mine," Vaughn said.

"And fresh apple mixed with cranberry is mine," Barbara said, setting down the third pie. She had to rearrange other dishes on the crowded counter to find room for it.

"Apple mixed with cranberry," Hassie mused aloud. "That sounds delicious."

"I'm willing to share," Barbara said with a laugh.

The meal was even better than Hassie had dared hope. The turkey was moist and succulent, and the sage dressing was her finest ever, if she did say so herself. The four of them sat around the table and passed the serving dishes to one another. They talked and laughed as if each was part of Hassie's family. Anyone seeing them would never have guessed there'd been a thirty-three-year lapse in their relationship.

This was the way Christmas was meant to be, Hassie thought, immersing herself in the good feelings. Barbara had always been a talker, and she effortlessly kept the conversation going. The years had changed Rick Kyle considerably,

Hassie noted, smiling over at him. She doubted she would've recognized him now.

The last time Hassie had seen Rick, he'd had shoulder-length brown hair, a bushy mustache and narrow-rimmed glasses. A wooden peace sign had dangled from his neck. As she recalled, he'd worn the craziest color combinations with tie-dyed bell-bottom jeans and sandals.

His hair was mostly gone now, but Barbara claimed bald men could be exceedingly sexy. Hassie wouldn't know about that, but it did her good to see that they were happy and obviously still in love.

Perhaps it was selfish of her, but she liked to believe that if her son had lived, Vaughn would've found the same happiness with Barbara.

"If I eat another bite, I swear someone might mistake me for a stuffed sausage," Barbara declared, pushing back her chair.

"Me, too." Rick wrapped his arms around his belly and groaned.

Hassie looked at Vaughn, who winked and said, "Could someone pass me the mashed potatoes and gravy?"

Laughing, Barbara hurled a roll at him from across the table. Vaughn deftly caught it. "Hey, I'm a growing boy."

When they'd finished, the men cleared off the table and Hassie brewed a pot of coffee. They gathered in the living room around the small Christmas tree, where Hassie had tucked three small gifts, one for each of her guests. Shopping in Buffalo Valley was limited and there hadn't been much time, so Hassie had found items with special meaning to share with her friends. Three little gifts she knew each would treasure.

For Barbara, it was a pearl pin Jerry had given her after Vaughn's birth. For Rick it was a fountain pen—an antique. Choosing a gift for Vaughn had been difficult. In the end she'd parted with one of the medals the army had awarded her son for bravery. Since Vaughn had recently been in the military himself, she felt he'd appreciate what this medal represented.

They seemed truly touched by her gifts. Barbara's eyes brimmed with tears and she pinned the pearl to her silk blouse. Rick, who didn't appear to be the demonstrative sort, hugged her. And Vaughn seemed at a loss for words.

"I have something to tell you," Vaughn said after several minutes of silence.

"This sounds serious." Hassie saw the look Barbara and Rick exchanged and wondered at its meaning.

Vaughn leaned forward and took Hassie's hands in both his own. "I told Mom and Dad earlier, and they urged me to be honest with you, as well. First, I want you to know I'd never deliberately do anything to hurt you."

"I know that. Honest about what?"

"Value-X. When I left Seattle, I'd accepted a job with them."

Hassie gasped, and her hand flew to her mouth. This was almost more than she could take in. Vaughn an employee of Value-X?

"I knew the company was planning to expand into Buffalo Valley, but I didn't understand the threat they represented to the community."

"He isn't working for them any longer," Barbara quickly inserted.

"Since I wasn't going to be officially an employee until after the first of the year, one of the vice presidents suggested I not mention my association with the company," Vaughn explained. "It was never my intention to deceive you or anyone in Buffalo Valley." He took a deep breath. "I faxed in my resignation and made it effective immediately."

Hassie felt a little dizzy. It was hard enough to grasp what he was saying, and she could only imagine what Carrie must think, so she asked, "Does Carrie know?"

Vaughn nodded. "I told her the night of the play. I didn't want to wait until after the holidays."

"What did she say?" Hassie asked. She feared that the news might mean the end for this budding relationship, which would be a dreadful shame.

"I haven't had a chance to speak to her since."

Barbara moved forward to the edge of the sofa. "There's more."

Vaughn cast his mother a look that suggested he'd rather she hadn't said anything.

"Tell me." As far as Hassie was concerned, it was too late for secrets now.

Vaughn glanced at his mother again. "I don't want to get anyone's hopes up, because it's much too soon."

"Yes, yes, we know that," Barbara interjected, then waited for him to continue.

Vaughn's reluctance was evident. At last he said, "I'm investigating the possibility of opening a feed store here in town."

For the second time in as many moments, Hassie gasped. Only this time, the shock was one of excitement and pleasure. "Oh, Vaughn, that's an excellent idea. The town could use a feed store."

Rick wrapped his arm around his wife's shoulders, and both of them smiled broadly.

"Vaughn spoke with two of the Hendrickson brothers about it yesterday morning," Barbara said. "They actually suggested it."

Hassie's heart surged with hope. Vaughn was right of course; there was no reason to get carried away. But she couldn't help it. The thought of having Vaughn right here in Buffalo Valley—she was almost afraid to believe it could happen.

"I've got an appointment with Heath Quantrill first thing Wednesday morning," Vaughn explained. "I'll need to put together a business plan and look into financing. The Hendricksons recommended I start there."

"Yes—Heath will give you good advice." Some of the excitement left her as reality came rushing back. "Everything hinges on what happens with Value-X, doesn't it?"

"True." Vaughn gave her a lopsided smile. "But I have a good feeling about this." As Hassie fought the emotion that threatened to overwhelm her, he added, "I want to invest in Buffalo Valley."

Keeping the tears at bay was impossible now. "Why would you do such a thing?" she asked between sniffles. Reaching into her pocket, she withdrew a linen handkerchief and blew her nose. She must be getting old, because normally she wasn't a woman prone to tears.

"I arrived in North Dakota thinking I knew exactly what I wanted and where I was headed," Vaughn said, "but everything changed. I probably shouldn't have said anything about my idea." He frowned at his mother. "But now that it's out, I'm glad you know."

"God bless you," Hassie whispered, stretching her arms toward Vaughn for a hug. Their embrace was warm. "If God had seen fit to give me a grandson, I would have wanted him to be just like you."

"That's a high compliment," Vaughn said, sitting down again.

"I meant it to be," Hassie told him. She rubbed her wet cheek with the back of her hand. "Look what you did," she said. "It isn't just anyone who can make this old lady weep."

"Shame on you, son," Rick teased, and they all smiled.

It took Hassie a few moments to compose herself.

"Look," Barbara said, pointing outside, "it's snowing."

Sure enough, the flakes were falling thick and soft, creating a perfect Christmas scene. "This is the way I always dreamed Christmas would be," Hassie whispered. "Surrounded by family—" she used the word purposely "—on a beautiful winter day."

This was the best Christmas she'd had in many years, and all because of the Kyles—people who'd been brought into Hassie's life by her son. Somehow she could picture Vaughn smiling down, wishing them a Merry Christmas.

Hassie had invited Carrie to join Vaughn and his parents for dessert on Christmas Day, and Carrie had yet to decide if she'd go. Vaughn's confession about working for Value-X had shocked her. The fact that he'd come into town, gained her confidence and that of everyone else—so he could collect information for the company—had been a betrayal of trust and goodwill. He'd withheld the truth from her and she should be outraged. She *was* outraged.

All week Vaughn had listened to everyone's objections to Value-X and said nothing. As she thought back on their numerous conversations, she realized how often he'd defended the company. At the time she'd assumed he was playing devil's advocate. Now she knew otherwise. Carrie wasn't sure what had happened to make him resign. Whatever it was, she was grateful. Still...

Trust was a basic issue with Carrie. Vaughn had betrayed her, Hassie and the entire town, and she couldn't conveniently look the other way. *Forgive and forget* might work for others, but not for her.

She didn't think Vaughn had told anyone else. Carrie hadn't determined whether that was a good thing or not. She did know she had to hide this from Hassie, who would be heartbroken if she found out. If she didn't show up at Hassie's and then claimed she'd forgotten, Hassie would immediately conclude that something was wrong. Then she'd start asking questions. Questions Carrie didn't want to answer. She could invent plausible excuses, but the problem was that Carrie *did* want to see Vaughn again, despite what he'd told her.

She needed to talk to him, needed to vent her feelings. The shock of his confession had robbed her of that chance. But finding a private time to speak with him today might prove difficult, if not impossible. In any event, she hadn't given verbal shape to her emotions yet. Talking to him should probably wait, she rationalized.

"Where you going?" Ken asked, following her into the hallway as she gathered her coat, gloves and scarf.

"I bet she's going off to see that new friend of hers," Chuck teased.

"I'm going over to Hassie's," she informed her two younger brothers smugly.

"I suppose *he's* there."

How Pete knew that, Carrie could only guess. She shoved her arms into the silk-lined sleeves of her coat.

"He's there, all right," Tom said, leaning against the door jamb. "His car's parked outside Hassie's."

Carrie ignored him and went to get her purse. She and Hassie had exchanged their gifts on Christmas Eve, but Carrie had borrowed a book on traditional remedies that she needed to return. She retrieved it from the bookcase.

"Will you guys leave me alone?" she cried. All four of her

brothers were trailing her from room to room. "Don't you have anything better to do?"

Her brothers glanced at each other and shrugged, then Pete announced, "Not really."

"Do you want to hear what we think of your new boyfriend?" Ken asked.

If they could be this obstinate, so could she. "No."

Carrie headed for the front door. If her four guardian angels wanted to follow her into the cold and snow, that was their choice.

"I like him, Carrie," Ken called after her.

"Me, too." Tom crowded beside him in the doorway.

"He's all right," Pete concurred.

Chuck simply winked and gave her a thumbs-up. This had to be a record. Never before had she dated a man all four of her brothers approved of. Little did they know. She wondered what they'd say if they knew that, until recently, he'd been a Value-X employee. The answer didn't bear considering. She couldn't disillusion them any more than she could Hassie. Against her will, she'd been pulled into his subterfuge, and she hated it.

The snow was falling hard by the time Carrie reached Hassie's house; she barely noticed.

Vaughn answered the door and surprised her by closing it after him as he stepped onto the porch. "Merry Christmas," he said, his eyes never leaving hers.

As much as possible, she avoided looking at him.

"We need to talk, Carrie."

"Here? Now?" She faked a short laugh. "I don't think so, Vaughn."

"Later, then?"

She nodded.

He sighed with unmistakable relief. "Thank you."

She didn't *want* to feel anything. She longed to ignore him, make a token visit and then be on her way. But it was too late for that. Her emotions were painfully confused; she wanted to kiss him and at the same time, she wanted to scream and rage and throw his betrayal in his face.

He pressed his hand to her cheek. "I'm glad you're here."

She'd intended to slap his hand away, but instead, her fingers curled around his, and she closed her eyes and leaned toward him. Then she was angry with herself for being weak and jerked back.

"Come in out of the cold," Hassie called just as Vaughn opened the door and Carrie stepped inside. She took off her coat and tossed it onto the stair railing.

"Have you met my dad?" Vaughn asked, taking Carrie by the elbow and escorting her into the living room. He made the introductions.

"Pleased to meet you," she said, hoping none of the stiffness she felt came through in her voice.

Hassie was on her way to the kitchen. "You're just in time for pie."

"I'll help dish up," Barbara said, following Hassie.

"Me, too," Carrie offered, eager to escape Vaughn.

Barbara Kyle shook her head. "Well take care of it."

The two older women disappeared, which meant that Carrie was left alone with Vaughn and his father. She would've preferred the women's company and felt awkward alone with the two men. Vaughn was obviously eager to talk to her, and she was just as eager to avoid any conversation with him. Yes, there were things she needed to say; she wasn't ready, though—not nearly ready. She glanced in his direction and he mouthed something, but she looked away.

"Hassie and Barb are trying to keep you and Vaughn together," Rick confided to her frankly. Vaughn scowled fiercely. "So you may as well play along," he advised. "Here, sit down, Carrie, and make yourself comfortable."

She sat on the sofa and Vaughn joined her, sitting so close that their thighs brushed. In an effort to ignore him, she stared out the picture window.

"Isn't it a lovely day?" she asked, making conversation with his father. "The snow—" A flash of color outside caught her attention. It was her younger brothers. Gasping, she leaped to her feet.

"What?" Vaughn asked, getting up, too.

"It's Chuck and Ken," she said, and pointed at the window. Sure enough, they were outside—in an old-fashioned sleigh pulled by two draft horses.

"That's my great-great-grandfather's sleigh," Carrie explained. "He used it to deliver the mail. Dad and Mr. McKenna have been fixing it up. It's been in the barn for the last hundred years."

"That sleigh looks like something straight out of a Christmas movie," Vaughn's father remarked, standing by the window. "Whose horses are they?"

"I think they belong to a friend of Pete's," Carrie said.

Despite her mood, she giggled. Her brothers must have planned this all along. How they'd managed to keep it a secret she could only guess.

The doorbell chimed, and when Hassie answered it, she found Chuck grinning down at her.

"Anyone here interested in a sleigh ride?" he asked, looking around Hassie to where Carrie and Vaughn stood. "There's room for five."

"I'm game," Rick said. "Come on, Barb."

"Hassie?" Vaughn turned to their hostess.

She seemed about to refuse, then smiled broadly and said, "Don't mind if I do."

Vaughn helped Hassie on with her coat and made sure her boots were tightly laced before they ventured outside. Carrie tried not to be affected by the tenderness he displayed toward Hassie, especially when he bent down on one knee to lace her boots. There was nothing condescending in his action, only affection and concern. Meanwhile, Rick held Carrie's coat for her and then Barbara's. By the time they left the house, the old sleigh, pulled by twin chestnut geldings, had attracted quite a bit of attention from the neighborhood. The horses were festively decked out in harnesses decorated with jangling bells.

Barbara, Rick and Hassie sat in the backseat, which fortunately was nicely padded. Once they were settled, Ken handed them a blanket to place over their laps. Carrie and Vaughn took the front seat, which was narrower and made of wood, forcing them close together.

Chuck and Ken walked in front of the horses, leading them down the unfamiliar street.

"Where are you taking us?" Carrie shouted as her brothers climbed onto the sleigh.

"The park," Ken called back.

"Shouldn't we be singing Christmas songs?" Barbara asked.

"Go right ahead," Rick answered, and taking him at his word, Vaughn's mother started with "Jingle Bells." What could be more fitting? Even if it was a "two-horse open sleigh."

Moments later Hassie's rough voice joined Barbara's soft soprano.

Carrie began to sing, too, and soon Vaughn's rich baritone blended with the women's voices. He and Carrie looked at each other. Perhaps it was the magic of the season or the fact that they were in a sleigh singing while they dashed through the snow, their song accompanied by the muffled clopping of hooves and the jingling of harness bells. Whatever the reason, Carrie realized her anger had completely dissipated. Vaughn seemed to genuinely regret what he'd done. He wasn't involved in a plot to destroy Buffalo Valley. To his credit, as soon as he'd recognized the threat Value-X represented to the town, he'd resigned from the company. It couldn't have been easy to walk away from a high-paying job like that.

Vaughn noticed the transformation in her immediately. He stopped singing and leaned close enough to ask, "Am I forgiven?"

Carrie nodded.

His eyes brightened and he slid an arm around her shoulders. Carrie was convinced that if their circumstances had been different, he would've kissed her.

When they reached the middle of the park, they found Carrie's entire family waiting there, applauding their arrival.

Effortlessly they segued from one Christmas carol to another. Everyone seemed to have a favorite. Amid the singing and the laughter, Carrie's mother served hot chocolate from large thermoses.

Vaughn and Carrie left their places in order to give others an opportunity to try out the sleigh. After several trips around the park, Chuck and Ken drove Hassie and Vaughn's parents back to Hassie's. Carrie and Vaughn remained with her family.

With pride, Carrie took Vaughn around and introduced him to everyone he had yet to meet.

"What were Chuck and Ken talking about earlier?" Tom asked, standing next to his wife, Becky.

Vaughn glanced at Carrie. "We discussed a few ideas, nothing more."

"That's not what I understood," Tom said. "Chuck said you'd made an appointment to talk to Heath Quantrill."

"You've got an appointment to see Heath?" Carrie asked. "About what?" She'd suspected earlier that something was up involving her two younger brothers. Sunday night they'd sat with their father at the kitchen table, talking excitedly in low voices. Carrie couldn't figure out what they were doing, and when she asked, their replies had been vague.

Rather than answer her directly, Vaughn looked away.

"More secrets?" she asked him under her breath.

"Vaughn's thinking about opening up a feed store in town," Tom supplied.

"Is this true?" she asked. If so, it was the best kind of secret.

"Nothing's certain yet," he told her, and she could see that he wasn't pleased with her older brother for sharing the news. "Everything's just in the planning stages. The *early* planning stages."

"You'd actually consider moving to Buffalo Valley?"

Vaughn nodded and smiled down on her, but then his gaze clouded. "I still need to talk to you."

"Of course."

"Privately," he insisted.

The park was crowded with her family. Carrie knew that the instant they broke away, one of her brothers or nieces and nephews would seek her out. "We can try," she promised.

"It's important."

Her heart was in her eyes, but Carrie didn't care if he saw that or not. "I'm so excited you might move here."

"I'm excited, too."

He didn't sound it. If anything, he seemed anxious. "What is it?" she asked. She wanted to hear what he needed to say, and she wanted to hear it *now,* even if they couldn't escape her family.

"Someone from Value-X is coming to Buffalo Valley," he murmured.

"You mean the representative Lindsay mentioned?" Carrie was well aware that the company intended to wage a public-relations campaign to win over the community; that was part of their strategy. She suspected the corporate heads at Value-X had only the slightest idea how unwelcome the retailer was in Buffalo Valley. Whatever they were planning simply wouldn't work.

"Yes. Her name's Natalie Nichols and—"

"It doesn't matter," she told him.

"Yes, it does," he countered.

Carrie lowered her voice, wanting him to know he could trust her. "I didn't tell anyone—no one knows."

"Hassie does. I told her myself."

She didn't understand what had prompted that confession, but wasn't sure it had been the wisest thing.

"She deserves honesty, the same way you do." Vaughn's brow creased with concern. "I would've come to meet her, with or without Value-X."

"I know."

"It isn't going to be pretty, Carrie, when Natalie Nichols arrives. Value-X has proved that it's capable of bulldozing its way into a town. They've done it before."

"Not here, not in Buffalo Valley. We won't let it happen." When he shook his head, she whispered, "It's going to be all right, Vaughn." Because her fears about him had been laid to rest, she leaned forward and kissed him.

Vaughn wrapped his arms around her and held her close.

"Hey, what's this?" Pete shouted.

Carrie laughed. "Leave us be," she replied. "Go on! Shoo!" She wasn't about to let her brothers ruin the most romantic moment of her life.

"Never," Tom hollered.

"There's something else," Vaughn said, ignoring her brothers.

"I have a feeling it's going to have to wait," she said, and ducked just in time to miss a flying snowball. Vaughn, however, wasn't quick enough. Snow exploded across his shoulder and he whirled around to face four large Hendrickson males.

"You shouldn't have done that," he said mildly.

"You gonna make me sorry?"

"Oh, yeah." Vaughn's chuckle was full of threat. "Prepare to die, Hendrickson."

Three hours later a cold and exhausted Vaughn made his way back to Hassie's. The snowball fight had eventually involved everyone in Carrie's large family, from two-year-old Eli to his grandfather. They'd stopped only long enough to build snow forts before the battle had resumed with peals of laughter and more hilarity than Vaughn could remember in years.

He'd sincerely meant to tell Carrie about his relationship with Natalie, but the opportunity never arose again. It became easy to let it ride once they were caught up in the family fun. Come morning, he was driving back to town to meet with Heath; he'd stop by the pharmacy and tell her then.

It was dark when he returned to Hassie's, and his parents were ready to head home to Grand Forks. When they got there, he discovered that Natalie had left five messages on his parents' machine. He was stunned to learn that she'd already arived in North Dakota.

The first message, from the Seattle airport, had been soft

and coaxing, claiming she needed to speak to him at his ear-
liest convenience. By the final one, her tone had become hard
and demanding. The last part of the message, telling him
she'd call early the next morning, had sounded more than a
little annoyed.

"Trouble?" his father asked, standing next to the phone as
the message finished playing.

Vaughn shook his head. "Nothing I can't handle."

"Good."

"This has been the most wonderful Christmas," his mother
said as she turned off the lights. They all went to bed, wishing
each other good-night and a final Merry Christmas.

The following morning Vaughn woke early. He showered,
shaved and dressed for his meeting with Heath. Sooner or later,
he'd have to talk to Natalie, but he wanted as much information as he could gather before the inevitable confrontation.
He gulped down a cup of coffee, eager to be on his way, to
begin this new phase of his life. His mother hugged him before
he left. "What do you want me to say if Natalie shows up?"

"No need to tell her anything," he advised. He'd deal with
her when he had to, but not before. The letter she'd mentioned
would be in the community post office soon and with that,
the campaign would officially start. Vaughn was prepared to
do whatever was necessary to keep the retailer out of Buffalo
Valley. He had a stake in the town's future now.

He parked near the bank, then hurried inside; to his surprise, Heath's glass-enclosed office looked empty.

"I have an appointment with Mr. Quantrill," Vaughn told
the receptionist.

"You're Mr. Kyle?"

Vaughn nodded.

"Mr. Quantrill left a message. He had some last-minute

business to attend to and said I should reschedule the appointment. He sent his apologies and asked me to tell you that the Kohn property has sold."

It wasn't until he was standing outside that Vaughn understood the significance of the message. The Kohn property was the land Value-X wanted. So the battle lines had been drawn. No wonder Quantrill was out of the office. There was no longer any reason for Vaughn to meet with him; Quantrill and the community had far more important issues to worry about.

Vaughn walked over to the pharmacy, his steps slow. No doubt Hassie and everyone else in town had heard the news. He knew how discouraged they'd be.

When he entered the pharmacy, Carrie was behind the prescription counter. As the bells over the door cheerfully announced his arrival, she glanced up, and from her disheartened expression, it was clear she'd heard. Her eyes seemed dull and lifeless. For a long moment she stared at him, almost as though he was a stranger.

"I guess you know?" he asked, stepping toward her.

"Oh, yes," she said with such sadness it nearly broke his heart.

"I'll help, Carrie," he told her. "We can beat Value-X if we stand together." He tried to sound positive, but truth was, he didn't know if they could.

"That's not the news I'm talking about," she said, moving out from behind the counter. "I wonder if you've ever heard the old saying, *Fool me once, shame on you, fool me twice, shame on me.*"

Vaughn frowned, not understanding. "What are you talking about?"

"You mentioned the name Natalie Nichols yesterday."

"Yes, she works for Value-X. She—"

"I met her this morning."

"Natalie's here?" Foolishly he'd assumed she'd spent the night in Grand Forks.

"She stayed at the 3 of a Kind last night. She's been trying to reach you—and here you are, right under her nose."

"I don't know what she told you, but—"

"She told me she was your fiancée."

It was all starting to make sense to Vaughn, a sick kind of sense. Natalie's declaration certainly explained that "shame me twice" stuff. "She spoke to your mother this morning," Carrie went on. "Your mother said if you weren't over at the bank to check here with Hassie. Only it was me she found."

"I can explain," he began.

"I'm sure you can, but frankly I'm not interested in listening." With that, she returned to the pharmaceutical counter and resumed her work as if he was no longer there.

Vaughn waited uncertainly for a moment, but she didn't look anywhere except at her task, at the pills she was counting out.

It was too late for explanations. Too late to regain her trust. Too late for him.

Ten

Vaughn didn't think anything could happen to make this day any worse, but he was wrong.

As soon as he pulled into the driveway at his parents' home, he saw the unfamiliar car. Even before he'd climbed out of his own vehicle, he knew who'd come to visit.

Natalie.

Sure enough, the instant he walked into the house, his father cast him a sympathetic glance.

"You're back," his mother said, her voice strained and unnaturally high.

"Hello, Vaughn," Natalie said from the living room. She held a cup of coffee balanced on her knee. She looked out of place—and decidedly irritated.

He nodded in her direction.

"I think we'll leave the two of you to talk," his mother announced, and exited the room with the speed of someone who's relieved to escape. His father was directly behind her.

With a silent groan, Vaughn turned toward Natalie.

"You didn't answer my phone messages." She set aside her coffee, glaring at him. "When I couldn't find you, I drove straight to Buffalo Valley, where I spent the night at some hole-in-the-wall. Merry Christmas, Natalie," she said bitterly.

She didn't appear to expect a comment, so he sat down across from her and waited. When she didn't immediately continue, he figured he'd better take his stand.

"I'm finished with Value-X." Nothing she could say or offer him would influence his decision. "You aren't going to change my mind."

"I'll say you're finished. I'll be fortunate to have a job my-self after this."

Vaughn doubted that. Natalie was the type who'd always land on her feet. Yes, she'd recommended Vaughn to the company, but they couldn't hold that against her.

"You intend to go through with this...this craziness, don't you?"

No use hedging. "Yes, I do. I've resigned, and since I hadn't officially started work yet, I didn't bother to give any notice."

She sighed and stared down at her coffee. "I wonder if I ever knew you."

Vaughn said nothing. He'd let her say what she wanted, de-nounce him, threaten him, whatever. She had cause; he wasn't exactly blameless in all this.

"You think I don't know what this is about?" she chal-lenged. She stood, crossing her arms. "It all has to do with you and me."

Vaughn didn't know a kind way to tell her there *wasn't* any "you and me." There'd probably never been a "you and me." Not with Natalie. Looking at her, Vaughn wondered how he could ever have believed he was in love with her. The very traits that had once attracted him now repulsed him. Her ambition blinded her to everything that was unique and special about Buffalo Valley.

"Say something!" she shrilled.

"I'm sorry."

"That's a good start." Her stance relaxed somewhat.

"It doesn't change anything, though." He wasn't being purposely cruel, only frank. "I'm going to do everything I can to keep Value-X out of Buffalo Valley."

"You're mad at me," she insisted. "All this craziness about moving to some backwoods town is a form of punishment. You're trying to make me regret what I said. Vaughn, you simply don't understand how important Value-X is to me and to our future."

"Natalie—"

She ignored him and started pacing. "We've always been good together, Vaughn, you know that."

"Have we, Natalie?" he asked, hoping she was capable of admitting the truth.

"I can't let you do this," she said, clenching her fists.

He shook his head. "It's done."

"But you're destroying your career!"

"I don't want to work for a company like Value-X. Not now and not in the future."

"What are you going to do, then?"

"I don't know," he told her, and it was true. He'd fight the big retailer for as long as his money held out, but after that... he didn't have any answers.

"I can help you," she said. "You're this rough-and-ready Airborne Ranger, trying to be a hero. But you've got to face reality. No one goes against Value-X and walks away a winner. This will cost you more than you can afford to lose."

He ignored her threat. "Thanks but no thanks," he muttered.

She looked crestfallen.

Vaughn had a few questions of his own. "Why did you tell Carrie we're engaged?"

"Because we are!" she cried. "Did we or did we not discuss marriage?"

He didn't respond. She already had her answer.

"Oh, I get it," Natalie raged, her eyes spitting fire. "You found yourself a little side dish while you were away visiting Mom and Dad. You forgot all about me. Is *that* it?"

"We aren't engaged and we aren't getting married." She couldn't seriously believe he intended to continue this relationship when it was obviously a dead end for both of them.

"But we *did* discuss marriage on more than one occasion, and I never said I *wouldn't* marry you. We both understood we'd get married someday."

"I didn't see it that way. Yes, we talked about marriage, but there was no commitment—and very little interest on your part."

"Now you're lying, too."

He bristled, but bit his tongue before he said something he'd regret.

"Well…it's sort of a lie." Natalie lowered her head. "I made a mistake, but not once did I say anything about breaking off our relationship."

"It's over." He didn't know how much plainer he could be.

"I know." She sighed. "Well, if you insist on this lunacy, you're on your own."

He nodded.

"We could've been very good together," she whispered.

"I'm sorry."

"I know, and you'll be a whole lot sorrier once Value-X is through with this town." She rallied then, jerking her head up, chin tilted. "If you want to freeze your butt off in this horrible place, then go right ahead." She reached for her coat and yanked it toward her.

The sound of several car doors closing distracted Vaughn. He glanced out the window to see all four of Carrie's brothers standing in the driveway. He could only surmise that they'd come en masse to finish him off.

"Who's here?" Natalie asked.

"The firing squad," Vaughn answered.

"Terrific. Can I fire the first shot?"

Vaughn didn't respond to her sarcasm. He headed toward the front door, opening it for the four men who marched, single file, into the house. Soon Carrie's brothers stood in the middle of the room, looking from Vaughn to Natalie and then back.

"What happened?" Chuck demanded. "You left town without saying a word."

"I didn't meet with Heath," Vaughn started to explain, but wasn't given the opportunity before another question was hurled at him.

"Aren't you going to introduce us to your sister?"

"I'm Natalie Nichols." She introduced herself, stepping forward and offering each of the Hendrickson brothers her hand. "And I'm not Vaughn's sister."

"Then who are you?" Ken asked, frowning.

"His fiancée. Or I was," she said, "until recently, but now Vaughn's met someone else. He just told me that he no longer wishes to marry me." She appeared to be making a brave effort to hold her chin high and keep her lower lip from trembling. He'd never realized what a good actress Natalie was.

Vaughn resisted rolling his eyes. He remained silent, preferring not to get drawn into a theatrical scene in which *he*
was identified as the villain.

"Someone will need to give me directions back to my
hotel." She pulled a tissue from her pocket and dabbed at her
eyes, being careful not to smear her mascara.

"I can get you there." Ken stepped forward. "I'll be happy
to help."

Tom's gaze narrowed on Vaughn. "Did she have something
to do with the fact that you didn't see Heath?"

Vaughn shook his head, surprised the Hendrickson brothers hadn't already heard. "The land sold."

"What the hell?"

All four brothers started speaking at once. As luck would
have it, Vaughn's parents chose that precise moment to reap-
pear.

"I thought I heard voices," his mother said as she came into
the living room.

Tom motioned with his head toward Natalie. "You'd better have a good explanation," he muttered. "You'd better not
be engaged to her and seeing Carrie."

"Yeah," Pete agreed. "This is all some kind of misunder-
standing, isn't it? Didn't I tell you I'd make you pay if you
hurt my sister?"

"He was never actually engaged," his mother said, hurrying to defend Vaughn. "What he told us is—"

That was when his father stepped into the fray. "Barbara,
let Vaughn answer for himself, would you?"

This was impossible. Everyone talked at once. Part of the
conversation had to do with the land; everyone was clearly
upset about that. Then Pete and his mother got involved in a
debate about whether Vaughn should be dating Carrie. In the

meantime, Ken and Natalie had apparently struck up a friendly conversation. They sat next to each other on the sofa, so close that their knees touched. Vaughn could only guess what she was saying, but frankly, he couldn't care less.

Before everything blew up in his face, Vaughn walked through the kitchen, grabbed his coat and stepped out the back door. He got into his car, which fortunately hadn't been blocked by the other vehicles. Glancing toward the house, he saw everyone gathered in front of the big window in the living room, staring at him. They must have been dumbfounded, because no one seemed to be speaking.

When he reached the end of the long driveway, Vaughn had to make a decision. He could go searching for solitude, a quiet place to recover his dignity. Or he could drive back to Buffalo Valley.

He chose Buffalo Valley. When he'd finished breaking Hassie's heart, he'd do what he could to mend Carrie's.

He'd never meant to hurt Carrie, but that didn't discount the fact that he'd misled her. This wasn't exactly his finest hour.

When they'd first met, he'd found her charming. Later, when he got to know her, he'd been enchanted by her warmth, delighted by her love of family and home. Those were qualities that had come to mean a great deal to him. Carrie was *genuine,* and she was authentic in her relationships. Unlike him...

Vaughn wanted to kick himself for not being honest with her from the start. He didn't have a single excuse. All he could do now was pray that she'd be willing to accept him—and that she'd give him an opportunity to prove himself.

The hour's drive into town passed in a blur, and practically before he knew it he'd pulled off the highway and turned onto what were now familiar roads. Buffalo Valley stretched before him, but he viewed it with new eyes. He recalled his first visit, recalled how stark and bare the town had seemed, almost as if it were devoid of personality. He'd soon recognized how wrong he was.

While the buildings might be outdated and the lampposts antiques, the town itself represented the very heart of the country. The heart of America's heartland. It was where he wanted to be, how he wanted to live.

His mind was clear now. Easing the car into a parking space on Main Street, Vaughn forced himself to consider what he'd say to Hassie. It wasn't a task he relished.

All his talk of opening a feed store had done nothing but build up her hopes. Now he was about to disillusion an old woman who'd invested her whole life in a town that couldn't be saved. Whatever happened, though, he was staying in Buffalo Valley; he'd be part of its struggle and part of its future.

He dared not put this off any longer, and drawing a deep breath, he walked into the pharmacy.

The instant she saw him, Hassie cried out his name. "Vaughn, oh, Vaughn." Tears streaked her weathered cheeks as she hurried across the store, her arms stretched out toward him.

Apparently someone had already brought her the news. Holding open his own arms as she came to him, he hugged her, the sound of her sobs echoing in his ears.

"I'm so sorry," Vaughn whispered, wondering what he could say that would comfort her.

"Sorry?" Hassie eased back, gazing at him through watery eyes. "In the name of heaven, why would you be *sorry?* This is what we've hoped for all along."

Vaughn stared at her, not knowing what to think. "The land sold, Hassie."

"Yes, I know." She clapped her hands, eyes sparkling with delight. "This is better than anything I could've imagined."

"I'm...confused."

"I know." She patted his back and led him to the soda fountain. "Sit down," she ordered. "If there was ever a time for one of my chocolate sodas, this is it."

"What about Value-X?"

"They lost the land. The women of Buffalo Valley got to Ambrose before he signed the deal with Value-X and they bought it out from under the company. The ladies convinced Ambrose he'd be making a mistake."

Vaughn knew that several of the women in town owned businesses; he knew they had a big stake in the community. It floored him that they'd managed to do what no one else had deemed possible.

"But how...when?"

"Do you recall when the women got together?" Hassie asked, leaning over the refrigeration unit, scooping up the ice cream.

"I remember a cookie exchange." Carrie had mentioned something along those lines earlier in the week.

"The meeting took place after that," Hassie said. "Then a committee of six paid Ambrose a visit. I don't know everything they said, but apparently they convinced him to sell *them* those twenty acres. I hear they twisted his arm by appealing to his vanity—promising to name the school after him. He liked that. He also liked the fact that he could sell his land at the same price Value-X offered."

"Is Value-X seeking out any other property?"

Hassie grinned. "They can try, but there isn't a single person in this area who'd sell to them—not at any price."

Vaughn nodded, still feeling a little numb. "What do the women intend to do with the property?" he asked.

Hassie's grin widened. "You mean you don't know?"

He didn't. Since they were all capable, business-minded individuals, Vaughn suspected they already had plans.

Hassie chuckled softly. "You'll have to ask them, but my guess is they'd be willing to sell you a portion of it—that is, if you're still inclined to settle in Buffalo Valley."

Vaughn could barely take it in. "You mean that?"

"Talk to Sarah Urlacher and she'll give you all the details."

"I need to see Carrie first."

Hassie set the glass on the counter. "Ah, yes, Carrie." She made a tsking sound and plunked a paper straw into the thick chocolate soda. "You've got your work cut out there."

Vaughn wrapped his hand around the glass, feeling the cold against his palm. "I assume she's upset."

"That's one way of putting it."

Vaughn slid off the stool. He didn't want to offend Hassie by not drinking the soda, but he'd feel worlds better once he resolved the situation with Carrie. "She at home?"

"Doubt it." Hassie reached for the soda herself and took a long sip before she continued. "My guess is she's sitting on the swings over in the park. I found she likes to go there when something's troubling her. Look there first and if you can't find her, then check the house."

Vaughn thanked her and left immediately. He jogged across the street to the park. The snow forts he'd helped build on Christmas Day—was that only yesterday?—were still standing, a little the worse for wear. Following the freshly shoveled walk, Vaughn made his way toward the play equipment.

Hassie had, as always, given him the right advice. Carrie

sat in the middle swing. Her face was red from the cold, and he wondered how long she'd been there.

Vaughn ached to tell her how sorry he was, but he feared that if he said or did the wrong thing now, he might lose her forever.

As he approached, Carrie glanced up, but she didn't acknowledge him. Vaughn, needing to gather his thoughts, didn't say anything, either. Instead, he settled into the swing beside her and waited for the words to come.

"I hurt you, didn't I?" he asked after an awkward moment.

"Were you engaged to her when you came to town?"

This was the difficult part. "No. No, I wasn't."

"She seemed to think so."

He gripped the chain and shifted sideways to see Carrie more clearly. "Before I left Seattle, Natalie and I talked about marriage."

The words seemed to hit her hard.

"She wasn't interested."

"Apparently she's changed her mind."

Vaughn saw that Carrie was staring straight ahead, as though mesmerized by whatever she was watching. "So have I."

Carrie turned toward him, but when their eyes met, she turned away again. "Why?"

"I met someone else."

"You must be a very fickle man, Vaughn Kyle, to ask one woman to marry you and then, while she's making up her mind, start seeing another."

"I realize how bad it sounds."

"Sounds, nothing! Underhanded and unfair is more like it."

"You're right," he said simply. "I have no excuse."

"You must've really enjoyed hearing me spill out my heart."

She covered her cheeks with both hands and closed her eyes,

as if remembering the things she'd said. They seemed to embarrass her now.

"Carrie, no! It wasn't like that." He thought about the afternoon she'd told him about her ex-husband. He didn't know how to put into words what her trust had done for him. How her straightforward devotion had wiped out the cynicism he'd felt after Natalie's opportunistic approach to love and marriage.

"You're certainly not the kind of man I'd want in my life."

"I need you, Carrie...."

"For what, comic relief?"

"We've only known each other a short while. Who can say where this relationship will take us? Maybe you're right. After you get to know me better, you could very well decide you don't want any more to do with me. If that's the case, I'll accept it. All I'm asking for is a chance."

"To break my heart?"

"No, to give you mine."

She didn't answer him for the longest time. Finally her mouth twisted wryly and she said, "You're afraid of what my brothers will do to you once they learn about...Natalie, aren't you?"

"No man in his right mind would voluntarily tangle with your brothers," he replied, deciding this was not the moment to tell her they'd already met the woman in question. "However, I figure I can take them on if it comes to that. What I'm telling you now has nothing to do with your brothers. It's how I feel about you."

"Don't!" she cried with such passion that Vaughn jumped. "Don't say things you don't mean."

"I am completely sincere." He slid off the swing and crouched down in front of her. He wanted her to see how vulnerable he was to her. Taking her right hand in his, he removed her glove and kissed the inside of her palm.

She pulled back her hand.

"I plan to stay in Buffalo Valley," he continued, undaunted.

Her eyes widened, but she bit her lower lip as if to suppress her reaction.

"I'm going to invest in the community, become part of it, make a contribution."

Carrie's gaze darted away and then returned. "Don't tell me things like that just because you think it's what I want to hear."

"It's true, Carrie."

She closed her eyes and lowered her chin. "I want so badly to believe you."

"Believe me," he whispered, then nuzzled her throat. He didn't kiss her, although the temptation was strong. "All I'm asking for is another chance," he said again.

"Oh, Vaughn." She pressed her hands against his shoulders—to bring him closer or push him away?

Vaughn helped make the decision for her. Crouched down as he was, his face level with her own, he leaned toward her and grazed her lips with his. Her mouth was cold, yet moist and welcoming. She moaned softly and he rubbed his warm lips over hers, seducing her into deepening the kiss.

One moment he was crouched in front of Carrie and she was leaning forward, giving herself to the kiss. The next he was losing his balance and tumbling backward.

Carrie let out a small cry of alarm as she went with him. Vaughn did what he could to protect her. He threw his arms around her waist and took the brunt of the impact as she landed on top of him in the snow.

"You've knocked me off balance from the moment we met," he said.

Carrie smiled then, for the first time since he'd joined her. "You've done the same thing to me."

"Good."

"No promises, Vaughn."

"I disagree." He brushed the hair from her face, barely aware of the snow and the cold.

She frowned. "What do you mean?"

"There's promise every time I look at you, Carrie Hendrickson. Promise each time I kiss you." Then, because he couldn't keep himself from doing so, he showed her exactly what he meant.

As soon as their lips met, Carrie whimpered and he wrapped his arms more firmly around her.

"This is only the beginning for us," he whispered.

Carrie placed her head on his shoulder and gave a shuddering sigh.

"I was never really worried about your brothers," Vaughn confessed. "*You* were always the one who terrified me." He laughed and rolled, reversing their positions in the snow. Her eyes were smiling as he gazed down on her.

"So you want to give me your heart?" she said, looking up at him. She flattened her hand against his coat.

"Don't you know?" he asked her.

"Know what?"

"You already have it." And then he went about proving it.

Mr. and Mrs. William Hendrickson

and

Mr. and Mrs. Richard Kyle

Request the honor of your presence at a reception

to celebrate

the marriage of their children

Carrie Ann Hendrickson

and

Vaughn Richard Kyle

When: December 15th

Where: Buffalo Bob's 3 of a Kind

Main Street,

Buffalo Valley, North Dakota

RSVP

★ ★ ★ ★ ★